Eugene S. Talbot

Degeneracy
Its Causes, Signs and Results

Outlook

Eugene S. Talbot

Degeneracy
Its Causes, Signs and Results

1. Auflage | ISBN: 978-3-73262-566-6

Erscheinungsort: Frankfurt am Main, Deutschland

Erscheinungsjahr: 2018

Outlook Verlag GmbH, Frankfurt.

Reproduction of the original.

Eugene S. Talbot

Degeneracy
Its Causes, Signs and Results

Outlook

THE CONTEMPORARY SCIENCE SERIES

EDITED BY HAVELOCK ELLIS

DEGENERACY

DWARFISM AND GIANTISM.

DEGENERACY

ITS CAUSES, SIGNS, AND RESULTS

BY

EUGENE S. TALBOT, M.D., D.D.S.,

FELLOW OF THE CHICAGO ACADEMY OF MEDICINE; MEMBER OF THE CHICAGO
ACADEMY OF SCIENCES; HONORARY MEMBER OF THE BERLIN
ODONTOLOGISCHEN GESELLSCHAFT, AND THE ASSOCIATION
GÉNÉRALE DES DENTISTES DE FRANCE; PROFESSOR OF
DENTAL AND ORAL SURGERY, WOMAN'S MEDICAL
SCHOOL, NORTH-WESTERN UNIVERSITY, U.S.A.

WITH 120 ILLUSTRATIONS

LONDON
WALTER SCOTT, LTD., PATERNOSTER SQUARE
1898

PREFACE

The present work is the result of more than twenty years' labour in a limited medical department of biology. It demonstrates once more the truth of the scientific principle, that the truth or falsity of any theory or working hypothesis becomes more and more demonstrable the further its application is attempted in the explanation of new lines of facts. The truth of the degeneracy doctrine had forced itself on the writer long before its popular apotheosis under Lombroso and Nordau, because it alone sufficed for an explanation of constitutional and local defects (encountered in a seemingly limited speciality of medicine), which local causes failed entirely to explain. The investigations thereon resultant have appeared in medical and dental journals for the past two decades. The present work is chiefly based on these researches. At the same time, the author has drawn largely from all fields of biology cultivated by European investigators, while he must acknowledge a particular indebtedness to the investigations (of which he has made large use beside that elsewhere specifically acknowledged) of certain American investigators— Rush, Parkmen, Ray, G. Frank Lydston, C. L. Dana, C. F. Folsom, W. W. Godding, E. C. Spitzka, E. D. Cope, D. R. Brower, Marsh, B. Sachs, Harriet C. B. Alexander, Clara Barrus, H. M. Bannister, Delia E. Howe, Grace Peckham, Adolph Meyer, Kerlin, Wiley, J. G. Kiernan, W. E. Allison, Osborn, R. Dewey, Frederick Peterson, Gihon, Cowles, W. A. Hammond, A. B. Holder, C. H. Hughes, F. W. Starr, F. C. Hoyt, J. H. McBride, C. K. Mills, C. B. Burr, T. D. Crothers, W. S. Christopher, W. X. Sudduth, A. Lagorio, J. Workman, Wilmarth, and others. These scientists had raised an exceedingly stable foundation for the doctrine of degeneracy long before Lombroso and Nordau (forcing one phase of the subject into popular recognition) compelled an examination of the entire doctrine.

The work has been written with a special intention of reaching educators and parents. With this object, it has avoided laying stress on any one cause of degeneracy, and ignoring factors which produce it and are aggravated by it. The doctrinaire reformer will here find no support for any limited theory. While it does not pretend in the slightest degree to give all the details of degeneracy, it attempts to lay down general principles for practical purposes in a way that permits their application to the solution of sociologic problems.

From a sense of scientific accuracy no attempts have been made to demarcate, rigidly, abnormality from disease, or atavism from arrested development, except as may be done by the features of the cases in which the terms are used. The guiding principle adopted has been that the factors of degeneracy affect in the ancestor the checks on excessive action acquired during the evolution of the race, thus producing a state of nervous exhaustion. The descendant in consequence is unable to reach the state of the ancestor thus nervously exhausted.

For the illustrations, other than those that are original, the author is indebted to the *Journal of the American Medical Association, Dental Cosmos, The International Dental Journal, The St. Louis Clinical Record,* to M. Félix Alcan, and to the officers of the New York State Reformatory and Illinois State Reformatory, Drs. Geo. T. Carpenter, W. A. Pusey, F. S. Coolidge, Ch. Féré, Zuckerkandl, John E. Greves, Amsterdam; Ernst Sjoberg, Stockholm; Bastian, J. G. Kiernan, E. C. Spitzka, John Ridlon, James W. Walker, and Ignatius Donnelly.

E. S. T.

DEGENERACY

CHAPTER I

INTRODUCTION

Considered as a condition hurtful to the type, the conception of degeneracy may be said to appear even in the precursors of man, since animals destroy soon after birth offspring which, to them, appear peculiar.

With that stage of development of the religious sense marked by assigning malign occult powers to natural objects and forces, this view of degeneracy became systematised, and exposed weakly or deformed offspring, charged to evil powers, to death. This occult conception of degeneracy is even yet a part of American folklore. Against degenerate children charms are still used by the "witch-doctors" among the "Pennsylvania Dutch." These people are on the level of culture of the early seventeenth century middle class English, if not a little below it. The folklore of these, as embodied in Shakespeare, demonstrates, according to J. G. Kiernan,[1] that ere the seventeenth century the fact that "mental and moral defect expressed itself in physical stigmata was recognised and even the term used." Thistleton Dyer[2] remarks that it is an old prejudice, not yet extinct, that those who are defective or deformed are marked by nature as prone to mischief. Thus in *King Richard III.* (i. 3) Margaret calls Richard—

> "Thou elvish-marked, abortive, rootinghog!
> Thou that wast sealed in thy nativity
> The slave of nature and the son of hell!"

She calls him hog in allusion to his cognisance, which was a boar. A popular expression in Shakespeare's day for a deformed person was "stigmatic." It denoted any one who had been stigmatised or burnt with iron (an ignominious punishment), and hence was employed to represent a person on whom nature had set a mark of deformity. Thus in the Third Part of *Henry VI.* (ii. 2) Queen Margaret says—

> "But thou art neither like thy sire nor dam;
> But like a foul misshapen stigmatic,
> Marked by the destinies to be avoided,
> As venom toads, or lizards' dreadful stings."

Again in the Second Part of *Henry VI.* (v. 1) young Clifford says to Richard—

> "Foul stigmatic, that's more than thou canst tell."

In *A Midsummer Night's Dream* (v. 1) Oberon wards off degeneracy from the issue of the happy lovers by the following charm—

> "And the blots of Nature's hand
> Shall not in their issue stand;
> Never mole, hare-lip nor scar,
> Nor mark prodigious, such as are
> Despised in nativity,
> Shall upon their children be."

Constant allusions to this subject occur in old writers, showing how strong was the belief of the early English on this point. King John (iv. 2) calls Hubert, the supposed murderer of Prince Arthur,—

> "A fellow by the hand of Nature marked,
> Quoted and signed to do a deed of shame."

Concerning this adaptation of the mind to the deformity of the body Francis Bacon remarks: "Deformed persons are commonly even with Nature, for as Nature hath done ill by them so do they by Nature, being void of natural affection, and so they have their revenge on Nature."

The quaint old "Anatomist of Melancholy,"[3] Burton, seems but to paraphrase modern curers of degeneracy when, at the end of his chapter on the inheritance of defects, he remarks concerning this fetichistic notion: "So many several ways are we plagued and published for our father's defaults; in so much that as Fernelius truly saith: 'It is the greatest part of our felicity to be well born, and it were happy for human kind, if only such parents as are sound of body and mind should be suffered to marry.' An husbandman will sow none but the best and choicest seed upon his land, he will not rear a bull or an horse, except he be right shapen in all parts, or permit him to cover a mare, except he be well assured of his breed; we make choice of the best rams for our sheep, rear the neatest kine, and keep the best dogs, *quanto id diligentius in procreandis liberis observandum!* And how careful, then, should we be in begetting of our children! In former times some countries have been so chary in this behalf, so stern, that if a child were crooked or deformed in body or mind, they made him away; so did the Indians of old by the relation of Curtius, and many other well-governed commonwealths according to the discipline of those times. 'Heretofore in Scotland,' saith Hect Boethius, 'if any were visited with the falling sickness, madness, gout, leprosy, or any such dangerous disease which was likely to be propagated from the father to the son, he was instantly gelded; a woman kept from all company of men; and if by chance having some such disease she were found to be with child, she with her brood were buried alive'; and this was done for the common good, lest the whole nation should be injured or corrupted. A severe doom, you will say, and not to be used amongst Christians, yet more to be looked into than it is. For now by our too much facility in this kind, in giving way for all to marry that will, too much liberty and indulgence in tolerating all sorts, there is a vast confusion of hereditary diseases, no family secure, no man almost free, from some grievous infirmity or other, when no choice is had, but still the eldest must marry, as so many stallions of the race; or if rich, be they fools or dizzards, lame or maimed, unable, intemperate, dissolute, exhaust through riot, as he said, they must be wise and able by inheritance. It comes to pass that our generation is corrupt, we have many weak persons both in body and mind, many feral diseases raging among us, crazed familiies; our fathers bad, and we are like to be worse."

This conception gradually developed into the widespread myth of a primevally perfect man through the natural operation of that psychological law whereby, as Macaulay remarks, society, constantly moving forward with eager speed, is as constantly looking backward with tender regret. They turn their eyes and see a lake where an hour before they were toiling through sand.

From this view came the belief that man as existing is degenerate. This degeneracy, while popularly charged to occult influences, was early ascribed by scientists to physical causes. Aristotle, as Osborn[4] points out, appears to have recognised degeneration or the gradual decline of structures in form and usefulness, in his analysis of "movement" in connection with development. Degeneration is first met with as a term in an explanation of the origin of species by Buffon in the eighteenth century. The conception itself occurs in a criticism by Sylvius of Vesalius (1514-64), who had asserted that the anatomy of Galen could not have been founded upon the human body, because he had described an intermaxillary bone. This bone, Vesalius observed, is found in the lower animals but not in man. Sylvius (1614-72) defends Galen on the ground that though man had no intermaxillary bone at present this is no proof of its absence in Galen's time. "It is luxury, it is sensuality, which has gradually deprived man of this bone." This passage, as Osborn remarks, proves that the idea of degeneration of structures through disuse, as well as the idea of the inheritance of the effect of habit, or the "transmission of acquired characters," is a very ancient one. Sylvius, while here recognising factors of degeneracy, erred in considering disappearance of the intermaxillary bone, not reappearance, as degeneracy. He failed to recognise, moreover, the law of economy of growth by which one structure is sacrificed for another or for the organism as a whole. This law, indicated by Aristotle, but clearly outlined by Goethe in 1807, and Geoffroy St. Hilaire in 1818, underlies the physiological atrophies and hypertrophies which play such a part in degeneracy.

The *Twelve Cæsars* of Suetonius (that stud book of imperial degeneracy as it has been styled) stamps the decided impression on its readers that Hippocratian notions of degenerate heredity strongly permeated Roman thought, to revive in those Arabic, Italian, and British (Roger Bacon) thinkers who created the scientific phase of the revival of learning.

In the science of medicine, as developed by Hippocrates,[5] the modern conception of degeneracy is evident. Hippocrates argues against the "sacred" nature of epilepsy, since it is a hereditary disease and hence comes under the operation of physical law. He furthermore points out, as did Aristotle, that epilepsy produced in the ancestor by traumatism and other physical causes may be inherited by the child.

As the degeneration phase of evolution was less antagonistic to the religious theory forced into biblical dogma by the Jesuit Suarez (in opposition to the evolutionary views of St. Augustine and St. Thomas Aquinas), being supported by biblical dicta (that when the fathers had eaten sour grapes the children's teeth were set on edge) and fetichistic folklore, it retained a dominance that the advanced phase lost. From the time of Hippocrates, psychiatry (the science devoted to mental disorders) continued to accumulate data of the origin and transmission of human defects. The impetus given the evolutionary explanation of these data by the seventeenth and eighteenth century biologists (Harvey, Buffon, Lamarck, Erasmus Darwin, and others) laid the foundation for the modern doctrine of degeneracy.

Buffon[6] remarks that many species are being perfected or degenerated by the great changes in land and sea, by the favours or disfavours of Nature, by food, by the prolonged influences of climate, contrary or favourable, and are no longer what they formerly were. He regarded temperature, food, and climate as the three great factors in the alteration and degeneration of animals.

Erasmus Darwin[7] considers that all life starts from a living filament having the capability of being excited into action by certain stimuli. This capability is that whereby plants and animals react to their environment, causing changes in them which are transmitted to their offspring. All animals undergo transformations which are in part produced by their own exertions in response to pleasures and pains, and many of these acquired forms or propensities are transmitted to their posterity. Other effects of this excitability (such as constitute hereditary diseases, like scrofula, epilepsy, insanity) have their origin in one or perhaps two generations, as in the progeny of those who drink much vinous spirits. Those hereditary propensities cease again if one or two sober generations succeed, otherwise the family becomes extinct.

Benjamin Rush[8] (greatly influenced by the Erasmus Darwin school) remarks that through hereditary sameness of organisation of the nerves, brain and blood vessels, the predisposition to insanity pervades whole families and renders them liable to this disease from a transient and feeble operation of its causes. Insanity when hereditary is excited by more feeble causes than in persons in whom this predisposition has been acquired. It generally attacks the descendants in those stages of life in which it has appeared in the ancestors. Children born previously to the attack of madness in their parents are less liable to inherit it than those who are born after it. Children born of parents who are in the decline of life are more predisposed to insanity than children born under contrary circumstances. A predisposition to certain diseases, seated in parts contiguous to the seat of insanity, often descends from parents to their children. Thus it occurs in a son whose father or mother has been afflicted only with hysteria or habitual headaches. The reverse likewise takes place. There are families in which insanity has existed where the disease has spared the mind in the posterity, but appeared in great strength and eccentricity of the memory and of the passions, or in great perversion of their moral faculties. Sometimes it passes by all the faculties of the mind, and appears only in the nervous system of persons descended from deranged parents; again, madness occurs in children whose parents were remarkable only for eccentricity of mind. Among the diseases that attack the children of the insane, but did not exist in their ancestors, are consumption and epilepsy.

Similar studies were later published by Pinel, Tissot, Chiarrurgi, Stedman, Parkman, Brigham, Prichard, Esquirol, Jacobi, and other American, English, French, Italian, and German alienists. Based upon the data thus obtained, and upon the general principles thus outlined, then appeared—nearly at the same time as the like epoch-making work (on another phase of evolution), Darwin's *Origin of Species*—Morel's *Treatise on Human Degeneracy*, wherein the principle of natural selection was shown to involve the recognition of the physical conditions that constitute degeneracy, and, necessarily, to exclude primeval perfection. Morel's definition of degeneration as a marked departure from the original type tending more or less rapidly to the extinction of it, forms the basis of commonly accepted definitions.

While Morel practically outlined the modern study of degeneracy, his theologic timidity forced an absolute definition of a state which, according to his own admission, was purely relative. After fencing somewhat with the position that there was a primevally perfect man,[9] he admits with Tessier the primeval lowness of man, but also thinks that the fall of man could create new conditions which, in his descendants, from heredity and from causes acting on their health, tended to make them depart from the primitive type. These departures from the primitive type have led to varieties, some of which constitute races capable of transmitting racial characteristics. Other varieties in the races themselves have created the abnormal states which Morel has denominated degeneracies. Each of these degeneracies has its own stamp from the cause that produces it. Their common characteristic is hereditary transmission under graver conditions than normal heredity. With certain exceptional instances of regeneration, the progeny of degenerates presents progressive degradation. This may reach such limits that humanity is preserved by its excess. It is not necessary, however, that the ultimate stage of degradation be reached before sterility occurs. Morel confines degeneracy to a pathologic type, criticising F. Heusinger[10] for applying the term degenerate to domestic animals which "throw back" to the wild or original type. Morel's admission that causes influencing health produce deviations which, under favouring conditions, become racial types capable of indefinite transmission, saves him from absolute scientific inaccuracy, but renders inconsistent his limitation of degeneracy. It may be convenient to separate diseased states from anomalies, but such separation can only be very relative. From his conservatism and his plentiful data, Morel aroused much less antagonism than did a contemporary, Moreau (de Tours), who bore to him the relation of Darwin to Wallace.[11] While Moreau devotes much attention to the factors of degeneracy and its stigmata (or marks), like Morel, his main point is the expansion of the theory of Aristotle which Dryden epigrammatised into—

> "Great wit to madness nearly is allied,
> And thin partitions do their bounds divide."

As J. G. Kiernan shows,[12] this doctrine, early in the history of the race, obtained dominance through the evolution of arts, sciences, and religions from fetichism. Phenomena manifested by fetich priests (of the Shaman type) so closely resembled epileptic insanity in its frenzies and visions that the two states were long regarded as identical, whence the term *"morbus sacer."* The supernatural influences which, in current belief, underlay epilepsy were, at the outset, malign or benign as they were offended or placated. They became benign, and the insane were under protection of a deity, as in Mussulman countries. Later still the demon-possession theory gained dominance, and at length the demon sank into disease. Throughout all this evolution the belief in an inherent affinity between insanity and genius persisted.

Aristotle, in whose day the disease notion was becoming dominant, asserts that, under the influence of head congestion, persons sometimes become prophets, sybils, and poets. Thus Mark, the Syracusan, was a pretty fair poet during a maniacal attack, but could not compose when sane. Men illustrious in poetry, arts, and statesmanship are often insane, like Ajax, or misanthropic like Bellerophon. Even at a recent period similar dispositions are evident in

Plato, Socrates, Empedocles, and many others, above all, the poets.

According to Plato, "Delirium is by no means evil, but when it comes by gift of the gods, a very great benefit. In delirium the sibyls of Delphi and Dodona were of great service to Greece, but when in cold blood were of little or none. Frequently, when the gods afflicted men with epidemics, a sacred delirium inspired some men with a remedy for these. The Muses excite some souls to delirium to glorify heroes with poetry, or to instruct future generations."

Precedent to the works of Morel and Moreau appeared their source and inspiration, Prosper Lucas's *Natural Heredity*.[13] Here the biologic current of thought encountered the sociologic current; although the waves clashed, the two currents merged into and modified each other. The biologist demonstrated that degenerate types often "threw back" in their structures, and this very "throwing back" made them the fittest to survive. The sociologist found that the only test of acquired or inherited degeneracy in man was disaccord with environment. The co-existent moral and physical defects resultant on heredity found by Erasmus Darwin, Rush, Parkman, Grohmann, and others tended to show that all types of defectives might be a product of heredity.

These stimulating researches into the sources of crime led to a controversy which reached its height two decades ere the treatise of Morel. To this controversy three suggestive works owed their origin: a psychological treatise by Dr. Lauvergne[14] on felons, a romance with a purpose by Eugène Sue,[15] and a suggestively practical brochure by a rather corrupt police official, Vidocq.[16] Seemingly conflicting as were these productions, all strikingly illustrated the influence of heredity and environment in the production of defectives. To these productions were soon added those of Moreau (de Tours), [17] Attemyer, Eliza Farnham,[18] the American Sampson,[19] Dally, Lélut, Camper, and the older Voisin.

Morel[20] laid the foundation of what is widely known as the Lombroso School by a brochure wherein he proposed to entitle morbid anthropology, "that part of the science of man the aim of which is to study phenomena due to morbid influences and to malign heredity."

To the factor of atavism, inconsistently ignored by Morel, the early embryologic studies of Von Baer and the biologic studies resultant on the transmutation of species lent special emphasis. Three possibilities of life await, as Wilson[21] remarks, each living being: either it remains primitive and unchanged, or it progresses toward a higher type, or it backslides and retrogresses. The factors underlying the stable state force the animal to remain as it is; those underlying the progressive tendency make it more elaborate, while the factors of degeneration, on the other hand, tend to simplify its structure. It requires no special thought to perceive that progress is a great fact of nature. The development of every animal and plant shows the possibilities of nature in this direction. But the bearings of physiological backsliding are not so clearly seen.

That certain animals degenerate or retrogress in their development is susceptible of ready and familiar illustration. No better illustration is needed than is derived from the domain of parasitic existence. When an animal or plant attaches itself partly or wholly to another living being, and becomes more or less dependent upon the latter for support and nourishment, it exhibits, as a rule, retrogression and degeneration. The parasitic "guest" dependent on its "host" for lodging alone, or it may be for both board and lodging, is in a fair way to become degraded in structure, and, as a rule, exhibits marked degradation where the association has persisted sufficiently long. Parasitism and servile dependence act very much in structural lower life as analogous instances of mental dependence on others act on man.

The destruction of characteristic individuality and the extinction of personality are natural results of that form of association wherein one form becomes absolutely dependent on another for all the conditions of life. A life of mere attachment exhibits similar results, and organs of movement disappear by the law of disuse. A digestive system is a superfluity to an animal which, like the tapeworm, obtains its food ready made in the very kitchen, so to speak, of its host. Hence the lack of digestive apparatus follows the finding of a free commissariat by the parasite. Organs of sense are not necessary for an attached and rooted animal; these latter, therefore, go by the board and the nervous system itself becomes modified and altered. Degradation wholesale and complete is the penalty the parasite has to pay for its free board and lodging; and in this fashion Nature may be said to revenge the host for the pains and troubles wherewith, like Job of old, he may be tormented.

The most emphatic biologic degeneration is that discovered by Kowalevsky[22] in the sea squirt, which, in its larval state, is a vertebrate, and when adult is an ascidian, seemingly far below the cuttlefish and the worms. This strikingly illustrates that, as Ray Lankester[23] has said, degeneration is a gradual change of structure by which the organism becomes adapted to less varied and less complex conditions of life; a reverse of evolution which proceeds from the indefinite and homogeneous to the definite and heterogeneous with a loss of explosive force due to the acquirement of inhibitions or checks.

This principle of biologic degeneration, long recognised, was most lucidly enforced by Dohrn[24], whose views were later extended by Ray Lankester. The parallelism of animal degeneracy with that of man, so clearly evident even in the parasitic nature of defectives, was, as Meynert[25] showed, due to the fact that the fore-brain is an inhibitory apparatus against the lower and more instinctive natural impulses. The higher its development the greater is the tendency to subordinate the particular to the general. Even in insects a high social growth occurs, as in the bee and ant communities. The same is the case in the development of man; in the infant, a being entirely wrapped in its instincts of self-preservation, the "primary ego" is predominant and the child is an egotistic parasite. As development goes on this standpoint is passed, conscience assumes its priority, the fore-brain acts as a check on the purely vegetative functions and the "secondary ego" takes precedence over the primary one; this is the general order of society, designated as civilisation or social order. If this inhibition become weakened or disordered, predominance of the natural instincts or impulses occurs, and when it is totally lost the individual is in the position of a criminal who opposes the ethical order of society—a parasite, and one of the worst kind who not only lives upon his host but destroys him in doing so.

Hence degenerate tendencies are reversions in type indicating the original source of the inhibition.

The tree of Moreau[26] illustrates clearly the essential principles of these inter-relations of defect, further elucidated by the observations of Sander[27] on the connection of deformed central nervous systems with mental and moral disorder.

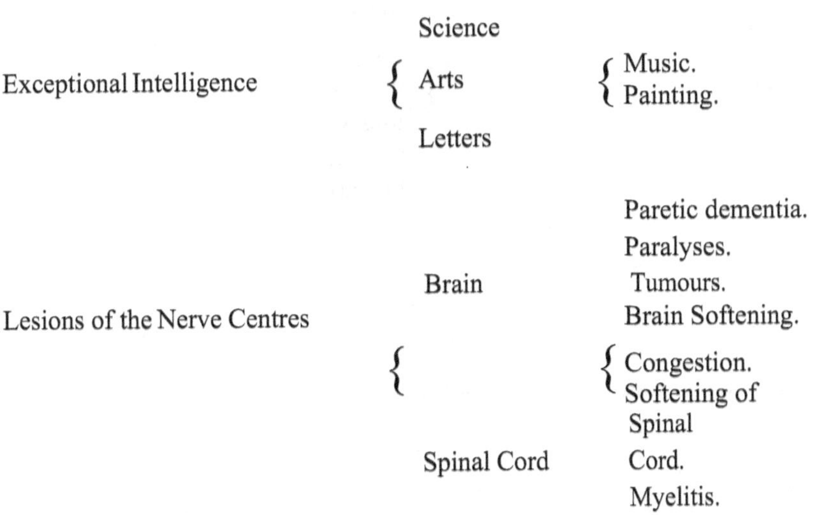

Neuroses

{ Epilepsy.
Chorea.
Stammering.
Convulsive
Fits.
Hysteria.

Intellectual States

{ Utopians.
Eccentrics.
Mixed
Conditions.

Emotional States

{ Prostitutes.
Criminals.
Unstable.

Neuralgia

{ External.
Internal.

Psychoses

{ Acute Insanity { Symptomatical.
Idiopathic.
Alcoholic.

Imbecility
Idiocy
Chronic
Insanity

General Insanity.

{ Dementia.

Partial Insanity.

Special and General Conditions of the

Senses

{ Congenital
Blindness.
Anæsthesiæ.

Deafness.

Hyperæsthesiæ.

Nutritional Defect.

The extensive studies of Niepce,[28] Vogt,[29] and others on idiot biology sought to show that the brain was not merely arrested in development, but sometimes reverted even as low as the sauropsida type (reptiles and birds). Grohmann,[30] as early as 1820, had "often been impressed in criminals, especially in those of defective development, by the prominent ears, the shape of the cranium, the projecting cheek-bones, the large lower jaws, the deeply placed eyes, the shifty, animal-like gaze."

Maudsley[31] observes that in the case of such an extreme morbid variety as a congenital idiot we have to do with a defective nervous organisation. Marchand, in the brain of two idiots of European descent, found the convolutions fewer in number, individually less complex, broader and smoother than in the apes. The condition results neither from atrophy nor mere arrest of growth, but consists essentially in an imperfect evolution of the cerebral hemispheres or their parts, dependent on an arrest of development. The proportion of the weight of brain to that of body is extraordinarily diminished. With the brain of the orang type comes a corresponding defect of function. With this animal type of brain in idiocy sometimes appear animal traits and instincts. One class of idiots is justly designated theroid, so brute-like are its members.

The human brain in the course of fœtal development passes through the same stages as other vertebrate brains, and to some extent these transitional stages resemble the permanent forms of their brain. Summing up, as it were, in itself the leading forms of vertebrate type, there is truly a brute brain within the man's, and when the latter stops short of its characteristic development, it is natural that it should manifest only its most primitive functions.

It must, however, be pointed out that the human brain, even of the idiot or microcephales, never resembles, *as a whole*, the brain of any anthropoid or lower animal form. Such a position was maintained by Vogt, but has long since been abandoned. The existing anthropoid apes are not the ancestors of man, and have pursued a different development.[32]

Despine's[33] researches revealed the absence of human checks on the instinctive tendencies in criminals. He, however, started from the doctrine of moral imbecility as elaborated by Rush, Prichard, Brigham, Ray, Galt, and others. Bruce Thomson,[34] testing Despine's results by primitive races and Scotch criminals, found that defective, abnormal, and anomalous states of the instinctive faculties exist in entire races and in the "moral idiots" that occur in the best races. Criminals form a variety of the human family quite distinct from law-abiding men. A low type of physique indicating a deteriorated character gives a family likeness due to the fact that they form a community which retrogrades from generation to generation. The low physical condition of juvenile criminals in reformatories, &c., becomes at once obvious if they be compared with healthy, active school children. They are puny, sickly, scrofulous, often deformed, with peculiar, unnaturally developed heads, sluggish, stupid, liable to fits, mean in figure, and defective in vital energy, while at the same time they are irritable, violent, and too often quite incorrigible. The adults usually have a singularly stupid and insensate look. The complexion is bad. The outlines of the head are harsh and angular. The boys are ugly in feature, and have, as a rule, repulsive appearances. These diseases of criminals are a proof of their low type and deteriorated condition. Their deaths are mainly due to tubercular diseases and affections of the nervous system. In the greater number crime is hereditary, a tendency which is, in most cases, associated with bodily defect, such as spinal deformities, stammering or other imperfect speech, club-foot, cleft-palate, hare-lip, deformed jaws and teeth, deaf-mutism, congenital blindness, paralysis, epilepsy, and scrofula.

Elisha Harris,[35] of New York, among 233 convicts found 54 to belong to families in which insanity, epilepsy, and other neuroses existed. Eighty-three per cent. belonged to a criminal, pauper, or inebriate stock, and were, therefore, hereditarily or congenitally affected. Nearly 76 per cent. of their number hence proved habitual criminals. According to Harris, crime, pauperism, and insanity revert into each other, so that insanity in the parent produces crime or pauperism in the offspring, or, *vice versâ*, crime or pauperism in the parent produces disease or insanity in the offspring. Campagne, Broca, G. Wilson, and others about the same time made similar researches.

The American sociologist, Samuel Royce, after a careful study of American and European defective classes,[36] found that observation of the hereditary nature of pauperism which congenitally reverts into insanity, disease or crime, leaves no doubt but that pauperism is one of the worst forms of race deterioration, and that the paralysis of the human will and its energies is but the result of a fearful dissolution in progress.

Extensive researches made by Charles S. Hoyt,[37] of the New York State Board of Charities (1874), into the origin of the defective classes of that state, show that the pauper, hysteric, epileptic, prostitute, criminal, born-blind, deaf- mute, paranoiac, recurrent lunatic and idiot were buds of the same tree of degenerate heredity. E. C. Spitzka,[38] basing his researches on the principles of Morel as expanded and critically applied by Meynert,[39] reached essentially the same results as also did Westphal, Krafft-Ebing, Grille, Kerlin,

Axel Key, Magnan, Foville, Bjornstrom, Amadei, Schüle, Nicolson,[40] Tonnini, Tamburini, Verga, Tamassia, Kowalevsky, and it may be said the German Psychiatrical Society (which, by accepting a conception of the distortion of mental faculties otherwise seemingly high, based on brain deformity rather than disease, accepted the degeneracy doctrine of to-day).

For several decades, moreover, the stigmata of degeneracy have appeared in French, German, Austrian, Russian, Italian, and Scandinavian court reports as evidence of hereditary defects.

As often happens in science—

> "Thought by thought is piled till some great truth
> Is loosened and the nations echo round."

Wherefore about this period (1870-78) appeared the first volume of the epoch-making work of Cesare Lombroso,[41] who, erroneously credited with being the apostle of the modern doctrine of degeneracy, has admittedly done more to stimulate research than any other investigator. This work exerted an influence at first in Austria, France, Germany, Italy, Russia, and the Scandinavian countries, while on the English-speaking countries, despite the apparently fertile soil prepared for it, its influence was seemingly slight. Under the degradation produced in many American charitable and correctional institutions by corruption, naturally resultant on a civil war, science therein was at a decided discount between 1861 and 1881. A school arose which, defying the individualistic rule of English common law underlying the institutions of the United States, pandered to mob-law and theologic prejudice by denying certain well-ascertained facts in human degeneracy. This school, represented at the Guiteau trial by the experts for the prosecution, denied heredity and that moral defect could result from physical abnormality. This school, however, was by no means representative of American psychiatry or sociology. Rush, Brigham, James MacDonald, Gait, McFarland, W. W. Godding, Ray, C. H. Hughes, Kerlin, Patterson, Wilbur, Fisher, J. H. McBride, C. H. Nichols, C. A. Folsom, Cowles, and others accepted Morel's principles. Spitzka,[42] long ere the trial, pointed out that criminals displayed the stigmata of Morel, and that the more intellectual types of insanity were based on brain deformity rather than disease.

Benedikt,[43] of Vienna, in 1879 stated that "criminals generally have nothing analogous to monomaniacs. They tend to develop distinct peculiarities of organisation and psychic features, and these peculiarities are the product of their social condition." J. G. Kiernan,[44] reviewing his work, remarked that any one who had at all examined the question would be convinced that between the true criminal type, the imbecile and the paranoiac (*primäre verrückt*) the psychological relations and their anatomical bases are intimate and close. Had Benedikt examined the insane and criminals, not for convolutional aberrations alone, but also for heterotopias, &c., he would never have written the sentence just quoted.

W. W. Godding,[45] commenting on the evidence of J. P. Gray,[46] the leader of the American school that denies degeneracy, feelingly remarked that "the disordered mind does not cease to be a unit although the observed manifestations of its insanity may seem to be confined in some cases to the emotion; in others to the affection; and in still others to the intellectual powers. We cannot deny that the old masters were as keen-sighted observers as ourselves. I dislike to hear drunkenness called dipsomania, as I so often do; but I do not therefore say that dipsomania is only drunkenness. It might improve my standing with the legal fraternity if I should pronounce kleptomania only another name for stealing, but my personal observations convince me that the insane have sometimes a disposition to steal, which is a direct result of their disease, and for which they are no more accountable than the puerperal maniac is for her oaths.

"And now, after all these years of careful research, and our asylum reports[47] rendered bulky with long tables prepared with so much care, involving inquiry on the origin of the disease not alone in the direct family line, but in the collateral branches also; just when the medical profession has come to believe that if one fact in medical science be better established than another, it is that insanity is hereditary, and we undertake in the present case to look up hereditary predisposition, and the family disposition likewise, we are met with the withering conundrum, 'Can a man inherit insanity from his uncle?' and we are told that there is no such thing as hereditary insanity. Yes, gentlemen, I understand you; the tendency to the disease is inherited. And so in the strict use of language there is no such thing as insane delusion; but we know that language is seldom used with scientific exactness, and no one is at a loss to understand what we mean when we say that Jones is full of insane delusions, insanity being hereditary in his family. Yes, and if Jones should marry an insane woman, the chances are good that Jones's son will turn out crazy, no matter how carefully he may be brought up under the direction of the most eminent psychist, for that little germ which you call 'a tendency'— so minute that it will elude your most careful scrutiny with scalpel and microscope—is a fixed fact, and will prove more potent than all theories. Not born there; develops. Ah, how is it that science shows us that syphilis and small-pox and tubercle are born in the offspring, that the infant comes into the world with spina bifida, idiotic, hydrocephalic, acephalic, that the child is blind and mute and misshapen in his mother's womb, but is never insane? Because, forsooth, we have seen fit to limit insanity to disease of the brain, and disease is not inherited. Is it possible that in all these years it has not been

Dr. Gray's lot as it has been mine to be consulted about those 'queer' children of insane parentage, who are perverse from the start? Will he say that the perverseness is only a 'badness' which should be whipped out of the child? But that has generally been thoroughly tried before the physician is consulted. Heterodox I know it is, but observed facts compel me to be heterodox with Prichard and Esquirol and Ray, with Morel and Griesinger and Maudsley, and I know not how many others, in recognising in some cases a condition of inherent defect born in the individual, and not a result of education—a condition which writers have recognised under various names as hereditary mental disorder, insane diathesis, insane temperament."

The Guiteau trial so stimulated studies of degeneracy that two experts for the prosecution, A. McL. Hamilton[48] and H. M. Stearns,[49] later changed their views as to degeneracy, while C. L. Dana, a strong supporter of the Gray school in 1881, subsequently made valuable contributions to the literature of the degeneracy stigmata. The position then taken by Spitzka and Kiernan as to the cerebral basis of degeneracy was in 1882 supported by H. Howard,[50] of Montreal; Workman,[51] of Toronto; Kerlin,[52] of Pennsylvania; Osler,[53] of Baltimore; and C. K. Mills,[54] of Philadelphia.

It was during 1881, moreover, that Jacobi made extensive studies of degeneracy in royalty and aristocracy,[55] as earlier had Ireland.[56]

From the time of Itard degenerate phenomena in idiots had been traced to cerebral mal-development. Kerlin[57] pointed out that "epileptic change" in them was marked by moral alteration similar in explosive characters to that so frequently observed in criminals. In England students of idiocy like Clouston, Shuttleworth, Beach, Ireland, Langdon Down, and others, had early brought the recognition of its inter-relations with insanity, crime and neuroses into strong relief. To the studies of Bruce Thomson, Maudsley, and Nicolson, Tyndall[58] gave strong support from the actual experience of a governor of a great British prison, who found that the prisoners in his charge might be divided into three distinct classes: the first class consisted of persons who ought never to have been in prison; external accident and not internal taint had brought them within the grasp of the law, and what had happened to them might happen to most of us; they were essentially men of sound moral stamina, though wearing the prison garb. Then came the largest class, formed of individuals possessing no strong bias, moral or immoral, plastic to the touch of circumstances which would mould them into either good or evil members of society. Thirdly, came a class, happily not a large one, whom no kindness could conciliate and no discipline tame. They were sent into the world labelled "incorrigible," wickedness being stamped, as it were, upon their organisation.

With the close of the year 1883 the degeneracy doctrine may be regarded as having practically been accepted in biology, in anthropology, in sociology, in criminology, in psychiatry, and general pathology. Debate was henceforth not as to its existence, but as to its limitations. Precedent to 1835 determinism in popular thought due to Calvinistic predestination had, in English-speaking countries, fought for the doctrine; subsequent thereto the theologic reaction against Calvinism was a strong opposing force, whose influence was finally destroyed by the practically general acceptance of the doctrine of evolution in the late seventies.

CHAPTER II

THE STIGMATA OF DEGENERACY

THE attempt made by Morel to limit the doctrine of degeneracy to the domain of the morbid proved impossible, because of the rapid accumulation of data by his own school, which demonstrated that atavistic deformity played a larger part in the production of diseases. Bland Sutton does not too forcibly put this result when he states[59] that if it be difficult to define disease when restricted to the human family, it becomes obviously more difficult when disease is investigated on a broad biological basis. As the great barrier which exists between man and those members of his class most closely allied to him consists not in structural characters but in mental power, it necessarily follows that there should be a similarity in the structural alterations induced by diseased conditions in all kinds of animals, allowing of course for the difference in environment. This is known to be the case, and it is clear that as there has been a gradual evolution of complex from simple organisms, it necessarily follows that the principles of evolution ought to apply to diseased conditions if they hold good for the normal or healthy states or organism; in plain words, there has been an evolution of disease *pari passu* with evolution of animal forms. For a long time it has been customary to talk of physiologic types of diseased tissues; Sutton's earlier efforts were directed to searching among animals for the purpose of detecting in them the occurrence of tissues, which in man are only found under abnormal conditions. The statement proved to be true in a limited sense. At the same time the truth of an opinion held by nearly all thoughtful physicians, that disease may in many instances be regarded as an exaggerated function, was forcibly illustrated; the manifestations of disease were found to be regulated by the same law which governs physiological processes in general, and many conditions regarded as pathological in one animal were revealed as physiological in another.

The doctrine, therefore, has its scope limited only by biologic data. It of necessity begins with the cell itself in its relation to other cells of that practically compound organism which constitutes a single vertebrate. The cell may, therefore, degenerate as a single member of that organism, producing danger or benefit to the other cells. Thus the cancer cell degenerates in its power of reproduction below the tissue to which it belongs. It is peculiarly true here, as has been said by Herbert Spencer, that every vertebrate is an aggregate whose internal actions are adapted to counterbalance its external actions; hence the preservation of its movable equilibrium depends upon its development and the proper number of these actions; the movable equilibrium may be ruined when one of these actions is too great or too small, and through deficiency or need of some organic or inorganic cause in its surroundings. Every individual can adapt itself to these changeable influences in two ways, either directly or by producing new individuals who will take the place of those whom the equilibrium has destroyed. Therefore there exist forces preservative and destructive of the race. As it is impossible that these two kinds of force should counterbalance each other, it is necessary that the equilibrium should re-establish itself in an orderly way. Since there are two preservative forces of every animal group—the impulse of every individual to self-preservation and the impulse to the production of other individuals— these faculties must vary in an inverse ratio; the former must diminish when the second augments. Degeneration constitutes a process of disintegration, the reverse of integration. Hence, if the term individuation be applied to all the processes which complete and sustain the life of the individual, and that of generation to those which aid the formation and development of new individuals, individuation and generation are necessarily antagonistic.

In the phenomena of unisexual generation we see that the larger organisms never reproduce themselves in the unisexual way, while the smaller organisms reproduce themselves with the greatest rapidity by this method. Between these two extremes unisexual reproduction decreases while the size increases. In the history of all plants and animals is evident the physiologic truth, that while the general growth of the individual proceeds rapidly, the reproductive organs remain imperfectly developed and inactive. On the contrary, the principle of reproduction indicates decrease in the intensity of growth and becomes a cause of cessation.

Great fecundity is always attended by great mortality. Each superior degree of organic evolution is accompanied by an inferior degree of fecundity. The greater the germs the less is the individuation, and *vice versâ*. The greater and more complex the organisation, the less is the power of multiplication.

What is true of the cells is also true of organs composed of them. Each organ can be regarded as a distinct animal (a parasite is preferable for comparison) which has its own nervous system (the ganglia), but is fed and controlled by the organism as a whole. Degeneration of this organ may therefore be an expression of a local state peculiar to it and either beneficial or maleficent, or both in inverse degree, to the organism as a whole, or it may be the expression of a general defect in the whole organism. The sclerotic states of the appendix vermiformis in man and of the human liver are, as Kiernan has shown, two excellent illustrations of the degeneracies last described. Man, in common with the four anthropoid apes, has a little thin tube attached to the cæcum known as the appendix vermiformis. In the early embryo it is equal in calibre to the other bowels, but ceases to grow proportionately after a certain time. In the new-born child it is almost as large as in the adult. As this tube proved disadvantageous to man's precursor (as it does to certain mammals) from catching foreign bodies which form the nucleus of enteroliths or bowel stones, it has lost the nutritive supply of the other intestines and is tending to disappear. It is often absent in man. The defect in its structure, while predisposing to the attacks of germs and an expression of its own degeneracy, is an evidence of an advance in evolution in the organism as a whole by which great danger and waste of nutritive force are avoided.

Recent researches[60] have shown that "hob-nail" liver, once supposed to be due entirely to abuse of alcohol, usually occurs in states of congenital deficiency in persons of defective heredity. The change in the appendix which is tending to cause its disappearance is essentially a sclerosis, and hence is morbid, considered from the appendix standpoint alone. As the same process occurs in "hob-nail" liver, it is obvious that degeneracy may be an expression of general advance and local defect or may be a local expression of general defect. The same phenomenon is seen in the nervous system. The researches of Cunningham[61] have shown that in man the struggle for existence between the sympathetic and the cerebro-spinal system has ended in the victory of the latter, while the first is tending to disappear. Such changes must necessarily result in local degeneracies which are for the benefit of the organism as a whole. Degeneracy on this basis may express itself in simple disturbance of the lower or nutritive functions. The uric acid or gouty states, for example, are, as Fothergill long ago pointed out, assumptions by mammalian organs of the functions of those of birds and reptiles. In conditions like myxœdema the skin, through thyroid gland disturbances, takes on features which resemble in result those found in certain mollusks and low fish. These nutritive disturbances may show themselves in disorders of the pituitary body (acromegaly, giantism, &c.), whereby the bony system of man reverts to conditions like those of the gorilla. The same conditions also appear in the diathesis of the "bleeders." All these conditions, however, may be an expression of a degenerate type assuming a normal equilibrium, as well as of a normal organism taking the first steps in degeneracy.

In a general way, therefore, as Dohrn has pointed out, this principle holds good of man not only as an organic unit but as a compound organism. Degeneracy[62] is a gradual change of structures by which the organism becomes adapted to less varied and less complex conditions of life. The opposite progression process of elaboration is a gradual change of structure in which the organism becomes adapted to more and more varied and complex conditions of existence. In elaboration there is a new expression of form corresponding to new perfection of work in the animal machine. In degeneracy there is suppression of form corresponding to the cessation of work. Elaboration of some one organ may be a necessary accompaniment of degeneracy in all the others. This is very generally the case. Only when the total result of the elaboration of some organs, and the degeneracy of others, is such as to leave the whole mass in a lower condition—that is, fitted to less complex action and reaction in regard to its surroundings than is the type—can the individual be regarded as an instance of degeneracy. These degeneracies appear at varying periods, since struggles for existence on the part of the different organs and systems of the body are most ardent during periods of body evolution and involution. During fœtal life, during the first dentition, during the second dentition (often as late as the thirteenth year), during puberty and adolescence (fourteen to twenty-five), during the climacteric (forty to sixty), when uterine involution occurs in woman and prostatic involution in man, and finally during senility (sixty and upwards), during all these periods degeneracy may be shown by mental or physical defect, a congenital tendency to which has remained latent until the period of stress. These defects may be such biochemic alterations (undemonstrable by existing methods) as lead to diminished inhibitory power or other altered function, or to secondary pathologic or teratologic change of decidedly demonstrable nature. Organs and structures checked at a certain phase of development may pursue a course of development differing from that pointed out in man but outlined in other vertebrates. The human cyclopean monstrosities, for example, might be regarded as reversions to the single-eyed sea-squirts, who are possibly the Ascidian precursors of the vertebrates.

The scope of degeneracy may therefore be limited to certain signs which are its sole expressions. These signs (stigmata as they were early called) may be the only expression of degeneracy, and their significance must be determined by a careful examination of the organism in which these expressions are found, since they may be merely defects produced by degeneracy, or may indicate how deep such degeneracy has penetrated. They may, therefore, indicate either slight or serious defect. In proportion to the depth of degeneracy in the organism will the stigmata affect the earlier simpler or later complicated acquisitions through evolution. Of necessity, when the organism is affected by degeneracy, the morbid element will take the line of least resistance, determined by the depth of degeneracy as well as the variability of the structures concerned. The same influence must equally affect functions of the structures. Furthermore, expressions of degeneracy will, as already stated, be influenced by the periods of stress; the first and second dentition, puberty, the climacteric and the senile period. In a general way these stigmata are divisible into mental and physical, and are best observable in their relations to the periods of stress. In certain races, as in certain animals, conditions appearing before puberty was completed cannot be considered as settling the position of the animal in evolution. What is true of individuals is also true of classes. The anthropoid apes and the negroes are much higher in physical characteristics, with potential mental results, before puberty than after. The infant ape, as Havelock Ellis[63] points out, is very much nearer to man than the adult ape. "The infant ape is higher in the line of evolution than the adult, and the female ape, by approximating to the infant type, is somewhat higher than the male. Man, in carrying on the line of evolution, started not from some adult male simian, but from the infant ape and, in a less degree, from the female ape. The human infant bears precisely the same relation to his species as the simian infant bears to his, and we are bound to conclude that his relation to the future evolution of the race is similar. The human infant presents, in an exaggerated form, the chief distinctive characteristics of humanity—the large head and brain, the small face, the hairlessness, the delicate bony system. By some strange confusion of thought we usually ignore this fact, and assume that the adult form is more highly developed than the infantile form. From the point of view of adaptation to the environment, it is undoubtedly true that the coarse, hairy, large-boned and small-brained gorilla is better fitted to make his way in the world than his delicate offspring; but from a zoological point of view we witness anything but progress. In man, from about the third year onwards, further growth—though an absolutely necessary adaptation to the environment—is to some extent growth in degeneration and senility. It is not carried to so low a degree as in the apes, although by it man is to some extent brought nearer to the apes, and among the higher human races the progress towards senility is less marked than among the lower human races. The child of many African races is scarcely, if at all, less intelligent than the European child, but while the African as he grows up becomes stupid and obtuse, and his whole social life falls into a state of hide-bound routine, the European retains much of his childlike vivacity. And if we turn to what we are accustomed to regard as the highest human types, as represented in men of genius, we shall find a striking approximation to the child type." The face, in its contest for existence with the brain, has finally caused both the cranium and the jaws to assume (for defence and food purposes) a lower type, although as regards existing functions and the higher standpoint of environment the infantile type must be considered the higher. Still a casual glance at the Ascidian tadpole shows that deficient as is the development of the ganglia afterward forming the medulla, the face is still more deficient. The face, as Minot shows,[64] is a characteristic of the higher vertebrates, and acquires increased importance with rise in the evolution. The position of the face in embryonic development is originally determined by the head-bend. If a median, longitudinal section of the head be imagined to occupy a rectangular area divided into quarters, then the lower posterior quarter corresponds to the mouth region, the other three-quarters to the brain. As development progresses, the mouth quarter so disproportionately enlarges in relation to the rest of the head as to project forward in front of the fore-brain. In this stage, which is represented by the adult amphibians, the bulk of the facial apparatus is very great, proportionately to the cranium. In the reptiles the mouth region is elongated still further in front of the brain- case, resulting in the long snout. In mammals a third stage is established by the great increase in size of the brain, especially of the cerebral hemispheres. In consequence the brain comes to extend over the snout, as it were; in man, whose brain has the maximum enlargement, the facial apparatus is almost entirely covered by the brain. In the course of evolution the face, while serviceable to the animal for certain reasons of general constitutional character (food-getting, means of defence and means of obtaining mates), is less so than brain growth. A struggle for existence, therefore, inevitably results between the tendency of the face to appropriate power of growth and the like tendency of the brain, which, in defective organisms, produces marked reversions of the one for the benefit of the other. This struggle is further complicated by the embryonic relations to both of the hypophysis, since this body admittedly exerts an influence over bone growth, most markedly (but abnormally) exhibited in acromegaly (excessive bone growth). In this contest for existence in the degenerate types, degeneracy will, of necessity, take the direction of least resistance. As the brain is the last acquirement in vertebrates, considered from the standpoint of necessity, while the face (also a late acquirement) is much less complex, the last, obviously, will present the derangements from degeneration in shape, while the former will show these in shape and function. Furthermore, during the embryonic period the development of the brain will, of necessity, be more immediately affected by degeneracy than the face, which will gain in evolution at its expense. The stigmata of degeneracy, therefore, most likely to attract attention are in the order given, those of the face, jaws, and teeth; ear, eye, cranium; body, bodily functions; brain and spinal cord. Under these last are to be included their mental and nervous functions.

The following table summarizes in practical form these stigmata[65]:—

Crime.

Ethical Degeneracy. { Prostitution and Sexual Degeneracy.
Moral Insanity, Pauperism, and Inebriety.

Paranoia.

Cerebral.

Intellectual
Degeneracy.
{ Adolescent Insanity.
Periodical Insanity.
Hysteria.
Epilepsy.
Neuroses.
One-sided Genius.
Idiocy.

Sensory
Degeneracy.
{ Deaf-Mutism.
Congenital Colour Blindness.
Smell Abnormalities.

Spinal

Various congenital and hereditary disorders

Nutritive
Degeneracy.
{ Exophthalmic Goître.
Lymphoid Degeneracy.
Acromegaly.
Tissue Instability.
Adenoids.
Myxœdema.
Plural Births.
Bleeders.
Cancer.
Excessive Fecundity.
Gout.
Early Lipomatosis.

Local

Jaws.
Cleft Palate.

Teeth.
Primitive Uteri.
Cloacal conditions (and allied male states)

Reversionary
Tendencies.
{ Horseshoe Kidney and allied states.

Cyclopian Monstrosities.

Plural mammæ.

Simian muscular and bony states.

Liver and other organ reversions.

The factors producing degeneration act by causing nervous exhaustion in the first generation. This implies a practical degeneration in function since tone is lost.

Every nerve cell has two functions, one connected with sensation or motion, and the other with growth. If the cell be tired by excessive work along the line of sensation or motion the function as regards growth becomes later impaired, and it not only ceases to continue in strength, but becomes self-poisoned. Each of the organs (heart, liver, kidneys, &c.) has its own system of nerves (the sympathetic ganglia), which while under control by the spinal cord and brain act independently. If these nerves become tired the organ fails to perform its function, the general system becomes both poisoned and ill-fed, and nervous exhaustion results. In most cases, however, the brain and spinal cord are first exhausted. The nerves of the organs are thus allowed too free play, and exhaust themselves later. This systemic exhaustion has local expression in the testicles in the male, in the womb and ovaries in the female. Through this the body is imperfectly supplied with natural tonics (antitoxins) formed by the structures, and the general nervous exhaustion becomes still more complete. All the organs of the body are weakened in their function. Practically the neurasthenic in regard to his organs has taken on a degenerative function albeit not degenerating in structure, since the restlessness of the organs is a return to the undue expenditure of force which occurs in the lower animals in proportion as it is unchecked by a central nervous system. Through the influence of various exhausting agencies the spinal cord and the brain lose the gains of evolution and the neurasthenic is no longer adjusted to environment. Since the reproductive organs suffer particularly, children born after the acquirement of nervous exhaustion, more or less checked in development as the influence of atavism is healthy or not, repeat degenerations in the structure of their organs, which in the parent were represented by neurasthenic disorders in function. As the ovaries of the neurasthenic women generally exhibit prominently the effects of the nervous exhaustion, the offspring of these do not retain enough vigour to pass through the normal process of development.

CHAPTER III

HEREDITY AND ATAVISM

HEREDITY, like other biologic factors, starts with the cell. As elsewhere pointed out, reproduction is first unicellular in type and involves an expenditure of nutritive force antagonistic to the growth of the cell. As Geddes remarks,[66] no one can dispute that the nutritive, vegetative, or self-regarding processes within the plant or animal are as opposed to the reproductive, multiplying, species-regarding processes, as income to expenditure or as building up to breaking down. But within the ordinary nutritive or vegetative functions of the body there is necessarily a continuous antithesis between two tissue-changing sets of processes, constructive and destructive metabolism. The contrast between these two processes is seen throughout nature, whether in the alternating phases of cell-life or in the great antithesis of growth and reproduction.

The starfish, deprived of an arm, replaces this by a fresh growth; crabs can renew the great claws which they have lost in fighting; even as high up as the lizard the loss of a leg or a tail can be made good. In a great variety of cases a kind of physiological forgiveness is shown in the reparation of even serious injuries. Now this "regeneration," as it is called, is a process of reproduction. By continuous growth the cells of a persistent stump are able to reproduce the entire number. A sponge, a hydra or a sea-anemone may be cut into pieces with the result that each fragment grows into a new organism. The same is done with many plants; and though the division is artificial the result shows how very far from unique is the process spoken of as reproduction, which is but more or less discontinuous growth. This is well shown in the evolution onward insensibly from cases of continuous budding, as in sponge or rosebush, to discontinuous budding in hydra zoophyte and tiger-lily, where the offspring vegetatively produced are sooner or later set free.

The enormous expenditure of force required for unicellular reproduction is lessened by conjugation with another cell through satisfaction of cell hunger; and this, by making two cells do the work of one, lessens the amount of nutritive force expended by each. Evolution in fertilisation has the following steps:—

> I. Formation of plasmodia.
>
> II. Multiple conjugation.
>
> III. Conjugation of the two similar cells.

IV. Union of incipiently dimorphic (different) cells.
V. Fertilisation of differentiated sex elements.

As Maupas has shown, by the time conjugation of two similar cells is reached, the paranucleus in both is incipiently hermaphroditic. The impelling force leading to conjugation is, as Rolph has shown, cell hunger. Conjugation, he remarks, is a necessity for satisfaction, a gnawing hunger which drives the animal to engulf its neighbour, to isophagy (self-eating). The process of conjugation is only a special form of nutrition which occurs because of a reduction of the nutritive income or an increase of the nutritive needs. It is an "isophagy" which occurs in place of "heterophagy" (eating of others). "The less nutritive, and therefore smaller, hungrier, and more mobile organism is the male, the more nutritive and usually relatively more quiescent organism the female. Therefore, too, is it that the small starving male seeks out the large, well-nourished female for purpose of conjugation, to which the latter, the larger and better nourished, is on its own motive less inclined." The unicellular type of reproduction long remains after sex differentiation has occurred and assumes the form of parthenogenesis (virgin generation). The phenomena of this demonstrate that the female element is the highest in evolution. Spitzka[67] has shown that the ovum possesses an inherent activity independently of fructification. How far this may extend in the direction of more mature development is shown by what is known about parthenogenesis. This is the development of living beings without a father. Bees, some butterflies, ants and wasps notoriously multiply their kind without sexual congress. As a rule the parthenogenetic offspring are themselves incapable of further procreating their kind. But to this there are remarkable exceptions. The aphides multiply for many generations without the intervention of a male. Weigenbergh has shown that the silk-moth can be propagated as long as the male element is permitted to act at every fourth generation. The *Artemsia salina*, a minute crustacean living in saline springs, reproduces its kind for years without a male being present, males being produced at definite intervals only (Von Siebold). Among the vertebrata parthenogenetic development has also been observed, though rarely reaching maturity. Thus, segmentation occurs in unfertilised ova of the chicken (Oellacher), of the fish (Burnett and Agassiz), and of frogs (Moquia-Tanden). Spitzka has seen a blastoderm form in unfertilised ova of the toad-fish (*Batrachus tau*). Hensen isolated the oviducts of a rabbit, thus rendering the admission of semen impossible, while the ova, discharged at heat, were compelled to remain in these oviducts. Three years later he killed the animal and found the ova had developed into twisted, club-shaped, hollow sacs. The development in the female ovary (also, though very rarely, in the male testicle and parotid gland, which show such a remarkable metastatic sympathy in mumps), of dermoid cysts (containing bones recognisable as maxillaries with teeth, hair, and skin, rudimentary bowel, gland, and brain traces), even in undoubted virgins, proves that even the human ovum is capable of parthenogenetic development. While such development, so far as known to science, is always abortive, and while, as Washington Irving remarks, the ingenious maiden who to-day would attribute conception to any other cause than sexual congress would find it difficult to overcome the prejudice of scientists, yet embryology, while declaring immaculate generation improbable, does not pronounce it impossible. A worker bee may be an offspring of an unimpregnated queen bee. What is a regular occurrence in one class of animals is sometimes observed as an exceptional one in another class. If the startling and apparently miraculous nature of a virgin generation of a living child be regarded as the sole objection to receiving such a fact, its defender might urge that the virgin generation of a dermoid cyst with all the traces, however aborted, of vertebrate organisation, is only a shade less startling and miraculous.

This power of parthenogenesis, however, cannot continue indefinitely without extinction. This has been shown by the careful experiments of Maupas, who had observed 215 generations of an infusorian without sexual union. He found that then the family became extinct. Powers of nutrition, division, and conjugation with unrelated forms come to a standstill. The first symptom of this senile degeneration is decrease in size, which may go on till the individuals only measure a quarter of their normal proportions. Various internal structures then follow suit "until at last formless abortions occur, incapable of living and reproducing themselves." The nuclear changes are no less momentous. The important paranucleus is fatally sterile. The larger nucleus may also become affected, "the chromatin gradually disappears altogether." Physiologically, too, the organisms become manifestly weaker, though there is excessive sexual excitation. Such senile decay of the individuals and of the isolated family inevitably ends in death. Sexual union in those infusorians, dangerous perhaps for the individual life, a loss of time so far as immediate multiplication is concerned, is, in a new sense, necessary for the species. The life runs in cycles of a sexual division which are strictly limited. Conjugation with unrelated forms must occur else the whole life ebbs. Without it the protozoa, which some have called "immortal," die a natural death. Conjugation is the necessary condition of their eternal youth and immortality.

Starting from this standpoint the relative functions of the two sexes in heredity are apparent. The original function of reproduction, that of cell division, is the part of the female. The male in the lower instances simply supplies the female with nutriment. Thus in certain plants there is nothing but a subtle osmosis between the sexes. This is also the case with some of the lower infusoria. With a rise in evolution protoplasm becomes differentiated. At the outset of the subject of heredity it is evident, therefore, that the female furnishes the type which is best capable of development when properly nourished by a highly developed male. To deficiencies in both particulars are due defects and variations in the offspring. As the product of fructification is longest under the nutritive control of the female, her influence is most emphatic in either redeeming defects or producing them. Heredity, according to Ribot, Spitzka, Féré, and others, is divisible into direct heredity, indirect heredity, and, more dubiously, telegony. Direct heredity consists in the transmission of paternal and maternal qualities to the children. This form of heredity has two aspects: (1) The child takes after father and mother equally as regards both physical and moral characters, a case strictly speaking of very rare occurrence; or (2) the child, while taking after both parents, more especially resembles one of them. Here again distinction must be made between two cases. The first of these is when the heredity takes place in the same sex from father to son, from mother to daughter. The other which occurs more frequently, is where heredity occurs between different sexes—from father to daughter or from mother to son. Reversional heredity or atavism consists in the reproduction in the descendants of the moral or physical qualities of their ancestors. It occurs frequently between grandfather and grandson, as well as between grandmother and granddaughter. Collateral or indirect heredity, which is of rarer occurrence than the foregoing, and is simply a form of atavism, subsists, as indicated by the name, between individuals and their ancestors in the indirect line—uncle, or grand-uncle and nephew, aunt and niece. Finally (3) there is telegony, or the heredity of influence, very rare from the physiological point of view, which consists in reproduction in the children by a second marriage of some peculiarity belonging to a former spouse.

In dealing with heredity the position of Weismann and others, that acquired characters cannot be inherited, needs a short examination. In his later work Weismann has practically abandoned the essential basis of his position by admitting that maternal nutrition may play a part in determining variation. He[68] now asserts that the origin of a variation is equally independent of selection and amphimixis, and is due to the constant occurrence of slight inequalities of nutrition in the germ plasm. As acquired characters affecting the constitution of the parents are certain to affect the nutrition of the germ plasm, it is therefore obvious, according to Weismann's admission, that acquired characters or their consequences will be inherited. This is an emphatic though concealed abandonment of the central position of Weismann.

One of the stock arguments of the Weismann school is drawn from results of the Jewish rite of circumcision. While the operation is not calculated to make a profound impression on the constitution, and furthermore, as being performed on the male, less likely to affect the race, still the alleged non-inheritance of its results is much over-estimated. William Wolf,[69] of Baltimore, Maryland, who has circumcised six hundred Jewish children, finds on careful examination, that 2 per cent. were born partially circumcised and 6 per cent. were born with a short prepuce. P. C. Remondino,[70] of Los Angeles, California, has seen a large number of cases of absence of the prepuce which proved to be hereditary. After a confinement his attention was once called to the child by the nurse, who thought it was deformed. The nurse was astonished at the size and appearance of the glans penis. On examination the prepuce was found to be completely absent. On inquiry, the father and another son, born more than twenty years previously (comprising every male member of the family), were found to have been born with the glands fully exposed. He has seen a French family similarly affected.

Similar, but much stronger, results have been obtained by me through the courtesy of the Reverend Drs. S. Bauer, M. A. Cohen, and B. Gordon, all of Chicago. Dr. Bauer, who has been seventeen years in the practice of the religious rite of circumcision, has circumcised 3,400 boys and has found preputial absence in about 3½ per cent. of the cases. Dr. Cohen, who has been two decades in the practice, has performed 10,000 circumcisions. He has found the prepuce wanting in 500 cases; partially developed in 300 cases; slightly developed in 2,000 cases. Dr. Gordon has performed 4,400 circumcisions in twenty-five years. He has found the prepuce absent in 15 cases; partly wanting in 200, and slightly developed in 2,200 cases. These, it should be remembered, are only cases where preputial change forced itself on the observer, who was not pursuing investigations on this point.

The volume of Hebrew casuistic religious literature collected in the Medrash, evidences as I have elsewhere[71] shown the frequency of congenital preputial defect.

That acquired characters can be transmitted has been definitely shown by the experiments of George Roe Lockwood,[72] of New York, anent hereditary transmission of mutilations. White mice were selected, as they begin to breed when thirty days old, and breed every thirty days. He bred in-and-in for thirty-six generations, destroying the weakly, and thus obtained finer animals than the first pair. He selected a pair, caged them by themselves, and clipped the tails of the young. When they were old enough to breed, he selected a pair and clipped the tails of their progeny. In the seventh generation he obtained some tailless mice, and finally a tailless breed. The experiments have one possible element of error; white mice, like all albinoes, are a degenerate type. At the same time these experiments show that accidental mutilations favoured by circumstances are inherited.

Eimer[73] reports the case of a pair of long-tailed pointers which had once produced a litter of long-tailed pups. In order to obtain short-tailed pups the owner had the tails of both shortened. The bitch from that time produced repeatedly short-tailed pups only. As the most careful attention was paid to the parents, no error can be suspected in this case, which, moreover, excites no surprise among dog-breeders.

Brown-Séquard[74] has shown that a peculiar alteration of the shape of the ear or a partial closing of the eyelids is inherited by the offspring of animals in which these changes were caused by dividing the sympathetic. Exophthalmia (eye protrusion) was inherited by guinea-pigs in whose parents this protrusion of the eyes had occurred after an injury to the spinal cord, and so were bruises and dry gangrene, as well as other trophic disturbances in the ear, due in the parents to an injury to the restiform body of the brain. Loss of certain phalanges or of whole toes of the hind feet which had occurred in the parents in consequence of division of the sciatic nerve was inherited. Diseased conditions of the sciatic nerve occurred in the offspring of guinea-pigs in which this nerve was divided. Forty guinea-pigs in which one or both eyes showed more or less morbid change were descended from three individuals in which one eye had become diseased in consequence of transverse section of the restiform body. Twenty guinea-pigs exhibited muscular atrophy on the upper and lower sides of the thigh, when in the parents such atrophy had been caused by section of the sciatic nerve.

The experiments of Brown-Séquard, Westphal, Dupuy[75] and Obersteiner, which show that artificially induced epilepsy is inherited, still further bear out the conclusions resultant on the inheritance of these mutilations. Indeed, Weismann has been forced to that *reductio ad absurdum* in science, narrowly limited definitions, in order to maintain his position. "But although I hold it improbable," he remarks, "that individual variability can depend on a direct action of external influences upon the germ cells and their contained germ plasm, because, as follows from sundry facts, the molecular structure of the germ plasm must be very difficult to change, yet it is by no means to be implied that this structure may not possibly be altered by influences of the same kind continuing for a very long time. This much may be maintained: that influences which are mostly of variable nature, tending now in one direction, now in another, can hardly produce a change in the structure of the germ plasm, and this is the reason why the cause of inheritable individual differences must be sought elsewhere than in these varying influences." "No one has doubted," he says, in reply to objections made by Virchow, "that there are a number of congenital deformities, birth-marks, and other individual peculiarities which are inherited. But these are acquired characters in the above sense. True, they must once have appeared for the first time, but we cannot say exactly from what causes; we only know that at least a great proportion of them proceed from the germ itself, and must therefore be due to alterations of the germinal substance. If Virchow could show that any single one of these hereditary deformities had its origin in the action of some external cause upon the already formed body (soma) of the individual and not upon the germ cell, then the inheritance of acquired characters would be proved. But this no one has yet succeeded in proving, often as it has been maintained."

The crucial test which Weismann demands is furnished by Dupuy,[76] who made one thousand experiments on guinea-pigs to the fifth generation, critically rejecting all results which did not correspond to the most rigid tests of direct heredity, excluding all instances of indirect heredity, however demonstrable. He found that certain lesions of the spinal cord, or the brain or the sciatic nerve, give rise in guinea-pigs to epilepsy.

In from three to six weeks after the operation an alteration in the nutrition takes place in an area of skin which is limited by a line starting from the outer canthus of the eye, and running to the median line on the upper lip, enclosing the nostril, thence backward enclosing the lower jaw, to the anterior portion of the shoulder to the median dorsal line, to the base of the ear and inner canthus of the eye. The alteration in nutrition occurs on the side corresponding to the injury. The pain, heat and cold sense disappear by degrees, while touch appears to be exalted. Very soon, tickling this zone of skin gives rise to twitchings limited to the muscles of the eye and the eyelids on the same side. Later, the muscles of the mouth and of the face are affected, still later the contractions become more general, until the whole side is the seat of convulsions, then the convulsions attack the other side also. When things have come to this point the convulsions precede by a very short time complete loss of consciousness. If the subject of experiment be white, it is found that there is paleness of the face, but in all cases there is little foam at the mouth and dilatation of the pupils. The animal sometimes utters a cry corresponding to the epileptic cry in the man. Not only are the convulsions identical with those in epileptic man, but there is also loss of consciousness, a state of torpor, stupor, and even sometimes insanity. When epilepsy is due to the destruction of the sciatic nerve, the foot of the affected side loses the two outer toes, so that the animal has only one toe, the inner. When young are born to such a parent or parents (for it matters not whether one or both of the parents have been operated upon), they have very often only one toe on the posterior foot. Sometimes, however, they have additional toes, which, in this case, are attached by a pedicle to the limb.

Those peculiarities observed in the parents are in all their details witnessed in the guinea-pigs hereditarily born toeless, who have developed epileptic phenomena. In Dupuy's cases not only is the epileptic tendency (of which Weismann gives a wholly imaginative microbic explanation) inherited, but the very stigmata (loss of toes) which mark development of the parental epilepsy.

E. D. Cope's[77] careful studies of the effects of impacts and strains on the feet of mammals are testimony difficult for Weismann to explain, since they also meet his requirements.

Weismann's admission of the inheritance of a tuberculous habit must logically, from the standpoint of degeneracy, be regarded as destroying his claims.

Kiernan has observed the case of a female cat in which brain mutilation had been induced to secure secondary cerebro-spinal degenerations. The mutilations were made under antiseptic precautions. The descendants of this cat had traces of the mutilation, and its results until the fourth generation, when the breed became extinct. This instance certainly fulfils all Weismann requirements.

In the Lambert family a skin deformity, the last result of degeneracy in previous generations, was transmitted. This peculiarity appeared first, according to Proctor,[78] in the person of Edward Lambert, whose whole body, except his face, the palms of the hands and the soles of the feet, was covered with a horny excrescence. He was the father of six children, all of whom as soon as they had reached the age of six weeks presented the same peculiarity. The only one of them who lived transmitted the peculiarity to all his sons. For five generations all the male members of the family were distinguished by the horny excrescence which had adorned the body of Edward Lambert.

Shwe-Maong, one of the hairless Burmese, when thirty years old had his whole body covered with silky hairs, which attained a length of nearly five inches on the shoulders and spine. He had four daughters, but only one of them resembled him. She had a son who was hairy like his grandfather. The case of this family illustrates rather curiously the relation between the hair and teeth; for Shwe-Maong retained his milk teeth till he was twenty (when he attained puberty); then they were replaced by nine teeth only, five in the upper and four in the lower jaw. Eight of these were incisors, the ninth (in the upper jaw) being a cuspid tooth.

Certain motor expressions of disturbed functions are also inherited. Galton describes the case of a man who, when he lay fast asleep on his back in bed, had the curious trick of raising his right arm slowly in front of his face, up to his forehead, and then dropping it with a jerk, so that the wrist fell heavily on the bridge of his nose. The trick did not occur every night, but occasionally, and was independent of any ascertained cause. Sometimes it was repeated incessantly for an hour or more. The gentleman's nose was prominent and its bridge often became sore from blows which it received. At one time an awkward sore was produced that was long in healing on account of the recurrence, night after night, of the blows which first caused it. His wife had to remove the buttons from the wrist of his nightgown, as it made severe scratches, and some means were attempted of tying his arm. Many years after his death his son married a lady who had never heard of the family incident. She, however, observed precisely the same peculiarity in her husband; but his nose, from not being particularly prominent, has never as yet suffered from the blows. The trick does not occur when he is half asleep, as, for example, when he is dozing in his armchair, but the moment he is fast asleep he is apt to begin. It, as with his father, is intermittent, sometimes ceasing for many nights, and sometimes almost incessant during a part of every night. It is performed, as it was with his father, with his right hand. One of his children, a girl, has inherited the same trick. She performs it likewise with the right hand but in a slightly modified form; for after raising the arm she does not allow the wrist to drop upon the bridge of the nose, but the palm of her half-closed hand falls over and down the nose, striking it rather rapidly, a decided improvement on the father's and grandfather's method. The trick is intermittent in the girl's case also, sometimes not occurring for periods of several months, but sometimes almost incessantly. These "tricks" suggest nocturnal epilepsy, however.

The face of a child is often fully developed, yet, owing to some of the constitutional diseases, arrested development of the face at this point takes place. The second generation inherits this deformity, while the grandparents possess normally developed faces.

The following case came under my own immediate observation. The grandfather was in the habit of sitting in front of the fire with fingers locked together twirling the thumbs in one direction, and then occasionally knocking the thumb nails together. Two of his three sons inherited this habit; the third brother had the habit of biting his nails when in a fit of abstraction. The nephew of the last has a similar habit under the like conditions. The children of this nephew have in two instances shown a tendency to pick at the nails when in an unconscious state, from acute disease. The third child has a periodical tendency to do the same since it was four months old.

X. P. Gibney,[79] of New York, has reported a family consisting of father and mother, five children, and one grandchild. The father and mother are semi-ambidextrous. All of the children and the grandchild are semi-ambidextrous to an annoying degree; all of the movements which they perform with one hand are simultaneously performed by the other hand. The girls are obliged to use only one hand when dressing themselves, or when cutting patterns, and hold the other hand down by their side, because the two hands perform the same movements at the same time and would interfere with each other.

One factor in heredity concerning which there has been much dispute, and whose existence has been denied because of certain theories anent the nerve connection of the mother and fœtus, is that of maternal impressions. As Féré[80] has shown, the fœtus exhibits very decided reaction to sensory impressions on the mother. He cites cases of several women who, often in the midst of an ordinary dream, producing but very moderate excitation, not generally interrupting sleep, were awakened by fœtal movements. The dreams had nothing of the nightmare which would cause sudden contraction under the influence of a terrifying idea. They were merely the ordinary phenomena of sleep. Mental changes of the mother hence excite motor reactions in the fœtus, and, as with sensorial excitations, these reactions are stronger in the fœtus than in the mother. The mechanism of these motor reactions is, Féré points out, obviously due to unconscious and involuntary movement of the muscle walls of the womb. The organisation of a morbid predisposition may be largely influenced by an accident accompanying conception or gestation. In some degenerates cannot be found a trace of hereditary defect. The fact cited explains how sensorial excitations or repeated and violent emotions in the mother during pregnancy give rise to profound nutritive troubles in the fœtus, and especially in its nervous system. These congenitally degenerated beings (*ab utero*) can hardly be distinguished from those having direct heredity. A considerable number of cases of epilepsy, idiocy, &c., are recognised as having arisen from alcoholism in the mother. Psychic troubles in the mother may react upon the fœtus in an analogous way. The prominent facts which show the influence of the psychic state of the mother upon the somatic condition of the fœtus explain the action of the imagination of the mother upon the development of the product of conception. The opinion which refers the origin of birth-marks to intense mental impressions on the part of the mother is not without physiological foundation. Concurrently with the motor phenomena, stigmata[81] may become developed by vascular and nutritive troubles produced under the influence of a strong excitation or by the imagination.

Spitzka,[82] who approached maternal impressions from an actively sceptical standpoint, had his scepticism shaken by specimens (preserved in the British Museum) of newly hatched chicks, all of which had a curved beak like a parrot, and the toes set back as in that bird. According to the report of the curator the hens in the farmyard where these monstrosities were hatched had been frightened by a parrot which, having escaped, fluttered among them some time before the eggs were laid and greatly frightened those from whom the malformed chicks were received. It is certain that the chief argument of those who deny that maternal impressions are transmitted is defeated by this case. They have usually asserted that the explanation of the nature and cause of a birth-mark was always an after-thought on the part of the mother. But there was no after-thought in this case. The hens did not publish a theory as to the malformation of their chicks. It was their owner, a gentleman of intelligence and culture, who observed the casual occurrence, and who verified the almost photographic truthfulness of the germ monstrosity by depositing it in a museum as a permanent record at which none may cavil.

Since then, the singular freaks attributable to maternal impressions of women, seen by Spitzka, have become so numerous that he has been compelled to negative the argument that they were merely accidental coincidences. He has never seen an idiotic, malformed child or one afflicted with morbid impulses derived from healthy parents free from hereditary taint in which a maternal impression could not be traced.

In a large number a direct correspondence between the maternal impression and the nature of the deformity or peculiarity could be discovered. He reports the case of a woman, about five months pregnant, who, while standing in her yard, saw her husband stab into the belly of a goat he had slaughtered. The sight of the suddenly protruding visceral mass, which happened to be imperfectly bilobar, shocked her extremely, and, starting back, she, in her great revulsion, feeling a strange sensation at the nape of the neck or back of the head, clutched the former with her right hand. The impression continued to haunt her. When the child was born and she saw its deformity she instantly exclaimed, "Oh, the intestines of that goat!" At the back of its head the child had a large tumour of the consistency of a loose sac of a bluish colour, showing convolutions interpreted by the mother as a reproduction of the intestinal convolutions that had so shocked her. In reality they were the convolutions of a hernia containing the posterior ends of both cerebral hemispheres. The accidental resemblance of the deformity to the mental impressions was striking.

A. Lagorio[83] brought before the Chicago Medical Society several cases in which maternal impressions had produced decidedly abnormal births with deformities resembling those feared by the mother. Kiernan, in discussing these, pointed out that all were instances of checked development. He was of opinion that moral shock, generally directed, played the chief part in maternal impressions through checking development and causing either general or local reversion. Here, as Spitzka[84] shows, the statistical method can be applied. It has been long known that profound grief, mental or physical shock acting on the mother, produce cerebral defect or generally arrested development in the offspring. Of 92 children born in Paris during the great siege, 1870-71, 64 had mental or physical anomalies and the remaining 28 were weakly, 21 were intellectually defective (imbecile or idiotic), and 8 showed moral or emotional insanity. These figures, furnished by Legrand du Saulle, justify the popular designation by the working men of Paris of the defective children born in 1871 as "*enfants du siège*."

After the great Chicago fire in 1871 birth-marks, deformities, and mental defects were noticed to occur among the offspring whose mothers were pregnant with them pending the exciting time during and after the conflagration.

Spitzka has seen in practice, constitutionally melancholic or mentally defective children in whom no other predisposing cause could be discovered than that the mother was struggling with direct or indirect results of the financial crisis of 1873. In several of these cases the death of the father was a contributory cause of maternal depression. In Berlin the financial crisis of 1875-80 was followed by an increase in the number of idiots born. Lombroso attributes a series of cases of microcephaly to profound mental impressions occurring during pregnancy. To the same class of cases belong the hermaphrodites born by mothers who have been frightened in their first pregnancy and who continue to bear hermaphrodites. The continual and not ill-founded dread that the succeeding children may resemble the first is to be regarded as a contributory cause. Observers who have had a large experience with illegitimate births believe that the mental agony suffered by the unfortunate mother reacts upon the fœtus, causing arrest of development, and thus accounting for the frequent occurrence of idiocy in illegitimate children.

The influence of maternal diet on the fœtus is excellently illustrated in the results of the "fruit diet" advised by certain vegetarians. Here the children[85] become, as Elise Berwig has recently shown, rickety, irritable, peevish, liable to convulsions, morally peculiar, and otherwise defective in contrast with children born of the same parents without "fruit diet" during pregnancy.

Kiernan,[86] after citing instances reported by Amabile, Carson, F. B. Earle, Erlenmeyer, F. H. Hubbard, C. H. Hughes, Mattison, and others, of congenital opium habit where opium was needed to preserve the infant during the first months of life, states that inheritance of the opium habit seems at first an isolated phenomenon, but zoologists have pointed out that pigeons whose ancestors were fed on poppies became intractable to opium. Murrell found that the same was relatively true in England of persons descended from Bedfordshire ancestors who used infusions of poppies as a prophylactic against malaria. Nervous diseases were, however, relatively prevalent in these districts. Narcotic habits in the ancestors produces descendants in whom the normal checks on excessive nervous action are removed, so that paranoiacs, periodical lunatics, epileptics, hysterics, congenital criminals, congenital paupers, or other degenerates result. This influence is most strongly exerted when the maternal ancestor is the one affected, for to her is committed the development of the ovum prior to conception and of the child subsequently. If either is interfered with by a habit, a being defective in some respects is the result. The direct inheritance of the opium habit has been shown experimentally by Levenstein, who found by experiments on pregnant dogs and rabbits that the use of opium during pregnancy produced either abortion or still-births, or rapidly dying offspring.

In a similar manner Rennert[87] has shown that lead-poisoning occurring in the mother is apt to produce macrocephalism with frequent idiocy in the child.

This brings the observer face to face with the problem of morbid heredity. It may at once be admitted that, as has been claimed by a large number of observers, morbid heredity, especially in its graver forms, is much less frequent than at first would be expected. J. P. Gray, of Utica, New York, went so far as to claim that disease is never transmitted, but this is contradicted by his own hospital reports, which, to the day of his death, contained a table headed, "Statistics of hereditary transmission of the disease." It is true, however, that the descendants of a victim of morbidity or abnormality do not always exhibit the morbidity or abnormality of the ancestor. In some cases all apparent morbidity or abnormality is wanting. In other cases slighter abnormalities are to be detected. Here the observer is brought face to face with the operation of two general principles which are interdependent: the transmutation of heredity and atavism, or "throwing back" as the cattle breeders call it. Tennyson voices the general erroneous opinion of the always evil effects of atavism in his "Locksley Hall Sixty Years After":—

> "Evolution ever climbing after some ideal good
> And Reversion ever dragging Evolution in the mud."

As Kiernan has shown, atavism at times tends to preserve the type, and offsets the influence of degeneracy. This element of atavism underlies not merely the production of the sound scions of degenerate stock, but also those in whom the degeneracy affects the earlier and not the later acquirements of the race. The contrast of the moral imbecile who is unable to acquire an idea of right, or the idiot of the lowest grade who can hardly be taught to keep himself clean, with the otherwise sound, sane, able victim of hereditary gout, is very great. Yet all the links of the chain connecting, in the same family, these contrasted types, can often be found. The law laid down as to absolute extinction through degeneracy by Morel and others can only be regarded as absolutely true when applied to a given type rather than the race as a whole. Indeed, environment may play a part in preserving a degenerate who would otherwise die out. Thus in societies at a certain stage of culture imbeciles, paupers, lunatics, and congenital criminals live at large and even propagate through legal marriage. The seemingly enormous increase of the defective class which occurs in frontier communities when the classes begin to be placed in public institutions is an excellent illustration of this.

Manifestations of morbid heredity result not in inheritance of the whole defect but in disturbance of relations of structure and hence of function, producing, as Kiernan remarks, a constitutional deficiency which takes the line of least resistance. The extent and direction of this line of least resistance depend on the amount of healthy atavism which separate organs and structures of the body preserve. The line of least resistance sometimes taken is excellently illustrated in the occurrence of stigmata already pointed out in the case of epileptic guinea-pigs.

This unilateral predisposition (which, as Kiernan has shown, is due usually to heredity or intra-uterine causes) may be artificially produced. Kasparek[88] cut one sciatic nerve of a guinea-pig and (after all inflammatory symptoms had subsided) injected the opposite ear with cultures of pus microbes. He killed the animal after some days. The sound side was found free from suppuration, but immense abscesses existed on the side of the cut nerve. Such local predisposition was pointed out by Merrill[89] over forty years ago. This condition occurs, as Féré has shown,[90] in many systemic and infectious diseases which presents a localisation due to heredity, or determined by anterior morbid state of the nervous symptom. Sometimes these manifestations are limited to the side free from nervous trouble.

As a rule they attack the side which is the predominant seat of nervous symptoms. Féré points out that in chromatic iris asymmetry the iris (coloured part of the eye) is most coloured on the side most affected by arrest of development. Localisation of nervous trouble occurs on the side most affected by hare-lip. Heuse has observed the co-existence on the same side of congenital cataract and of deformities of the skull and chest.

Hernia is often an expression of hereditary defect (Le Double) taking the unilateral line of least resistance. Testicle inflammations of microbic origin (venereal or otherwise) occur as a rule on the side where hernia is located in the groin. In one-sided malformations of ovary or testicle (decreased or increased in size, or changed in shape or location) microbe inflammation almost always occurs at the seat of the anomaly. This principle is illustrated in the experiments of Dupuy.[91] Here, while as a rule, the scions of guinea-pigs (rendered epileptic by section of the sciatic nerve) were epileptics and had deficient toes, still in some epilepsy resulted without the toe anomaly, while still more rarely the toe anomaly was present without the epilepsy.

The same principle is shown by certain observations of Charin and Gley,[92] who for five years conducted experiments calculated to throw light on the influence on the offspring of parental reception of virus. Either both male and female have been inoculated with the bacillus of blue pus or its toxins, or but one animal has been inoculated. The results have not been uniform. Most frequently there ensues sterility, abortion, or birth of progeny that die immediately. In rare instances the offspring survive; more rarely still are they healthy. Certain rabbits (born of these undeveloped animals) were provided with enormous epiphyses (ends of bones), the shafts of the bones being shortened. Two rabbits were born of a couple of which the male alone received inoculations of sterilised culture. Five rabbits were born of these two, of which two were normal, and a third (whose ears were rudimentary) died in a few days. In the remaining two the ears comprised only fragments with jagged upper edges. The tails were but two centimetres long. The external orifice of the vagina (one rabbit was a male and the other a female) was oblique. One of the limbs (the hind in the male and the fore in the female) was much shorter than its fellow, the difference being four centimetres. The shortened limb ended in a kind of stump, there being no foot or toes.

These experiments illustrate the transformation of heredity, that is the manifestations which show the line of least resistance that the morbid heredity has taken. As Moreau (de Tours) remarks,[93] "An incorrect conception of the law of heredity looks for identical phenomena in each succeeding generation. Some have refused to admit that mental faculties were subject to heredity, because the mental characters of the descendants were not precisely those of the progenitors. Each generation must copy the preceding. Father and son must present the spectacle of one being, having two births, and each time leading the same life, under the same conditions. But it is not in the heredity of functions, or of organic or intellectual facts that the application of the law of heredity must be sought, but at the very fountain-head of the organism, in its inmost constitution. A family whose head is insane or epileptic does not of necessity consist of lunatics or epileptics, but the children may be idiotic, paralytic, or scrofulous. What the parents transmit to the children is not insanity, but a vicious constitution which will manifest itself under various forms in epilepsy, hysteria, scrofula, rickets, &c. This is what is to be understood by hereditary transmission."

The same position has been taken by Rush,[94] the pioneer American alienist; by Maudsley,[95] by Krafft-Ebing,[96] by Meynert, by Mercier, by Féré,[97] and others. Morel,[98] the chief accepted apostle of the doctrine of degeneracy, remarked, nearly at the same time as Moreau, that "heredity does not mean the very disorder of the parents transmitted to the children with the identical mental and physical symptoms observed in the progenitors, but means transmission of organic disposition from parents to children. Alienists have, perhaps, more frequent occasion than others for observing not merely this hereditary transmission, but likewise various transformations which occur in the descendants. They are aware that simple neuropathy (nervous tendency) of the parents may produce in the children an organic disposition resulting in mania or melancholia, nervous affections which in turn may produce more serious degeneracy and terminate in the idiocy or imbecility of those who form the last link in the chain of hereditary transmission."

What is true of the organism as a whole is true of the cells forming its organs. It should be remembered that while cell life is altruistic or subordinated to the life of the organ, through the law of economy of growth, recognised by Aristotle, and through it to the life of the organism as a whole, altruism is not complete enough to prevent entirely a struggle for existence on the part of the cells or the individual organs. With rise in evolution this struggle decreases, to increase with the opposite procedure of degeneracy. From it results the phenomenon of arrested and excessive development.

As Dareste has shown (and the fact has been corroborated by Spitzka[99]), embryologists can imitate natural malformation of the nerve centres by artificial methods. By wounding the embryonic and vascular areas of the chick's germ with a cataract needle, malformations are induced, varying in intensity and character with the earliness of the injury and its precise extent. More delicate injuries produce less monstrous development. Partial varnishing or irregular heating of the egg-shell, in particular, results in anomalies comparable to microcephaly (little head) and cerebral asymmetry. This latter fact (showing the constancy of the injurious effect of so apparently slight an impression as the partial varnishing of a structure not connected with the embryo at all directly) suggests the line of research to be followed in determining the source of the maternal and other impressions acting on the germ. What delicate problems are to be solved in this connection may be inferred from the fact that eggs subjected to the vibration and shocks of a railroad journey are checked in development for several days, or permanently arrested. A more delicate molecular shock during the maturation of the ovum, during its fertilisation, or finally during embryonic stages of the more complex, and therefore more readily disturbed and distorted human germ, accounts for the disastrous effect of insanity, emotion, or other mental or physical shock of the parent on the offspring. The cause of the majority of cerebral deformities exists in the germ prior to the appearance of the separate organs of the body. Artificial deformities produce analogous results because they imitate original germ defects, either by mechanical removal, or by some other interference with a special part of the germ. Early involvement of the germ is shown by the fact that the somatic malformations of the hereditary forms of insanity often involve the body elsewhere than in the nervous axis. The stigmata of heredity—defective development of the uro-genital system, deformities of the face and skull, irregular development of the teeth, misshapen ears and limbs—owe their grave significance to this fact. Like deformities of the brain, these anomalies are also more marked and constant with the lower forms of the hereditarily based systematised perversions of the mind than the higher. It is easy from these results to understand how far and how the nervous system has its part in the disorders of general development. It can be easily understood how the individuals who present most deformities are equally those who suffer from most decided disorders of the nervous system.

These morbid manifestations of heredity occur in certain categories, either local as to organs or structures, or affecting the body as a whole. These categories Moreau (de Tours) lucidly sums up as: First, absence of conception; second, retardation of conception; third, imperfect conception; fourth, incomplete products (monstrosities); fifth, products whose mental, moral, and physical constitution is imperfect; sixth, products specially exposed to nervous disorders in order of frequency as follows—epilepsy, imbecility or idiocy, deaf-mutism, insanity, cerebral paralysis, and other cerebral disorders; seventh, lymphatic products; eighth, products which die in infancy in a greater proportion than sound infants under like conditions; ninth, products which, although they escape the stress of infancy, are less adapted than others to resist disease and death.

The explanation of these morbid manifestations lies in the very foundations of embryology. Bearing in mind the principles of individuation pointed out by Spencer, it is easily understood how reversal of this principle would produce greater and greater destruction of the complex functions, resultant on increased reproductive power of cells (whose environment is not suited to such reproductions) and thus lead to such a struggle for existence as to produce sterility (from interdestruction of the ovum cells, or the cells forming the spermatozoon). This condition is further increased by the operation of two biologic principles. The first relates to the cells or organs forming an organism. The second, as Von Baer has shown, deals with the relation of the organs to each other.

Vertebrate embryos of a common type, at their origin, assume successively a number of common forms before definitely differentiating. Dareste points out that supernumerary organs do exist in these common forms at one phase of embryonic life. This community of embryonic types and this last fact explain repetition of teratologic types or monstrosities in vertebrates. This community of origin, moreover, indicates that a higher vertebrate embryo contains in essence the organs and potentialities of lower vertebrates, and that under the influence of heredity or accidental defect an organ belonging to another species may develop, or an organ constant in a species may be lacking in an individual, without the necessity of explaining the immediate effects by distant atavism. Some anomalies found among degenerates recall types less elevated than man, and very distant from him, even his possible Lemurian precursor.

It is obvious from the principles already demonstrated that the secondary effects of infectious disorders and injuries are reproduced in various types in the offspring. The malformations of the limbs experimentally demonstrated to be due to ancestral infection by Charin and Gley, and to injury by Dupuy, noticeably occur in men. Moor has observed supernumerary fingers in an imbecile girl; her grandfather and one uncle are polydactylous and insane. F. S. Coolidge has had under observation a case which excellently depicts these deformities in men. Kiernan[100] reports the case of a man whose grandfather and father had been prophets of the Lord, as shown by the fact that on one side of the body they had six toes and six fingers, and the two sides of the body were unequal, the six-fingered one being smaller than the other. This father and grandfather were highly regarded in a secluded vale in Norway as religious teachers and for their power to cure disease by charm. The father had ten children, of whom three were born dead and six died in infancy. Kiernan's patient was the only survivor of this family. During boyhood he experienced various persecutions, some by unseen agencies, some on the part of the villagers, who towards the end of his father's life also persecuted the father. These persecutions seem to have been withdrawal by the peasants of their belief in the father's ability to charm sickness out of cattle, evidently due to growing popular intelligence. This was regarded by the father as the result of persecution by the devil, who was desirous of trying him as Job was tried. It was revealed to him that his son should likewise suffer persecution, which would also be the work of the devil. The son heard unseen persons, who pointed him out in school as the son of the sham wizard. In consequence he was avoided by all his schoolmates except the members of one family who still retained their belief in the father's supernatural powers. Into this family the son married; then, pressed by his unseen persecutors, he came to the United States. Here he worked at his trade as a carpenter, and had no return of any persecutory delusions, although he still believed he was a prophet. On admission to the insane hospital, twenty years after his arrival in the United

States, he was found to have such a decidedly asymmetrical body that suspicions of general hemiatrophy were excited, but the condition was found to be congenital. The hand and foot of the seemingly atrophic side had six fingers and toes. The man had been sent to the insane hospital in consequence of an altercation with a neighbour who was clearly in the wrong; but both being arrested, the patient's *amour propre* was aroused and he declared his prophetship, which led to his trial and commitment as a lunatic. His wife, who applied for his discharge, was also a paranoiac. They had had ten children, of whom three were still living at the ages of six, eight, and ten. Two of these were six-toed and six-fingered unilaterally, and one of them, a boy, had the peculiar general asymmetry of the father. The third child was seemingly normal.

The experimental results of Charin and Gley, on the degeneration produced in offspring by ancestral microbic infection, tend to show that not merely are the extremities affected, but in certain cases the whole organism, along lines laid down by Moreau's categories. This is demonstrated by study of the degeneracy stigmata of phthisical families. Alex. James, Ricochon,[101] C. E. Paddock,[102] and others have shown that (in addition to the ordinary stigmata) the biologic stigmata of degeneracy (such as plural and quickly repeated births) are frequent among phthisical families. The same phenomena often occur in families whose scions are attacked with diabetes, obesity, articular rheumatism, cancer and gout. De Giovanni[103] finds that particular nervous states exist in those predisposed to tuberculosis, whom he divides into erethists (restless), torpids, and energetics. There is a diminutive heart, whose right ventricle has comparatively exaggerated dimensions, while the arteries have lessened calibre.

A family illustrating excellently the transmutation of morbid heredity is one followed through five generations by Kiernan.[104] A farmer lived twenty miles distant from his nearest neighbour, whose only child he married. The daughter had led a lonely life till her courtship at the age of 28 by the farmer, then three years younger. The farmer married her for $300, after having impregnated her. He then found lead on his farm and went to a city. A stock- company bought his farm and launched him into the stock market, where he made money more as a cunning tool than an adventurer. He became a high liver, gouty and dyspeptic, and died with symptoms of gouty kidney at 70. The couple had five children. The eldest, a son, became a "Napoleon of Finance," but, inheriting his father's cunning, died wealthy and within the pale of the law. He married a society woman, the last scion of an old family. The second child, a daughter, was club-footed and early suffered from gouty tophi. She married a society man of old family who had cleft palate. The third child, a daughter, had congenital squint. She married a man who suffered from migraine of a periodical type. The fourth child, a daughter, was normal. She married a thirty-year-old active business man, in whom ataxia developed a year after marriage. The fifth child, a son, was ataxic at eighteen. The children of the "Napoleon of Finance" and the society woman were an imbecile son, a nymphomaniac, a hysteric, a female epileptic who had a double uterus, and a son who wrote verses and was a society man. The cleft- palated society man and club-footed woman had triplets born dead and a squinting, migrainous son who, left penniless by his parents, married his cousin the nymphomaniac daughter of the "Napoleon of Finance," after being detected in an intrigue with her. The migrainous man and squinting daughter of the farmer stockbroker had a sexually inverted masculine daughter, a daughter subject to periodical bleeding at the nose irrespective of menstruation, as well as chorea during childhood, a normal daughter, a deaf- mute phthisical son, a daughter with cloacal formation of the perineum, an ameliac son, a cyclopian daughter (with one central eye) born dead, and, finally, a normal son. The sexual invert married the versifier son of the "Napoleon of Finance." The progeny of the normal daughter of the farmer stockbroker and the ataxic husband were a dead-born, sarcomatous son, a gouty son, twin boys paralysed in infancy, twin girls normal, a normal son, and a son ataxic at fourteen. The progeny of the nymphomaniac daughter and her strabismic, migrainous cousin were a ne'er-do-well, a periodical lunatic, a dipsomaniac daughter who died of cancer of the stomach, deformed triplets who died at birth, an epileptic imbecile son, a hermaphrodite, a prostitute, a double monster born dead, a normal daughter, and a paranoiac son. The ne'er- do-well married his nose-bleeding cousin. The gouty son of the farmer's normal daughter married the hysteric daughter of the "Napoleon of Finance." They had a son born with such general asymmetry as to seem hemiatrophic, a prostitute, dead triplets, a male sexual invert, a colour-blind daughter, and a normal son. The colour-blind daughter married the paranoiac grandson of the "Napoleon of Finance." The progeny of the sexual invert and the versifier, who were soon divorced, were a daughter with periodical nymphomania, who had some artistic and literary ability, and a son who died of gastric cancer. The scions of the ne'er-do-well and his nose-bleeding cousin were a moral imbecile, a "bleeder," a stammering daughter who had an uvular deformity, a deaf-mute with undescended testicle, dead-born triplets, an infantile paralytic son, and dead-born quadruplets. The progeny of the paranoiac and his colour- blind cousin were an exophthalmic daughter, an epileptic with undescended testicle, a cleft-palated imbecile with a cloaca, dead-born quadruplets, an idiot boy, and a "bleeder."

Doutrebente reports the following family history: First generation: Father intelligent, became melancholic, and died insane. Mother nervous and emotional. Second generation: Ten children; three died in childhood, seven reach maturity as follows: Daughter A, melancholiac; daughter B, insane at twenty; daughter C, imbecile; daughter D, a suicide; son E, imbecile; son F, melancholic; son G, a melancholic. Third generation: A has ten children; five die in childhood, one is deformed, one has fits of insanity, one is eccentric and extravagant, two are intelligent and marry, but are childless. B leaves no issue. C has one child, a deformed imbecile. D has three children; one is an imbecile, one dies of apoplexy at twenty-three, and the third is an artist described as "extravagant." E has two children; one dies insane, the other disappears and is supposed to have committed suicide. F is childless. G has one child, who is imbecile.[105]

Strahan[106] gives a genealogy which shows very clearly the close kinship existing between the cancerous diathesis and other forms of constitutional degeneration whose outward manifestations are infantile convulsions, suicide, epilepsy, insanity, lymphatism, and sterility. The father of this family died of stomach cancer at sixty. He had a brother who cut his throat at fifty-six; the mother, an apparently healthy woman, died of a fit, at the age of fifty-four. To this pair seven children were born: 1. A son who died of stomach cancer at fifty-eight. 2. A son who died in convulsions at thirteen weeks. 3, 4, and 5. Three daughters who died of phthisis, one at sixteen, the other two later in life, and after being married for many years; none left any issue. 6. A son who is epileptic, and has twice been confined in lunatic asylums; married, but no issue. 7. A son who is sane, and enjoying fair health. Here the taint in the mother appears to have been slight; still, it was there, and while certainly preventing reversion, it doubtless deepened the degeneration of the father in the children. In the father's stock the taint was much deeper. While it was exhibited as cancer in him, it took the form of suicidal impulse in his brother. In the children of this pair the disease of the father is transmitted to the eldest son; but can it be denied, Strahan asks, that the infantile convulsions, the liability to tubercular disease, the epilepsy, the insanity, and the marked sterility were but the varying evidences of the degenerate nature, inherited from a father who might have died earlier of some acute disease, taking the secret of his nature with him?

The value of the principle of atavism in off-setting degeneracy is nowhere better illustrated than in the history of famous families of degenerates like those of the Binswangers, of "Margaret," of the Jukes, as well as those reported in France, Germany, Austria, Russia, and the Scandinavian countries. The Rougon-Macquart family of Zola (which had its actual prototype in the Kerangal family described by Aubry[107]) had, like these, several scions in whom former normality regained its power through atavism. Sometimes this atavism is not shown to any greater extent than a slight modification of the abnormality or morbidity.

Telegony, the so-called and much-debated heredity of influence, whereby the children of a second marriage resemble the first husband, may be explained by a biologic principle demonstrable in the lower animals, whereby conjugation not sufficient to fecundate ova is sufficient so to impress them that when finally fecundated they bear characteristics of the first conjugation. Its part in either normal or degenerate heredity is but slight. Some instances charged to it might be attributed to mental impression on the mother.

Luys[108] excellently sums up the whole question of heredity when he remarks: "Heredity governs all the phenomena of degeneracy with the same results and the same energy as it controls moral and physical resemblances in the offspring. The individual who comes into the world is not an isolated being separated from his kindred. He is one link in a long chain which is unrolled by time, and of which the first links are lost in the past. He is bound to those who follow him, and to the atavic influences which he possesses; he serves for their temporary resting-place, and he transmits them to his descendants. If he come from a race well endowed and well formed, he possesses the characters of organisation which his ancestors have given him. He is ready for the combat of life, and to pursue his way by his own virtues and energies. But inversely, if he spring from a stock which is already marked with an hereditary blemish, and in which the development of the nervous system is incomplete, he comes into existence with a badly balanced organisation; and his natural defects, existing as germs, and in a measure latent, are ready to be developed when some accidental cause arises to start them into activity."

CHAPTER IV

Consanguineous and Neurotic Intermarriage

BYRON has sung[109] of the old popular belief in the advantages of cross-breeding, which arose originally in the practice of exogamy (marriage outside the tribe), or, more often, outside those having the same totem, or coat-of-arms. In all probability casual observation of deformities after intermarriage enforced the prohibition which arose after the killing of female children had led to exogamy. Totemic relationship was often far from being consanguineous. The idea of incest is, as Byron's stanza denotes, of religious origin rather than innate.[110] Its criminal nature is often removed by priestly dispensation in Latin countries. From this practice sprang the medical, theologic, and legal notions to which D. H. Tuke[111] thus refers: "The danger arising from marriages of consanguinity has been insisted upon from time to time by medical writers, and has been recognised by ecclesiastical authority, civil law, and by popular feeling. As regards ecclesiastical and civil law, it would be more correct to say that the marriage of those very nearly related has been forbidden on other grounds than that of the alleged danger to mental health. At the same time the justice of such laws receives support if medical observation leads to the conclusion that consanguineous marriages tend to generate idiocy and insanity."

The biologic evidence from the experiments of Maupas on parthenogenesis, elsewhere cited, is seemingly supported by the results of animals breeding in-and-in. The evidence advanced against such marriages seems at first sight exceedingly strong from a biologic standpoint in man.

Rilliet[112] cites cases tending to show that consanguineous marriages, in themselves pernicious, tend with certainty to lower vital force. The effects he divides into two categories; those which relate to the parents, under which head are:—

a. Failure of conception.

b. Retardation of conception.

c. Imperfect conception.

Those which relate to the progeny:—

a. Imperfections of various kinds.

b. Monstrosities.

c. Imperfect physical and mental organisation.

d. Tendency to diseases of the nervous system, such as epilepsy, imbecility, idiocy, deaf-mutism, paralysis, and various cerebral affections.

e. Tendency to strumous diseases.

f. Tending to die young.

g. Tendency to succumb to disease which others would easily resist.

C. H. S. Davis,[113] of Meriden, Connecticut, states that intermarriages in families lead to a degeneration that manifests itself in deaf-mutism, albinism, and idiocy. Isaac Ray[114] is of the opinion that consanguineous marriages repeated through successive generations account for the numerous instances of insanity and idiocy occurring in quiet rural populations of New England, far from the excitements of city life, which are generally supposed to be more productive of mental unsoundness.

S. M. Bemiss,[115] of New Orleans, Louisiana, giving a report of the condition of the offspring of 580 intermarriages of first cousins, gathered mostly by medical men from nearly every State in the Union, says: 2,778 children were born of these cousins, of whom 793 were defective, 117 deaf and dumb, 63 blind, 231 idiotic, 24 insane, 44 epileptic, 189 scrofulous, 53 deformed, and 637 died early.

While these figures seem very demonstrative, they contain a great many elements of error. One of these is incidentally pointed out by Arthur Mitchell, [116] who finds that under favourable conditions of life the apparent ill effects of consanguineous marriages are frequently almost nil, whilst if the children are ill-fed, badly housed and clothed, the evil may become very marked. He calculates that the percentage of consanguineous marriages generally in Scotland is 1·3, or ten times less than with the parents of idiots. Taking his figures a strong case seems to be made out in support of the opinion that idiocy, among other evils, results from intermarriage. Langdon Down, although his figures are not of so unfavourable a character, admits consanguinity as one of the causes of deterioration.

George H. Darwin concluded from a careful investigation that about 4 per cent. of all marriages in England are between first cousins, and between 2 and 3 per cent. in the smaller towns and in the country; with these he compared the rate of similar marriages among the parents of lunatics and idiots in asylums, and found it to be about 3 or 4 per cent.—not higher, therefore, than in the general population.

Huth[117] cites instances occurring regularly at the present day among certain isolated communities (St. Kilda, Pitcairn, and Iceland) without apparent evil consequences to the race. Such marriages were common among the North American Indians and the South Sea Islanders, people among whom idiocy and other degenerate hereditary conditions were remarkably rare. These cases, Strahan remarks, deal with peculiarly healthy communities. Therein lies the secret of such intermarriage proving innocent of evil to the offspring. Were such intermarriage common among the degenerates the result would be disastrous.

In 1869 the New York State Medical Society[118] appointed a committee to investigate the influence of consanguineous marriages upon the offspring. Their results show clearly that if the family be free from degenerate taint, marriage among its members in no way diminishes the chances of healthy offspring. This conclusion is in accord with the findings of recent investigators like Anstie, George Darwin, and A. H. Huth, according to whom there is no greater amount of morbidity or abnormality among the offspring of consanguineous parents than among the children of parents not so related, provided the parents be equally free from tendency to disease or degeneration. With a perfectly healthy stock, as every breeder of animals knows, remarks Strahan,[119] "in-and-in breeding" may be practised with impunity, but where the stock is tainted with disease or imperfection, safety is only to be found in "crossing."

Where the error lay in the old doctrine, upon which was founded the prohibition of consanguineous unions, was not, as Strahan remarks, in asserting that disease and deformity were more often met with in children of these than in those of other unions, for such is true, but attributing these unhappy results to the mere fact that the parents were related by blood. Over and above the fact that these consanguineous marriages are almost certain to transmit in an accentuated form any defect or tendency to disease already present in the family, there is no physiological reason why such marriages should not take place. Breeders of prize stock frequently breed "in and in," not only with impunity, but with marked benefit. But this fact, while going to prove that it is not the mere blood relationship of the parents which induces the degeneration so often found in the children of consanguineous marriages, can but rarely be advanced as an argument in support of the marriage of blood relations. The stock-raiser only permits the more perfect members of his flocks and herds to continue their kind, and for this reason the "in-and-in" breeding is innocuous, just as it would be in the human family under like conditions. But where shall we find the perfect human family? Such families are certainly rare. The laws of natural life have been so strained and perverted that almost every family nowadays has a taint or twist of some kind, and as all such imperfections are transmitted and rapidly deepened and fixed in the family by the intermarriage of its members, it is best that such unions should be forbidden.

Recently acquired characters, whether physiologic or pathologic, are very liable to disappear when the individual bearing such characters intermarries with another not having the same character. The natural tendency in all such cases is to revert in the offspring to the normal or healthy type, so that unless the new character be very deeply impressed upon the parental organism it is almost certain it will not appear in the offspring, if the other parents have nothing of the character. But when both parents are possessed of the character, whether it be physiologic or pathologic, this natural tendency to revert to the original is often overborne and the character is repeated in an accentuated form in the offspring.

Now this accentuation of all family characters is what must always happen in the case of consanguineous marriages. If there be any taint in the family each member of the family will have inherited more or less of it from the common ancestor. Take the case of cousins, the descendants of a common grandparent who was insane and of an insane stock. Here the cousins are certain to have inherited more or less of the insane diathesis. Even if the taint has been largely diluted in their case by the wise, or, more likely, fortunate marriages of their blood-related parents, yet will they have inherited a certain tendency to nervous disease, and if they marry they must not be surprised if that taint appears in an aggravated form in their children. Some of the children of such parents are generally idiotic, epileptic, dumb, or lymphatic, and the parents marvel whence came the imperfection. It may be in some cases that the parents, and possibly the grandparent, of the unfortunate children, have not up till that time displayed any outward evidence of the tendency to disease which they have inherited and handed on to their descendants; and, not looking farther back, the parents boldly assert that such a thing as insanity, epilepsy, scrofula, &c., is unknown to their family. They themselves have never been insane; why, then, should their children? In like manner children may be epileptic, blind, deaf-mute, lymphatic, cancerous, criminal, drunkards, or deformed from direct inheritance, and yet the family line be honestly declared to be healthy. Hence the truth of Sir William Aitken's maxim, that "a family history including less than three generations is useless and may even be misleading." From the foregoing it is evident that the similarity of temperament induced by a common environment, and which Strahan would call "social consanguinity," must be a potent factor in the production of all hereditary degenerations. Living under similar customs, habits and surroundings, labouring at the same occupation, indulging in the same dissipation, tend to engender like diseases and degenerations, irrespective of any blood relationship. Hence it not seldom happens that persons not even distantly related by blood are, in reality, much more nearly related in temperament than cousins, or even nearer blood relations who have experienced widely different modes of life. This "social consanguinity" is the great curse which dogs every exclusive tribe and class, and hurries them to extinction. It has largely aided real or family consanguinity in the production of the diseases and degenerations which have so heavily fallen upon the aristocracies and royal families of Europe.

A crucial test of the opposing positions taken respectively in such a positive manner by Bemiss and Strahan would be a family intermarrying extensively, but placed under favouring conditions unlikely of themselves to create degeneracy. Excellent cases of this kind are furnished by Bourgeois[120] and Thiébault.[121] Bourgeois gives the history of his own family, which was the issue of a union of the third degree of consanguinity. During the ensuing 160 years there were ninety-one marriages, of which sixteen were consanguineous. All of these latter were productive. There was not a single case of malformation, or other physical or mental disease in the offspring.

Thiébault reports the case of a slave-dealer who died in the year 1849 at Whidah, Dahomey, leaving behind him four hundred disconsolate widows, and about one hundred children. By the order of the king the whole family were interned in a particular district, where reigned the most complete promiscuity. In 1863 there were children of the third generation. Thiébault, after verifying these facts, states that at that time, although these people were born from all degrees of incestuous unions, there was not a single instance of deaf-mutism, albinism, blindness, cretinism, or other congenital malformation. From these cases it is evident that the position of Strahan is not too strongly taken.

While it is true that "like clings to like," still this does not imply kinship, but it very often implies likeness in mental characteristics. This tendency has been shown to be present in the neurotic by Roller,[122] De Monteyel,[123] Kiernan,[124] Bannister,[125] and Manning,[126] so far as Germany, France, the United States, and Australia are concerned. Bannister puts the statistical proof of this tendency very forcibly as follows: "There are in Illinois, according to the most recent estimates, in round numbers, about 6,000 insane, or one to a little over 500 of the population. Even if we double, treble, or quadruple this frequency to include all that have been or are to be insane, as well as those insane at the present time, it would not appear that there was much probability of two insane persons being married according to any ordinary law of chances. In fact, we find four out of the 104 with insane heredity had both father and mother insane. In one of these cases the insane heredity involved both parents and both grandparents on each side, though in the case of the latter the histories show it only as collateral. Besides these, three patients had direct paternal and collateral maternal heredity; two had direct maternal and collateral paternal heredity, and in one case there was collateral heredity of insanity on both sides. This makes altogether nearly 10 per cent. of those with insane heredity with it on both sides, maternal and paternal, and thus favoured with a double opportunity to inherit mental disease. If we add to this the instances where, with insanity of one parent, there is reported either epilepsy, hysteria, or drunkenness, 'brain disease,' nervousness, &c., of the other, the ratio of double inheritance rises to over 20 per cent."

The beneficial effects which may result from atavism are, it will be obvious, offset by this tendency of the neurotic to intermarry, thus perverting the principle of atavism to the assistance of degeneracy.

The age of the parent plays a part in degeneracy. Conger[127] (whose results have been corroborated by Joseph Workman, of Toronto, and Kiernan,[128] of Chicago) points out that in all degenerative forms we must take into consideration this factor, since it determines the development of degeneracy in childhood. Hereditary taint may be transmitted to descendants as a simple neuropathy, as a neurosis, or as a defect of development reaching even to idiocy. Conger finds the prevailing age, especially the age of the mothers of degenerates, is often between twenty and twenty-five years, and that hence there exists a relation between this age and the greater transmission of degeneracy to the offspring. Marro, who has specially investigated the influence of the age of the parents, both in the normal population and among criminals,[129] finds that among all classes of criminals there is an excess of immature parents (under 26) or senile parents (over 40), and that only petty offenders possessed a normal number of mature parents (26 to 40 years). A man between 20 and 25 is in as favourable condition for procreating degenerates as the very aged. Because of incompleted organic development he has been unable to free himself from hereditary taint which he transmits to his descendants, but which in maturer age, through the influence of adaptation, evolution, or education, might perhaps be more or less notably modified.

The organism between 20 and 25 is yet incomplete; education has not been able to exert much influence in determining those possible changes which are adapted to modify congenital tendencies. In a word, the individual between 20 and 25 feels too much the influence of atavic characters, and too readily transmits to his posterity the brands of degeneracy. Experience has made it well known that the children of the aged readily show degenerate types. Many children of old fathers have undoubtedly inherited all the characters of the weakness of the age in which they were begotten. Old age represents the period of retrogression, of involution, and hence readily transmits the mark of degeneracy. The children of either too young or too old parents, failing to escape hereditary predisposition, may from birth inherit those characters which are proper to incomplete organic development or to the period of involution.

Kiernan has had under observation a Nova Scotian family of Scotch extraction, the mother of which continued to bear children until she was 63 years old. There had been no pregnancy between 50 and 56. At 56 a son was born who had ear, jaw and skull stigmata, and became a periodical lunatic at
25. A son, born a year after, was a six-fingered idiot, with retinitis pigmentosa. (These last expressions of degeneracy are, as Darier[130] has shown, often associated. Darier's cases had the following hereditary antecedents: One father had hemeralopia; one mother had defective vision; a grandfather was blind at 30; a grandfather was blind in one eye, and an uncle had congenital iris coloboma. Only one patient examined did not have hemeralopic descendants. Six patients examined belonged to five different families, all consisting of five or six children, one-third of whom had hemeralopia. Among thirty-five children there were eleven hemeralopes and two six-fingered children, who died too young to determine the existence of retinitis pigmentosa. The disease in all began in childhood, and hemeralopia was absent in but one case.) Three of the next children (two boys and a girl) became paralytic idiots in infancy. Here the degeneracy was expressed in that tendency to miliary aneurismal weakness of arteries to which E. C. Spitzka,
[131] called attention over a decade ago. One of the next children was a periodically sexual invert female. The last child was an epileptic. The children born before the age of fifty were normal and averaged 60 years of age.

Matthews Duncan,[132] Arthur Mitchell, and Langdon Down, have called attention to the influence of premature and late marriage in the production of idiocy. Factors capable of producing idiocy are of course capable of producing less decided expressions of degeneracy.

CHAPTER V

INTERMIXTURE OF RACES

D EFOE, in his *Trueborn Englishman*, outlines a factor of great importance in degeneracy.[133] Race intermixture is much more common than is generally believed, owing to that ethnologic error consequent on the discovery of Sanscrit, which tests race by speech. Keane[134] excellently explodes this error by the following table:

Peoples.	Race.	Speech.
English	Kelto-Teutonic	Teutonic
Scotch	Kelto-Teutonic	Teutonic
Cornish	Siluro-Kelto-Teutonic	Teutonic
Irish (West)	Siluro-Kelto-Teutonic	Keltic
Welsh	Siluro-Kelto-Teutonic	Keltic
French	Ibero-Kelto-Teutonic	Italic
Spanish	Ibero-Keltic	Italic
Germans	Slavo-Kelto-Teutonic	Teutonic
Bohemians	Kelto-Teuto-Slavonic	Slavonic
Russians (many)	Finno-Slavonic	Slavonic
Hungarians	Ugro-Slavonic	Slavonic
Bulgarians	Ugro-Teuto-Slavonic	Finnic
Prussians (East)	Letto-Teuto-Slavonic	Teutonic
Rumanians	Italo-Slavo-Illyric	Italic
Italians	Liguro-Kelto-Italic	Italic

Profoundly mixed as this table indicates European races to be, it is far from representing the full extent of race mingling. The primitive worship of the Slavonic Czernebog by the Saxons in England demonstrates a Slavonic strain, derivable, as Kiernan[135] remarks, from their contact with the Wends of the Baltic. Not merely are the Aryan races of Europe mixed together, but the blood of all has a pre-Aryan and a Turanian dash. In Great Britain, as Taylor[136] and others have shown, the Iberian type is found in Wales and Scotland as well as elsewhere, though in lesser degree. These admixtures date back to palæolithic times when, although, as Keane remarks, the predominant type of skull was dolicocephalic (or long-headed), the brachycephalic (or round-headed type) had begun to appear in America, then connected by land with both Africa and Europe. In the subsequent neolithic time, while the type is at first generally brachycephalic, it soon becomes mesatocephalic (mixed long and round-headed), pure brachycephals and dolicocephals becoming rare. Vogt went so far as to maintain that were the three chief anthropoid apes developed further, two dolicocephalic and one brachycephalic type of man would result; the first two from the chimpanzee and gorilla, the last from the orang. The orang descendant would have long arms and red hair. The chimpanzee descendant would be of small size, dark colour with slender bones and jaws. The gorilla race would have massive chest, big bones, massive jaws and teeth. These three types appear in Great Britain and Ireland and traces of their blood are still detectable in living men. Sir Walter Scott draws an excellent picture of the "orang" type in *Rob Roy*, whose hero, according to reliable tradition, represented the Pict type. Gomme[137] has lately shown that these races persisted long enough to stamp their savage beliefs on coming races and intermingled with them. The Neolithic race in Great Britain was dark, of feeble build, short stature, with dolicocephalic skulls. This race remained to the historic period, as the Silures in Great Britain and the Firbolgs in Ireland. It had high cheek-bones and oblique eyes, as Kiernan[138] points out. Towards the middle of the neolithic period this race was conquered by a brachycephalic, tall, long-armed, muscular race, with florid complexion and yellowish or red hair.[139] Scott's *Rob Roy* is an example of this type. A third race of fair complexion with prognathous face, dolicocephalic skulls, of tall stature, great bones, great chest development and massive jaws, later invaded Great Britain. While these races resemble Vogt's hypothetical descendants of the anthropoid apes, it should be stated that there is not the slightest evidence for this line of descent. Writers who ignore these race characteristics have often brought serious criticism and even discredit on the doctrine of degeneracy. Lombroso, starting from the correct premise, that wide departure from the race type is evidence of degeneracy, erroneously cites in illustration Virchow's departure from the German type, Byron's departure from the English type, O'Connell's dolicocephalic departure from the mesatocephalic Irish type, and Robert Bruce's neanderthaloid departure from the Scandinavian type. As Kiernan has shown,[140] Virchow, as his name denotes, is a German-speaking Slavonic Wend; Byron was a Celto- Scandinavian Scotchman; O'Connell was born in a district conquered by the tall dolicocephalic race which invaded Ireland. The Bruce type of skull is still found among the purer Norwegians, Frisians, Swedes, and Danes, and was common just before his day and just after, as has been shown by Taylor.

As the intermingling of races began early, the question of the existence of pure races to-day, or even during the historic period, is an open one. The Hebrews have been comparatively pure since the return from the Captivity.

Before that, as the history of Solomon's foreign marriages demonstrates, they were a raceless chaos, the Semitic element predominating. Researches by Flinders Petrie[141] and others show that the Egyptians were a mixture of Turanians, Hamites, Aryan and Semite peoples imposed on a negroid basis. When these elements were finally fused, the race bred relatively true, although the lower classes tend to the negroid type and the higher to the Caucasic.

The Koreans, as Keane remarks, are a mixture of two primitive races, one white and one yellow. The Japanese, whose ancestors emigrated to Japan from Korea are, according to Topinard,[142] the product of the addition of three distinct types to that forming their Korean ancestors. The Caucasic to a small extent, the Polynesian to a greater, and the Malay to a still greater, are mixed with the original Korean.

The Chinese are neither a homogeneous people nor a pure race, albeit the relatively few Mantchus are dominant. The Aryan of India, on whom Max Müller laid such stress, is known to be, despite a rigid caste system, a non-Aryan race, feebly infused with a modicum of Aryan blood. The so-called "Gypsy" seems, of all the races of India, to have retained most Aryan speech and type as well as its original semi-nomadic waggon-journeying tendencies in the midst of settled civilisation. Ghetto seclusion long helped to preserve relative purity of race in the Jew, but despite vagabond surroundings the "Gypsy" has remained even purer.

Great as has been the mixture of even widely separated types like the three races described as mingling in Great Britain and Ireland, even greater admixture occurred in comparatively late historic times. The so-called Scotch-Irish (whose blood enters so largely into the dominant race of the United States) are, despite their speech (much more Teutonic and monosyllabic than English), as Kiernan[143] has shown, a raceless chaos of Gaelic and Cymric Celts, Lowland Scotch, French Huguenots, Danes (Celto- Teuto-Slaves),[144] Palatinate Germans, Magyars, English Puritans, Hollanders, Swedes, Protestant Italians, Poles, and Spaniards. The intermixture of the dark, small-boned, dolichocephalic, orthognathous (with in-drawn jaws) race first with the brachycephalic, prognathous, big-boned, red-haired race, and then with the dolichocephalic prognathous, deep-chested, big-boned, fair race, must have produced in the British Isles as marked variations in type as now occur from the admixture of the Indian and negro. These are especially noticeable in the Marshpee Indians of Cape Cod, the Long Island tribes and the "Red Bones" of South Carolina. The Marshpee tribe is an admixture of Anglo-Saxon, Portuguese, Indian, and negro. The Indian element, while still demonstrable, is lessening. Some of the older people still retain Indian characteristics. A girl of ten was negro in all respects except her hair. An adult whose mother was half white, half Marshpee, while the father is negro, had all the negro characteristics except the skin, which was Indian in type, and the jaws, which were slender. Another adult who had a negro great-grandfather, Marshpee mother, and a three-fourths Marshpee father, had large, negro-like jaws, Indian hair, skin, and cheek-bones. Another adult had a Portuguese maternal grandmother, negro grandfather, an Indian-white paternal grandmother and Indian-negro paternal grandfather. His hair, jaws, and nose were negro, his cheek-bones were high, his upper and lower jaws met so that the front teeth occluded.[145] The like condition obtains in the Long Island Indians, but to a less extent with the "Red Bones," who, after the type was formed, avoided admixture with the negro.

The influence of race intermixture in the production of degeneracy is easily settled. Basing their opinion on the notorious sterility of the hybrid offspring of the horse and ass, certain biologists have assumed like results in man and have cited the alleged absence of Australian half-breeds in evidence. Since the hare and rabbit, dog and wolf, sheep and goat produce breeds intermediate between the parents, fertile while environment is unchanged, horse and ass sterility cannot be accepted as of much value in settling the question. Recent researches have shown that the half-breeds which survived birth among the Australians were killed in accordance with tribal usages regulating population in accordance with food supply.

Whether the results of race intermixture prove degenerate or not will turn largely on the environment. The mulatto is certainly better adapted to the white environment than the pure negro, albeit less so than the white. That race intermixture may, however, determine degeneration, is shown by the relapse into voodooism and cannibalism of the Haiti and Louisiana French hybrids, and the Anglo-Saxon hybrids of Liberia, who contrast disadvantageously with the Arabianised Moslem Mandingoes and Veys, which last have advanced so far as to devise a system of writing. The extent of the influence of environment is shown in the career of the Dumas family, which is of Haitian- negro origin. The grandfather was a general in the French army, the father and son were two stars in the literary firmament. The sculptor, Edmonia Lewis, was of similar stock to these. Evidences of degeneracy were rare among the Marshpee Indians, as I have elsewhere shown.[146]

The Abyssinians have preserved that antique type of Christianity which had Jewish usages; they had their own literature, alphabet, and old type of civilisation. According to Keane, the present inhabitants of Abyssinia form an extremely complex ethnical group in which it is not always possible to distinguish the constituent elements. The prevailing colour is a distinct brown, shading northwards to a light, olive, fair complexion, southwards to a deep chocolate and an almost sooty black. There are Abyssinians who may certainly be called black, and in whom the negro strain is revealed in the somewhat tumid lip, small nose, broad at base, and frizzly, black hair. But the majority may be described as a mixed Hamito-Semitic people, who, beyond question, belong fundamentally to the Caucasic division. While the Hamitic, Semitic, and the Latin branch of the Aryans are admitted to form a fertile, progressive admixture with the negro, the reverse is commonly assumed to be the case with the English speaking Celto-Teutons. Daniel Wilson[147] is of opinion that this is not true as to millions of the coloured race who now constitute the indigenous population of the Southern States. They are at home there in a climate to which the white race adapts itself with very partial success. The offspring of white fathers and of mothers of the African races, they have multiplied to millions; and now, with the recently acquired rights of citizenship, and with the advantage of education within their reach, the country is their town. The very social prejudices against miscegenation protect them from the effacing influence to which the Indian half-breed is exposed, by ever-recurrent intermarriage with the dominant race. As yet there are discernible the various degrees of heredity from the mulatto to the quinteron. But the abolition of slavery has placed the coloured race on an entirely new footing. Left as it now is, free to enjoy the healthful, social relations of a civilised community, and protected, by the very prejudices of race and caste, from any large intermixture with the white race, it can scarcely admit of doubt that there will survive on the American Continent a Melanochroi of its own, more distinctly separated from the white race, not only by heredity but also by climate influences, than the "dark Whites" of Europe are from the blonde types of Hellenic, Slavic, Teutonic, or Scandinavian stock. This condition will be modified by the fact that the negro American, like the others, is a traveller and, with a rise of culture, tends to city life.

The admixture with the white has reduced negro prognathism and dolichocephaly. It must, however, be admitted that these reductions had already been begun in Africa. Sir H. H. Johnston, however, fully agrees with the negro writer[148] who holds that the "pure and unadulterated Negro cannot, as a rule, advance with any certainty of stability above his present level of culture; that he requires the admixture of a superior type of man." But the white and black races are "too widely separated in type to produce a satisfactory hybrid"; hence Johnston thinks that, "the admixture of yellow that the Negro requires should come from India, and that Western Africa and British Central Africa should become the America of the Hindu. The mixture of the two races would give the Indian the physical development which he lacks, and he, in his turn, would transmit to his half Negro offspring the industry, ambition, and aspiration toward a civilised life which the Negro so markedly lacks."

On the whole, race intermixture will not tend to elevate the race where there is a decided difference in the state of evolution of the two races, and moreover especially where, as is usually the case, the mother is of the inferior race. It must be obvious that, given a negro pelvis and the head of a white, results damaging to the offspring cannot but occur. And these results are of a nature likely to be transmitted by heredity. The same would hold true with other races as well. Although the differences between the Hawaiian and the white are much less than those between the negro and the white, it is notorious that while the labours with pure Hawaiians are easy, those with half-whites are difficult. The same conditions have been observed from time to time between different breeds of dogs, whose pelves vary. Therefore it is safe to assume that admixtures of races of different grades of evolution will, if carried to any great extent, tend to render the superior race more liable to the action of the factors producing degeneracy. Dixon[149] has shown that mulatto families tend to disappear, if they be not crossed with either black or white, and that the limit of descent is the fourth generation. He has also pointed out that morbid proclivities and retrogressive tendencies are peculiarly rife among mulattoes. The fact, long ago shown by Menatta,[150] that the conflict for existence between brain growth and reproductive organ growth at puberty, results, in the mulatto, as in the negro and anthropoids, in the triumph of the reproductive, indicates that the mulatto has factors of degeneracy which would be fatal to the establishment of an intermediate type on the environment of the white. While Menatta is in error in regarding skull mal- development as the cause, when it and brain growth disturbance are defects due to the same cause, still general observation supports his opinion that "negro children are sharp, intelligent, and full of vivacity, but on approaching the adult period a gradual change sets in. The intellect seems to become clouded, animation giving place to a sort of lethargy, briskness yielding to indolence. We must necessarily infer that the development of the negro and white proceeds on different lines. While with the latter the volume of brain grows with the expansion of the brain pan, in the former the growth of the brain is, on the contrary, arrested by the premature closing of the cranial sutures and laternal pressure of the frontal bone." Since, as Havelock Ellis remarks,[151] even the highest races do not fulfil the promise of evolution they make before puberty, anything which tends still further to impede the fulfilment must be regarded as a factor of degeneracy. Hence intermixture with an inferior race, having an inferior type of pelvis, would tend to degeneracy.

CHAPTER VI

TOXIC AGENTS

THE toxic agents which influence the race toward degeneracy, exert that deterioration in a mode which closely resembles that of the degenerative powers of the acute and chronic contagions and infections. The acute poisonings by these toxic agencies resemble the acute, nervous and other exhaustion caused by the toxin of the germs underlying the infections and contagions. The chronic conditions due to these toxic agents agree in many respects with the chronic states produced by the infections and contagions. The toxic agencies are divisible into those belonging to the condiments, medicines, foods and beverages, and those arising from occupations.

Tobacco is the most common, while alcohol and opium contend for second place both as to use and as to deleterious effects. Alcohol has been repeatedly charged with being *the* factor in degeneracy. Statistics of the first half of the present century seem to justify the conclusion that it is apparently the most potent factor, yet these statistics as a rule confound coincidence and cause, or effect and cause, or the vicious circles thereby resulting, to a remarkable degree. There are but few races in which alcohol has not been used and abused. The American Indians[152] had tizwein, chica, and pulque long ere Columbus; the Tartars and Russians, bouza, kvas, and kumyss; the South Sea Islanders ava and toddy (from the cocoanut); the Tunisians, laymi. The vast majority of the races of mankind have used alcoholic beverages. Each was called by a local name and not by a loan word, a most demonstrable evidence of local origin.

Even the social insects (bees and ants) at times indulge in fruit ferments. The claim, therefore, that alcohol is the product of high civilisation, hence of recent origin, and hence peculiarly destructive, is untenable. That excess in alcohol frequently occurs in degenerate stocks is, however, undeniable. But as Krafft-Ebing, Kiernan, Spitzka and others have shown, intolerance of alcohol is an expression of degeneracy. The person intolerant of alcohol becomes either a total abstainer because of a personal idiosyncrasy (like that which forbids certain people to eat shell-fish lest nettle-rash occur), or because of parsimony, or for both reasons combined. Such total abstainers leave degenerate offspring in which degeneracy assumes the type of excess in alcohol as well as even lower phases. The race tests of the deteriorating influence of alcohol are practically valueless, nor are statistics concerning alcoholism in the ancestry of degenerates of much more use. The enormous amount of idiocy, for example, in the Scandinavian countries, charged by Huss, Langdon Down and others to alcoholism in the parents, has been, by the most recent researches, cut down by Roof to less than 7 per cent. Insane hospital statistics vary to a like degree. Bad faith, however, is out of the question in these statistics. Lack of analytic skill, and that dangerous unscientific, canting, philanthropic tendency which rebels at statistics unfavourable to preconceived sociologic theories, explain these discrepancies. The ignoring of all but the alcoholic factor produces also great elements of error. Kiernan[153] cites twenty-three cases in which degenerate stocks were charged to alcoholic parentage, but which on analysis proved to be due to a degenerative factor in the parents of which alcoholism was merely an expression. Nearly all the offspring born after inebriety were prematurely born, defective, epileptic, hysteric, insane, idiots or criminals. Some few were healthy, apart from their intolerance of alcohol. In eighteen cases both father and mother were alcoholists. The fathers in four of these cases had been temperate, industrious, and affectionate ere being sunstruck. Following this came periods of irritability, excessive drinking and spendthriftiness. The mothers had remained for some years after the fathers' breakdown free from the use of alcohol, but were nervously exhausted from the strain. One became depressed during pregnancy, was given gin for the depression, and the habit persisted after the delivery. In the three other cases painful menses developed during the nervous exhaustion. The popular prescription for these, gin, was given, with the result of producing inebriety. In ten cases skull injury to the father had like results on both mother and father. In two cases the mother became a victim of painful menstruation after a railroad accident; gin drinking, to relieve this, followed and became a habit. The father's nervous system broke down under the strain and both became inebriates. In two other cases nervous exhaustion from typhoid and typhus fever produced the same outcome in inebriety on the part of the father and mother. In the remaining cases the inebriety was an expression of nerve exhaustion after various protracted infections. The alcoholism in these cases was clearly an expression of the factors of race deterioration producing degeneracy, and not its cause.

The influence of alcohol must therefore first be studied on the individual to determine its value and method of action as a cause of race deterioration. Careful medical researches have shown that alcohol produces a nervous state, closely resembling that induced by the contagions and infections, often accompanied with mental disturbance (delirium tremens and acute types of insanity). The acute nervous state to which the term alcoholism was applied by Magnus Huss has all the essential characteristics of the nervous state due to the contagions and infections. There is, however, a greater tendency to impotence and sterility in the alcohol nervous state than in the others, and consequently a lesser influence on race deterioration. The condition, moreover, has a tendency to set into action degenerative tendencies latent in the liver and kidneys. This action of alcohol on the liver and kidneys so interferes with their functions as to produce the effect already described as resulting in the contagions and infections from their toxins. Alcohol exerts a similarly deteriorating influence on the antitoxin-forming organs (especially on the testicles, ovaries and their appendages), to that already described as exerted by the toxins of the contagions and infections. To the direct toxic effects of alcohol are therefore added results of imperfect liver and kidney action and defective strengthening powers from deficient antitoxin secretion. Like all toxic agents, alcohol interferes with the functions of the eye and ear nerves. Special weakness thus created is transmissible to the offspring. The chronic type of alcoholism may well be compared in its effect with chronic contagions. There is, however, less tendency to infection with the microbes forming pus. There is a greater tendency to deteriorating action on the nervous system. There is in chronic alcoholism, as in syphilis, special tendency to that formation of connective tissue which destroys organs. The chronic mental disorders of chronic alcoholism resemble those of tuberculosis except that the capricious state and exaltation are less frequent than the suspicional tendency which is deeper, and takes the direction of delusions of poisoning and insane jealousy. The last are due to the deteriorating influence of alcohol on the generative organs. Alcohol may limit its action to the central nervous system, and thus produce hereditary losses of power. It causes changes in the peripheral nerves which in the offspring find expression in spinal cord and brain disorder through extension of the morbid process. But for its deteriorating effects on the ovaries and testicles, alcohol would be a most serious social danger. Through its action on the generative organs it tends to prevent the survival of the unfit, rather than to develop degenerates.

Opium seems to be the Charybdis on which the human bark strikes when escaping from the Scylla of alcohol. Its abuse as a narcotic is much older, even among the English-speaking races, than is generally suspected. Murrell, over ten years ago, demonstrated that the inhabitants of the fens of Lincolnshire had long employed opium as a prophylactic against malaria. The ratio of insanity in these regions proved to be very great. The same conditions obtained in certain malarial regions of New Jersey and Pennsylvania, where the use of strong infusions of poppy was common. The statistics of Rush[154] as to opium-caused insanity in Pennsylvania, indicate that the percentage of American opium abuses at the beginning of the nineteenth century was very great. The drug differs in two serious respects from alcohol. It is nearer in chemical composition to nerve tissue, and the tendency to its use may be transmitted by the mother directly to the fœtus. This, as Bureau and Ringer have shown, receives through the placenta from its opium-using mother a certain amount of morphine. In consequence, the child in the first month of infancy must be nourished on the milk of an opium-using woman, or given opium in some other way lest it perish. To this fact Calkins[155] was the first to call attention. His results were corroborated later by Hubbard; Kiernan, of Chicago[156]; Erlenmeyer, of Berlin; F. B. Earle, of Chicago; Mattison, of Brooklyn; Hughes, of St. Louis; and others. Amabile, of New York, showed that not only were the children of opium-using mothers born with tendency to the opium habit, but that the mothers aborted frequently with twins, and that the children who survived were very liable to convulsions. Independently of this factor the mental state produced by opium habit resembles in many respects that of the lunatic, in that the victim of opium is as unable to distinguish between his wishes and the facts, and therefore often utters what appear to be sheer lies. Hence he is totally unreliable and has taken a step in mental and moral degeneracy that, by the ordinary laws of heredity, must greatly increase, unless corrected by healthy atavism and training in the next generation. Opium is a more dangerous factor of degeneracy than alcohol, since the opium user must be in a continuous state of intoxication to carry on his usual avocation, while abstinence is perfectly compatible with proper work on the part of the drunkard. The opium habit is increased by the peculiar propaganda carried on by the *habitués* who justify their position by urging the use of opium for any ailment, however minimal. Opium, like alcohol, causes nervous exhaustion similar to, but greater than, that of the contagions and infections. From the affinity of opium to nerve tissue, from its tendency to stimulate the heart, thus causing increased blood supply to the brain; from its action on the bowels and the increased resultant work of the liver, this nervous state is much intensified. Opium does not have as great tendencies to interfere with the structure of the ovary and testicles as alcohol, hence the greater danger of the opium *habitué's* children surviving. Opium, when smoked, stimulates the reproductive apparatus, and thus would greatly increase the number of degenerates due to this habit but for the defects due to the inheritance of the habit and their consequences.

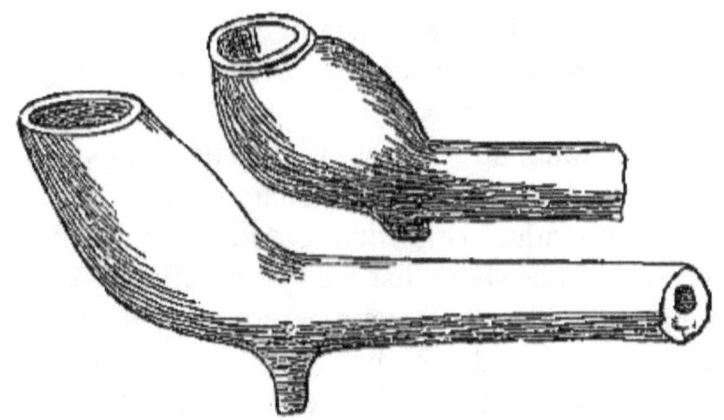

FIG. 1.—ANTE-CHRISTIAN IRISH PIPES.

FIG. 2.—ANTE-COLUMBIAN PIPES FROM SCULPTURE
AT STRATFORD-UPON-AVON.

The origin of the use of tobacco is usually ascribed to the New World. There
is no doubt that immediately subsequent to the discovery of America, the use
of tobacco spread over the world, and that its employment by Sir Walter
Raleigh made it fashionable. It is certain, however, that the Romans and Irish
employed pipes for smoking long ere the Christian era (Fig. 1), but the
substances smoked were not tobacco but dried aromatic leaves. The English

before Columbus (Fig. 2) did the same. In Western Asia historic botanical evidence leaves no doubt that tobacco was indigenous. Tobacco from the East hence probably encountered tobacco from the West, both currents meeting in Asia Minor. As with alcohol and opium the statistic method generally adopted proves fallacious when applied to the degenerative effects of tobacco. Study of its effects on the individual is needed to determine its effects on the race. The most careful researches show that the typical effects occur as a rule after long-continued use of tobacco, sometimes not until twenty years or more. While many smokers reach old age, many fail to live to old age because they are smokers. The skin is the subject of itching and reddening, the nerves of taste are blunted, and patches develop in the throat; loss of appetite, epigastric fulness, pain, vomiting, and disturbance of bowel function are common. Menstrual disturbance occurs in women. In female cigar-makers abortion and pluriparity are frequent. The sexual appetite is impaired and sometimes sterility and impotence occur; also disturbed heart action, palpitation, rapid and intermitting pulse, precordial anxiety, weakness, faintness and collapse, with sclerosis of the coronary arteries of the heart and left ventricular hypertrophy. Cigars and cigarettes produce irritation of the nose, mucous membrane, diminished smell, chronic hyperæmia of the epiglottis and larynx, and sometimes of the trachea and bronchi predisposing to consumption. Nicotine amblyopia, or sight weakness, is common, with central disturbances of the field of vision and with colour-weakness of sight. Often there is disorder of the ear tubes and congestion of drum, with loss of power of the hearing nerves, and consequent noises in the ear. The central nervous system is affected. In high schools, non-smokers get on better than smokers. Children from 9 to 15 years of age exhibit less intelligence, laziness, or other degenerative tendencies. Adults have head-pressure, sleeplessness, or drowsy stupor, depression, apathy, and dizziness. There may also be ataxic symptoms, paretic weakness of bowel and bladder, trembling and spasms. Tobacco insanities are comparatively rare in smokers, but are common in snuffers and still oftener in chewers.[157] In the precursory stage, which lasts about three months, there is general uneasiness, restlessness, anxiety, sleeplessness, and mental depression, often of a religious type. After this occurs precordial anxiety, and finally the psychosis proper consisting of three stages: 1. Hallucinations of all senses, suicidal tendency, depression of spirits, attacks of fright with tendency to violence and sleeplessness. 2. Exhilaration, slight emotional exaltation, agreeable hallucinations after from two to four weeks' relaxation, again followed by excitement. 3. The intervals between exaltation and depression diminish, the patient becomes irritable, but otherwise not alive to his surroundings, and perception and attention are lessened. The patient may be cured in five or six months if he stop tobacco during the first stage. In a year or so he may recover during the second stage. After the third stage the disease is frequently incurable. As the patient often becomes (especially by the use of the cigarette) an *habitué* ere puberty, the proper development and balance of the sexual and intellectual system is checked. These patients break down mentally and physically between 14 and 25. The moral delinquencies, other than sexual, are often an especial tendency to forgery and deceit of parents. Frequently the insanity of puberty (hebephrenia) is precipitated by tobacco. The cigarette, if used moderately, may be a sedative, but as used is a stimulant, and is often made of spoiled tobacco, resembling in reaction morphine, and on animals acting in a somewhat similar manner. As tobacco turns the salivary glands (which are concerned in digestion of starch) into excretory glands, it leads to imperfect digestion of starch, to consequent irregular fermentation in the bowel, thus at once furnishing a culture medium for microbes, to form more violent toxins from, and also creating leucomaines, to interfere especially with a nervous system overstimulated by nicotine. This is one great reason why those who snuff and chew tobacco more frequently become insane from tobacco than smokers, albeit these last are not exempt.

Statistics from the female employés of the Spanish, French, Cuban, and American tobacco factories, while defective and somewhat vitiated by the co-existence of other conditions producing degeneracy, support the opinion that the maternal tobacco habit (whether intentional or the result of an atmosphere consequent on occupation) is the cause of frequent miscarriage, of high infantile mortality, of defective children, and of infantile convulsions.[158]

Tobacco, therefore, in its influence on the paternal and maternal organism, exhausts the nervous system so that an acquired neurosis results in such a way as to be transmissible.

Professional tea-tasters have long been known to suffer from nervous symptoms; very early in the practice of their occupation the head pressure symptoms of neurasthenia occur. Tremor also occurs early. While changes in the optic nerve have not been demonstrated beyond a doubt, still eye disorders have been observed in the pauper tea-drinkers of the United States and in the tea-tasters of Russia, thus indicating that similar changes to those produced by tobacco and alcohol are likely to occur in the optic nerve from tea. Bullard[159] has found that tea has a cumulative effect. In his experience toxic effects are not produced by less than five cups daily. The symptoms manifested are those of nervous excitement resembling hysteria, at times almost amounting to fury; nervous dyspepsia; rapid and irregular heart action; neuralgia of the heart; helmet-like sensation on the head, and tenderness along the spine. James Wood,[160] of Brooklyn, found that 10 per cent. of those under treatment at the city hospitals exhibited similar symptoms. Of these 69 per cent. were females. Every symptom ascribed by Bullard to tea was found by Wood in his cases, who also found that the women manifested irregularities in menstruation of neurasthenic or hysteria type. He has found these symptoms to be produced by one-half of the quantity of tea charged with these effects by Bullard. The *Lancet*[161] several years ago, from an editorial analysis of the effects of tea-tippling, took the position that in no small degree nervous symptoms occurring in children during infancy were due to the practice of the mothers, both of the working and society class, indulging in the excessive use of tea, the excess being judged by its effects on the individual and not by the amount taken. Convulsions and resultant infantile paralysis were frequently noticed among the children of these tea- tipplers. Observations among the factory population and the workers in the clothing sweating-shops show that tea neurasthenia, presenting all the ordinary symptoms of nervous exhaustion, is especially common among these. It is evident that tea produces a grave form of neurasthenia readily transmissible to descendants. In addition to its effects directly upon the nervous system, tea tends to check both stomach and bowel digestion, and thus increases the self-poisoning which is so prominent a cause, consequence, and aggravation of these nervous conditions.

Coffee exerts a very similar action to that of tea, albeit the nervous symptoms produced by it are usually secondary to the disturbances of the stomach and bowel digestion. Coffee produces tremor, insomnia, nervous dyspepsia, and helmet sensations. With the exception of certain districts of the United States, coffee abuse is not carried to such an extent as tea, albeit in these, as in some portions of Germany, the habit is an excessive one. The conditions described result in Germany as frequently as they do in the United States. Mendel[162] finds that in Germany coffee inebriety is increasing and supplanting alcohol. Profound depression with sleeplessness and frequent vertex headache are early symptoms. Strong coffee will remove these temporarily, but it soon loses its effects, and they recur. There is much tremor, especially of the hands. The heart's action is rapid and irregular. Nervous dyspepsia is frequent. L. Bremer, of St. Louis, Mo., has observed similar conditions among both Germans and Americans there.

While coca took its place only recently among the toxic causes of degeneracy, it was old as a factor in the degeneration of the Peruvian long ere the discovery of America by Columbus. Forty-three years ago Johnston[163] wrote that even Europeans in different parts of Peru had fallen into the coca habit long practised by the Indians. A confirmed chewer of coca is called a *coquero*, and he becomes more thoroughly a slave to the leaf than the inveterate drunkard is to alcohol. Sometimes the *coquero* is overtaken by an irresistible craving, and betakes himself for days together to the woods, and there indulges unrestrainedly in coca. Young men of the best families of Peru are considered incurable when addicted to this extreme degree of excess. They abandon white society, and live in the woods or in Indian villages. In Peru the term white *coquero* has the same sense as irreclaimable drunken tramp. The inveterate *coquero* has an unsteady gait, yellow skin, quivering lips, hesitant speech, and general apathy. The drug has assumed an unusual prominence in the field of degeneracy since the discovery of its alkaloid, cocaine. Since then there has sprung into existence in both Europe and the English-speaking countries the world over, a habit which, while much over- estimated, is undoubtedly growing, and aggravating as well as producing degeneracy. Many of the cases reported as due to cocaine are, however, chargeable to the desire of the hysteric or neurasthenic to secure a new sensation, or the desire on the part of the opium or whisky *habitué* to try a dodge for forgiveness by friends. The habit is very frequently induced by patent medicines taken to cure catarrh by the neurasthenic, or to cure nervousness by hysterics as well. As the deformities of the nose passages predispose to what is called "catarrh," patent medicines for local application containing cocaine are frequently employed in the treatment of this supposed constitutional disease, with the result of aggravating the original degeneracy. As the youth under the stress of puberty frequently ascribes all his ills to catarrh, he also employs very frequently snuffs containing cocaine, and has his nervous condition much aggravated thereby. Among the nostrums urged in the newspapers and magazines for this condition, so often resultant on nerve stress, is a certain notorious snuff containing 3 per cent. of cocaine. From the description given by Johnson of the *coquero* there can be no doubt but tramps, errabund lunatics, and paupers result from this habit, to give birth to degenerates in the next generation.

Lead has been found to produce in those exposed to its fumes a systemic nervous exhaustion, characterised by local paralysis about the wrist as well as the general symptoms of profound systemic nerve tire. This may result, as Tanquerel des Planches[164] pointed out nearly half a century ago, in acute insanity of the confusional type followed very often by forms of mental disorder of a chronic type resembling paretic dementia. In some cases the patient recovers from the acute insanity to suffer thereafter from epilepsy. In other cases, as Kiernan has shown,[165] an irritable suspicional condition results, in which the patient may live for years, marry, and leave offspring. This last condition and the epileptic are the most dangerous as to the production of degeneracy. As has already been pointed out, the women employed in the pottery factories in Germany suffer according to Rennert[166] from a form of lead poisoning which produces decidedly degenerative effects upon the offspring. These women had frequent abortions, often produced deaf-mutes, and very frequently macrocephalic children.

Brass workers suffer from a very similar nervous condition to that produced by lead. Hogden,[167] of Birmingham, called attention to the grave forms of nervous exhaustion produced among brass-workers. The period during which the patient is able to pursue the occupation without breaking down is longer than that of the lead workers. Women, like men, are exposed to this condition. The chief effect produced, so far as offspring have been observed, is chiefly frequent abortions and infantile paralysis.

The occupations employing mercury, whether mining, mirror-making, or gilding, produce forms of systemic nervous exhaustion in which the most marked symptom (but less important from a sanitary standpoint) is a tremor amounting at times almost to shaking-palsy. Like all other systemic nervous exhaustions, the mercurial one may appear as degeneracy in the offspring. The employment of women in match factories and tenement house sweating shops is growing. The chief toxic effect of phosphorus is not the localised jaw necrosis. This is but an evidence of the progressive system saturation with phosphorus. It bears the same relation to the more dangerous effects of phosphorus that "blue gum" does to the systemic effects of lead.

Every condition arising from a toxic cause capable of producing profound systemic nervous exhaustion in the ancestor, and especially the ancestress, is likely to be transmitted as degeneracy to the descendant. Undoubtedly with the growing tendency of woman to pass from the ill-paid work of the seamstress to the better paid but dangerous occupations, a certain seeming increase in degeneracy must result.

CHAPTER VII

Contagious and Infectious Disease

AMONG the gains of human advance in evolution stand out prominently complete immunity from certain diseases due to germs, and partial immunity from others, which last immunity results in chronic types, rather than in acute, because of increased vital resistance in man. Tuberculosis and dourine, acute diseases in the cow and horse, have become chronic diseases, tuberculosis (or consumption) and syphilis, in man. Such chronicity is evidence of advance, yet it constitutes an element of degeneracy, since the victim of the chronic disease is able to leave more offspring than would be possible were the disorder acute. In other respects acute and chronic contagions and infections exert the same influence in regard to degeneracy. The germ of the disease may be inherited, or general nutrition of the fœtus may be so checked in development that the child inherits a predisposition to disease.

Through this check to fœtal development the phagocytes, or white blood cells, become so weakened that they are unable to devour fœtal structures as useless to man as the tadpole's tail (which it devours) is useless to the developed frog. This power being weakened, the organs which form antitoxins (or protective tonics against disease), from lack of development fail to perform their function. For this reason in the degenerate many infections and contagions assume their old destructive type.

The influence of these disorders in the parent may result in the bony mal-development shown to occur in animals by Charrin and Gley, and in man by Coolidge. The facial bones, jaw, and teeth are peculiarly liable to be thus affected. Though the effect of the disease on the parent be but temporary, the child's development may be checked as to higher tendencies. Thus mothers have borne moral imbeciles, epileptics or lunatics, after a pregnancy during which they were attacked by contagious disease, albeit the children of subsequent and previous pregnancies were normal.

The children of pregnancies previous to the one complicated by the contagious disease may be healthy, while those of subsequent pregnancies are defective. Any contagious or infectious disease may not only interfere temporarily with the bodily strength, but may produce complete change in the parent's system extending even to the highest acquirement of man. In some occur changes thus graphically described by Bulwer: "There have been men who, after an illness in which life itself seemed suspended, have arisen as out of a sleep with characters wholly changed. Before gentle, good, and truthful, they now become bitter, malignant, and false. To those whom they before loved they evince repugnance and loathing. Sometimes this change is so marked and irrational that their kindred ascribe it to madness. Not the madness which affects them in the ordinary business of life, but that which turns into harshness and discord the moral harmony which results from natures whole and complete."

The nerve centres controlling nutrition, growth, repair, secretion, and excretion are often as deeply affected as those checks constituting morality. At the periods of physiologic stress these effects are especially noticeable. Moral insanity, intellectual insanity, unequal mental balance, hysteria, precocious sexuality, unconscious mendacity, mental parasitism (the germ of pauperism), epilepsy, neuroses, and all types of nutritive and constitutional defects result. The nutritional defects may appear chiefly in the walls of the blood vessels and lymphatics. While these are most common in the chronic infections and contagions, they often occur in acute typhoid fever, scarlatina, diphtheria, whooping-cough, &c. Proper blood supply and utilisation of waste is thus prevented. Organs cannot perform their function, and are predisposed to disease from disuse and from weakness of the disease-fighting phagocytes and antitoxins. From this results irregularity of organ function, which is hereditarily transmissible. The weakened vessel walls yield to strain, and thus produce local stomach, bowel, liver, gland, and kidney disorders. This organ weakness may alone be transmitted to the offspring. The functions of the great glands (thyroid, thymus, suprarenals, pituitary body, bone-marrow, testicles and ovaries) which secrete principles necessary to the equal balance of nutrition are perverted. The liver, in the acute but more particularly the chronic contagions, paralysed in nerve tone, fails in its function of poison- destroyer, as for the same reason the kidneys fail in their power of ejecting hurtful waste. Through this interaction of perverted nutrition, imperfect poison-destruction, and deficient waste ejection result and continue the states of nervous exhaustion after the contagions and infections. Thus nerve exhaustion with its suspicion, its capricious hopefulness and gaiety, is practically continuous in tuberculosis, syphilis, and leprosy.

The acute and chronic contagions and infections so lower cell vitality through the perverted functions described that inert connective tissue replaces healthy working cells. This is especially the case with syphilis, which, when driven from the system, leaves behind it a tendency to disease based on this connective tissue increase. This tendency, latent in the ancestor, may be so intensified in the descendant as to produce the hereditary ataxias (loss of movement power), and like neuroses. At the periods of stress such tendencies are peculiarly potent, and not only check, but reverse development. The chronic contagions and infections are most fertile sources of human degeneracy since their weakened products are enabled to survive under modern beneficence. Of these chronic contagions two (tuberculosis and syphilis) alone deserve attention, since the third (leprosy) exerts but little influence. Despite its existence for more than a century (New Brunswick and Nova Scotia on the north and Louisiana on the south) on the borders of the United States, despite its subsequent importation from Norway, Sweden, China, and Hawaii, its spread has been infinitesimal, and its influence on race deterioration is still less demonstrable.

Tuberculosis ("the white death") is from every standpoint a social danger more serious than syphilis. The father, as in syphilis, can infect the mother, but sterility is much less likely. As has already been shown in the chapter on heredity, plural and quickly repeated birth are common in tuberculous families. The tuberculous diathesis (or "habit," as Weismann calls it) was very early observed in the United States. Nearly seventy years ago W. P. Dewees, of Philadelphia, pointed out its frequency and its early observation by the Greek and Roman physicians. He cites a case illustrative of the extent and uniformity of diathesis in a very numerous family. This predisposition arose on the side of the mother, though she lived herself to the age of forty-three, a period much exceeding that of any of her children, with the exception of a son, who died in his forty-fifth year. This lady bore twenty-three children without being able to suckle any but the two first. The males much exceed the females in number, yet there did not appear to be any exception to their favour in the transmission of the phthisical taint, except that they attained in general a greater age before they died. Some died about puberty, others at manhood or womanhood; but all, with the exception just stated, under thirty. The disease was never very rapid; they generally complained from one to two years before they died. The men had a healthy, even in some instances an athletic, appearance until the disease became open and decided. In their growth and stature they altogether resembled the father, who was not only a remarkably stout man, but lived beyond the eightieth year. The females, who passed puberty (two in number) were rather stout women, while the mother was both delicate and small. This family lived in the country, was very wealthy, and always accustomed to the various means generally found successful either in destroying the predisposition or lessening its influence, yet in no one instance in this family were they successful, though the open form of the disease was retarded perhaps in all. The females died the earliest.
[168]

The blood vessel system is affected as regards development in such families. The heart is often diminutive; the right ventricle is exaggerated. Two great types of degenerate constitutions are produced in children of the tuberculous.

One of these may well come under De Giovanni's category of the torpid. The victim is usually coarse-featured and coarse-skinned, with peculiarly unstable mentality; slowness of comprehension is combined with power of continuity of thought; at times mental apathy alternates with quickness of perception. Decided exaggeration of the lymphatic system (connected with utilising of material elsewhere than at the point where it has been rendered unfit) with deficient function occurs, resulting in fitting a soil for germs. In other respects the torpid resembles the second type, the erethistic (nervously fussy type) of De Giovanni. This is generally characterised by the presence of a clear complexion, a fine skin, and features well cut and often beautiful. The lips are red and the teeth pearly white, though liable to early decay, and the eyes are large and full, the pupil being widely dilated and the white of the eye beautifully clear. The eyelashes are long, curved and silky, and the blue veins show distinctly through the clear thin skin. The bones are light, the hands and feet well formed, the stature often tall, and the whole figure slightly and gracefully built. The erethists generally remain spare, and have a strong dislike to fatty food. They are vivacious and excitable, and the intellectual faculties are often highly developed. At an early age they show marvellous activity. The regularity with which such precocious tubercular children die has given rise to proverbs anent exceptionally clever children that they are "too wise to live long." Wanting in stamina, they are incapable of prolonged exertion either of mind or body, and break down under conditions which would not prove injurious to the healthy. They are continually taking "cold," and are prone throughout life to affections of an inflammatory character. Multiple and frequent pregnancies occur. The children, deficient in vitality, are carried off in numbers during infancy by convulsions, brain fever, water on the brain, exhaustion, diarrhœa, teething, and other ailments, or they succumb at the second detention or at puberty. A small proportion reach maturity. Few live beyond thirty-five or forty years of age. However brilliant intellectually, they are equally emotional, impressionable, and impulsive. There is a marked absence of mental stability. They are suspiciously capricious. The great secreting and eliminating glands undergo with peculiar frequency the perversions already described.

Neuroses and psychoses are peculiarly frequent in childhood and youth. The degenerative power of tuberculosis is not always due to the influence of the germ, or even of the toxin produced by it, but to the state of nerve weakness resultant on the disorder. The victim of tuberculosis (especially if affecting the lung) is a suspicious, yet hopeful, nervous invalid, whose functions are irregularly performed and who is therefore likely to leave scions with greater defect, especially as the maternal factor, either through infection or worry, can hardly escape being weakened. Tuberculosis attacks the bones of the offspring, especially the spine and hip-joint, but the victim of these last frequently regain health after apparent recovery from the local disease through surgical procedures. If the victim of the hip-joint disorder be of the erethist type marriage is not unlikely. Despite the deformity produced by spine disorder, popular superstition as to the "good luck" of a hunchback leads to marriage among the working class. Monetary and social considerations effect the same result among the wealthy classes. Here deformity does not prevent marriage, but predisposes to sterility through birth difficulty.

The influence of syphilis is, in a general sense, the same as that of tuberculosis, except that by reversing the principle of individuation it leads to greater sterility. Furthermore it exhibits greater tendencies to revert towards health, and yields (even in the inherited form) more to medicinal treatment. The inherited form at times presents itself in two types closely simulating those due to tuberculosis. Like the bacillus of tuberculosis, the syphilitic germ attacks every structure and organ of the body. Its reversal of the principle of individuation, causing excessive cell formation, produces more decidedly demonstrable effects. As syphilis is more apt to attack the central nervous system than tuberculosis, it would seem that it is a greater race-deteriorating factor. The excessive tendency to cell formation, however, produces impotence in man, sterility and abortion in woman. There are very good reasons for believing that the race is becoming immune to syphilis, and that this disease will disappear. Its greatest race-deteriorating effect is in preparing the soil for tuberculosis and other infections and contagions.

The influence of contagions and infections on degeneracy is therefore by no means slight. Each disease can produce grave constitutional defects in the ancestor likely to be intensified in the offspring. The greatest social dangers result from tuberculosis; the next from syphilis. Typhoid fever, scarlatina, small-pox, measles, diphtheria, whooping-cough, and all other contagions, however, may produce these constitutional defects, either through the mother during pregnancy or through their secondary effects on the ancestor's constitution. If the subject be attacked before the close of the periods of dental stress an arrest of development of the bones of the face may result with irregularities in the shape and position of the teeth. These, then, are stigmata of degeneracy, especially due, in the individual presenting them, to the contagions and infections rather than to inheritance alone.

CHAPTER VIII

Climate, Soil, and Food

AMONG the factors constituting environment few have impressed the biologist so much as climate, soil, and food. The seeming modifications produced by these have made a very decided impression on the sceptical Weismann, who stated that "the possibility is not to be rejected that influences continued for a long time, that is, for generations, such as temperature, climate, kind of nourishment, &c., which may affect the germ plasm, as well as any other part of the organism, may produce a change in the constitution of the germ plasm. But such influences would not then produce individual variations, but would necessarily modify, in the same way, all the individuals of a species living in a certain district. It is possible, though it cannot be proved, that many climatic varieties have arisen in this manner. Possibly other phenomena of variation must be referred to a variation in the structure of the germ plasm produced directly by external influences."

Considering the changes brought about in European plants and animals in Australia, those occurring in the East Indian mongoose in Jamaica, the changes in European plants and animals in America, or American animals in Europe and European animals in Asia, Weismann's position seems judicial.

The influences dependent on food, soil, and climate producing normal modifications have been remarkably illustrated in the gilled batrachian Axolotl. This, under the nourishment and change of surroundings of the Jardin des Plantes, was transformed into a gill-less batrachian, which had hitherto been regarded as belonging to a totally distinct family.

According to Darwin,[169] English dogs degenerate in India in a few generations, losing the peculiarities of form and mental character which distinguish their particular race, in spite of the greatest care in selection and prevention of crossing. An instance which well deserves the consideration of those anthropologists who attach but little importance to the influence of the environment and to the value of speech as an aid to the ethnologist is that of the Wurtemburgers, who settled (1816) near Tiflis in Russia. They had originally fair or red hair, light or blue eyes and coarse, broad features. In the first generation brown hair and black eyes began to appear; in the second black hair and eyes became the rule, while the face acquired an oval form. These changes were due entirely to the surroundings, no instance of crossing with Georgian natives being on record. At the same time, these transformed

Wurtemburgers continue to speak their German mother-tongue uninfluenced by the local dialects.[170]

The alleged transformation of the British into the Yankee is commonly cited in illustration of the supposed effects of soil and climate. Three decades[171] ago Vogt remarked that American Anglo-Saxons or Yankees were instanced as illustration of change of character. Already, after the second generation, according to Pruner-Bey, the Yankee presents features of the Indian type. At a later period the glandular system is reduced to the minimum of its normal development. The skin becomes like leather; the colour of the cheeks is replaced by sallowness. The head becomes smaller and rounder, and is covered with stiff, dark hair; the neck becomes longer, and there is greater development of the cheek-bones and the masseters. The temporal fossæ becomes deeper, the jaw-bones more massive, the eyes lie in deep approximated sockets. The iris is dark, the glance is piercing and wild. The long bones, especially in the superior extremities, are lengthened so that the gloves manufactured in England and France for the American market are of a particular make, with very long fingers. The female pelvis approaches that of the male. According to Quatrefages, America has thus, from the English race, produced a new white race which might be called the Yankee race. Vogt believes that America dries up the skin and reduces the fat, an effect to which all the above differences might be reduced. That the head becomes smaller he utterly denies. Exact cranial measurements by Morton show that the skull of the Yankee is at least as large as that of the Englishman.

Similar changes have been noted in the Anglo-Saxon Australians. The true explanation of this is that early rigorous environment tended to cause reversion to types not uncommon even now in Great Britain, Ireland, and Scandinavia, resultant on the admixture of primitive types to which reference has been made. The same error has been made about the pelvis as about the skull. The male pelvis in the American is approximating the female in accordance with advance, since, as Havelock Ellis has shown,[172] not only by his skull, but by his pelvis, modern man is following a path first marked out by woman. The skull of the modern woman is more markedly feminine than that of the savage woman, while that of the modern man has approximated to it. Not only is the pelvis of the modern woman much more feminine in character than that of the primitive woman, but the modern man's pelvis is also becoming more feminine.

The validity of Vogt's position anent the "Yankee" change of type is fully demonstrated by the following portraits of four generations of a noted American family with a Scandinavian patronymic, coming originally from a district in England where the alleged "Yankee" type (even to its nasal tone and so-called "Americanisms") occurs. The first "American" of the family (Fig. 3) was born in Connecticut in 1761 and died in 1826. He had a dolichocephalic head with massive jaws, prominent lips, especially the upper. The nose is long and the eyes are set close together, the forehead very high and straight. Quite a change is noticeable in the second generation (Fig. 4). The face is not so long, the lateral diameter of the head is larger, the forehead more prominent, and the eyes are a little farther apart. The nose is about the same length and while there is a resemblance about the mouth and chin, the distance from the front of the chin to the tip of the nose is not quite so long. The change seems to be due to shortening of the chin.

FIG. 3.—DOLICHOCEPHALIC.

FIG. 4.—MESOCEPHALIC.

FIG. 5.—MESOCEPHALIC.

FIG. 6.—BRACHYCEPHALIC.

The next generation (Fig. 5) shows still further changes. The forehead is broader and less retreating than either. There is perceptibly lest prognathism. There is less prominence in the supraorbital region.

The fourth generation exhibits (Fig. 6) a nearly brachycephalic head. The head is nearly round, forehead full, eyes set in the head to correspond with its width, nose broad, upper lips short, and the lower jaw is evidently much shorter in a perpendicular line. These changes are due to a protruding forehead, receding chin, and delicate features.

The climate of the United States exercises, according to certain sociologists, on the first generation of European immigrants, a deleterious influence in regard to fecundity. The decrease in the fecundity of the American woman has been charged to various anti-social causes (abortion and prevention of conception) and to a "nervousness" induced by the climate. A seemingly fair test of the influence of the climate would be a race elsewhere fecund, and whose religion encourages fecundity, decreasing in the first generation after immigration to the United States. Such a race is the Jewish. According to Gihon's analysis of the United States census of 1890[173] the Jewish birth rate is diminishing. From the mothers born in the United States the average is 3·56 children, as against 5·24 for those born in Germany, 5·36 for those in Russia and Poland, 5·27 for those in Hungary, and 5·44 for those in Bohemia. These figures, however, do not demonstrate the influence of climate, but of environment. The Jew, unlike the earlier American colonists, is not exposed to the stress of frontier life. He has a more favourable mental and physical environment than on the continent of Europe. This fact, therefore, does not demonstrate the effects of climate, but is really chargeable to climate, food, soil, and other factors constituting environment. That climate cannot be considered apart from these factors is shown, as I pointed out several years ago, by the fact that the United States surveyors in Minnesota reported to the national authorities that it was impossible to live the whole year in that state because of the extremely cold winter. Now, not only do people live and cultivate the soil throughout the entire state, but large cities have sprung up still farther north, and the country around has become well populated. Hence, in dealing with influences of climate, change of food and hygienic conditions must be taken into account. The error of the American surveyors as to the acclimatisation of the white race in cold climates has been emphasised as to the tropics and arctics. Here, however, the same error has been demonstrated by very careful researches. The experience of the Arctic regions as to necessity for change in diet and hygiene has been fully borne out by observations on the Anglo-Saxon in the tropics. The early experience of the English in India, upon which a fatal prognosis as to the future of British India was based, turns out to have been erroneous.

The influence of climate involves more than temperature. Stokvis, in a paper read before the Tenth International Medical Congress, at Berlin, on the comparative pathology of the human races with reference to the vital resistance of Europeans in tropical climates,[174] finds that the European immigrant in the tropics is assailed by two hostile forces: tropico-thermal and tropico-infectious agencies. The expression of innate racial peculiarities, like the variations of vegetable life and the varieties of animal life from effects of increased temperature, are such as occur in the inhabitants of temperate regions during the height of summer.

Marestang and Eykman find that neither high temperature alone nor meteorological agencies, apart from other deleterious influences, can produce that impoverishment of blood called "tropical anæmia." Stokvis shows that the tropical European does not prove inferior to the aboriginal with respect to thermal agencies. He is less susceptible to chill than the native. Mortality statistics of respiratory organ affections are greater for the native. While the European suffers more from liver disease than the native, the latter is less addicted to alcoholic drinks and pork. The percentage of deaths from cases treated is, however, more than twice as great with the native as with the European. Variations of physiologic life under tropical thermal conditions have little to do with the race. The vital resistance of the immigrant European (the European transformed into a permanent high-summer man) is somewhat greater than that of the native races.

Respecting the disease-producing effects of tropical infectious agencies, the experience of the last ten years (1880-90) is very different from that prior to 1860.

Average annual death-rate per thousand:—

		European Soldiers.	Native Soldiers.
	1819-28	170·0	138·0
Dutch East India Army	{ 1869-78	60·4	38·7
	1879-88	30·6	40·7
	1800-28	84·6	18·03
British India Army	{ 1828-56	56·7	
	1869-78	19·37	
	1876-88	16·27	21·6
	1820-36	121·0	30·0

British Army, Jamaica $\left\{\begin{array}{l} \end{array}\right.$ 1879-88   11·02   11·62

These changes are the consequence of sound sanitation. "The fairest laurel practical hygiene may boast of to-day is, doubtless, the laurel acquired in ameliorating the sanitary conditions of the European soldiers in tropical climates." A century ago James Lind said, "Much more than to the climate you are indebted to your own ignorance and negligence for the disease from which you suffer in tropical climates."

These statistics do not entirely support the declaration of Hippocrates that "races are the daughter of climates," but tend to show that the vital resistance of the different races in tropical climates depends more on external conditions than on race. Acclimatibility of strong, healthy, adult Europeans of both sexes in tropical climates must be admitted without any reserve, provided that they assiduously observe all hygienic rules. Stokvis disproves the allegation that the European is not able to produce in tropical regions more than three or four generations of true European blood, and that from the third or fourth generation onward sterility is the rule.

So accustomed, remarked Felken, however, is a man to his environment that it is difficult to remove an European from his home in the temperate region to any other, and yet for him to retain his health. Much may be done in the tropics to render climate more salubrious and sanitary precautions will do a great deal for the health of the community. But when all is done permanent residence for Europeans under European conditions is out of the question in the low-lying regions of the tropics. Comparatively few areas exist in the tropics where any great success for European colonisation can be prophesied from altitude alone. The influence of altitude on the physiologic characteristics is, however, very evident. The residents at high altitudes are strong, robust, buoyant, and of great mental and physical endurance.

In disproof of this position of Felken, Viault, of Bordeaux, has shown that the phenomena resultant on the acclimation of man at great altitudes comes neither from the frequency of respiratory movements nor from greater activity of the pulmonary circulation as has been asserted, but from increase of red blood globules. While the effects of both excessive heat and excessive cold may be admitted, even there other factors play a part. Very high mean temperature with low humidity is more likely to result in sunstroke and allied conditions than high temperature with high humidity. Low temperature of the Arctic regions tends to produce anæmia in natives of temperate zones. Food and depressing circumstances have, however, to be taken into consideration.

Sunstroke produces the ordinary phenomena of nervous exhaustion, but the patient becomes more irritable, suspicious, and extremely proud. As these patients are not recognised for a long times as insane they often marry and produce degenerates. Kiernan reports a case in which father and mother (both of healthy stock) were overcome by the heat during one of the processions of the American Centenaries. The children born before the sunstroke were healthy, but there had been no children for five years previously. A year subsequent to the sunstroke (which was followed by a change in character in both parents) the woman had triplets, one of which died soon after birth from convulsions. The second of the triplets, a girl, became epileptic at 2, a prostitute at 16, and chronically insane at 20. The third triplet became a puberty lunatic at 16. Of three children subsequently born, two are epileptics and one is a moral imbecile who manifests premonitory evidences of paranoia. Sunstroke, however, underlies many cases of alcoholism. Not a few of the instances of degeneration charged to alcoholism are, in reality, due to the nervous condition arising from the exhaustion produced by sunstroke. To this factor was in no small degree due the extremely large infant mortality of the English in India of the first half of the present century. While temperature plays a part in producing degeneracy in the offspring through its production of systemic disorder in the ancestor, it is usually associated with other factors which aid or predispose to its effects. It also predisposes to the greater action of other causes. Very frequently the sun-struck person, rendered incapable of continued labour by irritability, becomes a tramp or a pauper, either of which conditions tends to accelerate the degenerative process and furthermore to increase the possible chances of passing down the effect through heredity by the ease with which illicit relationships are contracted. The least intelligent of the prostitute class, or rather, of that class of nymphomaniacs who have not fully entered upon a prostitute career, are driven into the workhouse or almshouse, where they often remain for years, or depart at intervals, leaving their offspring to be reared at public expense. The number of such children born yearly in almshouses is at least ten thousand in the United States.[175] An enormous proportion of these die in infancy but sufficient survive to form a potent source of degenerates.

The influence of overheating further predisposes to the attack of microbes even in the temperate climates, and to constitutional defects resultant on these.

A factor of degeneracy as related to soil on which much stress has been laid, is that of goitre. This has been carefully studied by Munson[176] among the Indians on the reservation in the United States. The number was 77,173, of whom 2·36 per cent. had goitre. As regards geographic distribution the disease is more prevalent in the southern part of Montana. Goitre was reported as practically unknown among the white settlers living about the reservations where goitre was prevalent among the Indians. Fully 80 per cent. of the cases occur in Indian women, the disease being not only much less frequent, but also less decided and less extensive in the male. The average age of onset of the disease was from 12 to 14 years. There are many instances illustrating the apparent heredity of goitre. Several consecutive generations show its development. Only one case is reported in which goitre was associated with cretinism. Goitre among Indians cannot be traced to high altitudes, climate or water containing excess of calcium magnesium salts. The disease is apparently due to insanitary surroundings, depressing constitutional conditions, improper and excessively nitrogenous diet. This condition of things among the Indians bears an important relation to the facts pointed out by C. K. Clarke,[177] of Kingston, Ontario, who found in the Canadian asylums a large number of goitrous patients and one goitrous attendant. The goitrous patients, who were of long residence, had come from all parts of the dominion. The size of the goitre was in proportion to the length of the residence. It is possible that local influence may have much to do with the disease, though it is evident that the insane are much more liable to it than normal persons. W. B. Fletcher, of Indianapolis, has observed similar frequency as to goitre among the insane there, especially among the foreigners and their immediate descendants. Cretinism, according to Morel, was degeneracy due to a special action which a toxic principle exercises on a cerebro-spinal system, whether by the air that is breathed or by the substances ingested in the economy, and which, above all, appears to have some relation to a soil where predominates the magnesian limestone. That the last factor has some influence is shown by the fact that goitrous enlargements are encountered in medical practice in Chicago much more frequently than among the corresponding classes in the East. The water in Chicago contains magnesium-lime salts, whether it be derived from the lake or from the artesian well. The fact, however, that the Indians and the insane exhibit a tendency to goitre indicates that behind the influence of the soil or of diet lies a neuropathic constitution, whether this be inherited or acquired. Cretinism is much more frequent in the United States than was apparent ere the discovery of the value of the thyroid glands in treatment. Under the stimulus of investigation for cases in which to try this treatment, medical literature from all parts of the United States has been filled with reports of authenticated cases. Among these are scions of families which have been American for more than three generations and which may, therefore, be considered as products of an American environment. The same condition of things has occurred in both Great Britain and on the European continent in districts which, prior to 1890, were supposed to be free from cretinism. This illustrates the results of stimulus given investigation in biology rather than increase of the disorder.

The influence of spoiled maize in producing the mixed skin, nervous and mental disorder known as pellagra in the Italians, would seem, from the results of the researches of Billod,[178] to be chiefly due to the conjoined effects of unhygienic surroundings, the offspring of climate and soil. The fungus on maize (ustilago), like the fungus on rye (ergot), produces rather long-lasting neurosis of an epileptic character, susceptible to transmission to the offspring of women poisoned by these fungi. The Italian disease,pellagra, manifests the features one would expect from an improper food taken under unhygienic conditions. While this is undoubtedly exaggerated by the habits of the peasantry in Italy, still in a lesser degree like effects of food are observable in other races.

The influence of the potato diet in degenerating the Irish Celt in comparison with the Scottish Celt under the same conditions, is difficult at present to determine for lack of data. Certainly the descendants of this class of Irish Celts rapidly regain a handsome, healthy status under mixed American diet, even though the hygienic surroundings in the great cities be not the best. He who has to treat a class of neurasthenics in whom starch digestion is impaired finds that a diet of potatoes (undoubtedly through the auto-intoxication it produces) will increase certain nervous symptoms, and hence the tendency to transmission to the next generation.

In the families of the pioneers in the United States, as well as the families of farmers in secluded valleys in Norway, Switzerland, and elsewhere, the influence of monotony of diet, aggravated by monotony of surroundings, has undoubtedly produced a large amount of degeneracy. Ray Brigham of New York, Awl of Ohio, and Patterson of Illinois have shown that there is an unusual frequency of insanity in farmers' wives which is undoubtedly traceable to these conditions. Kiernan, of Chicago, has reported a case fairly typical of those earlier described by the American alienists just cited. The first generation was a woman of New England stock, of tireless energy, to whom work was a pleasure and rest an abhorrence, and who lived on a farm miles from the town. She did all her own work and brought up a large family, chiefly on maize, potatoes, and bread, pork being the meat diet. At 50 this woman removed with her husband, who had grown wealthy, to a small country town. Here she conducted the entire work of the household without a servant. At 52 she broke down with neurasthenia, which rapidly passed into periodical gloomy spells, in one of which she committed suicide. Her youngest daughter, who had an asymmetrical face, has the periodical gloomy tendency of the mother, alternating with periods of restlessness, which evince themselves in doing unnecessarily the work of the servants and other labours inconsistent with her husband's social status. She had at times suicidal and homicidal impulses. She has three children; one exhibits no special abnormality; the eldest, a boy of eleven, dislikes to play with boys because they are rough, and plays with girls, to whom he is at times mischievously cruel. He likes to sew and make doll's clothing and purchase dolls, while there are other indications of sexual abnormality. The youngest, a girl, has frequent attacks of epileptic-like fury, although between these she is kind- hearted, good-humoured, and very affectionate. In dealing with the question of soil, the factors predisposing to the attacks of the parasite of malaria have to be taken into consideration; certainly the inhabitants of certain malarial districts exhibit all the characteristics of degenerates.

The influence of nutrition in producing nervous states likely to be transmitted as degeneracy in the offspring are excellently illustrated in the nervous disorders due to improper nutrition during youth. This may, as W. S. Christopher[179] of Chicago has shown, produce all possible neuroses to which the organism may be liable. Such neuroses relate to—

    A. Psychic faculties.

    B. Sensation.
        1. Anæsthesia.
        2. Hyperæsthesia.
        3. Hyperalgia (increased pain sense).

    C. Heat production.
        1. Elevation of temperature.
        2. Depression of temperature.

    D. Muscular tissues.
        1. Hypertrophy.
        2. Atrophy.
        3. Paralysis.
        4. Convulsions.

    E. Skeletal muscles.
        1. General convulsions.
        2. Chorea.
        3. Tetany (toe and finger jerks).

    F. Pharynx.
        1. Dyspnœa (difficult breathing).

    G. Œsophagus.
        1. Dysphagia (difficult swallowing).

H. Stomach.
    1. Vomiting.
    2. Merycism (rumination).

I. Intestines.
    1. Increased peristalsis (movement of bowel).
    2. Decreased peristalsis.

J. Larynx.
    1. Dyspnœa.
    2. Laryngismus stridulus (croup spasm).
    3. Chorea.

K. Bronchi.
    1. Asthma.
    2. Bronchorrhœa (excessive secretion).

L. Bladder.
    1. Incontinence.
    2. Retention.

M. Urethra.
    1. Spasmodic stricture.

N. Uterus.
    1. Neuralgias.
    2. Spasms.

O. Vagina.
    1. Vaginismus (painful spasm).

P. Heart.
    1. Chorea.
    2. Disturbance of rate.
    3. Disturbance of rhythm.

Q. Secretory organs.
    1. Decrease of secretion.
    2. Modification of composition of secretion.

R. Absorptive organs.

S. Elaborative organs.

T. Respiratory organs. Other than those cited.

U. Excretory organs.

V. Reproductory organs.

Those of the genital organs only exist in precocious childhood, while still others occur, some occasionally, some very frequently.

Of the psychic neuroses, perhaps the commonest are the night terrors, which occur in ill-nourished children with great frequency. Hyperesthesia (or increased sensitiveness) is a starvation neurosis occurring especially in unrecognised scurvy. Variations of temperature, both increased and subnormal, occur in children suffering from evident in-nutrition.

Of the starvation neuroses, the commonest are muscular convulsions. Naturally enough, any muscle or any group of muscles may be affected, and the manifestations may present all the varieties of convulsive movements to which muscles are liable. Probably no child whose nutrition is perfect ever has general convulsions except as the result of actual brain disease or at the onset of some infectious process where the convulsion takes the place of the initial chill of the adult. The so-called reflex convulsions occur only in children whose nutrition is below par. In a rickety child the slight irritation produced by an erupting tooth may be sufficient to weaken the mechanism which checks explosive action, just as in the same child it may be the determining cause of bronchorrhœa. In the healthy child teething can cause no such effect. Both these manifestations, the convulsions and the bronchorrhœa, are starvation neuroses. In such children many other trivial conditions may weaken the controlling mechanism.

In older children chorea, whatever be its cause, is evidently connected with the developmental process. The beneficial effects in chorea of absolute rest in bed and forced feeding are a matter of common observation. Dysphagia as a neurosis in children is uncommon. Vomiting and diarrhœa occur so frequently in infants from a wide variety of causes, that it is very difficult to say when they are merely starvation neuroses. In rickets, diarrhœa often occurs, with no adequate explanation in the conditions present in the intestinal canal, and which is an essential feature of the disease itself.

Laryngismus stridulus is a very common manifestation of muscular starvation neurosis. Spasmodic asthma occurs in ill-nourished children. Incontinence of urine in older children is often a starvation neurosis.

The younger the child the more rapid are its processes of growth. Hence in infants the results of defective nutrition are quickly manifested, and the curative effects of food arranged to supply the nutritive deficiencies also become apparent very soon. In older children with more stable tissues a defective food supply is longer borne without apparent effect; but, on the other hand, the beneficial effect of an antidotal diet becomes apparent only after a prolonged use.

The relatively simple diet of the infant makes it easy to discover the particular kind of food which is supplied in sufficient quantity, and makes the supply of the deficiency comparatively easy. But in older children with a more varied diet the defect is less readily discovered and less readily supplied.

The effects of climate, soil, and food in the production of degeneracy are first shown in the causation of general loss of nerve tone in the ancestor, often with special local expressions. This loss of nerve tone may show itself in the offspring by any type of degeneracy from nutritive defect to loss of moral tone.

CHAPTER IX

School Strain

LIKE all factors of degeneracy, school strain evinces itself in a systemic nervous exhaustion manifest along lines of least resistance, as in the neuroses of Christopher. The first types of his neuroses are due to overstrain of certain territories related with memory, as contrasted with diminished use of the association fibres connecting these. As Schopenhauer has excellently observed, man is one-third intellect and two-thirds will, and much of this last two-thirds is the result of training. Capacity for training may be greater in one individual than another, because of inherited or congenital deficiencies. It is, as Sully[180] remarks, "a happy circumstance in healthy children that that most prolific excitant of fear, the presentation of something new and uncanny, is also provocative of curiosity, with its impulse to look and examine. A very tiny child, on first making acquaintance with some form of physical pain, as a bump on the head, will deliberately repeat the experience by knocking his head against something as if experimenting and watching the effect. A clearer case of curiosity overpowering fear is that of a child who, after pulling the tail of a cat in a bush and getting scratched, proceeded to dive into the bush again. Still more interesting here are gradual transitions from actual fear, before the new and strange, to bold inspection. The child who was frightened by her Japanese doll insisted on seeing it every day. The behaviour of one of these small persons on the arrival at the house of a strange dog, of a dark foreigner or some other startling novelty is a pretty and amusing sight. The first overpowering timidity, the shrinking back to the mother's breast, followed by curious peers, then by bolder outstretchings of head and arms, mark the stage by which curiosity and interest gain on fear, and finally leave it far behind. Very soon the small, timorous creatures will grow into bold adventurers. They will make playthings of the alarming animals and of the alarming shadows too. Later on still perhaps they will love nothing so much as to probe the awful mysteries of gunpowder."

In degenerate children, because of deficiencies of proper inter-association of the memory territories in the brain, healthy curiosity, and the instinct of sheltering are deficient, so that states of uncertainty, producing terror, result. These become permanent in after life, even when training as an adult is strongly antagonistic to them.

This is illustrated, as Harriet C. B. Alexander has shown,[181] in George Eliot, who during childhood "suffered from a low general state of health and great susceptibility to terror at night, and the liability to have all her soul become a quivering fear," which remained during life. She had periods of depression and vertex headache, which latter gave place to sick headache, often attended with rheumatoid phenomena. "She was an awkward girl, reserved and serious far beyond her years, but observant, and addicted to the habit of sitting in corners and watching her elders." Fear of the unknown in childhood, seemingly a reversion to the fear of the unknown of savages, tends, like it, to produce occult belief. Despite the German rationalism of George Eliot, such fear found utterance in her *Behind the Veil*, a mystically occult contrast with her novels and with the positivism which was her religion. Theoretically the philosophy of George Eliot should have destroyed much mysticism, yet as a survival of "night terrors" it came to the surface. A very vivid autobiographical narrative of night-terrors and similar nervous phenomena in the childhood of a distinguished man of letters will be found in Horatio Brown's *Life of John Addington Symonds*.

School over-pressure in certain respects checks, even in well-developed minds, the transition from the terror of the unknown of childhood into the calm of maturity. Morbid fears, imperative conceptions, and imperative acts which torture the individual during an otherwise healthy career unquestionably originate in the early periods of life.

Degenerate children, as Kiernan[182] remarks, early manifest decided neurotic excitability, and tend to neuroses at physiologic crises like the first and second dentition, and the onset and close of puberty. Slight physical or mental perturbation is followed by sleeplessness, delirium, hallucinations, &c. Hyperæsthesia and excessive reaction to pleasant or offensive impressions exist. Vasomotor instability is present, pallor, blushing, palpitations or pre-cardial anxiety result from trivial moral or physical excitants. There is no precocity or aberration of the sexual instinct. The disposition is irritable. The grasshopper is a burden. Psychic pain arises from the most trivial cause, and finds expression in emotional outbursts. Sympathies and antipathies are equally intense. The mental life swings between periods of exaltation and depression, alternating with brief epochs of healthy indifference. Egotism is supreme, and morality absent or perverted. This absence or perversion is often concealed under the guise of moral superiority, religiosity, or cant. Vanity and jealous suspiciousness are common. The intellect and temper are exceedingly irregular. Monotonously feeble, scanty ideation passes readily into seeming brilliance, even to the extent of hallucinations. But ideas are barren as a rule, because generated so rapidly as to destroy each other ere they pass into action. Energy fails ere aught can be completed. The inability to distinguish between desires and facts produces seeming mendacity. The will in its apparent exuberance, its capricious energy, and innate futility, matches and distorts the one-sided talent or whimsical genius which may exist. The whole of this mental state may not be present. The tendency to introspection, to morbid fear, to gloom, to hallucinations, to alternations of depression and exaltation, may occur in a degenerate child in whom has been otherwise preserved that secondary ego which is the latest and greatest acquirement of the race.

In the same class, according to George Parkman,[183] an American alienist of more than eighty years ago, brilliant talents, astonishing facility of receiving and communicating ideas often appear suddenly at puberty, especially in females, to be later followed by mediocrity, disappointment, and supineness.

These degenerate children have a tendency, as C. F. Folsom[184] remarks, to manifest aberrant tendencies at the periods of stress, which may, in Folsom's judgment, be congenital, or due to early interference with normal brain development. These show themselves in childhood and infancy by irregularity or disturbed sleep, irritability, apprehension, strange ideas, great sensitiveness to external impressions, high temperature, delirium or convulsions from slight causes, disagreeable dreams and visions, romancing, intense feeling, periodic headache, muscular twitching, capricious appetite, and great intolerance of stimulants and narcotics. At puberty developmental anomalies, and not infrequently perverted sexual instincts, are observed in both sexes. During adolescence there is often excessive shyness or bravado, always introspection and self-consciousness, and sometimes abeyance or absence of the sexual instinct, which, however, is frequently of extraordinary intensity. The imitative and imaginative faculties may be quick. The affections or emotions are vehement but shallow. Vehement dislikes are formed, and intense personal attachments result in extraordinary friendships, which not seldom swing around suddenly into bitter enmity or indifference. The passions are unduly a force in the character, which lacks will power. The individual's higher brain centres are not well inhibited, and he dashes about like a ship without a rudder, fairly well if the winds be fair and the seas be calm, but dependent on the elements for the character and the time of the final wreck. Invention, poetry, music, artistic taste, philanthropy, intensity, and originality, are sometimes of a higher order among these persons, but desultory, half-finished work and shiftlessness are much more common. With many of them concentrated, sustained effort, and attempts to keep them to it are impossible. Their common-sense perception of the relations of life, executive or business faculty and judgment are seldom well developed. The memory is now and then extraordinary. They are apt to be self-conscious, egotistic, and morbidly conscious. They easily become victims of insomnia, neurasthenia, hypochondria, neuroticism, hysteria, or insanity. They offend against the proprieties of life and commit crime with less cause or provocation than other persons. While many of them are among the most gifted and attractive people in their community, the majority are otherwise, and possess an uncommon capacity for making fools of themselves, and of being a nuisance to their friends and of little use to the world.

These conditions occur from heredity in degenerates, but, as Francis Warner[185] remarks, while "it is very common to see disordered conditions of the nervous system in children with defective construction of body, these nerve disturbances may also be seen in children with normal construction of body. Such signs result from the disorder, produced by special circumstances, aiding as well as producing defect which results from, or in the next generation becomes, defect in original construction. Among the signs of fatigue in children is the slight amount of force expended in movement, often with asymmetry of balance in the body. The fatigued centres may be unequally exhausted; spontaneous finger twitches like those of younger children may be seen, and slight movements may be excited by noises. The head is often held on one side. The arms when extended are not held horizontally. Usually the left is lower. The face is no evidence of bodily nutrition. It may be well nourished, yet the body be thin. Three per cent. of the children seen in school are below par in nutrition. These children are of lower general constitutional power. They tend to an ill-nourished condition under the stress of life, and many cases of mental excitement which, while they render them sharper mentally, militate against general nutrition."

Colin A. Scott has found corroborative evidences of similar effects of strain in the children of the New England and Illinois schools.

These systemic nervous exhaustions may, as W. S. Christopher, of Chicago, has shown (in remarks on neuroses already cited), take unexpected local directions, especially involving, in accordance with the general law of reversal, evolution or degeneracy checks on excessive action. Among the conditions produced by school strain of serious consequence in after-life are headaches, usually charged to anæmia or neurasthenia. These headaches, as Sachs,[186] of New York, has shown, usually appear after emotional excitement or fatiguing ordeal. There are other symptoms expressive of neurasthenia, such as slight tremor of the tongue and fingers and exaggeration of the deep reflexes, but, above all, the very persistent vertex headache, and the child's description of pressure or heat there. In children emotional conditions, school strain, rivalry between class-mates, are as liable to produce neurasthenia as are the more serious struggles for existence in later life. These headaches may pass very readily at periods of stress into migraine. The vertigo characteristic of migraine is not rarely found in the neurasthenic headache of childhood. What is true of migraine is also true of epilepsy. The tremors, &c., accompanying neurasthenic headache become the convulsions of epilepsy. G. B. Fowler reports a case emphasising very clearly the position of Christopher. It was that of a seven-year-old boy of mushroom growth and hothouse culture. He began every day before breakfast with an hour at Spanish, and until three in the afternoon was unceasingly occupied with French, German, music, and the ordinary school curriculum. This policy, initiated four years before, the pressure being gradually increased, had been maintained almost without interruption. The child had consequently developed into a sort of phonograph, capable of starting automatic expressions which afforded much entertainment to visitors, and gave the ambitious father great hope and comfort. Under such conditions it is not to be wondered at that something gave way, and, fortunately for the brain, it was the sphincter of the anus. When this deplorable occurrence first took place the child was sharply reprimanded; the accident repeating itself, however, two or three times weekly, and later about once a day, more pronounced measures were instituted. The boy was often severely flogged, deprived of liberty, luxuries, &c., yet without avail. The lower bowel was perfectly normal. The sphincter was tight, grasped the finger with the usual firmness, and there were no sources of irritation about the anus. The abnormal conditions under which the child had been living very naturally at the outset were the cause of the difficulty. Cessation of the punishment and release from books was ordered. The result was satisfactory. In three weeks the involuntary discharge became gradually less frequent, and finally ceased altogether.

Mental strain produces precisely similar effects on the nerve control of the stomach. All types of nervous disturbances of the stomach—merycism (cud-chewing), bulimia (ox appetite), acoria (incapacity for getting enough)—result, as Ewald[187] has shown, from nerve strain, and increase this through auto-intoxication.

The sphincter of bladder often gives way, and is a very frequent expression of nervous exhaustion in the child, often increased by the effects of nerve strain on the kidneys, which do their work of purification imperfectly, while excreting nearly pure water. The enormous quantity of clear urine passed during worry is a generally recognised expression of such strain. This nerve- strain interference with the purifying work of the kidneys leads to increased strain on the liver and other glands, whence result migraine, the uric acid states, rheumatisms, and the other perversions of nutrition. Nerve-strain on either liver, bowel, or other glands, has similar secondary effects on the kidneys. In part this is an organ degeneracy in function whereby man's liver and kidneys do the work of the sauropsidal liver and kidneys.

Among the nutritive disturbances resulting from nerve-strain is the fatty anæmia of Weir Mitchell, the juvenile obesity of Féré and others. This is generally associated with the uric acid states which so often result from school strain. The apparent improvement shown in increased weight leads to increased strain, and many of these fat victims of school over-pressure enter insane hospitals as puberty lunatics.

Other effects of the nutritive disturbances produced by school strain are local irritations about the sexual organs. These may arise from irritation by uric acid of the mouth of the bladder in boys, or of the vagina and bladder in girls. Neurotic persons are liable to nerve storms, which express themselves in emotional displays or restlessness or nagging tendencies. These often coincide with the uric acid tendency to express itself in "storms," like other periodical phenomena of the nervous system. In consequence, "sexual storms" result in neuropaths, whether the neuropathy be inherited or acquired. Local genital organ irritation leads to scratching. From this are produced "masturbation storms," which the subject loathes but cannot control. These occur also from the direct effects of constipation, as well as from the worms and other parasites which constipation fosters in the bowel. Teachers, by compelling children to retain urine through fear of masturbation, often lead to what they intend to prevent. At the outset masturbation and sexual explosions are often a physical expression of school strain destitute of moral significance. They are removable by removing the school strain and its consequences. If strengthened by protracted existence they intensify degeneracy due to school strain.

The states of imperfect nutrition, resultant from nerve strains on gland function, in this way and in others, interfere with the proper evolution of puberty and the involutional changes at the "change of life," which occurs in both sexes. The conditions of "nervous cough," of so-called "catarrh," and its ally, bronchorrhœa, are often found as expressions of the systemic exhaustion from school strain, and are treated as purely local conditions.

School strain, therefore, produces, like all the acquired factors of degeneracy, a systemic nervous exhaustion which may be expressed either in general neuropathy or hysteria after puberty, or in the tropho-neuroses, like gout and allied states, or in epilepsy or arterial change, predisposing to rupture of arteries at periods of stress, with resultant convulsions and paralysis.

CHAPTER X

THE DEGENERATE CRANIUM

THE cranium or skull is a development in part of the vertebræ or bones forming the backbone, and in part of dermal or membranous bones, which of old in reptiles, as in the alligator to-day, formed the protective armour of the skin of the head. As the head end of the spinal cord of the lancelet developed, the cartilage enclosing it developed to protect it. This was the earlier evolution. Later, another skull developed in connection with this. The cranium or skull therefore has, as Minot remarks,[188] a double origin, or, rather, there are two skulls which were originally distinct. In evolution from the lowest fish to the highest mammal, and in the embryonic development of man, these become united.

The primary skull, as already stated, is practically an extension of the vertebræ, which send side outgrowths to cover the brain as the backbone covers the spinal cord. This primary skull extended in front of the notochord (the spinal cord of the human embryo, and the permanent spinal cord of the lancelet), where it gave off two trabeculæ cranii or front skull plates. Behind, the primary skull or chondrocranium gives off two occipal or rear skull plates. It gives off also two plates midway between the trabeculæ and occipitals, which, as they gradually enclose the primitive hearing apparatus, the otocysts (permanent in fish, and embryonic in man), are called periotic capsules. This primary skull is at first cartilaginous, as in sharks. With the increase in the size of the brain in evolution and in human embryology, this cartilaginous primary skull became insufficient to roof over the brain, and thus resulted gaps in it. The fontanelles, or soft places at the top, sides, and back of the head of the new-born child, are the remains of this failure of the chondrocranium, or primary skull, to cover the gains of the nervous system in the struggle for existence. This deficiency, resultant on advance in evolution, would have been a long-standing serious block to further advance, were it not that the skin of the mammal retained a function inherited from the reptiles and bony fish.

These cavities were filled by dermal bones, which, at first serving merely as armour in the skin of the head, came to be protectors of the nervous system. The following bones represent these dermal bones in the embryonic human skull: The frontals, which form the chief part of the forehead; the sutures, or dovetails, of these normally disappear in the adult, so that the forehead seems to be but one bone. This union may not occur (Fig. 7), as in the case of the philosopher Kant, who had a frontal suture all his life. The dovetails are replaced by solid bone, through a process called synostosis. In the case of the frontal bone it is normal, and in the line of advance. Elsewhere in the skull it is often an expression of defect which may give rise to various cranial states which are either absolutely degenerate in type or degenerate only when occurring in certain races. The parietals and interparietals are also dermal bones which are united by synostosis to form the parietals or side bones of the normal adult skull. The nasal bones which, together with the vomer, form the nose, are likewise dermal bones, and so are the pterygoids and palatines. The maxillaries and præmaxillaries, which, with the mandibles, form the jaws, are dermal bones. The mandibles, however, are in part derived from the chondrocranium.

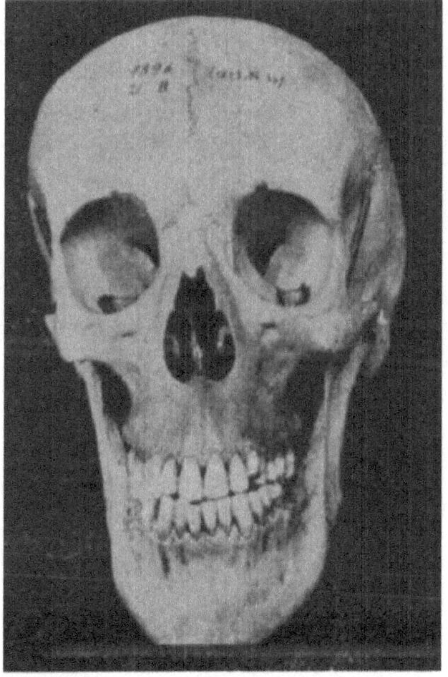

FIG. 7.

With rise in evolution, and during the progress of human embryonic development, these bones become fewer through their early gristly union or their synostosis. The openings in the skull resultant on the deficiencies in the chondrocranium are larger in the sauropsida (birds and reptiles) than in the ichthyopsida (amphibious and fish); in the monotremata (egg-laying mammals) than in the sauropsida; in the marsupials (pouched mammals) than in the monotremata, and in the higher mammals than in the marsupials. The development of the brain therefore depends on the growing and expanding power of the secondary skull formed by the dermal bones. These, considered as bones, are degenerate from the high type of the vertebræ, and are a mere reminiscence of that outer skeleton whereby early fish and reptiles emulated the lobster. The influence of any check to development such as produces degeneracy, is exerted first on the development of the bone itself, and finally on the relation to other bones by dovetailing.

In accordance with the general laws governing growth, deficiency in one place is apt to result in increase elsewhere. The brain-protective function of the dermal bones being later in development than their old armour function, is apt to be checked by degeneracy in two ways; in the first the bone does not grow in size or sufficiently to unite with its fellows, or this growth occurs only for the benefit of the bone itself, through Spencer's law of individuation, so that union with the other bones occurs too early for the benefit of the organism as a whole. To the factors underlying this is due the non-increase in intellect after puberty which occurs in the higher apes, and in some of the lower races of men.

These checks also tend to the nutritional benefit of the older primary skull, whence result the irregularities in development that constitute so many of the stigmata of the degenerate cranium. The sutures sometimes do not form because sufficient gristle is not produced to fill the gaps. (Fig. 8.) These secondary gaps are often filled by new dermal bones called Wormian. Sometimes this deficiency coexists with too early synostosis elsewhere.

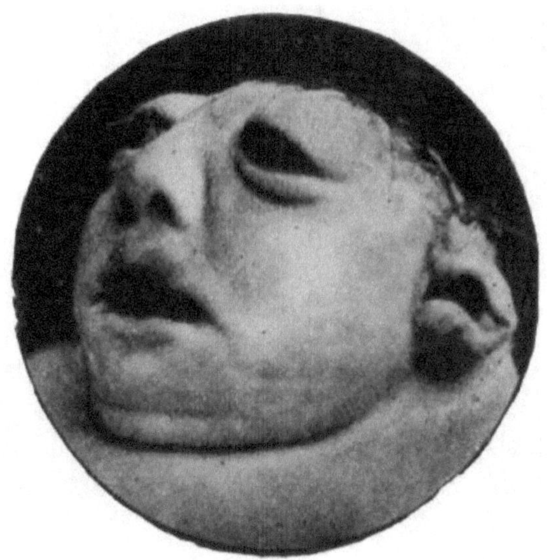

FIG. 8.

Degenerate skulls have therefore been divided from the standpoint of these various unions (by synostosis or otherwise) and non-unions of the sutures, on the principle that premature synostosis of a suture produces shortness of the diameter, perpendicular to the direction of the obliterated suture.[189] The bones stop growing prematurely at the seat of the synostosis, but the unaffected borders continue growing. The following types result on this principle:

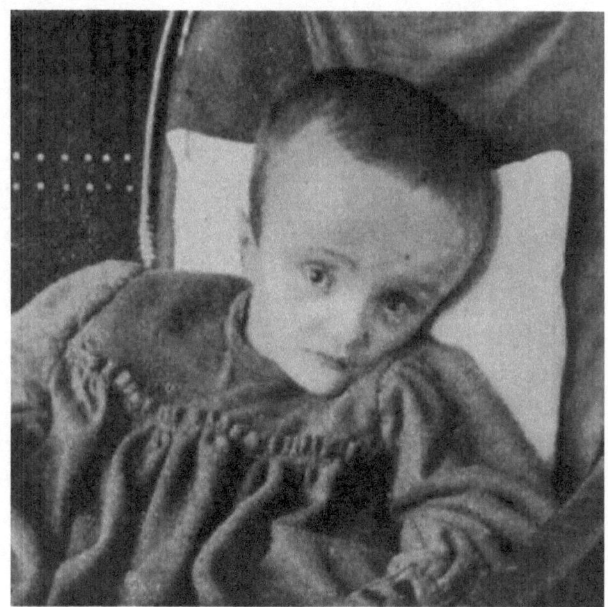

FIG. 9.

I. Simple macrocephaly (largeness of head). (*a*) Hydrocephaly (water in the head. Fig. 9.) (*b*) Kephalones (all heads. Fig. 10), without hydrocephaly. These two conditions result from the inability of the dermal bones to fill at the proper period the gaps in the chondrocranium. Neither of these denotes complete intellectual degeneracy on the one hand, nor vast intellect on the other. Cuvier was a case of healed-up hydrocephalus, whence his large brain and skull. In a case of kephalones observed by Kiernan there was a brain- weight of 68 ounces. The patient was an imbecile, practically unteachable.

[190] Both these conditions denote deep degeneracy, which, however, may find expression elsewhere than in the moral sense or intellect.

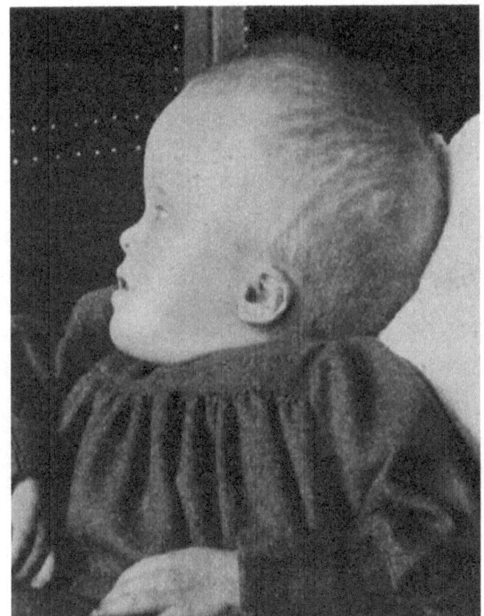

FIG. 10.

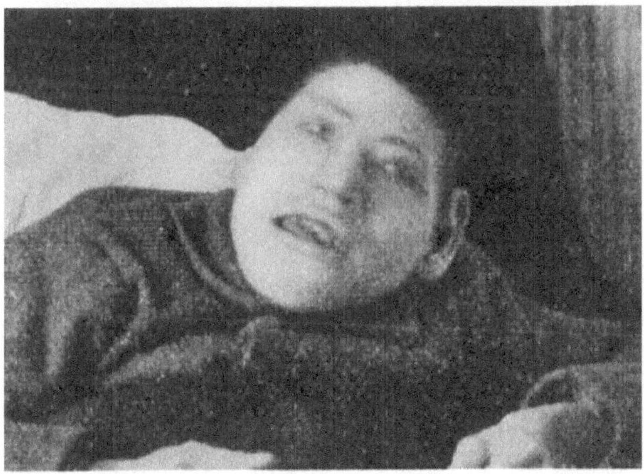

FIG. 11.

II. Simple microcephaly (smallness of head. Fig. 11) or nannocephaly (dwarf head). As a rule these are found among idiots, but much has been done by training, even for them. Many seemingly great intellects, however, have heads approaching, if not reaching this type.[191] Des Cartes, Foscolo, and Schumann had sub-microcephaly. The poet Shelley had a head belonging very nearly to this category, but while he exhibited many stigmata of degeneracy, that of intellectual deficiency was wanting. This type of skull, however, is usually associated with deep degeneracy. It represents in man the condition underlying the premature suture-closing which occurs in the ape. It sometimes may exist with considerable intellect, as in the case of Donizetti. Sometimes this suture-closing directly prevents brain growth. This condition is rarer than many surgeons admit, but it does occur, as witness the cases of Vico, Malebranche, and Clement VI. The fact that these three fractured their skulls in infancy saved them from being imbeciles and idiots like their brothers, sisters, and cousins.

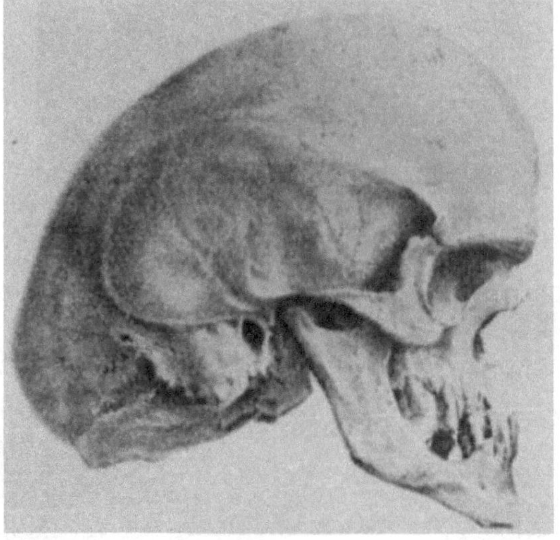

FIG. 12.

III. Dolichocephaly (long-headedness. Fig. 12). (*a*) Upper middle synostosis. (1) Simple dolichocephaly is due to synostosis of the sagittal, or antero-posterior suture of the skull. Whether this be due to degeneracy or not depends entirely on the race in which it occurs. The ultra-dolichocephaly of Daniel O'Connell was due, in Kiernan's opinion, to his birth in an Irish district settled by dolichocephalics. Undoubtedly dolichocephaly is tending to mesocephaly (medium size of head). Even the negro, generally regarded by ethnologists as dolichocephalic, is tending in this direction, as numerous observations of my own show. Dolichocephaly, however, while it does not demonstrate, suggests degeneracy, since it seems to be a disappearing type of skull. The changes in American families in this particular indicate this. (2) Sphenocephaly (wedge-shape of head. Fig. 13) is due to synostosis of the sagittal suture, with compensatory growth in the region of the large fontanelle. (*b*) Dolichocephalic states, resulting from inferior lateral synostosis are: (1) Leptocephaly (narrowness of head), due to synostosis of the frontal and sphenoid bones. (2) Klinocephaly (saddle-shaped head) is due to synostosis of the parietal bones with the greater wings of the sphenoid, or of the parietal with the squamous portion of the temporal bone.

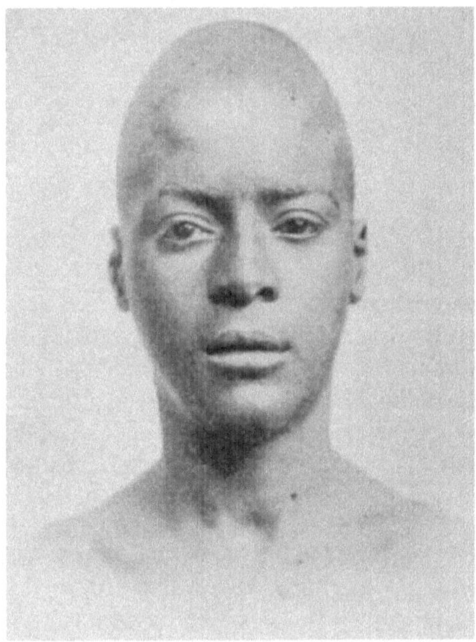

FIG. 13.

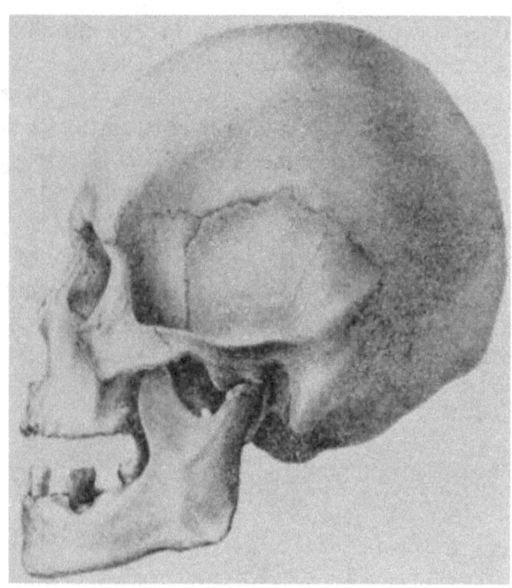

FIG. 14.

IV. Brachycephaly (shortness of head. Fig. 14). The pure type like pure dolichocephaly is not necessarily by itself evidence of degeneracy, as it may represent race. It is, however, a disappearing type of skull, and hence should lead to critical examination. In the case of the philosopher Kant his ultra-brachycephaly could not be charged to race, since he sprang from dolichocephalic Scotch on one side and dolichocephalic Germans on the other. (*a*) Posterior stenosis. (1) Pachycephaly (thickness of head) is due to synostosis of the parietal bone with the occipital. (2) Oxycephaly (sugar-loaf head) is due to synostosis of the parietal bones and the occipital with compensatory growth of the region of the anterior fontanelle; a variety of this is acrocephaly (spire head). (*b*) Upper, anterior, and lateral synostosis. (1) Platycephaly (flat head. Fig. 15), or chæmacephaly, is due to extensive synostosis of the temporal bones with the parietal. Kant, in addition to his cranial stigmata, had this condition. (2) Trochocephaly (roundness of head) is due to partial synostosis of the frontals and parietals in the centre of the coronal suture. (3) Plagiocephaly (wry head. Fig. 16) is due to unilateral synostosis of the frontal and parietal bones. (*c*) Brachycephaly due to inferior medium synostosis. Simple brachycephaly is due to early synostosis of the nasal and sphenoid.

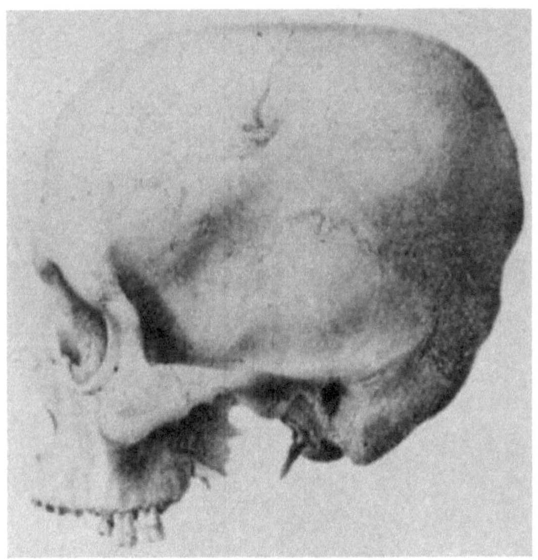

FIG. 15.

To these should be added kyphocephaly (lump head), due to synostosis of the posterior part of the squamous portion of the temporal and the parietal bones with Wormian bones in the lambdoid fissure. Tapeisocephaly (low head) is due to synostosis of the great wings of the sphenoid with the frontal. Scaphocephaly (boat-shaped head. Fig. 17) was a term applied by Von Baer to skulls which are very narrow and compressed at the sides, and in which there is no trace of the sagittal suture, but its region is so elevated that the skull cap has the form of a keel boat bottom upward. Trigonocephaly (triangular head) is a variety of scaphocephaly in which depression occurs in place of the keel. Sir Walter Scott had a skull in which premature closure of the sagittal suture produced the appearance of scaphocephaly, but compensation for this elsewhere produced a decidedly different type. Scott presented neurotic phenomena during youth, albeit the brain disease from which he died had anything but a degenerate origin.

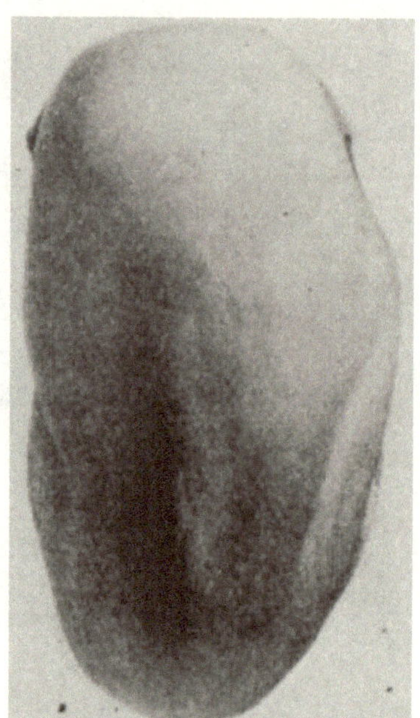

FIG. 16.

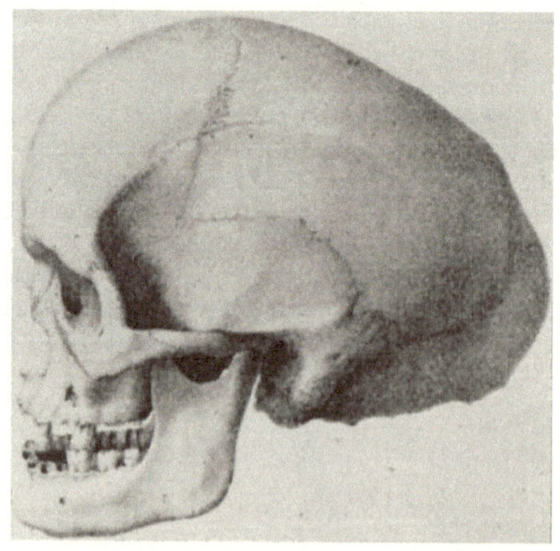

FIG. 17.

Morton and Catlin claim that while the artificial distortions of the cranium may play a part in developing synostosis these have no effect upon the intellectual functions. It has been stated further that there are no mental data to show the effect of artificial malformation of the child's head during development. Frederick Peterson expresses the opinion that this practice only exists among the lower races of mankind. In this he is in decided error, since, as Barnard Davis pointed out many years ago, the practice is far more widespread than is usually suspected. It was common all over Europe, was practised by the Turanians, by the Slaves, by the Scandinavians, Anglo- Saxons, and Celts. Less than half a century ago Foville[192] proved that the nurses in Normandy were still giving children's heads a sugar-loaf shape by bandages and a tight cap. In Britanny they preferred to press it round. In those districts Foville found that not only congenital cranial irregularities of all types, but epilepsy, idiocy, and insanity were exceedingly frequent. As customs like these survive in folklore long after the original superstition which gave them birth, it is exceedingly probable that such crop out in descendants of these races to the present day, to confront the anthropologist with some remarkable crania. Tylor[193] is of opinion that without respecting the repressive action of the Government, the Bretons and Normans secretly continue this practice. Despite the labours of Foville these people openly defied the Government for ten years.

Certain conditions of the occiput have been described as associated with degeneracy. As Obici[194] and Dei Vecchio[195] have shown, the occipital condyle, in man normally convex, abnormally varies between two extremes, the flat and angular condyles. The flat condyle indicates a degenerative type. In the angular condyle the anterior face is derived from that portion of the basi-occipital nucleus that normally takes part in the formation of the anterior condyle region; the posterior face forms the embryonal germ of the occipital.

The occipital of the adult is the final outcome of the fusion of an uncertain number of vertebræ. The occipital bone in man is practically made up of five bones, union between which does not occur completely until the fifth or sixth year. The deficiencies in the chondrocranium appear in the occipital bone, which requires a small portion of the dermal bone to complete it on each side.

The variability of the occipital bone which, as just shown, is so frequently associated with all forms of degeneracy, is still better understood when we remember that it is of vertebral character. The investing mass of the head and of the notochord is the skeleton of the occipital bone. Between this skeleton and the pituitary body the important portion of the brain formed by the occipital lobes takes its origin. As these lobes are practically, as Spitzka has shown, the great centres of sense and other inter-associations it is not astonishing that their imperfect development should be accompanied by changes in the occipital bone. As Crochley Clapham, Mickle, and Spitzka have shown, a flat occiput is common in imbecility and moral insanity. It has been found quite frequently in "reasoning maniacs" by Campagne. The proper development of the occiput influences the proper development of association tracts which serve as a balance wheel to the individual. The proper development of the occipital bone is, moreover, connected with the proper development of the two last vertebræ, which like it are losing their vertebral characteristics.

CHAPTER XI

The Degenerate Face and Nose

THE development of the face depends, as I have already shown, upon the enlargement and fusion of the mouth and nose cavities, and upon the later partial separation of the nose and mouth and the nose cavities, leaving the posterior nose open. It depends further upon the growth and specialisation of the face region, of which the elongation is the most prominent indication, and finally upon the development of a prominent external nose. The relations of face to cranium in embryology have already been described. When the medullary tube of the notochord enlarges to form the brain the end of the head bends over to make room for that enlargement. The bending of the head carries the mouth plate, which is to be the mouth, over to the front of the head. The changes which develop the mouth cavity are the growth of the brain and the increase in size of the heart cavity, which expand to the front, leaving the mouth cavity between them. The mouth cavity represents two gill- slits united in the front line. The nose is formed from two olfactory plates situated just in front of the mouth and in contact with the fore-brain. These olfactory plates grow in size by the increase of tissue, and the resulting pits pass away from the brain. At first these pits, although widely separated by what is called the nasal process, communicate freely with the mouth. The nasal process includes the origin of the future nose and of the future intermaxillary region of the upper lip.

The human face is modified backward from the vertebrate type. It is an additional illustration of the degeneracy of a series of related structures for the benefit of the organism as a whole. The progress of development of the face in the vertebrates is checked in man. First, as Minot remarks,[196] because the upright position renders it unnecessary to bend the head as in quadrupeds. Second, because the enormous cerebral development has rendered an enlargement of the brain cavity necessary. This has taken place by extending the cavity over the nose region as well as by enlarging the whole skull. Third, because the development of the face is arrested at an embryonic stage; the production of a long snout being really an advance of development which does not take place in man. From what has been said of the relations of the dermal bones to the nose and face in the chapter on the skull, it will be obvious that these must follow the same laws as to degeneracy as the skull itself. These checks from degeneracy in arrest of development are apt to affect most obviously the unilateral development of the face. From this results the exaggerated asymmetry so frequently observed.

Jacob Baumler, the founder of the Zoar community of the United States, a religious fanatic, had a very marked asymmetry of the face and the mind of a degenerate. His orbits were unequal, one being exceedingly large and the other correspondingly small.

The human face at birth is so near that of the monkeys that if only the heads of both were exposed to view at birth it would be difficult for a casual observer to distinguish one from the other. Cope[197] has made the following classification of the head and face for comparative study: The relative size of the cerebral to the facial regions, the prominence of the forehead, the prominence of the superciliary regions, the prominence of the alveolar borders of the jaws, the prominence and width of the chin, the relation of length to width of the skull, the prominence of the cheek-bones, the form of the nose, the relative size of the orbits and eyes, the size of the mouth and lips.

At birth in the infant ape the facial region of the skull is smaller than in the adult, the forehead is more prominent, the superciliary ridges are more prominent, the edges of the jaws are more prominent, the chin is less, while the cheek-bones are more prominent, the nose is without a bridge and has short and flat cartilages, the face is flattened, the orbits and eyes are smaller and closer together, the mouth is small and the lips thin.

In the typical infant child as he begins to develop the cerebral part of the skull predominates over the facial more than in the adult, the superciliary ridges are not developed, the alveolar borders are not prominent, the cheek-bones are not prominent, the nose is without a bridge and the cartilages are flat and generally short, the eyes are larger. In this last particular the human infant resembles the lemurs and thus retains an embryonic tendency. In some degenerates this tendency remains unchecked, and the result is unusually large orbits as in Fig. 18. In other instances the human fœtus passes through this lemurian stage to reach and even exceed the anthropoid in smallness and closeness together.

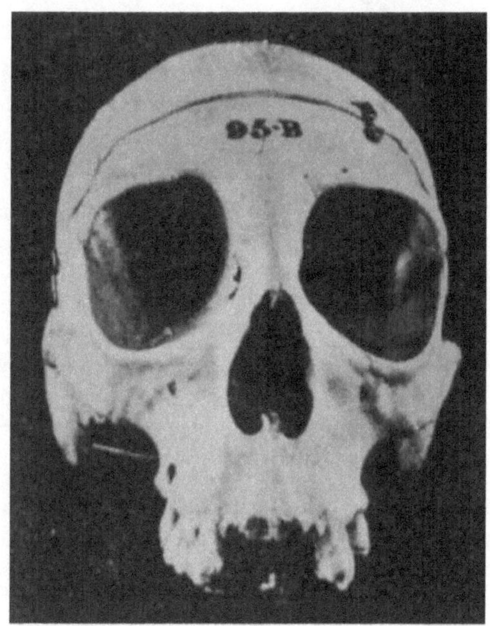

FIG. 18.

In determining a standard by which to measure the face two principles come into play: the general principle of evolution, and also that æsthetic principle governing profile, which has practically obtained supremacy, after long struggles for existence, from the Egyptian period of the first dynasty until its final acceptance by the Greeks, as shown, for instance, in the Apollo Belvedere. Indeed, so nearly does the modern standard approximate to the Greek, that Kingsley,[198] speaking of modern profiles, remarks that if he were to describe the American type he should be as much inclined to give that name to the form of features of the Apollo Belvedere as any other, since it is quite universal, distinctive, and possesses the same elements ofbeauty.

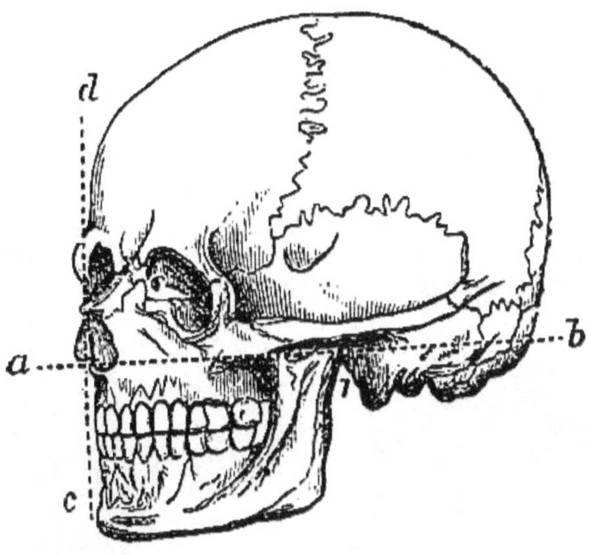

FIG. 19.

Among Aryan-speaking races this type would be accepted as the ideal one. Since each nationality, and peoples of the same nationality, living in different countries do not possess exactly the same type of face, the general presumption of evolution as modifying notions of beauty must also be taken into consideration. In the determination of the extent to which the profile exists the facial angle plays a part. This angle was early pointed out by Camper as a means of distinguishing the relative development of the skull and face. "The basis on which a distinction of nationality is founded," said Camper, "may be displayed by two straight lines (Fig. 19), one of which is to be drawn through the meatus auditorius to the base of the nose, and the other touching the prominent centre of the forehead and falling thence on the most advancing portion of the upper jaw, the head being used in profile. In the angle produced in these two lines may be said to consist not only the distinctions between the skulls of different species of animals, but also those which are found to exist between different races. The angle which the facial line or characteristic line of the visage makes varies from 70° to 80° in the race. All who raise it higher disobey the rules of art (from imitation of the antique). All who bring it lower fall into the likeness of the monkeys. If I cause the facial line to fall in front I have the antique head. If I incline it backward I have the head of a negro. If I incline it still further I have the head of a monkey; inclined still more I have the head of a dog; and, lastly, that of a goose."

This is excellently shown by the following illustrations. Fig. 20 is the head of Johanna, the female chimpanzee of Central Park, New York City. This head has (by Camper's method) an angle between 40° and 50°. The brain of this animal occupies one-third of the skull, and the jaws two-thirds. The negro criminal (Fig. 21) has an angle of about 70°. Here the brain is encroaching, while the jaws are receding. The Caucasic race (Fig. 22) has an angle of 75° to 80°. In many cases the frontal development of the brain and resultant recession of the jaws produce an angle of 90°, with a general result not unlike the Apollo.

FIG. 20.

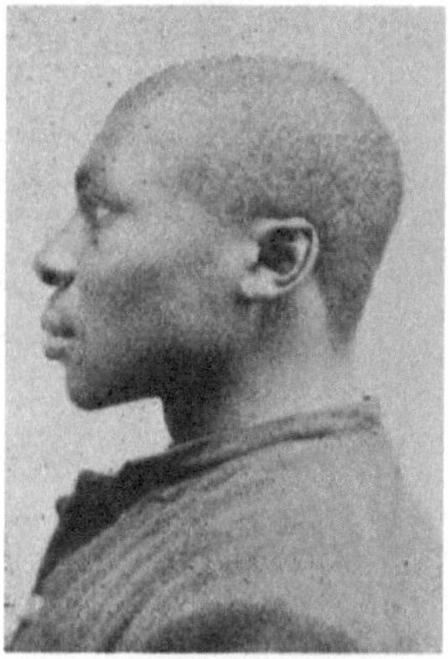

FIG. 21. COLOURED CRIMINAL YOUTH.

Although the general outlines of facial evolution as sighted by Camper are in accord with my own views, yet, as regards accuracy, this angle is not an ideal from whence to study face degeneracy, since the line does not fall low enough to include the chin, and also, as I have elsewhere shown, in the degenerate, the ear varies as much as one to one and one-half inches upon heads of different individuals. Frequently, in the degenerate classes, the ears of the same individual differ as much as one inch in height.

FIG. 22.

An ideal line, from whence to study a degenerate face, should be drawn perpendicularly from the supra-orbital ridge intersecting the upper and lower jaw and chin. While the chin of the Apollo Belvedere falls slightly inside of this line, yet this is hardly perceptible. Having now fixed a standard from which to study the degenerate face, it should be remembered that jaws which protrude beyond this line are atavistic, and those which recede are even more degenerate.

FIG. 23.

FIG. 24.

The angle between 80° and 90° may be accepted as an ideal by which to study degeneracy. This factor alone, however, can not be accepted: the evolution of the face itself must be also taken into consideration. It is obvious that in the struggle for existence and supremacy between the brain and the face (both expressions of vertebrate advance), stress may be concentrated on one particular part. Whence result certain factors which modify the conclusion to be drawn from the facial angle. The hollowed out condition of the face from the supra-orbital ridges down to and including the base of the nose (illustrated in Johanna) merits attention here. The same condition is observable in the negro, only it extends farther down and includes both jaws. One jaw, however, may alone be affected. Most of the Chinese, Japanese, Eskimo, Polynesians, Australians, Aryan Caucasic Africans, and some American Indians, possess this feature. As has been already remarked, the facial regions of man and the ape up to a certain point are similar. Not until the sense organs of man begin to develop are changes noticeable in facial expression. If, through heredity or constitutional defect, that part of the brain which presides over development of the facial bones lose its control, arrest of development of that particular tissue results at any period between birth and the twenty-fifth year, while other parts of the head and face continue to develop. With this understanding Camper's method can be safely applied to certain cases. If a line be dropped from the supra-orbital ridge to the upper lip in its most prominent part (Fig. 23), it will be found here that in place of the face presenting the full appearance illustrated in Fig. 19 and Fig. 22, it has the hollow appearance observable in Johanna and in Fig. 25. This is due to arrest of development of the bones of the face and the upper jaw. The extent of depression depends upon the time of arrest, the frontal development of the skull, and the position of the upper jaw. The nose may present and retain the appearance of that of a child six months old, or any other shape up to normal development, but will not protrude from the face nor present a normal symmetrical appearance. It has the appearance of having been driven into the face. It has been claimed that the bridge of the nose is pushed out by the advancing brain and cranium. This may be true to a certain extent, but one is not necessarily dependent on the other, since an arrested nose is frequently found in a fully developed cranium (Fig. 24), which is not unlike Fig. 23 and a "throw-back" to Fig. 20. This is due to the fact that in the struggle for existence the bones of the face and skull base became arrested early in life, while the brain and cranium continued to advance. The lower jaw is usually normal since, while the tendency to arrest may be present in a slight degree, mobility of the jaw often causes such increased nutrition of the part that normal development in many cases thereby results. Overlooking this fact has often led to the assertion that a large lower jaw exists when, in reality, this appearance is due to an arrest of the face and upper jaw, the lower remaining normal. The expression of degeneracy is rather in the arrest of the upper jaw than in the normal lower (see Fig. 23).

The criminals of the Elmira Reformatory, and those of the Pontiac Reformatory, present marked instances of this stigma, nearly 50 per cent.

being so affected. Arrest of the lower jaw may occur alone, or may be associated with arrest of development of the face (Fig. 25). When this is the case a deep, broad groove extends from below the eyes downward and backward to the lower jaw, also showing a lateral arrest of development, producing a hatchet-shaped face. The upper part of the face may be normal, and the lower jaw arrested antero-posteriorly.

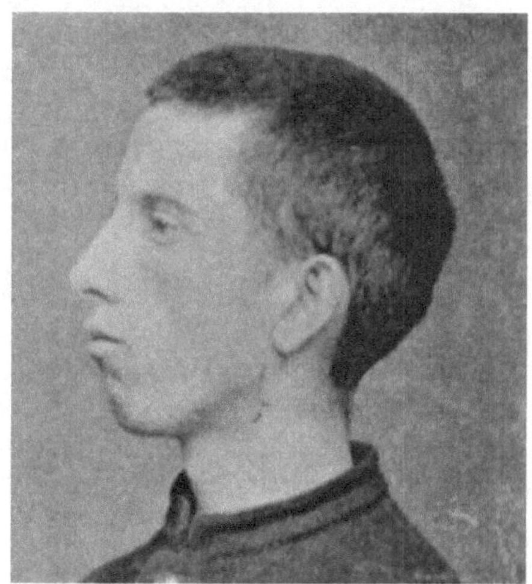

FIG. 25.

It has been broadly asserted that this is an atavism, but more probably it is an expression of that phase of evolution whereby both jaws are becoming subservient to the advance in evolution represented by the gains of the brain and cranium. When both jaws are arrested Camper's disobedience of the rules of art, whereby the facial angle is increased over 90°, occurs. This condition has been found in many degenerates. Almost invariably in connection with the arrest of development of the face occurs arrest of the bones of the nose. The diameter of the nasal cavities is much smaller than normal. Owing to the unstable condition of the nervous system there is also hypertrophy of the turbinate bone and mucous membrane of the nose and throat, tonsil hypertrophy, arrested development of the chest walls and lung tissue, and unstable mucous membranes throughout the lungs. Such a degenerate face, body, and unstable nervous system is a fruitful soil for the germs of tuberculosis. In these cases even a casual glance will show that the two halves of the face and head are not symmetrically developed. It looks as though the two halves were made separately and joined together, one half higher than the other. This condition is excellently illustrated in Fig. 26. In this case the left half is higher than the right. (Frequently the right side is the higher.) There is arrest of the upper and lower jaw. The left corner of the mouth is higher than the right. The left half of the lower jaw is higher than the right, the body of the lower jaw is longer, the ramus is shorter. The left eye and ear are higher. The left supra-orbital ridge is higher. The ears stand almost at right angles, while the malar processes are quite prominent. Viewing the face from a three-quarters' angle (which should always be done in making an examination, or photographing the degenerate face for study) it will be found that there is not only arrest of development of the bones of the face, but also of the lower jaw.

As already stated in the chapter on the cranium, the nasal bones belong to the dermal category, their special function as nose bones being a later acquisition. In their acquirement of this function they have passed through many changes, especially as the human face in its nasal features has assumed an embryonic type. In consequence, like all late embryonic acquisitions, degeneracy is apt to involve the nose.

When arrest of development of the face takes place stigmata of the nasal bones always result. Under such conditions narrowing or arrest of development of the entire nasal cavity ensues.

Deformities of the nasal septum, deflection, hypertrophy and atrophy of the turbinate bones, deformities of the maxillary sinus, hypertrophy of the mucous membrane and polypi are common. Deflection of the external nose is a very common stigma of degeneracy. Not only is the septum involved, but also the outer plates of the nasal cavity. So unstable are the bones of the face in their development that it is not an uncommon thing for the nasal process of the upper jaw on one side to be much more developed than the other. Not only is the nasal septum involved, but also the bones of the face as well, producing a fulness on the long side of the face. This stigma is very common among criminal youth. In such cases the deflected septum is due to the development of the outer plate and not *vice versâ*. Deflection of the septum to the left may entirely obliterate (as in Fig. 27) the left nasal cavity. If one nostril of a rabbit be permanently closed, after the animal has attained its full growth, the nasal cavity of the affected side remains undeveloped and facial asymmetry results.

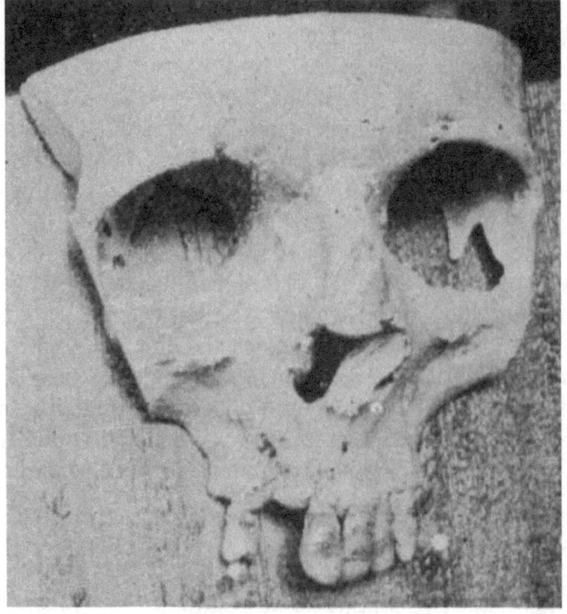

FIG. 27.

Therefore two factors are common: first, the arrest of development of the bones of the nose, and second, the clogging of the cavity, both active agents in producing a closure, resulting in mouth-breathing.

Coexisting with these is often (as in Fig. 27) smallness of the upper jaw. In the same connection grooved teeth occur, as in the same illustration.

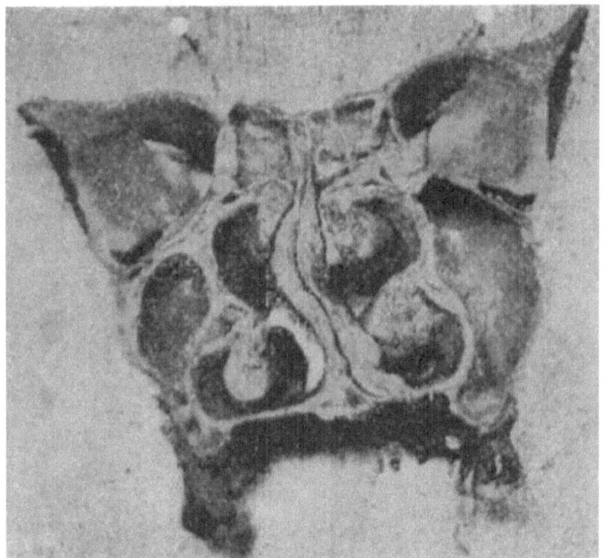

FIG. 28.

The turbinated (Fig. 28) bones are often hypertrophied, as is also the nasal septum (vomer or dividing bone) and the mucous membrane. This results from the general instability of the nervous system with its special expression in increased blood supply, whence occur overgrowth in and imperfect work by the mucous membrane, causing mouth-breathing and polypi, which again increase this defect. All these predispose to germ invasion.

In the figure are also shown grooves upon the teeth. Sufficient symptoms are here evident to stamp this as a marked degenerate skull.

Hypertrophy of the turbinate bones, septum, and mucous membrane, as it occurs among degenerates, appears in Fig. 29, and is due, first, to an unstable nervous system, and, second, a larger system of blood vessels which ramify through these parts. Stimulation, together with the stenosis (narrowing), tend to produce a closure. Still further, irritation and an unstable mucous membrane results, with polypi or adenoid vegetation following.

FIG. 29.

Not only do deflection of septum and hypertrophy of the nasal bones occur, but the antrum (cavity behind the nose) may be almost entirely obliterated, while the upper jaw is arrested (Fig. 29). The antrum may be entirely wanting, as in Fig. 30; so unstable may these tissues develop that the nasal cavities may become almost entirely obliterated, as observed in this figure.

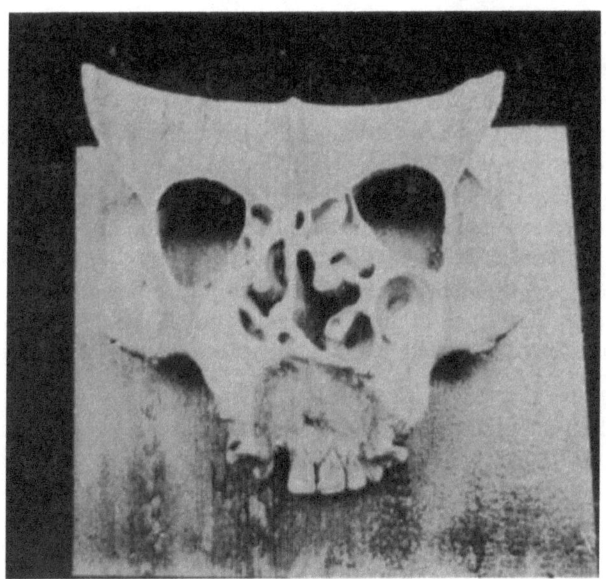

FIG. 30.

These conditions are due to the unstable structure and large nerve and blood supply. Perhaps one of the most interesting points in connection with degeneracy of the nose is the fact that in most cases the structures are either arrested or excessively developed, to the extent of the entire absence of the inferior turbinate bone. This was the case in a girl thirteen years of age who died of tuberculosis. Her skull revealed many other forms of degeneracy as well. The deviation in the development of the two nasal cavities results from the excessive and arrested development of the turbinates, thus preventing inhalation and exhalation of air, the free side developing and the closed side remaining undeveloped. In such case the nose is deflected to the right or left, depending on which side is arrested. When both nostrils are closed the nose becomes thin and pointed and mouth-breathing results. In degenerate nasal cavities polypi (tumours) are apt to occur.

Persons with long, thin noses, arrested nasal cavities, sunken faces (as a result mouth-breathers), and with contracted chest walls are the subjects for tuberculosis. In such cases, especially when the nervous system is unstable, the different forms of catarrh are present. This condition worries the youth under the strain of puberty. To the catarrh which is merely a result is ascribed his constitutional defects. These somatic signs are quite noticeable in most of these cases, and by early recognition proper treatment, with change of climate, frequently prolongs life for years.

The so-called erectile tissue of the nose (containing blood whose flow is checked through spasm to increase sensation), that relic of a time when smell played a greater part among the senses, is apt to be affected by degeneracy either as to its excessive or imperfect development. From this comes the bleeding of the nose, so frequently an expression of nerve strain at puberty, which may take the place of menstruation. It is to be noted that while true hæmophilia ("bleeder" tendency) occurs chiefly in boys, epistaxis shows itself very frequently in their sisters. A remarkable illustration of this was reported by Dr. Delia E. Howe,[199] of the Fort Wayne (Indiana) School for the Feeble-minded. In cases of so-called male menstruation[200] the symptom is apt to be epistaxis.

The irregularity in blood supply predisposes the nose to attacks on its structure from pathogenic germs. Hay fever is an expression of nervous instability of these structures, and is especially apt to occur in neurasthenics, hysterics, and degenerates.

CHAPTER XII

Degeneracy of the Lip, Palate, Eye, and Ear

Each part or sense organ may, independently of the face as a whole, exhibit signs of degeneracy. The palate, lip, nose, eye, and ear have their own expressions of degeneracy. The palate, so far as the joining of its two parts is concerned, resists degeneracy to a remarkable degree. The cleft, which results from non-union, is usually an expression of general degeneracy acted on by its nutritive expression, albeit cleft-palate may be associated with the graver degeneracies like idiocy.

As the subjects of the deeper degeneracies associated with cleft-palate usually perish in early infancy, the nutritive degeneracies are most frequently found associated with cleft-palate in adult life. The mouth in the vertebrates does not agree in character with the invertebrate mouth. The mouth has grown in proportion to evolution in the lower vertebrates. It is larger, however, in proportion in the human embryo than in the adult. In this it agrees with the general lower type of the human face. The human chin is at first retreating, and does not become distinctly prominent until the fifth month of fœtal life. The nose separates from the mouth toward the end of the second month. It is at first short and broad and resembles at three months the type of some of the lower negro races. When the nose is separated from the mouth a partition forms between the cavities of the nose and the mouth, later supplemented by the true palate, which divides the mouth into an upper respiratory passage and a lower digestive passage. This palate is partly composed of bone and partly of flesh. The fleshy part ends in what is called the uvula. This is very subject to abnormalities, as has been pointed out by C. L. Dana; it is a very frequent mark of degeneracy. Dickens noticed the uvular tone of voice in young thieves, due to deformity of the uvula.

Cleft palates are comparatively rare in proportion to other forms of nutritive degeneracy. Palatal embryology casts light on the causation. At a very early period of fœtal life a series of clefts appear on each side of the cephalic extremity, separated by rods of tissue called branchial arches. The clefts communicate with the alimentary canal. These various clefts have usually coalesced about the ninth and tenth week of fœtal life, but occasionally this coalescence fails or is incomplete. This leads to various deformities, the chief of which are cleft palate and hare-lip. Cleft palate has been known to affect several members of the same family, and to occur in the offspring of the affected members. There are instances of the transmission of this deformity from an affected pug-bitch to her offspring. If it were possible to practise selective breeding in man as in dogs a race of men with hare-lips and cleft palates could probably be produced.[201]

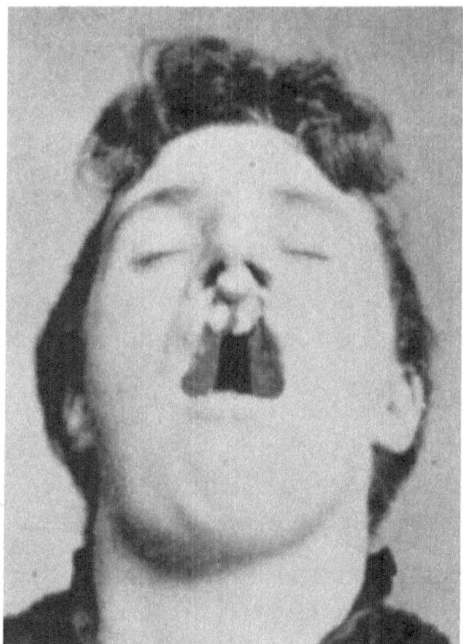

FIG. 31.

Cleft palate may be divided into two classes, congenital and acquired, acquired cleft palate being the result of disease either inherited or acquired, but only affecting the part after birth. Congenital cleft palate is divisible into two kinds, complete and partial; complete when the fissure extends the entire length, from the uvula to and including the anterior alveolar process and even the lips (Fig. 31), partial when only a small part of the structure is involved. Thus the cleft may extend through the anterior alveolar process, involving the incisive bone only, which is very rare; when present single or double hare-lip almost invariably coexists. I have observed in practice six cases where a small portion of the interior alveolar process was involved, with the jaw and one or two teeth. The hard palate only may be involved to the extent of a small fissure, or the whole palate may be wanting. The soft palate only may contain the cleft, or simply the uvula. Cases are on record in which the non- development of the intermaxillary bones produces fissures in the lip. *Apriori*, cleft palate is an evident expression of hereditary defect. Langdon Down found a constant relation between brain deformity, cleft palate, and deformed vaults.

In a case cited elsewhere,[202] three members of one family had cleft palate; one 17 years old, the other 30, and the third 35. The first and last are women, the other a married man with a family, who have no trace of the father's deformity. In these cases no instance of cleft palate could be found either among the ancestors or the collateral branches of the family.

Another family has a remarkable history. G. H. C., born 1853, perfect; L. C., born 1855, single hare-lip and cleft palate; J. F. C., born 1856, perfect; F. W. C., born 1860, double hare-lip and cleft palate; H. E. C., born 1868, perfect. The paternal grandmother also had cleft palate.

Knecht found that 5 per cent. of 1,200 criminals examined had cleft palate. Fourteen per cent. of the prostitutes examined by Pauline Tarnowsky had cleft palates. Langdon Down, among congenital idiots, found only a half per cent. of cleft palates. Grenzer found only nine cases in 14,466 children, or one in 1,607. I examined 1,977 feeble-minded children without finding a single case. In 207 blind only one case was observed. In 1,235 deaf mutes two cases were found. The percentage among the defective classes, while not large, is, undoubtedly, much larger than among normal individuals.

A keeper of the Zoological Gardens in Philadelphia observed cleft palate in the mouths of lion cubs born in the gardens. Cleft palates were also observed in a number of pups born in Buffalo. Dr. Ogle found that 99 per cent. of the lion cubs born in the London Zoological Gardens had cleft palates. He claims that this is due to the artificial diet, as the result of enforced captivity. Similar results observed in other gardens in Europe are charged to feeding the mothers with meat without bone, as feeding with the whole carcass of small animals greatly diminished these deformities. It would seem that if cleft palate is due to this cause other bony structures should also be involved, and, as a matter of fact, many of the lions born in captivity are rickety. Cleft palate has been observed among dogs, sheep, goats, &c. The question, therefore, whether domesticity here does not play the alleged part of civilisation in man can be solved only by a knowledge of the frequency of the condition among wild animals of the same genus. It is evident that, in dealing with the question of ætiology, the influence of shock on the mother's nervous system cannot be excluded in the cases charged to feeding.

It should be remembered that cleft palate is a factor which predisposes to death by infectious diseases whose local manifestations are in the mouth and throat; hence the majority of the degenerates in whom cleft palate occurs are liable to die before the completion of their fifth year. Hare-lip (Fig. 32) is an exceedingly hereditary disorder, as Murray, Demarquay, Trélat, Hutchinson,

Féré, Marsh, Lucas, Ireland, and others have shown. It occurs with great frequency in almost all forms of degeneracy. Kiernan, of Chicago, has found that 5 per cent. of the hereditary lunatics in that city and in New York City have hare-lip.

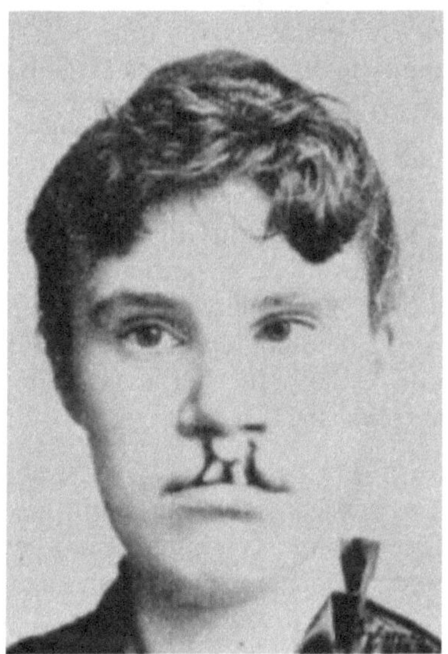

FIG. 32.

How far degeneracy may turn back the page of evolution is excellently illustrated in the cyclopian descendants of degenerate families elsewhere cited from Kiernan, of Chicago. While there is a seeming conflict as to the primitive eye type of vertebrates between morphologists represented by Howard Ayres[203] (who claims that the eyes were derived from the median eye of the ascidian lancelet) and Semper[204] (who is of the opinion that the existing vertebrate eyes represent the paired eyes of a hypothetical annelid precursor); still both opinions are fully reconcilable through the results of study of the ascidian and lancelet eye collated with cyclopian and triophthalmic (three-eyed) degeneracies in man, the human eye and the third eye of reptiles like the hatteria of New Zealand. The eye of the ascidian tadpole agrees fundamentally with the type of eye peculiar to the vertebrates in that the retina is derived from the wall of the brain. On this account it is called a myolonic eye. In the typical invertebrate eye, on the contrary, the retinal cells are differentiated from the external ectoderm.

The ascidian eye, however, differs, as Osborn[205] remarks, essentially from the paired eyes of the craniate (skulled) vertebrates in that the lens as well as the retina is derived from the wall of the brain. The lens of the lateral eye of the vertebrates is derived by an invagination of the ectoderm, which meets and fits in the retinal cup at the end of the optic vesicle. The ascidian eye, however, agrees in respect to the origin of its lens with the parietal or pineal eye of the lizard, in which the lens is likewise derived from cells which form part of the wall of the cerebral outgrowth which gives rise to the pineal body.

The pineal body is another of those remarkable rudimentary structures whose constant presence in all groups of vertebrates forms such an eminently characteristic median outgrowth from the dorsal wall of the brain (thalamencephalon), the distal extremity of which dilates into a vesicle and becomes separated from the proximal portion. The distal vesicle becomes entirely constricted off from the primary epiphysial (pineal) outgrowth of the brain, and the parietal nerve does not represent the primitive connection of the pineal eye with the roof of the brain, but arises quite independently of the proximal portion of the epiphysis.

The remote ancestors of the vertebrates possessed a median, unpaired, myolonic eye, which was subsequently replaced in function by the evolution of the paired eyes. The cyclopic condition occurs very frequently among human monstrosities, much more frequently than among animals, Hannover claims,[206] but this is clearly due to the fact that human monstrosities are much more frequently recorded. Of the 120 cases I have been able to collect from literature, 56 presented other evidences of degeneracy than cyclopic conditions, and 60 had neuropathic or other taint in the ancestry. Dareste[207] has shown that the production of a single eye, the changes in the structure of the mouth, the atrophy and abnormal situation of the olfactory apparatus and of the vesicle of the hemispheres, all result from an arrest of development. The determining influence must be exerted very early in the life history of the embryo.

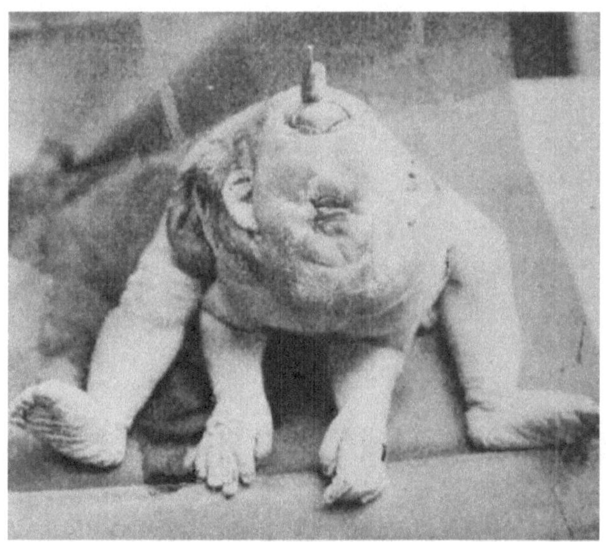

FIG. 33.

Hannover points out that there often is coincident hydrocephalus and harelip, imperfect genital development, and allied arrest of development. J. R. Folsom, of Cecil, Georgia, has reported a female, born alive to a negro multipara, who died two hours after birth. The eye was centrally located in the forehead, on a line with the nose. The brow was a complete arch, as was the upper eyelid. The lower lid had a mark midway, indicating an attempt at division. The nasal bones were wanting, but the soft part of the nose, destitute of the orifice, hung over the mouth, which was completely covered. The chin was recedent. C. Phisalix described a case in which the nose was wanting. Its place in the median was occupied by a single eye; on the horizontal diameter were two pupils separated by a narrow space. Landolt, discussing a case reported by Valude, points out that in cyclopic eyes all the parts may be double or united in every degree except that there is never a single lens or double vitreous. Bock and others, however, describe cases in which the eye has not been formed by the conglomeration of two separately developed eyes, but it is a single developed eye; the other being wanting entirely. Bruce reports a cyclop in which there was a single socket for the eye of a lozenge- shape, situated in the lower middle of the forehead. The socket was furnished with two pairs of eyelids, upper and lower. The eye was found to consist of two rudimentary eyes, with two rudimentary retinæ, apparently springing from a single optic vesicle. The nose was represented by a short process attached to the forehead, above the median eye.

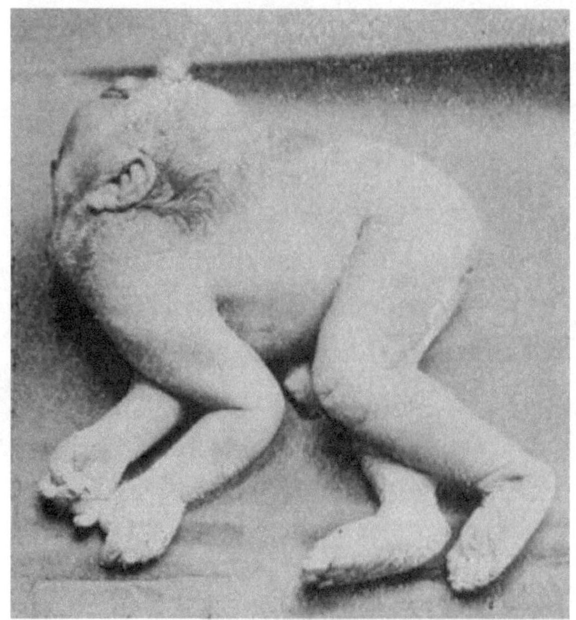

FIG. 34.

The cyclops illustrated (Figs. 33, 34) was born to a 17-year old neuropathic primipara, after a protracted labour. The child was living, but was killed by pressure on the funis. The mouth contained an ivory, tusk-like tooth at each corner. There was mane-like hair around the neck.

Cyclopia is very frequently associated with the absence of both the internal and external ear, and with synotia (joined ears).

In triophthalmic cases the three eyes are usually separate, two occupying the usual position, while the third is situated as illustrated in the case cited. Ninety families of degenerates, averaging eleven children each, had five cases of cyclops.

Degeneracy, which affects so deeply the development of the eye, naturally tends to evince itself in other anomalous states in the organ. As excessive asymmetry of the body is one of the most noticeable of the stigmata of degeneracy, it is not astonishing to find that this asymmetry expresses itself both in the position as well as in the size and structure of the eye. As Kiernan[208] pointed out, twenty years ago, asymmetrical irides are exceedingly frequent in the types of insanity due to hereditary defect. This observation has since been confirmed by Féré,[209] not only as to the insane, but as to other classes of the degenerate. The conditions of the eye known as microphthalmia (small eye), macrophthalmia (big eyes) and anophthalmia (absence of eyes), are found quite frequent in degenerate families. Very frequently the pupil of the eye is asymmetrical. This was pointed out by Kiernan in the case of Guiteau. Corectopia (displacement of the pupil so that it is not in the centre of the iris) often exists. Coloboma (eye fissure) is also not infrequent among the degenerate. These vary greatly in situation and general results. The iris is sometimes completely absent on one or both sides. Beside the anomalies, diseased conditions like retinitis pigmentosa, congenital cataract and the macular degeneracy cited by C. P. Pinckard,[210] of Chicago, are far from infrequent expressions of degenerate taint in the eye; the organ in this particular obeying the general law that degeneracy may show itself in the minute change resulting in disturbance of function or in that producing disease, or, finally, in atavism. The defects of the eyes requiring glasses are exceedingly frequent in degenerates, and often aggravate their morbidity. Here, as in the case of the teeth, the chief factor is often ignored.

The external ear is, of all organs, that most affected by degeneracy.[211] It is a cartilaginous organ extending from a bony base, without a bony framework for its support and with very deficient blood supply, on account of its distances from the great blood centres, so that any defect in the nerve centres which control the local blood supply is likely to affect its nutrition. As a cartilaginous organ it has no lymphatics, which of necessity affects its growth. The sensitiveness of the ear to vasomotor changes is evident by the results of the extremes in heat and cold, emotional blushing and fatigue. Galton reports a schoolmistress who judges the fatigue of her pupils by the condition of their ears. If the ears be white, flabby and pendant, she concludes that the children are much fatigued. If they be relaxed, but red, they are suffering, not from overwork, but from a struggle with the nervous system rarely under control in children. These states are very common among degenerates.

To appreciate the degeneracy observed in the ear its embryology requires study. Before the end of the first month[212] there appears around the external opening of the first gill-cleft (Fig. 35) a series of six tubercles, two in front on the hind edge of the first visceral arch, one above the cleft and three behind it (Fig. 36). A little later a vertical furrow appears down the middle of the hyoid arch, in such a way as to mark off a little ridge which joins on to tubercle 3 and descends behind tubercles 4 and 5. The second stage is reached by the growth of all the parts; the fusion of tubercles 2 and 3 and the growth of the ridge down behind tubercle 5 to become continuous with 6. After these changes it is not difficult to identify the parts.

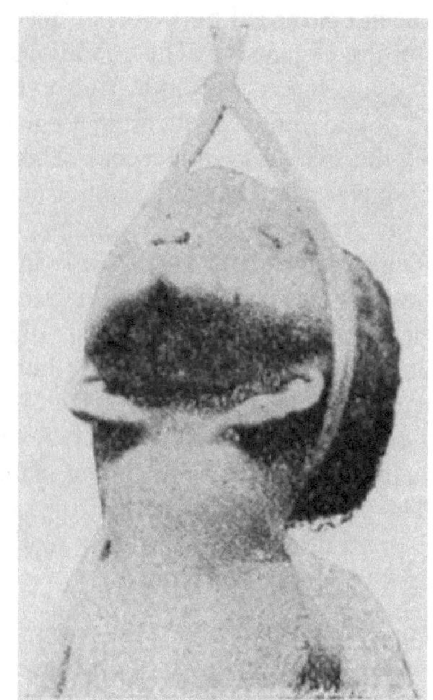

FIG. 35.

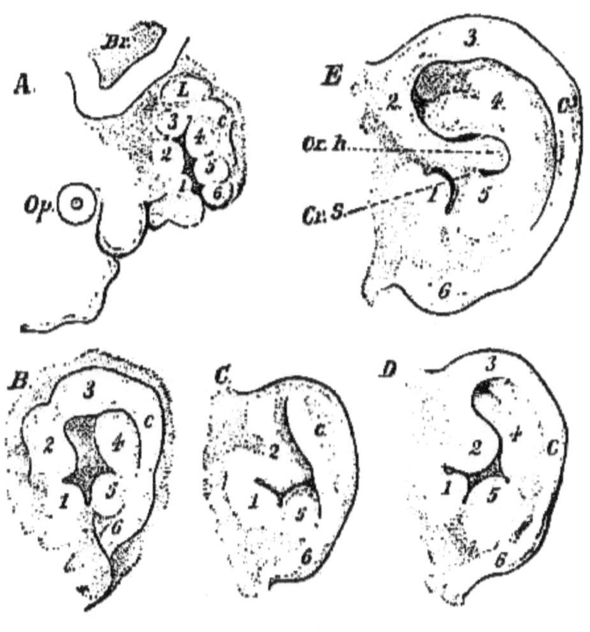

FIG. 36.

Tubercle No. 1 is the tragus; 2 and 3, together with the arching ridge, represent the helix; 4, the anti-helix; 5, the anti-tragus; and 6, the lobule; the pit between the tubercles the fossa angularis. During the latter part of the second month the ear changes in its proportion somewhat in the irregular development. The third stage begins at the third month. The upper and posterior part of the concha arises from the surface of the head, and gradually but rapidly bends forward so as to completely cover the anti-helix and the upper portion of the fossa angularis. During this stage in mammals the assumption of the pointed form of the ear commences. The fourth stage begins at the fourth month, when the tubercles, which are now joined together by cartilages, commence to unfold and are completed by the fifth month. Finally, the sixth tubercle develops to form the lobule. This unfolding or development of the tubercles to produce the different portions of the ear and make it complete is not unlike the development of a flower from the bud. By this process may be understood how if, by malnutrition in one tubercle or bud, or should there be a larger supply of nutriment in one than another, malformation of the ear would result. If arrest of development of all the tubercles should take place at any period, from the first to the fifth month of fœtal life, the ear would resemble a semi-developed flower! (Fig. 37).

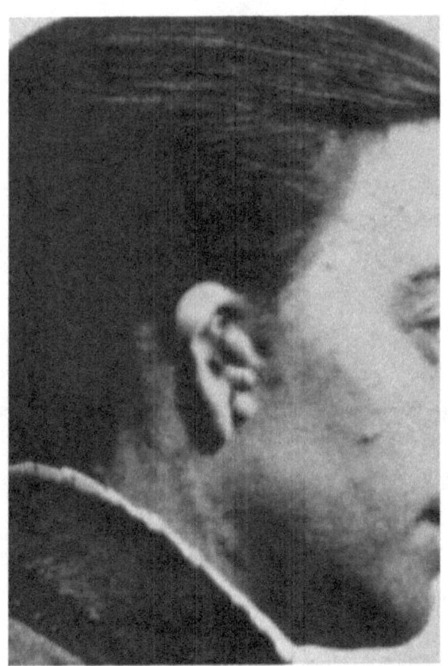

FIG. 37.

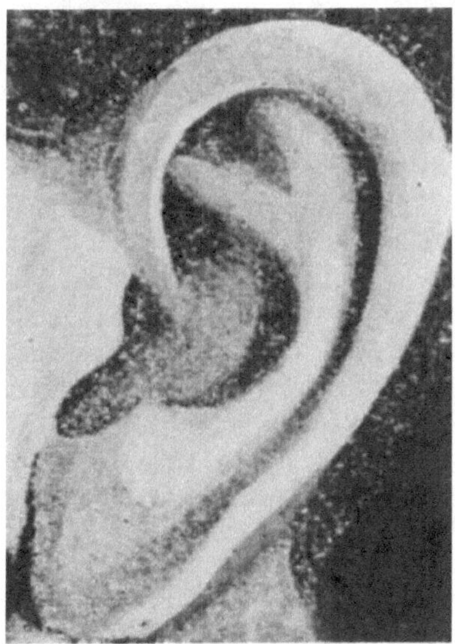

FIG. 38.

As in other cases, it is necessary to fix an approximately normal standard for the ear from the standpoint of man's status in evolution. The ear grows more or less through life, but, like the skeleton, practically reaches its full development about the twenty-sixth year. That this is not always the case, however, is demonstrated by the results of the examination of 546 persons. In an examination of 63 children between 6 and 18 months old the ears measured from 1·60 to 2·12, the average being 1·90 inches; in width from ·75 to 1, with an average of ·96. In 127 children from 8 to 12 years old the ear measured from 1·95 to 2·32 inches, the average being 2·19; width ·81 to 1·50, the average being 1·06. In 356 persons between 12 and 50 years old the shortest ear was 2, the longest 3, the average 2·50; width, smallest 1, largest 1·50, the average being 1·22 inches. The normal ear, or rather the ideal one (for few persons possess it in its entirety), should have a gracefully curved outline, be nowhere pointed or irregular, have a well-defined helix, separated from the anti-helix by a distinct scaphoid fossa extending down nearly to the level of the anti-tragus (Fig. 38). Its root should be lost in the concha before reaching the anti-helix. The anti-helix should not be unduly prominent, and should have a well-marked bifurcation at its superior extremity. The lobule should be shapely, not adherent, not too pendulous and free from grooves extending from the scaphoid fossa. The whole should be well shaped, and its proper proportion and size may be inferred from the table just given; in the adult it should not average over two and a half inches in length and one and a quarter in breadth.

The aural deformities that fall under the head of stigmata, or have been classed as such, affect all portions of the external ear. The helix may be imperfect, it may be angular, from Darwin's tubercle it may lack its inward roll, it may be interrupted, the root of the helix may extend inward completely across the concha, and in very rare instances it may be bifurcated. The anti- helix may be unduly prominent or be insignificant; the scaphoid fossa may extend through the lobule or be triple.[213] The lobule may be adherent and sometimes almost absent, thus producing the jug-handle-shaped, or so-called Morel ear. It may be exaggerated in size; the whole ear may be misshapen, too large or too small. These deformities may exist in nearly every degree, only when pronounced can they be considered as stigmata. Others have been noted, but their importance as signs of degeneracy is not very significant unless they co-exist with several of those above mentioned.

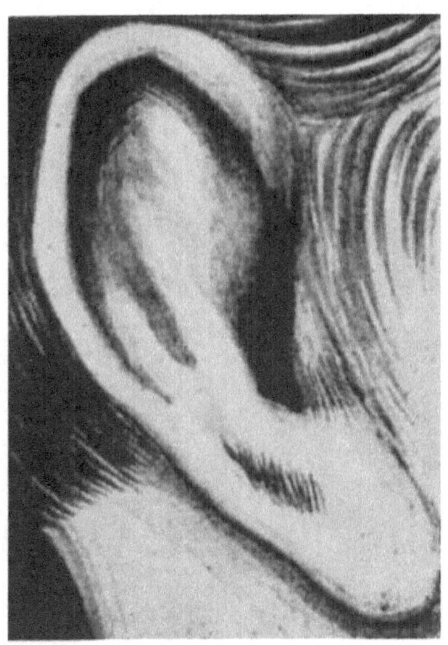

FIG. 39.

The ears of degenérates frequently grow in later life to an enormous size. On examination of 207 paupers over 50 years old the shortest ear was found to be 2·25 inches, the longest 3·36; the average on the right side was 2·73, on the left 2·76; the narrowest ear was ·88, the widest 1·50, the average 1·26. These results, compared with the results of the measurements of normal persons from 12 to 50 years, plainly demonstrate that the ears of degenerates grow after the twenty-sixth year, when the skeleton has completed its development. With such large ears other stigmata are generally associated. A few of the best types of stigmata of the ear illustrate better than any description the general characteristics. Fig. 39 illustrates the ear *par excellence* of degeneracy, the typical jug-handled ear first described by Morel and called by his name. This consists of a long, narrow ear attached its entire length, and tapering upward and outward from the lobe to the point where the Darwinian tubercle is located, and there it may take any shape—round, straight, or pointed—as illustrated in the drawing. The most singular deformity of the helix is the tubercle of Darwin, which is a little blunt point, projecting from the inwardly folded margin or helix. When present it is developed at birth and, according to Ludwig Meyer, more frequent in men than in women. Fig. 40 shows ear and tubercle taken from Darwin.[214] These points not only project in toward the centre of the ear, but open a little outwards (Fig. 41) from its plane, so as to be visible when the head is viewed from directly in front and behind. They are variable in size, number and somewhat in position (Fig. 42), standing either a little higher or lower, and they sometimes occur on one ear and not on the other. Another marked form of ear degeneracy is one in which the ear is developed backward at an angle of about 45° (Fig. 43). The general outline of the ear is fairly good. The anti-helix is much larger than it should be. Degeneracy usually extends deeply into the organisation of those in whom this ear is present.

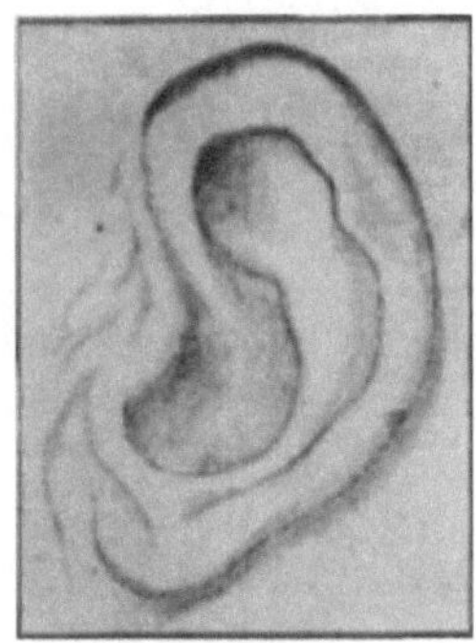

FIG. 40.

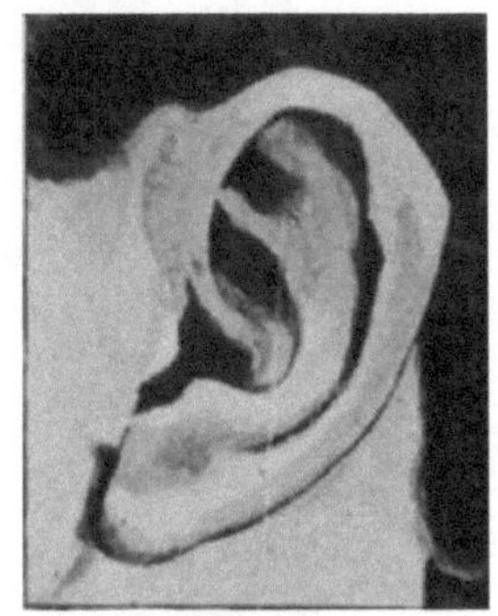

FIG. 41.

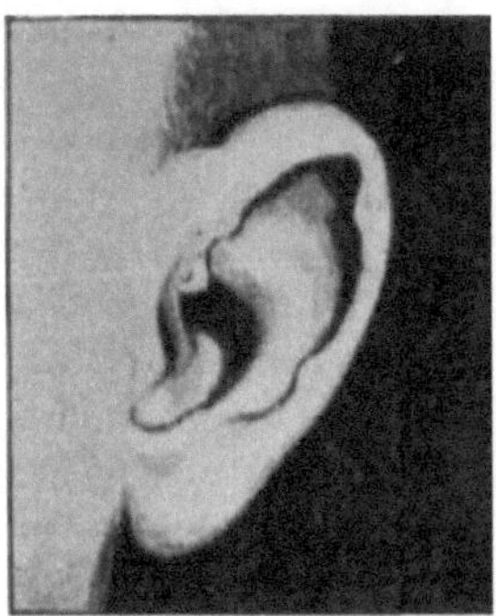

FIG. 42.

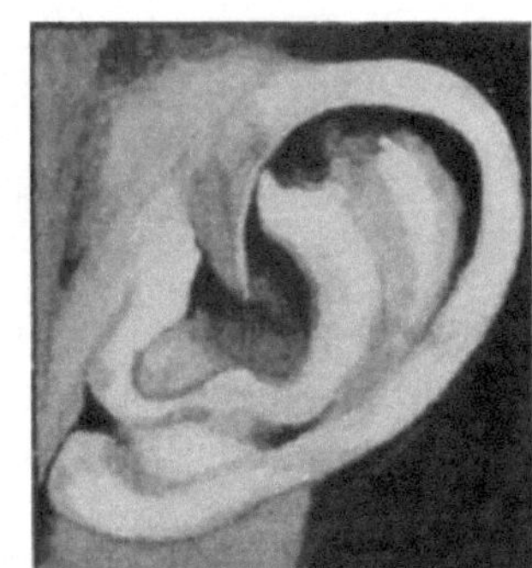

FIG. 43. EAR ALMOST HORIZONTAL
AND AT RIGHT ANGLES
WITH THE HEAD.

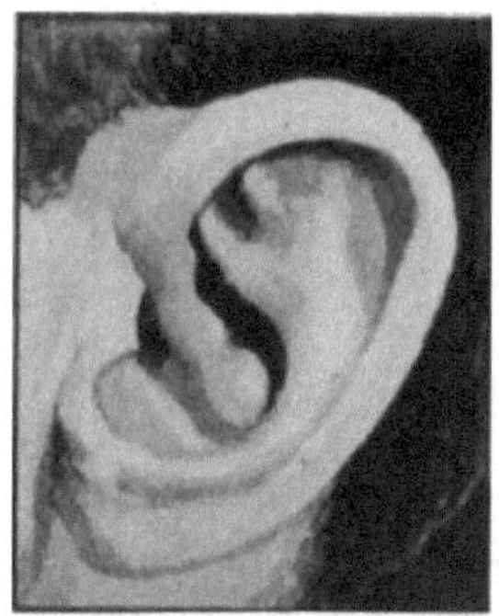

FIG. 44. EAR ALMOST ROUND
WITH THREE DARWINIAN
TUBERCLES AT
INNER BORDER.

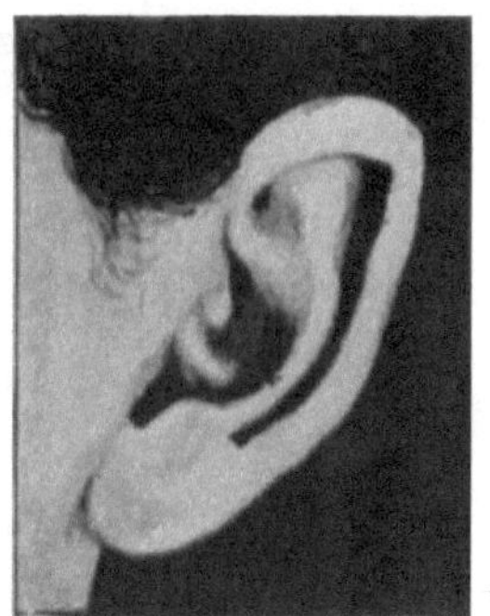

FIG. 45.

Fig. 44 illustrates noticeable stigmata. The ear stands at right angles with the head. It is, however, almost as broad as it is long and differs in shape. The outer helix is excessively developed. The scaphoid fossa extends through the lobe, which is continuous with the body of the ear and is not distinct. The root of the helix is excessively developed. There are three Darwinian tubercles on its border. The anti-tragus is undeveloped. The tragus is very small and divided into two parts. The auricle-temporal angle, for functional purposes, should not exceed, according to Buchanan, 30°, or be less than 15°. The difference in this respect is not clear, since free movement of head and body will readily adjust the auricle to receive sound. For functional purposes it would seem that the construction and shape of the ear, especially the anti- helix and concha, would be of greater importance than its position to the head, since it is necessary to collect the waves of sound for transmission. From a degeneracy standpoint, however, the position of the ear is important. Frigerio,

[215] from the examination of several hundred subjects, concludes that the auricle-temporal angle undergoes a gradual progress from below 90° in criminals and the insane to above 90° in apes. He found the large angle very marked in homicides, less so in thieves. There is no question but that Frigerio is correct in regard to this point. In an examination of the ears of 465 boy criminals at Pontiac, it was found that 198 were close to the head, or from 10 to 15°; 152 at an angle of 45°, and 115 at right angles or 90°. Of 1,041 criminals at Elmira 285 were close, 567 at an angle of 45°, and 187 at right angles.

FIG. 46.

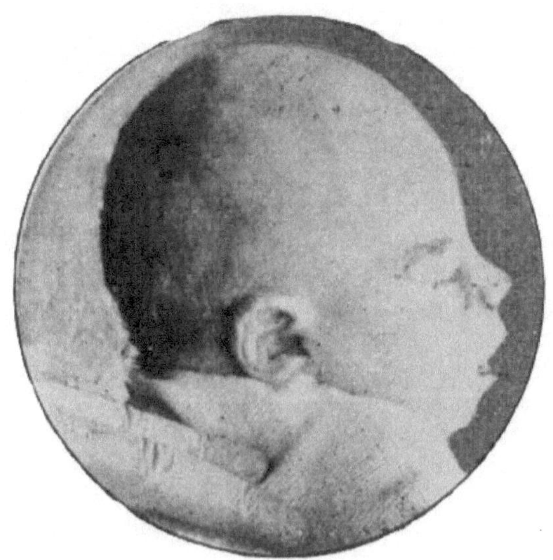

FIG. 47.

FIG. 48.

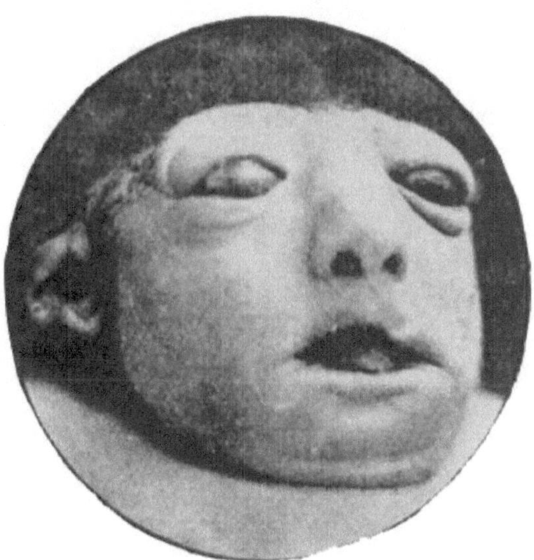

FIG. 49.

Fig. 45 shows the ear which Hawthorne gives Donatello in the *Marble Faun*;

it has been called the "Satanic" ear, because of the pointed extremities and its narrowness. The helix is rolled upon itself its entire length, giving the impression of great thickness. The anti-helix is excessively developed. Figs. 46, 47, 48 (ears of three illegitimate children at birth) show different stages of development as well as marked stigmata. Arrest of development occurs between the fourth and fifth month, owing to the trophic nerve centres being affected by the malnutrition of the mother. Fig. 49 exhibits the development of a congenital, elephantine ear in monstrosities. The resemblance to the large ear of the orang and chimpanzee is very marked.

CHAPTER XIII

The Degenerate Teeth and Jaws

NEXT to the ears, the jaws and teeth (as was to be expected from the variability of these organs in allied animals) are most affected by degeneracy. This is particularly true of the vertebrates, especially mammals, as might have been anticipated from their phylogeny. At the head of the vertebrates is man; at the foot is the lancelet (amphioxus), which is perhaps most akin to those semi-vertebrates the ascidians, who, in their larval phase, are higher than when adult, and whose life-history excellently illustrates that potent phase of evolution, degeneracy.

The lancelet has a spinal cord enclosed in a half-gristly canal (the notochord). It is practically destitute of a brain. The cerebral vesicle which represents this is a plain cavity without true subdivision into ventricles. There is no cranium. The eye (central in position) is a mere pigment spot with which it is able to distinguish light from darkness. The nose (behind this) is a small pit, lined with cilia, for purposes of smell. Into this the cerebral vesicle of the larval lancelet opens. The mouth is well guarded against the intrusion of noxious substances which have to pass through a vestibule richly provided with sensitive cells, resembling the taste buds of the human mouth. There is no heart. In this, as in the case of the eye, the lancelet is lower than the ascidians, the insects, crustaceans, and many molluscs. It approximates those worms which, despite a very elaborate vascular system, are destitute of a heart, the function of which is performed by contractile blood-vessels. From an embryologic and morphologic standpoint the proximate ancestor of the vertebrates may have been a free swimming animal, intermediate between an ascidian tadpole and the lancelet, and the primordial ancestor, a worm-like animal organised on a level with the star-fish. The vertebrates embryologically develop from this stage to the lampreys; thence to the cartilaginous fish (shark); to the amphibia (frog, toad, axolotl); to the reptiles; and thence to the oviparous mammals (duck-bill and echidna or spiny ant- eater); to the lemurs, and through forms like the *Pithecanthropus erectus* to man. Mammal teeth pass, in evolution, from the simple types found in that oviparous edentate, the spiny ant-eater of Australia, to those of the indeciduous ancestors of the sloths and armadilloes, and their descendants, inclusive of the dolphins and whales, whose teeth, both in the fetal Greenland and adult sperm whale, preserve this old type. (The whales have degenerated from the hoofed mammals to suit their environment.) While, as in the edentates, these teeth may be few, they may also, as in the insectivorous marsupials, approximate those of the reptilia in number (sixty or seventy on a side) and characteristic location.

The evolution of this primitive tooth to the bicuspid and molar type has been explained by two theories: that of concrescence and that of differentiation.[216]

A number of conical teeth, in line as they lie in the jaws of the sperm whale, represent the primitive dentition.[217] In time a number of these teeth, according to the concrescent theory, cluster together so as to form the four cusps of a human molar, each one of the whale tooth points forming one of the cusps of the mammalian tooth. Vertically succeeding teeth might also be grouped. What evidence is there in favour of this theory? and what is there against it? All primitive reptiles from which the mammals have descended, and many of the existing mammals, have a large number of isolated teeth of a conical form. Further, by shortening of the jaws, the embryonic germ from which each of the numerous tooth-caps is budded off in course of development could have been brought together in such a manner that any cusps originally stretched out in a line would form groups of a variable number of cusps, according to the more or less complex pattern of the crown. Against the acceptance of this theory stands the fact that cusps quite similar in all respects to each of the cusps which form the angles of the human molar are even now being added to the teeth in certain animals, such as the elephant, whose molar teeth cusps are being thus complicated. In the mesozoic period certain animals with tricuspid teeth occur. According to the theory of concrescence these teeth ought not to show any increase of cusps in later geologic periods, but down through the ages to the present time successors of those animals continue to present a very much larger number of cusps. How is this increase of cusps to be accounted for? Has there been a reserve store of conical teeth to increase the number? Most obviously to every student of the fossil history of cusps there is no reserve store, but new cusps are constantly rising upon the original crown itself by cusp addition.

In the Triassic occur the first mammalia with conical, round, reptilian teeth. There are also some aberrant types which possess complex or multitubercular teeth.

These teeth begin to show the first trace of cusp addition.

In Fig. 1, Plate A, the teeth of the dromatherium of the coal beds of North Carolina occur on the sides of the main cone, cusps or rudimentary cuspules. On either side of the main cone are two cuspules. In the same deposit occurred another animal represented by a single tooth (Fig. 3), in which these cusps are slightly larger. These cusps have obviously been added to the side of the teeth and are now growing. In teeth of the Jurassic period, found in large numbers both in America and in England, but still of very minute size, are observed the same three cusps. These cusps have now taken two different positions; in one case they have the arrangement presented in Plate B. The middle cusp is relatively lower, and the lateral cusps are relatively higher; in fact these cones are almost equal in size. These teeth are termed triconodont, as having three nearly equal cones. But associated with this is the spalacotherium, the teeth of which are represented in Plate A, Fig. 4. This tooth illustrates the transformation of a tooth (triconodont) with three cusps in line into a tooth with three cusps forming a triangle. Here the primitive cusp is the apex of a triangle of which the two lateral cusps are the base. This tooth, in this single genus, is the key of comparison of the teeth of all mammalia. By this can be determined that part of a human molar which corresponds with a conical reptilian tooth. This stage is the triangle stage; the next stage is the development of a heel or spur upon this triangle (see in the amphitherium, Fig. 5). The opossum still distinctly preserves the ancient triangle. Look at it in profile, inside or in top view, and see that the anterior part of the tooth is unmodified. This triangle is traceable through a number of intermediate types. In Miacia (Fig. 6), a primitive carnivore, is a high triangle and a heel; looked at from above (Fig. 6a), the heel is seen to have spread out broader so that it is as broad as the triangle. The three molars of this animal illustrate a most important principle, namely, that the anterior, triangular portion of the crown has been simply levelled down to the posterior portion.

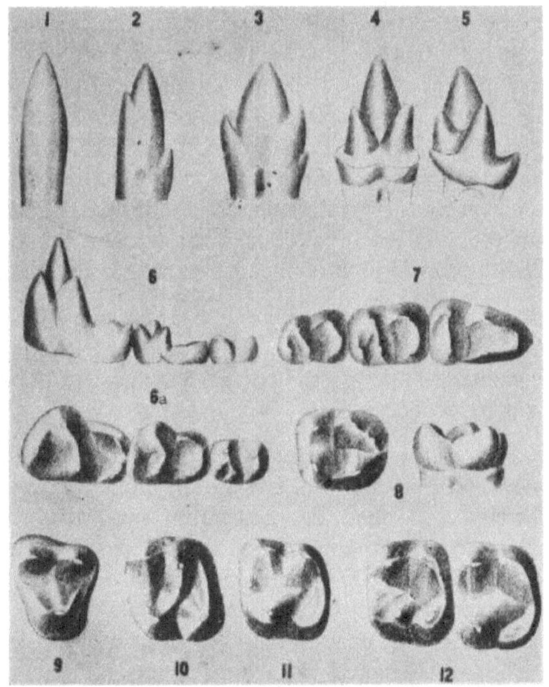

PLATE A.

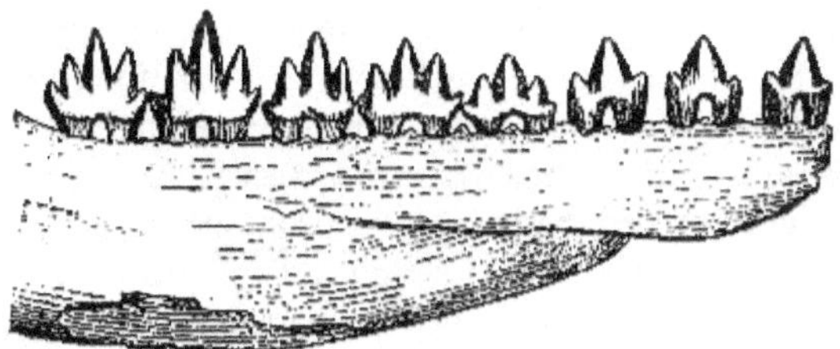

PLATE B.

These three teeth form a series of intermediate steps between a most ancient molar and the modern molar of the human type. The second tooth is halfway between the first and third. The second molar, seen from above, has exactly the same cusps as the first, so it is not difficult to recognise that each cusp has been directly derived from its fellow. The third tooth of the series (Fig. 7) has lost one of its cusps; it has lost a cusp of the triangle. It is now a tooth where only half the triangle is left on the anterior side and with a very long heel.

That tooth has exactly the same pattern as the lower human molar tooth (Fig. 8), the only difference is that the heel is somewhat more prolonged. These teeth belong to one of the oldest fossil monkeys, anaptomorphus. Human lower molars, not very exceptionally, instead of four cusps, have five. The fifth cusp always appears in the middle of the heel, or between the posterior lingual and the posterior buccal. This occurs in monkeys and other animals, but no record exists of the ancient anterior lingual reappearing. The human lower molar, with its low, quadritubercular crown, has hence evolved by addition of cusps and by gradual modelling from a high-crowned, simple, pointed tooth.

Human teeth are of excellent service in the initial determination of degeneracy in the child. For this purpose the teeth should be studied from the first evidence of their development until they are all in place, which occurs normally, in most cases, by the twenty-second year.

Teeth-enamel is formed from the epiblast, and dentine, cementum, pulp (except as to nerve tissue) from the mesoblast. The enamel organs of the first set appear during the seventh week of fœtal life; the dentine bulb during the ninth week. At this period the tooth obtains its periphery. This models the enamel cap which fits over the dentine like a glove. When imperfections in hand or fingers exist these deformities are distinctly observed upon the glove, and in precisely the same manner are observed the different shapes and sizes of the incisors, cuspids, and molars. Calcification of the teeth begins at the seventeenth week of fœtal life. The illustration (Fig. 50) shows the progress of calcification and development of the temporary set of teeth. Examination will show that any defect in nutrition, from conception to birth (due to inherited states or maternal impressions), has been registered upon the teeth. The state of the constitution and the locality register the date of such defects. Thus if the tooth, as a whole, be larger or smaller than normal, or abnormally irregular, taint is undoubtedly inherited from one or both parents. If, on the other hand, there be defect at any part on the crowns of the teeth, and the contour be perfect, the date of malnutrition can be easily determined from this chart. More or less than the normal number of teeth, abnormally placed, demonstrates the existence of inherited defect, since the germs must have been deposited at the period mentioned. No absolute rule can be laid down as to date of the eruption of the teeth. The teeth of the temporary set erupt nearly as follows:

	After Birth.	*Time of Eruption.*
Lower Central Incisors	7 months	1 to 10 weeks.
Upper ” ”	9 months	4 to 6 weeks.

Upper and Lower Lateral	12 months	4 to 6 weeks.
First Molars	14 months	1 to 2 months.
Cuspids	18 months	2 to 3 months.
Second Molars	26 months	3 to 5 months.

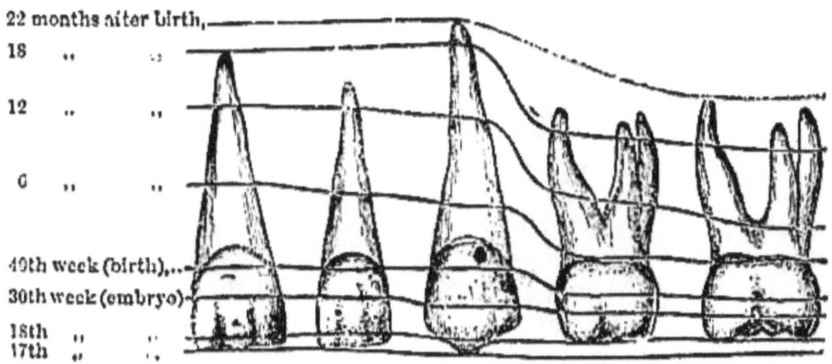

FIG. 50.

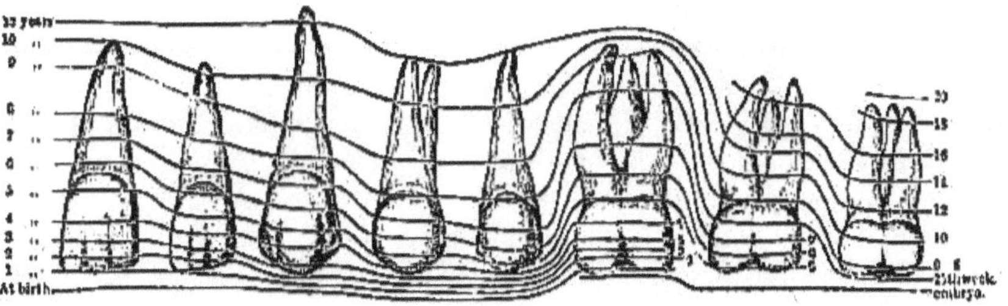

FIG. 51. SHOWS LINES OF DEVELOPMENT OF THE PERMANENT TEETH.

The enamel organs and dentine bulb for the permanent teeth form just before birth (Fig. 51) in like manner with the temporary set. They form just above the temporary set on the upper and below on the lower jaw. The permanent molars begin to calcify at the twenty-fifth week of fœtal life. The permanent incisors do not calcify until a year after birth. Any deviation in size or contour of the permanent teeth from the normal must hence be due to defect in nutrition in the dentine bulb, between the fifteenth and twenty-fifth week of fœtal life. Any deviation in calcification (except the cusps of the first permanent molars) must occur after birth. At the third year twenty-four teeth are fairly well calcified. At the fifth year the second permanent molars, and at the eighth year the third molars or wisdom teeth, begin to calcify.

The following table gives the age of eruption of permanent teeth:

First Permanent Molars	Circa	6 years.
Upper and Lower Central Incisors	"	7 years.
Upper and Lower Lateral "	"	8 years.
First Bicuspids	"	9 years.
Second Bicuspids	"	10 years.
Cuspids	"	11 years.
Second Permanent Molars	"	12 years.
Third Permanent Molars	" 17 to 24 years.	

Man, at this present stage of evolution, has twenty teeth in his temporary and thirty-two in his permanent set. Any deviation in number is the result of embryonic change occurring between the sixth and fifteenth week, for the temporary teeth, and the fifteenth week and birth for the permanent. The germs of teeth which erupt late in life, and are called third sets, of necessity appear ere birth and are completely formed at the beginning of the second year, although they remain protected in the jaw until eruption.

More than twenty teeth in the temporary set, or thirty-two in the permanent set, is hence an atavistic abnormality. From the maxillary and dental standpoint man reached his highest development when well-developed jaws held twenty temporary and thirty-two permanent teeth. Decrease in the numbers of teeth meant, from the dental standpoint, degeneracy, albeit it might mark advance in man's evolution as a complete being. In the New Mexican Lower Eocene occur monkeys like the lemurarius and limnotherium, each the type of a distinct family. The lemurarius, most nearly allied to the lemurs, is the most generalised monkey yet found. It had forty-four teeth in continuous series, above and below. The limnotherium, while related to the lemurs, had some affinities with the American marmosets. These solved the problem of the origin of the extra teeth (known as supernumeraries) that sometimes occur in man, and demonstrated that man, during his evolution from the lowest monkey, lost twelve teeth. These supernumerary teeth assume two forms; either they resemble the adjoining teeth or are cone-shaped. While they are rarely exactly counterparts, every tooth can be duplicated, as the following illustrations show.

Fig. 52 illustrates fairly well-formed duplicate central incisors, the normal incisors being outside the dental arch. They are crowded laterally by the large roots of the supernumerary incisors.

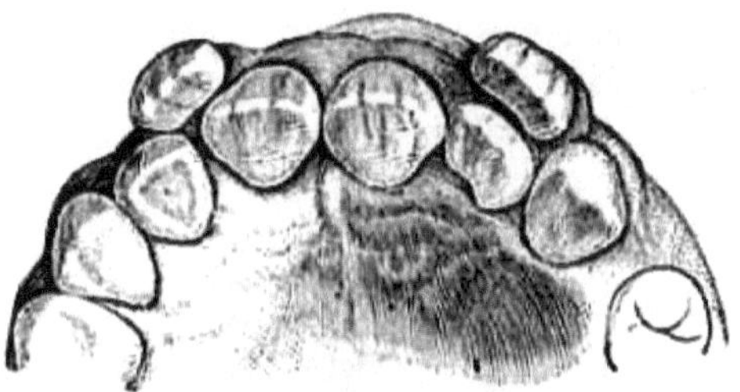

FIG. 52.

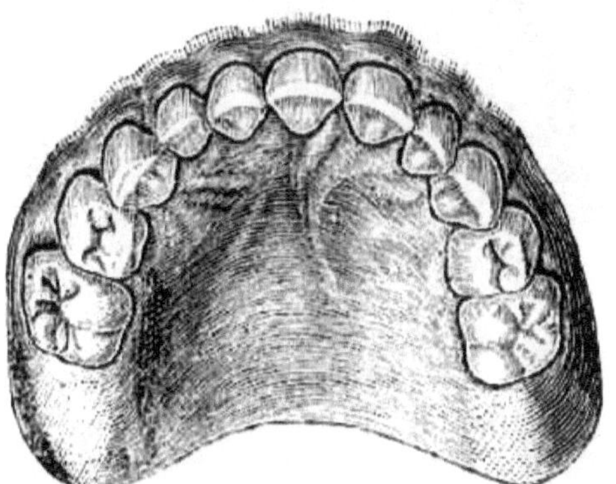

FIG. 53.

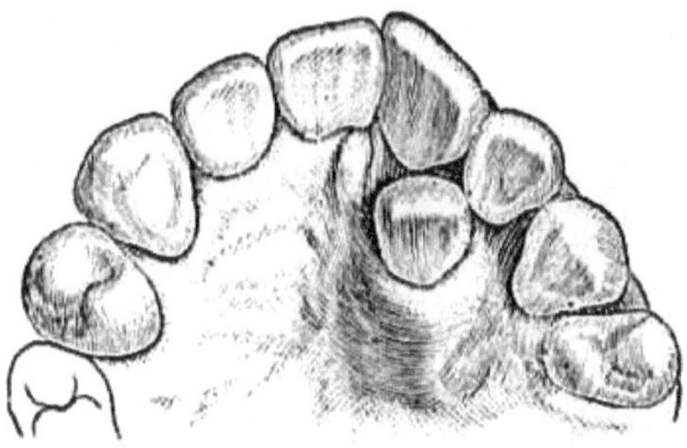

FIG. 54.

Fig. 53 shows an extra right lateral in a temporary set in the upper jaw. Fig. 54 an extra right lateral in the permanent set. Fig. 55 illustrates normally developed supernumerary cuspids which are all grouped together upon the right side, the bicuspid being also duplicated on each side; indeed, all but the molars are duplicate. Fig. 56 shows supernumerary third molars, easily demarcated from the normal molars. The teeth which fail to approximate their normal neighbours assume the cone shape of the primitive tooth.

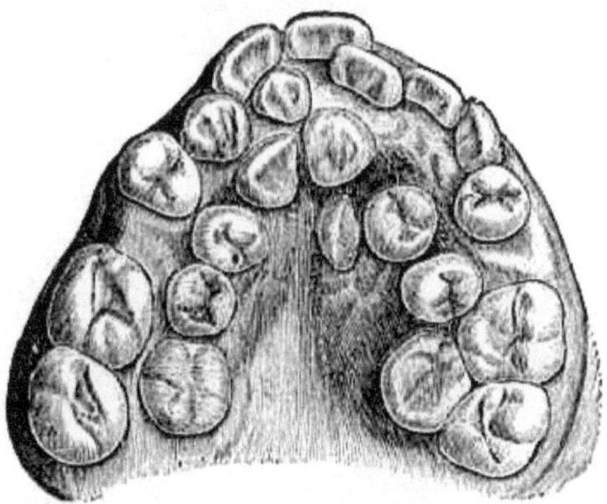

FIG. 55.

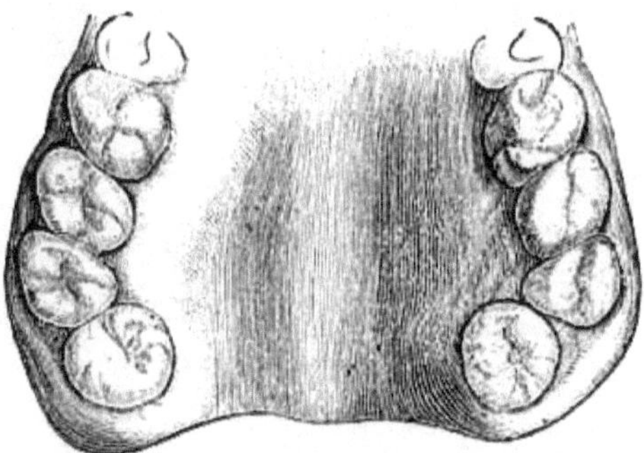

FIG. 56.

The fact that the cone-shaped tooth, as a rule perfect in construction, is found everywhere in the jaw, but especially in the anterior and posterior part of the mouth, is of much value in outlining tooth and jaw evolution, especially in the degeneracy phase. The upper jaw, being an integral part of the skull and fixed, is, of necessity, influenced by brain and skull growth; hence degeneracy is more detectable in it than in the lower.

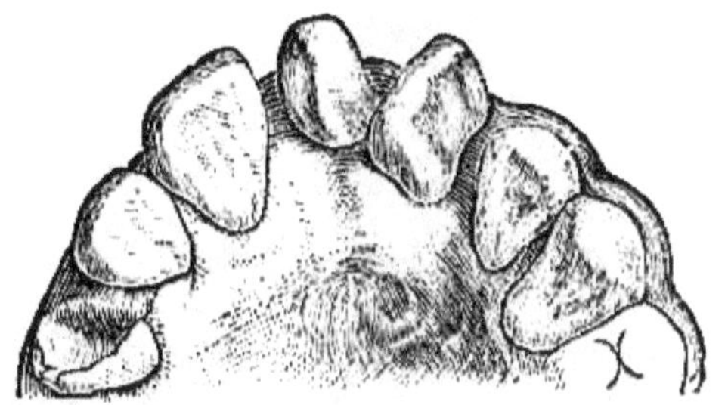

FIG. 57.

FIG. 58.

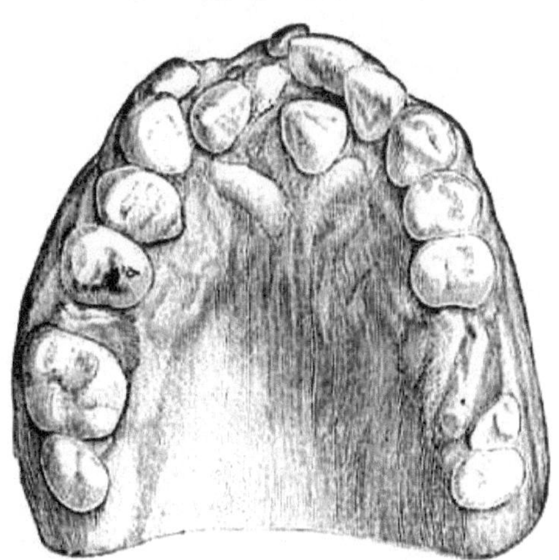

FIG. 59.

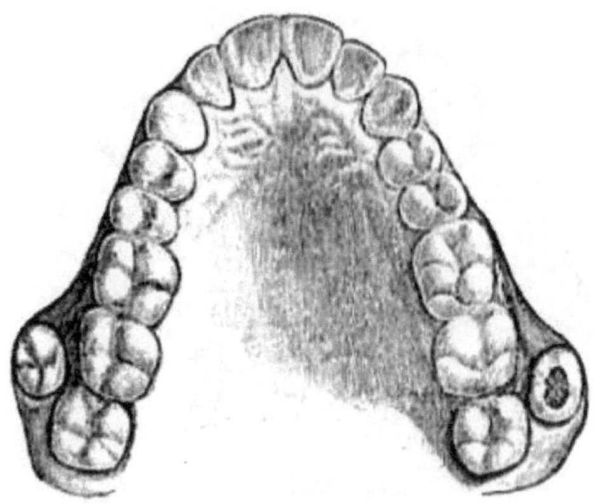

FIG. 60.

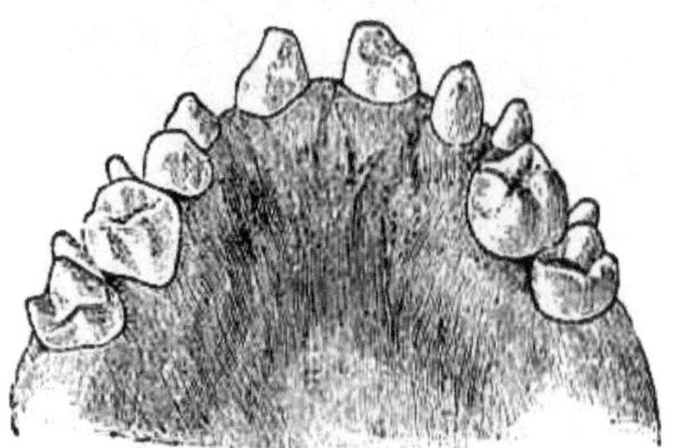

FIG. 61.

The evolution of the jaw is toward shortening in both directions. This shortening will continue so long as the jaw must be adjusted to a varying environment. The jaw of man having originally contained more teeth than at present, lack of adjustment to environment produces, from the shortening, degeneracy of the jaw and atavism of the teeth. While this may coincide with general advances of the individual, it indicates that he is not yet adjusted to his new environment. The shortening of the upper jaw causes supernumerary, cone-shaped teeth to erupt, in mass, at the extreme ends of the jaw, as shown in the following figures. Fig. 57 illustrates a cone-shaped tooth between the two central incisors, forcing them out of position. Fig. 58 shows three supernumerary teeth—a cone-shaped tooth between the central laterals, and the cuspids out of position. The left permanent lateral is at the median line; another cone-shaped tooth remains in the vault, while the supernumerary left lateral is in place. As many as eight are at times to be observed in the anterior vault. Posteriorly these teeth are most often noticed in connection with the third molars, usually on a line with other teeth posterior to the last molar. Fig. 59 shows two supernumerary teeth in the anterior and two in the posterior part of the left arch; the molars have been extracted. Supernumerary teeth are not confined to these localities, but may be observed at any point in the dental arch (Figs. 60 and 61). The primitive cone-shaped tooth is rarely observed in the lower jaw. In twenty-six years' practice I have not seen a case. The mobility of the lower jaw prevents that mal-adjustment to environment present in the upper. The continual shortening, in both directions, of the jaw causes the third molars frequently to wedge in between the angle of the jaw and the second molars, so that eruption, if possible, is difficult.

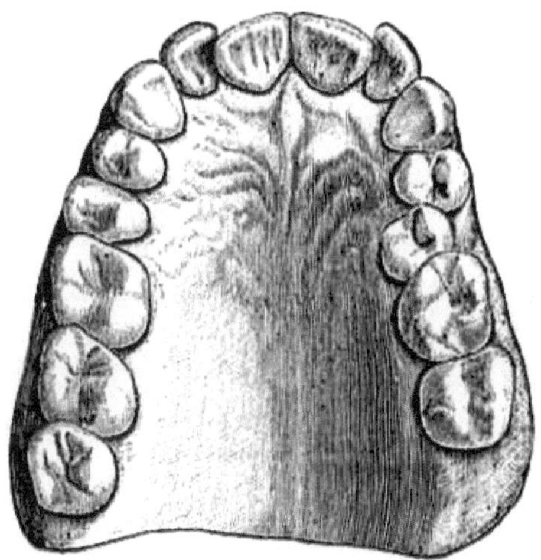

FIG. 62.

169

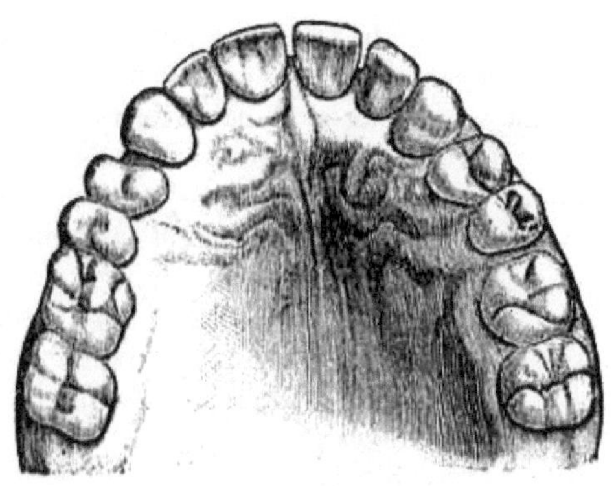

FIG. 63.

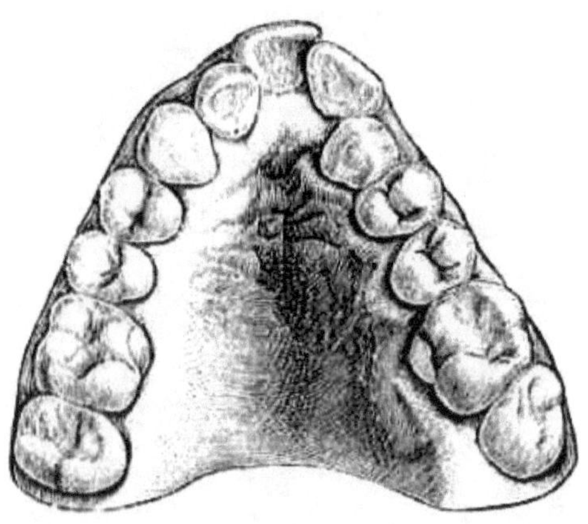

FIG. 64.

The third molar is often absent in the English-speaking and Scandinavian races. In 46 per cent. of 670 patients it was missing. Frequently its development is abortive. This tooth, in the struggle for existence, seems destined to disappear. It is more often absent from the upper than the lower jaw. When absent, or badly developed, the jaw is smaller and frequently teeth irregularities, nasal stenosis, hypertrophy of nasal bone and mucous membrane, adenoids and eye disorders coexist. Fig. 62 shows absence of the left third molar with irregularities of that side of the arch. In Fig. 63 both third molars are seen to be missing. Anteriorly, the lateral incisors are most often wanting; 14 per cent. of the laterals were wanting in 670 patients. In the progress of evolution man has lost one lateral upon each side of the mouth

170

and the second lateral seems also destined to disappear. In Fig. 64 the left lateral incisor has disappeared; and in Fig. 65 both lateral incisors are absent. Not infrequently does it occur that centrals, cuspids, bicuspids, and even molars are absent, even their germs not being detectable. Fig. 66 shows three supernumeraries in the anterior part of the mouth and but two molars. The absence of the teeth indicates lack of development of germs, due either to heredity or defective maternal nutrition at the time of conception or during early pregnancy.

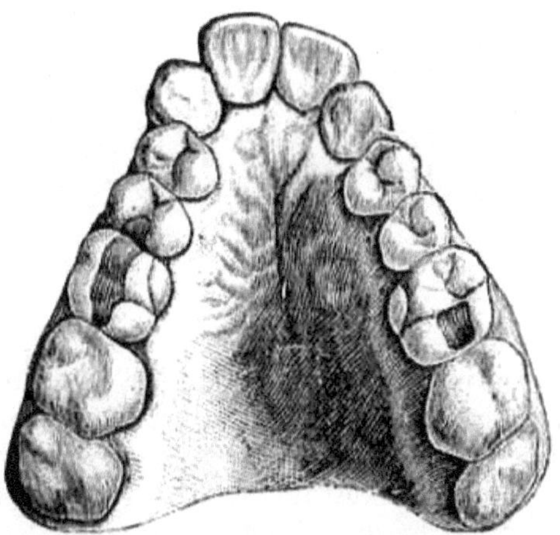

FIG. 65.

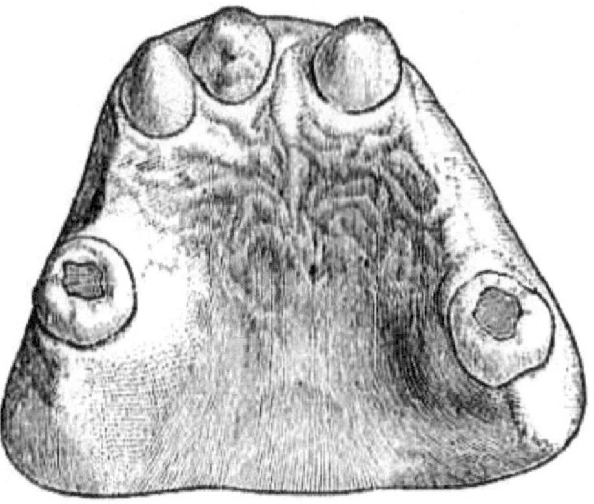

FIG. 66.

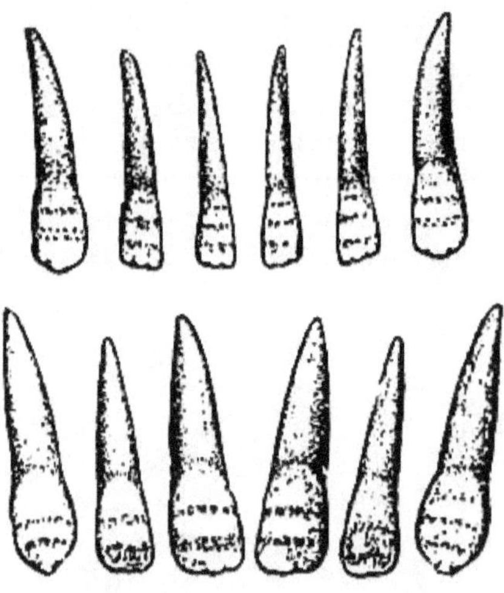

FIG. 67.

Crescent-shaped, bitubercular, and tribucular as well as deformed teeth, tend to be cone-shaped. The malformation of these teeth results from precongenital trophic change in dentine development, dwarfing and notching the cutting and grinding edges of the second set of teeth, of which a familiar example is the so-called Hutchinson's teeth, usually referred to a syphilitic causation. Hutchinson's position has, however, been more strongly stated than his words justify, since he admits that in at least one-tenth of the cases this cause could be excluded.

Syphilis only plays the part of a diathetic state profoundly affecting the maternal constitution at the time of dentine development; while these teeth may be due to secondary results of syphilis, they do not demonstrate syphilitic heredity.

In Fig. 67 are seen the teeth of an individual affected with constitutional disease (referring to Fig. 51 it becomes evident that the defective lines represent the respective ages, 2½, 4, and 5 years). The degree of pitting will depend, as a rule, on the severity of the constitutional disorder. In the case just cited, however, although nutrition was but slightly disordered, each tooth shows a tendency to conate. Not infrequently cavities extend completely through the tooth. The cusps of the (permanent) first molars, calcifying at the first year, are usually attacked also, and arrested in development, producing the cone shape. These data, together with the dates of eruption of the temporary and permanent teeth, furnish an absolute basis for calculation as to malnutrition producing excessive or arrested development, not only of the teeth and jaws but all parts of the body.

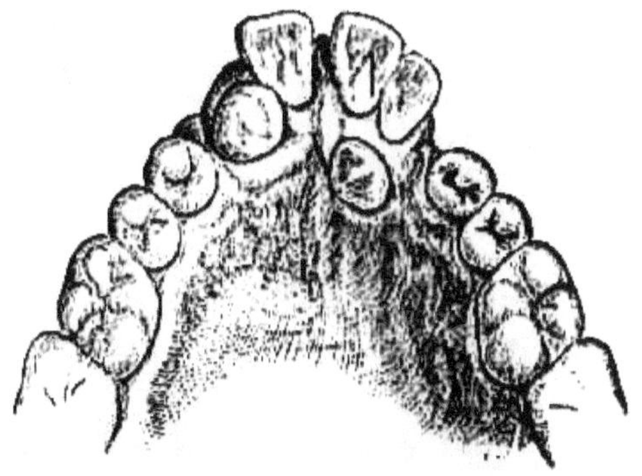

FIG. 68.

173

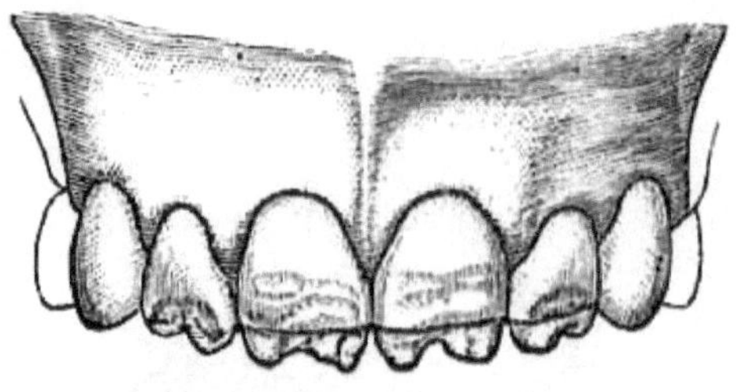

FIG. 69.

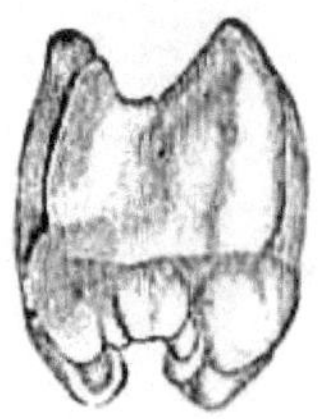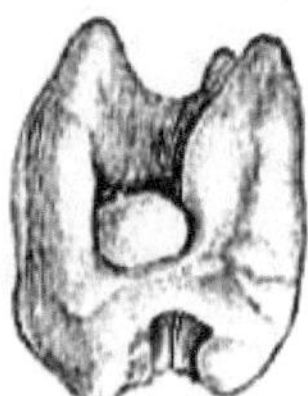

FIGS. 70, 71.

Fig. 68 shows a very degenerate jaw with cone-shaped, malformed bicuspids. The right lateral missing, the cuspids are erupting in the vault and the dental arch is assuming a V-shape. The jaw shows, as a whole, marked arrest in development. Fig. 69 shows Hutchinson's teeth. Were the first molars visible, they would present marked contraction of the outer surface with a malformed centre. Referring again to Fig. 51, it is observable that trophic changes affected the system at the age of birth. The outer surface exhibits a tendency to take the cone shape. Figs. 70, 71, 72, 73, and the molars in Fig. 66, exhibit malformations that assume the cone shape and the centre frequently associated with this type of teeth. The coincidence in form between Hutchinson's and malformed teeth and those of the chameleon suggests that tropho-neurotic change produces atavistic teeth. Fig. 74 illustrates the tendency of human bicuspids (when there is no antagonism) to rotate one- fourth round, thus again indicating an atavistic tendency toward the teeth of the chameleon. Fig. 75 exhibits extreme atavism; all teeth anterior to the molars are cone-shaped. The third molars are missing and would, probably, never erupt. In Fig. 76 appears more marked atavism. The upper and lower are both cone-shaped, and the superior first bicuspid exhibits tendency thereto. The right superior second bicuspid, second and third molars, the right inferior first and second bicuspids, with second and third molars are missing. The same condition, probably, exists on the left side. The space in the upper jaw is due to the insufficient width of the teeth. Alternation of teeth in the upper and lower jaw is a reptilian feature.

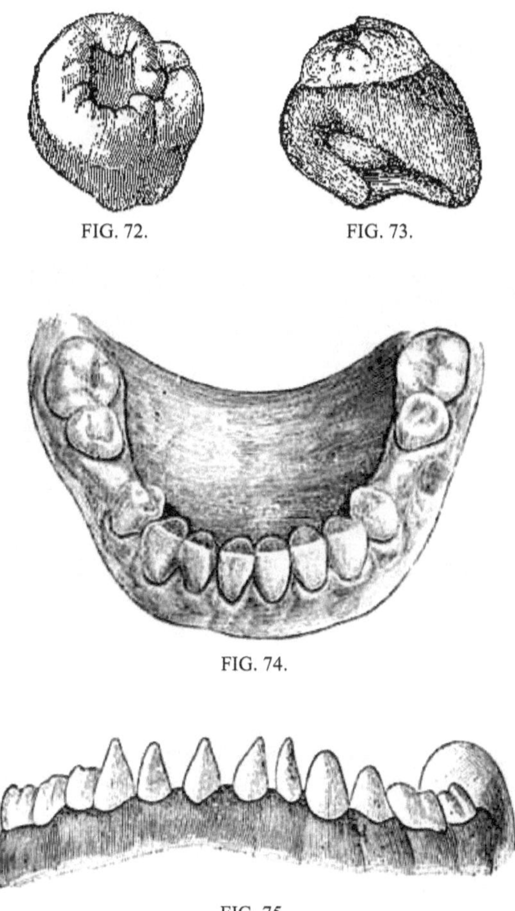

FIG. 72.

FIG. 73.

FIG. 74.

FIG. 75.

Fig. 76 furnishes excellent illustration of the principles already stated. In degenerate jaws every tooth in the jaw, at one point or another, may display rudimentary cusps. On the incisors they are always to be found on the lingual surface.

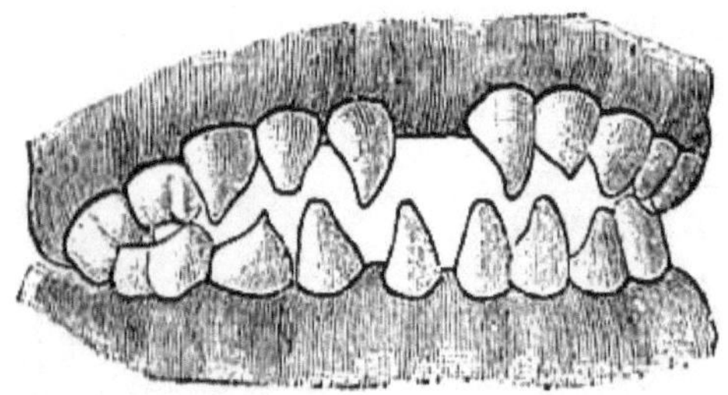

FIG. 76.

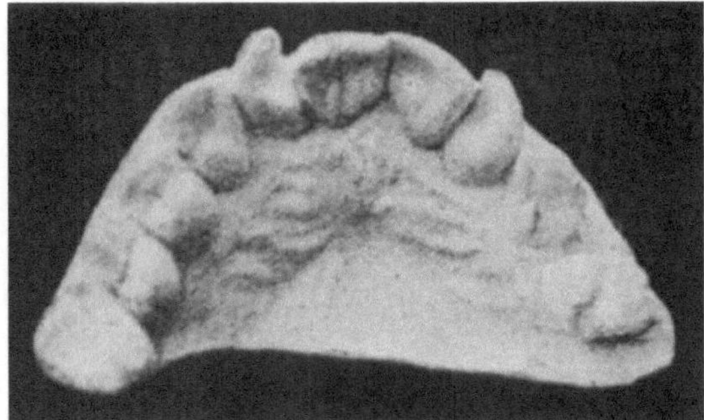

FIG. 77.

Fig. 77 illustrates the centrals with two rudimentary cusps, the laterals with one, and the cuspids with one also. Fig. 78 represents cusps upon the lingual surface of the molars. The cuspids are not unlike the lower cuspids with a rudimentary lingual cusp.

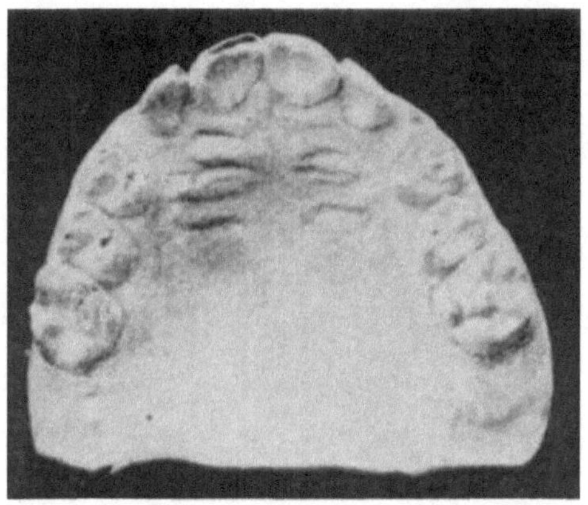

FIG. 78.

There is a gradation from central incisors toward the bicuspids, in evolution. This grading of form is not observed in passing from the cuspid to the bicuspid in man. But the cuspid often presents a cingulum on the lingual face that inclines it toward the bicuspid forms in lower mammals, like the mole, and the first premolar, or bicuspid, is then more caniniform, the inner tubercle being much more reduced. This inner tubercle is very variable and erratic as to its position. It appears as far front as the centrals and is often present on the lingual face of the laterals of man. The lingual tubercle is very constant on the first bicuspid of man and is as well developed as the buccal. But in some lower forms, as in the lemurs, it is quite deficient. It attains the highest development only in the anthropoids and man. Considering these stages of development, the grading from the cuspid to the bicuspid forms was more gradual in the earlier species than in the later, where the individual teeth have taken on special development.

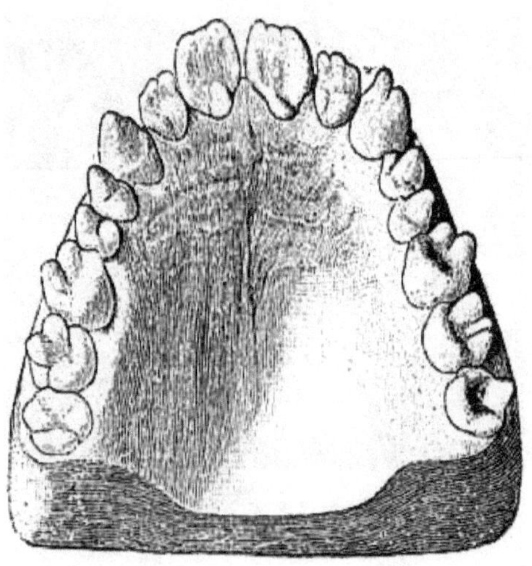

FIG. 79.

The skull of a degenerate girl who died from tuberculosis, at thirteen years, presented, among other stigmata, a cusp on the external surface of a right inferior cuspid. In Fig. 79, where every tooth is present, a most remarkable display of cusps occurs. The cusps upon the cutting and grinding edges are not obliterated. Commencing with the left superior central incisors, three cusps are present with a rudimentary palatine cusp. The laterals also show three cusps, while the cuspid has two very distinct. The first and second bicuspids have tubercular cusps, they being in line. The buccal cusps upon the molars, two or three, and are still in position. The palatine cusps are worn away. The same is the case upon the opposite side, except that the cuspid has cusps that have fused together, leaving a small projection upon the mesial side and a rudimentary palatine cusp. The cusp upon the third molar is lost. In another case (Fig. 61) the primitive cone teeth are seen trying to shape themselves into incisors. The lateral incisors, cuspids and bicuspids are still cone-shaped. The first permanent molar is fairly formed while the second molars are still in a primitive condition.

Degenerate teeth unite in twos, threes, fours, and fives. These single, cone-shaped teeth grow together and form bicuspids and molars. The germ of any two normal teeth may intermingle and unite; not only are the crowns found united with separate roots, but crowns and roots are united throughout.

Figs. 80 and 81 show two superior, central and lateral incisors joined together throughout the entire length of crown and root. In Fig. 82 two lower incisors are united throughout. Fig. 83 shows a cuspid with two roots. George T.

Carpenter, of Chicago, has a right superior, second bicuspid with three well formed roots. Fig. 84 illustrates two bicuspids united at the crowns. Fig. 85 shows two molars perfectly united. Fig. 86 illustrates central and lateral incisors of the permanent set perfectly united. Fig. 87 shows two molars united. Fig. 88 a molar and supernumerary taking the cone-shape with deformed centre. Fig. 89 shows three malformed teeth, each coated and completely united. It is not uncommon to find three molars united together, as, for instance, the second, third, and supernumerary molars. C. V. Rosser, of Atlanta, Georgia, has two small molars and a supernumerary cuspid perfectly united, from crown to root, and these three further united to the roots of a well-formed molar.

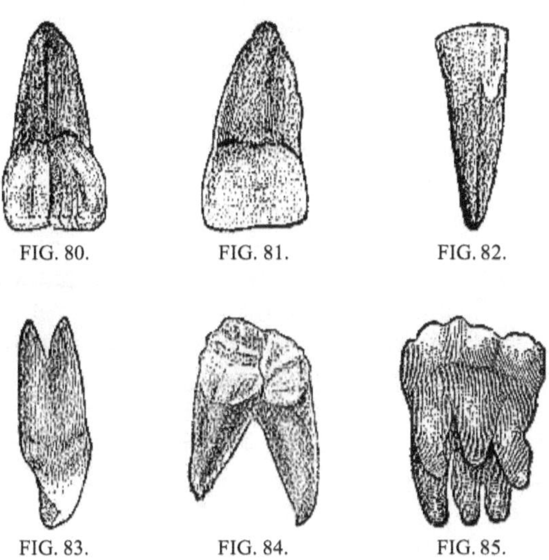

FIG. 80.　　FIG. 81.　　FIG. 82.

FIG. 83.　　FIG. 84.　　FIG. 85.

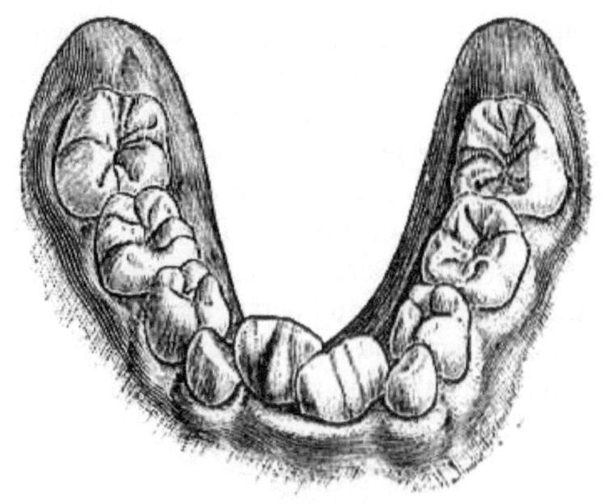

FIG. 86.

That human jaws, like human ears, are degenerating is demonstrable by actual measurements. Mummery, who examined the skulls of 200 Briton and Roman soldiers, found the narrowest 2·12 inches, the highest 2·62, with an average of 2·50. The width of jaws of 402 British soldiers to-day is: narrowest, 1·88; widest, 2·63; average 2·28. The highest width was very rare; only eight measured 2·50. The jaws of the mound builders, compared with the existing cliff dwellers, show similar results. The average width is about 2·50 inches. This is also true of nearly pure negro races. Measurements of normal jaws of 855 Italians of Central Italy were: narrowest, 1·88; widest, 2·63; average 2·17. Measurements of normal jaws of 4,935 Americans gave the following results: narrowest, 1·75; widest, only one case, 2·56; average 2·13. If in the highest type of physical man the width of the upper jaw from the outer surface of the permanent molars near the gum margin was originally 2·50 inches in diameter, the jaw of people now living in the same locality is from 0·25 to 0·33 inches smaller. Although the jaw has thus been growing smaller, since there are no breaks or deformities in the contour of the dental arch this must be regarded simply as an adaptation to environment, and not degeneracy in the proper sense of the term. The degeneracy of the jaws, on which I would lay special stress, is that in which deformity has resulted from inability to adjust structure to a changing environment. When arrest of development so takes place that deformities of the dental arch result, the jaws vary from two inches to one inch in width. As a rule, the teeth are the same size to-day that they were thousands of years ago. This is due to the fact that they are ante- natal and not influenced by post-natal systemic changes. The jaws do not contract as a result of mouth breathing.[218] If the jaw be arrested and be smaller in circumference than the teeth, a break takes place in the dental arch and deformity results. Two types of deformity occur, the V-shaped arch and the saddle arch. All other types of deformity, not due to local causes, are modifications of these two. These deformities always occur with the second teeth only. In these cases the facial profile assumes the perpendicular line or arrested face, as illustrated in the chapter on Degeneracy of the Face. They are never seen before the sixth year, when the second set begin to erupt and are complete with development of the second molars at 12. They may become exaggerated later in life from want of room, the eruption of the third molar and want of harmony in relation of the two jaws when closed.

FIG. 87.   FIG. 88. 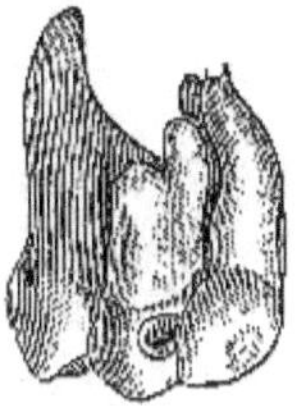   FIG. 89.

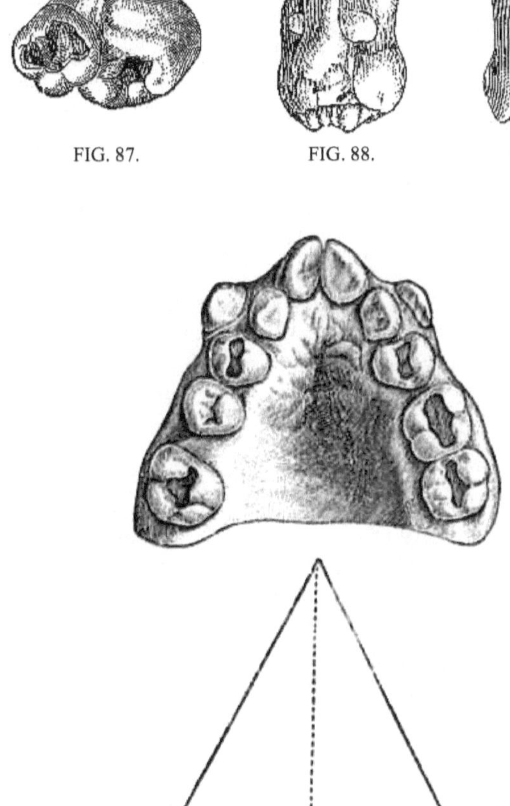
FIG. 90.

There are three characteristics of the normal arch. Independent of temperamental peculiarities, the line extending from one cuspid to the other should be an arc of a circle, not an angle or straight line; the lines from the cuspids to the third molar should be straight, curving neither in nor out, the sides not approximating parallel lines. Absolute bilateral uniformity is not implied in this, as the two sides of the human jaw are rarely, if ever, wholly alike. A uniform arch necessitates uniformity of development between the arch of the maxilla and the arch of the teeth and a correct position of the individual teeth in their relation to each other. When there is inharmonious development between the jaws and the teeth, as may happen when one parent has a small maxilla with correspondingly small teeth, and the other a large one, with correspondingly large teeth, if the child inherit the jaw of one and the teeth of the other, irregularities must follow. Such difference in diameter between the arch of the maxilla and that of the crowns of the teeth is a constitutional cause of irregularity. When there is a difference between these diameters the line formed by the teeth must either fall outside or within the arch of the maxilla and irregularities of arrangements result. The primary division of irregularities is the V-shaped and saddle-shaped arches. We have the V-shaped variety (Fig. 90, one of the typical forms), where the apex of a triangle is formed by the incisors, the base of the triangle being a line connecting the first two molars. If, because of premature or tardy extraction, the first molars move forward, or by coincidence of the arch of the maxilla and the arch of the crown of the teeth in trying to accommodate itself to the lesser arch of the maxilla, the arch becomes a broken line, forming an angle at the incisors. This angle results from two causes: the thinness of the process at this point and the diminution of resistance which must follow.

When the permanent bicuspids erupt under a favourable condition, so that their greatest diameter is in a line with the greater diameter of both cuspids and first molar, they will be held firmly in place, since the greatest pressure is on this very line. On the other hand, when the bicuspids are erupted after their proper time, while the cuspids progress duly, and meeting no resistance fall into their proper places, but the bicuspids adapt themselves as best they can to the space left for them, and if the arch of the maxilla does not coincide with that of the crowns, they must fall within or without the arch. Now, if the first molar have moved forward, diminishing the space, the bicuspid must erupt either within or without the arch.

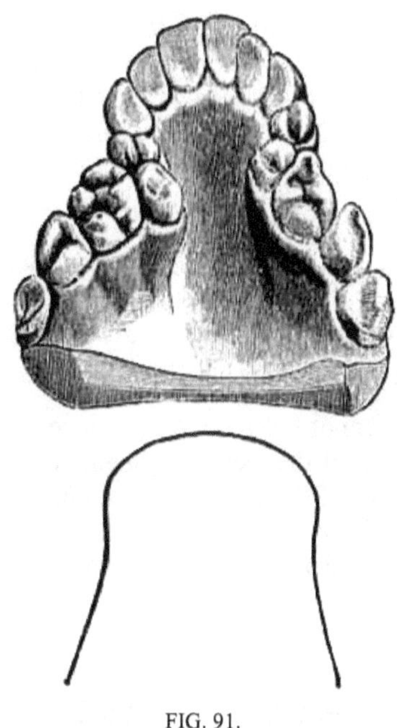

FIG. 91.

To understand why they are generally found within the arch, the shape of the molar and cuspids must be kept in mind. A transverse section of their crowns shows their proximal walls not to be parallel, but wedge-shaped, their diameter being greater on the buccal than on the palatal side. When the crowned bicuspid falls within the greatest diameter of these teeth, finding more room within the arch, they naturally slip in the direction of least resistance, *i.e.*, toward the palate. A local cause for the same condition is found in the fact that the crown of the bicuspids, before their eruption, was held between the roots of the temporary molars, and, as these form an arch of a smaller circle than that of the permanent teeth, the bicuspids will be found generally inside the arch. From both causes occurs an inward curvature, which is termed the saddle-shaped arch (Fig. 91). It should be noted here that, since the V-shaped irregularity is found anterior to the cuspid, the upper incisors are always projecting beyond the lower; the saddle-shaped irregularity is invariably posterior to the cuspid from an inward curve. The incisors never project. Both forms contract the arch; the V-shaped anteriorly, the saddle-shaped posteriorly. In both forms the forward movement of the first molar is the local cause.

Deformities of the dental arch are due, first, to arrest of development of the jaws, and, second, in the nature of the deformity, to the order of eruption of teeth, which rarely erupt twice alike. From an evolution standpoint these deformities are atavistic. The V-shaped reverts to the reptilian type; the saddle-shaped to the lower mammals. In the gorilla, the nearest to man in dentition, there is a very distinct approach to the saddle shape. In the chimpanzee it remains. The orang-outang exhibits less of this tendency. The arch of some of the cebidæ very nearly approaches man. It all depends upon the extent of prognathism. When that is reduced the arch appears and rectangular arrangements of the teeth are lost. Most carnivors exhibit a distinct approach to the saddle shape. Some felines have a shortening of the jaw, partly obliterating the tendency, but in most canidæ it is quite marked.

These are facts which cannot be overlooked, since, from the very nature of development and eruption of the teeth, they cannot take any other form. The arrangement of the crowns of the cuspid (canine) in the jaw before eruption is such that, no matter what the local condition of the jaws or teeth may be the V-shaped or saddle-shaped dental arch must be produced.

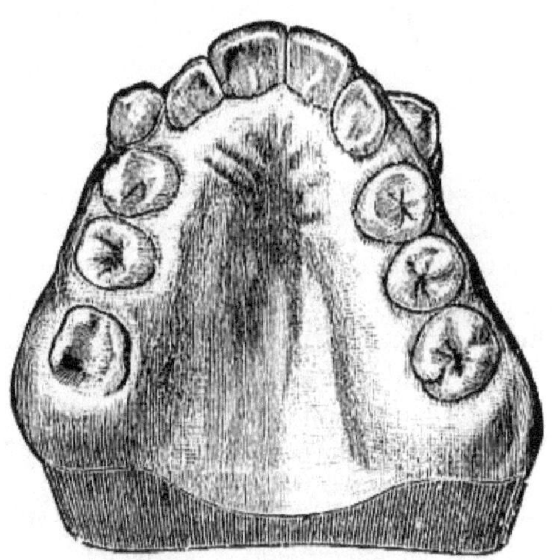

FIG. 92.

In no symptoms is degeneracy so evident as in the stigmata resultant on hypertrophy of the alveolar process. This occurs at all ages, but more particularly at the period of development of the permanent set of teeth. The entire alveolar process may become involved (Fig. 92), or only a portion (Fig. 93).

Hypertrophy of the alveolar process is the result of irritation incident upon eruption and the shedding of the temporary teeth, and eruption of the permanent teeth.

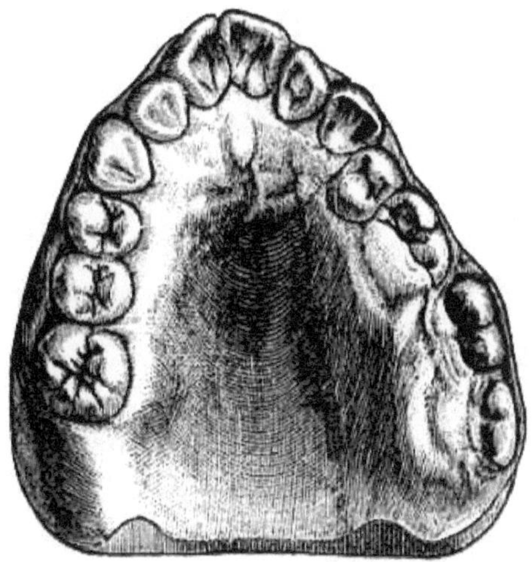

FIG. 93.

Laryngologists, rhinologists, and neurologists claim that certain vaults are deformities; in reality the alveolar process is hypertrophied. The jaws, as a whole, owing to an unstable and ill-balanced nervous system, are liable to become excessively developed, as well as arrested in development. Excessive development of the superior maxilla is evinced by a fulness of the upper lip. In these cases the upper maxilla is too large for the lower, and stands out beyond it. The lower may be quite normal. When there is simply a want of proportion between the two jaws, it is due to the diminutive or excessive size of one while the other is normal. The criterion in these cases must be the facial angle. The upper jaw is usually in harmony with the skeleton, while the lower jaw depends for its size largely upon function, its size being the result of accident rather than the result of general proportions.

FIG. 94.

When the upper jaw is normal, or smaller than the lower, the extent of the posterior portion is determined by the occlusion of the first permanent molar, which keeps the alveolar processes in permanent relation to each other at this point and allows freedom of development in front. If the occlusion be not normal, the upper jaw and alveolar process will develop laterally as well as anteriorly. The teeth of the anterior columns may either stand vertically, or they may be turned in toward the lower incisors. The latter defect is produced by the action of the lips. When the cuspids are in their normal position the upper incisors form a larger arch than the lower, and this permits of their being turned inward; but when the cuspids have moved so far forward that they are not normally interlocked with the lower teeth, the incisors are too crowded to permit this. While the jaws are growing smaller the teeth tend to cause reversion to the original form. Arrest of development of the superior maxilla is always associated with marked depression at the alæ of the nose, producing the appearance of having been hollowed out from a point at the floor of the orbit to the grinding surface of the lower teeth (Fig. 94).

FIG. 95.

Arrest of the lower jaw (Fig. 95) is common among degenerates. This consists of a shortening of the body of the jaw. Sometimes it is arrested to such an extent that there is apparently no chin. About 50 per cent. of criminals of Elmira, New York, have this deformity. The following table shows the number of deformities of the jaws and teeth which I have found among some of the degenerate classes.

JAWS.

	Number examined.	V-shaped.	Partial V.	Semi-V.	Saddle.	Partial Saddle.
Criminals at Pontiac, Ill.	465	75	71	3	66	63
Criminals at Elmira, N. Y.	1041	381	49	1	157	26
Criminals at						

Joliet, Ill.	468	13	79	19	59	92
Prostitutes at Chicago, Bridewell	30	10	17	7	27	10
Insane at Dunning, Ill.	700	26	47	…	12	…
Insane at Kankakee, Ill.	613	69	107	29	89	105
Idiots, imbeciles	1977	129	236	…	207	…
Deaf and Dumb	1935	169	192	…	203	…
Blind	207	7	9	…	11	…
Inebriates[219]	514	1·5	24·4	0·3	9·3	13·2

<hr>

CHAPTER XIV

DEGENERACY OF THE BODY

As degeneracy checks the natural course of embryonic development it necessarily finds expression in the body as well as in the skull. One most striking condition is that by which development of the bones enclosing the spinal cord is checked. The spinal cord is at first essentially a notochord as in the lowest types of vertebrates. The structures surrounding the cord are not divided into vertebræ. This condition is permanent in the lancelet. Around the notochord is later formed a species of membrane which protects it, called the perichord. This condition is the second stage of development of the cord and is the permanent condition in the lampreys. Later still the cartilaginous vertebræ develop, and then these ossify at the point in the perichord which is to form a vertebra, bows of dense tissue <u>form</u> which unite behind. In front similar bows form to constitute the bodies of the vertebræ. These bows remain ununited in some of the lower fish and at certain stages in the human embryo. As degeneracy checks the union of the bows of the vertebræ, imperfection, and even absence, of the union occur, which is called spina- bifida (Fig. 96). This condition when complete is rarely compatible with life. In a partial state it is often found among degenerates.[220] The seat of the trouble is frequently covered by an excessive development of hair (hypertrichosis), especially in the small of the back; this, which occurs very frequently in degenerates, resembles the tail which the ancients represented as that of the fauns.[221]

FIG. 96.

As the vertebræ unite irregularly, deviations or bends of the spine occur very frequently among degenerates. These may be of any of the types known to surgeons. In man the spinal column terminates in two bones. One of those (composed of five vertebræ) begins at eighteen years to unite slowly into a single bone called the sacrum. The bones of the sacral vertebræ form processes similar to those which are formed from the vertebræ of the chest region. These serve to cover the nerves of the sacral region. The bone immediately below the sacrum, called the coccyx, is essentially the representative of the tail in man. At a certain stage of human development, as in the tadpole, the tail disappears, the nine vertebræ forming the coccyx unite together and become a very diminutive bone which loses nearly all vertebral characteristics. Sometimes this bone retains its embryonic peculiarities to such an extent that it simulates in some degenerates a rudimentary tail. Of this many instances are on record. A greater degree of this condition has been found to occur, with comparative frequency, amongst the lowest negro races. In this respect these are below the anthropoid apes, where the tail, considered from the tail standpoint, has degenerated as in man for the benefit of the organism as a whole.

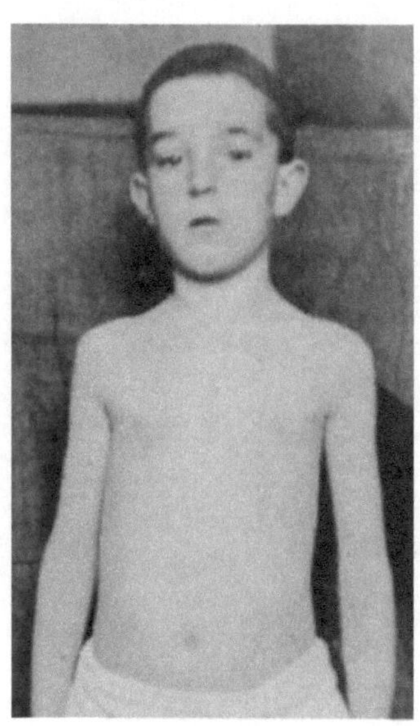

FIG. 97.

The ribs and breastbone develop from the processes of the vertebræ. It is probable that every vertebra originally had ribs. Traces of these exist in most vertebræ in the human embryo. In man, as a rule, there are but twelve vertebræ which develop true ribs. In degenerates, as in the gibbon, a thirteenth pair sometimes appears. Normally, the two lowest ribs are, however, very imperfectly developed as compared with the other ten, and one is sometimes absent. The rib develops from the ends of the vertebral bows, which, coming in contact with the muscle plates of their own segment of the body, are by the resulting bulging forced to expand, and later come together through the formation of the breastbone. Checking of these conditions produces various deformities of the chest which have been divided into "funnel-shaped" and "dropper" deformities.[222] Frequently the entire chest wall is arrested early in life (Fig. 97). The relation between the muscle plates and the course of development of the chest is illustrated by the fact that an arrest of development of important muscles often coexists with deformities of the chest. The human limbs are developments from the fin-folds as found in fishes and the human embryo. In one of these the fins are divided into four segments. The upper segment contains one long bone, the humerus (or arm bone), or the femur (or thigh bone). The second segment contains two long bones, the radius and ulna (or arm bones), or the tibia and fibula (or leg bones). The third segment consists of nine small bones, the carpals of the wrist or the tarsals of the ankle. The fourth segment consists of five separate digits. These limbs pass through three stages in embryonic development as to their position, which may be designated as amphibian, reptilian, and mammalian. Many of these bones fuse together (carpals and tarsals). The digits have long before the late fish stage been formed of more than one bone. At times this condition persists even after the completion of human embryonic development. Limb anomalies resulting from checks of development causing either excess or arrest of development are far from uncommon among degenerates, but are not so common as anomalies of form and proportion. Among such anomalies may be mentioned joined limbs (symelia), or the more or less complete absence of limbs (ectromelia), or the absence of a peripheric segment (hemimelia), or the complete or partial absence of a central segment (phocomelia). Among the other important degeneracies of the limbs are supernumerary digits. These Annadale[223] classifies as: First, a deficient digit loosely attached to the hand or foot or to another digit. Second, a more or less developed digit free at its extremity and articulating with other bones. Thirdly, a fully developed separate digit. Fourth, a digit united along its whole length with another digit. The first three types have been called polydactylia. The last has been called syndactylia. There is finally a condition in which union between the digits results in the disappearance of some of the fingers and toes (Fig. 98). This condition is called ectrodactylia. Supernumerary digits to the extent of six fingers and six toes are exceedingly common in the families of degenerates. The influence of heredity in this particular has been well demonstrated. The Kelleia family of Malta was one of the earliest reported. The condition may last for five generations,[224] but often disappears on marriage with normal persons outside the community or family. A family of the Arabian Hyabites, named Boldi, confined marriages to their own tribe. They all have twenty-four digits. Children born with a normal number are killed as being the offspring of adultery. The inhabitants of Cycaux, France, till the end of the eighteenth century, had nearly all supernumerary digits either on the hands or feet. Isolated in a mountainous region, they for years intermarried. On communication being opened, they emigrated or married strangers, and sexdigitism vanished. Maupertius reports the case of a German family whose members had twenty-four digits for many generations.[225] One of them refused to acknowledge a normal child. In one instance in the United States supernumerary digits lasted through five generations. A case reported[226] some years ago was the following: The first instance of the appearance of the deformity was in a man, born of a degenerate family in 1752, who had six toes on one foot. His son was born with six toes on one foot, but the daughter was normal. This daughter had five children; among them were a son and daughter, each of whom had six fingers on one hand. The granddaughter had eight children, including one son with six toes on one foot. Another son had two daughters, each having six fingers on each hand, and one daughter having twenty-four digits. This last girl had three children; the son was doubly deformed like his mother, while a second son had six fingers on each hand, the toes being normal. One of the two daughters of the fourth generation (with only the hands affected) had eight children, several of whom were normally developed, but the rest were deformed as follows: One daughter had an osseous thickening at the end of the digits, one son had twenty-four digits, another had twelve fingers, the toes being normal in number.

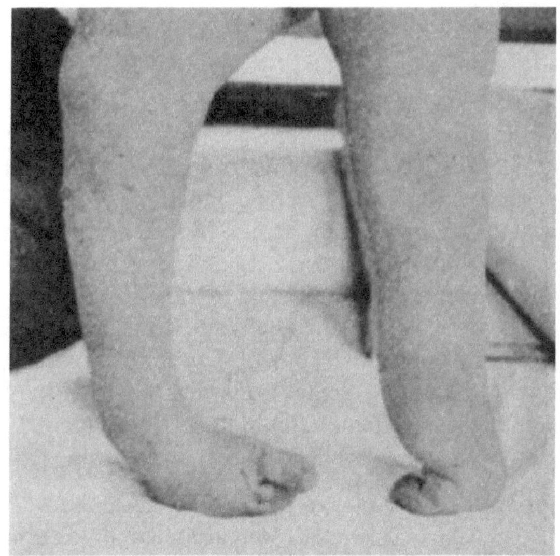

FIG. 98.

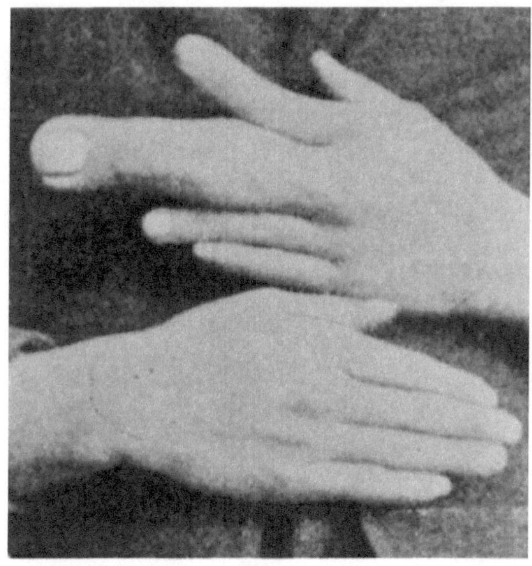

FIG. 99.

I have elsewhere cited an instance from Kiernan in which unilateral sexdigitism was found in four generations of Norwegian degenerates.

Not unfrequently polydactylia is associated with the absence or union or decrease in size of bones of the limbs. It happens that the upper or lower extremities may be increased or diminished disproportionately through the body. This disproportion in size of the fingers and toes is exceedingly frequent. Big digits (macrodactylia, Fig. 99) are comparatively rare, and may only involve a supernumerary bone in the thumb. Short digits (microdactylia) are much more frequent. This state may be constituted by the absence of one bone or the union of two bones, or the shortening of metacarpal or metatarsal bones, or the shortness of several phalangeal bones. There may be increased disproportion between the different fingers. The method of determining this is by comparison with the middle finger. This disproportion may vary greatly. Féré is of opinion that shortening of all the fingers constitutes a grave mark of degeneracy. Relative shortness is exceedingly common.

Under the conditions of development of the limbs from the fin-fold, itfollows that these may be checked completely so that the condition approximates the earlier development from the fish. On the other hand the large bones of the arm and thigh may be checked while the digits and the two lower bones (radius and ulna, tibia and fibula) go on to full development as do the digits. Sometimes the arms develop completely while the lower extremity remains in the fin-fold state. On the other hand the arms may be checked and remain in the fin-fold state while the legs go on to full development. Sometimes the bones of the arm and forearm are checked while the digits go on to full development. The lower extremities are sometimes fused together. This condition, from its resemblance to the like state in the seal, is called phocomelia, or seal limbs. They are also called sirens, on account of the resemblance to the sirens of mythology.[227]

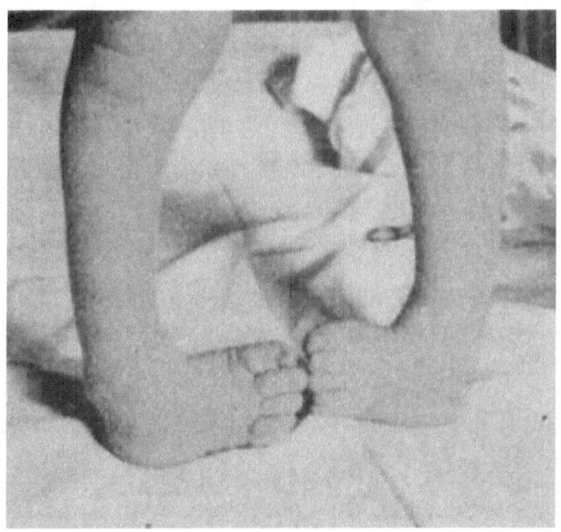

FIG. 100.

Other expressions of degeneracy, albeit sometimes secondary, are club-foot and club-hands (Fig. 100). In many instances these are retentions of positions assumed by the limbs of the fœtus in the course of evolution, and are therefore, in the adult, expressions of degeneracy. Club-foot was an expression of degeneracy which appeared in Byron, the poet, as a consequence of the degeneracy present in both the Byrons and the Gordons, as Kiernan has shown.[228] Commenting on this condition as found in Byron,
F. S. Coolidge, of Chicago, remarks: "Byron undoubtedly suffered from double congenital club-foot, the deformity being worse on the right." While in Coolidge's opinion congenital club-foot unquestionably arises from different causes, it is, however, so frequently an accompaniment of severe forms of mal-development and of congenital brain defects, that there can be no doubt but that imperfect constitutional development is one of its causes. That the deformity with the many limitations which it involves may tend to create morbidness is very likely to be an additional symptom of the degeneracy which, in certain cases, is the underlying cause for the deformity. Dareste, who has studied the club-foot and the club-hand from the standpoint of experimental teratology, finds that in no small number of cases club-foot and club-hand result from checked development. Absence of the kneecap or patella may, as H. N. Moyer has shown, be an expression of degeneracy.[229]

The conditions resultant on checked development may appear in any of the bony or muscular structures. At times muscles checked in development pass on to conditions present in the lower apes.[230] Sometimes the checked development of bones results in artery courses which are present in some of the lower animals. Just above the bend of the elbow in the embryo is an opening through which an artery passes in many quadrupeds. In adult man, as a rule, this has disappeared, but not rarely in degenerates the opening persists with the artery through it.

Hernias, of all varieties, are noticeably hereditary,[231] but what is hereditary is not the rupture, but the laxity of the orifice of the cavity of the abdomen. As descent of the testicles from the abdomen (where they are embryonically in man and normally in many animals) is often delayed and even does not occur in degenerates, hernia of the groin variety is particularly apt to occur in them. These hernias are often found united with defects of the testicles as well as deficiencies of the chest. Deformities of the nose are also especially apt to coexist with these.

Degenerate women frequently have supernumerary milk glands arranged on the abdomen as in some lemurs, while males may have supernumerary breasts of either male or female type. These breasts may be represented by nipples alone. In either sex arrested development of the face, middle ear, and palate often coexists with these supernumerary breasts.

The degeneracies of the body combine so frequently with those of the skull and the brain as to indicate a common origin. Polydactylia is found with almost all the degeneracies of the body. It occurs with all the degeneracies of the eye, from those which are purely atavistic like coloboma to those like retinitis pigmentosa and amauroses, which are atavistic in origin. Hare-lip, cleft palate, and deformities of the jaws and teeth are often found associated with all the bodily degeneracies and the nutritive, intellectual, and moral degeneracies as well. Phocomelia with brain deformity has been found associated with them. Anomalies of the genital organs are also quite frequently associated with these and with finger anomalies. In the subjects of juvenile obesity are frequently associated unstable mentality and will-power, and delayed or precocious sexual maturity. My own observations have shown this condition to be frequently associated with the jaw and teeth degeneracies.

FIG. 101.

Aside from their general significance as stigmata of degeneracy, anomalies of the external ear have been found frequently associated with mal-development of lungs, kidneys, liver, and intestines. Hidden spina-bifida is often associated with the same anomalies, and not rarely with irregular development of the genital organs of both sexes. Albinism or deficient pigment in the skin and hair is not only often associated with grave degeneracies, intellectual and moral, but appears combined with mal-development of the spleen, liver, and kidneys. The opposite state (melanoderma, or black skin) is often associated with similar deformities, especially with early precocity in development. It has also been found in connection with hairlessness and irregularities in development of the teeth and jaws.

The deformities of the chest and their resulting interferences with respiration are not only associated with conditions like narrowing of the pulmonary artery, of the aorta, and with cardiac deformities, but also lead to diminution of the respiratory power and, in consequence, to conditions predisposing to pneumonia and consumption. They are also, as my own observation has shown, associated with deformities of the face, of the nose, of the mouth cavity, of the palate, and of the jaws. These conditions result in mouth breathing and in other conditions which predispose to the attacks of microbes. The deformities of the arterial system coexisting with checked development of the chest are apt to extend to the blood vessels of the kidneys, and therefore to retain these in the embryonic condition, thus predisposing them to disease. To a somewhat lesser degree this arterial condition coexisting with checked development of the chest or with the other arrested conditions of development associated with it, may extend to the liver in such a degree as to prevent it destroying the toxins of typhoid fever and allied diseases, thereby increasing the dangers from these disorders. The same influence may be exerted on the spleen and suprarenal capsules, thus interfering with the physiologic guards these organs furnish against disease and its results. Not infrequently do these last conditions tend to give an epileptic character to degeneracies which would otherwise be destitute of it. With the interference with the proper blood supply, due to checked conditions of the organs named, may occur gout, diabetes, and many forms of rheumatism with their secondary consequences.

The imperfect and irregular action of the lungs associated with the arrests in development of the face, nose, palate, jaws, and chest may produce an irregular blood supply to the brain, which will exaggerate the mental instability of the degenerate.

Among the conditions which are expressions of degeneracy of the body, combined with degeneracy of the head and face, are three conditions known as infantilism, masculinism, and feminism. Practically all three are arrests of development of the promise of the child type. Owing to the struggle for existence which occurs at puberty between the old type of the chondrocranium and its new type as supplemented by the dermal bones, the nervous system takes a distorted ply which arrests both the bodily, nervous, and mental development at certain points. In infantilism the arrest is of the future promise of the child, so that the body and face remain at the childish point, or the body and nervous system are checked, or finally the nervous system or certain organs alone are checked while the body goes on to full development. Not infrequently the face is arrested at any period from birth to puberty (Fig. 101). Hence the reason many persons retain their youthful appearance throughout life. These people are often vain and egotistic. The mental stamina is weak, and they are frequently unreliable, while the females are often prostitutes or prurient prudes, hysteric reformers or gossip mongers.

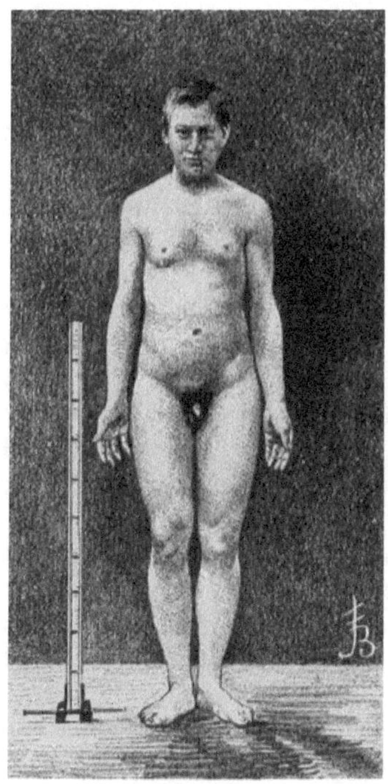

FIG. 102.

The female type, from the standpoint of bodily and nervous development, most nearly approximates the promise of the child type, and checks of development will result in masculinism and feminism. In the first the female has proceeded so far in development as to have female organs and their functions while retaining traces of a predominant character of the lower male type. In the second, the male has proceeded along the line of evolution toward the female type, but ere sex has been fixed, further development has been checked and the male type is finally assumed as the predominant one. Both sexes proceed embryologically from an indifferent type nearly resembling the hermaphroditic type found in the lower vertebrates. The arrest of development may therefore take place at any point in the embryonic evolution. The male may preserve only the female breasts[232] (Fig. 102), while normal in other respects; or, again (Fig. 103), present cryptorchidism or sloping shoulders, and be otherwise masculine. On the other hand, his nervous system may have taken such a ply that at the period of puberty the sexual instincts may be female in type. In some instances, this may extend merely to an extreme modesty toward males, to an intense liking for female occupations and disgust for male occupations. In the female precisely analogous conditions may occur. In certain cases the sex side is entirely dormant until awakened at puberty. Education of these cases of arrested development may give the sex direction rather than any in-born tendency. In one case, a male who had undergone arrest of development in his evolution towards the female type was brought up as a girl, had unusually pleasing womanly qualities; as a result was married twice to intensely devoted husbands, and the real sex was never even suspected until post-mortem examination revealed that the supposed woman was a male. In other cases where the nervous system has taken one sexual ply, while the body has taken another, an exceedingly unfortunate class of beings results. This class of beings needs especially careful training during puberty and adolescence. In some instances in addition to the sexual distortion there exist in these beings conditions of mental defect and moral obliquity. In the last case they approximate the criminal type. In the first case residence in an insane hospital protects the community and these beings against themselves. In some instances no mental defect nor, in a strict sense, moral obliquity occurs. Here the patient requires very careful study from every standpoint.[233] There is in the higher and lower races a tendency in different directions as to the predominance of sex. The woman of the lower races more nearly resembles the male of the race. The male of the higher races more nearly resembles in structure the female of his race than does this female the females of the lower race. This is in part due, in the course of evolution, to the intrusion of the male on female occupations, since all occupations, other than war, hunting, and fishing, were created by women.

[234] The male, however, in the higher races, while thus taking on the female intellectual and æsthetic qualities, retains the male sexual characteristics, mentally and physically, but in accordance with the law of evolution, these manifest themselves less explosively as in the case of the female. As the victim of masculinism or feminism is a degenerate the explosive manifestations are more marked. Every one of the stigmata of degeneracy already described may coexist with any one of the three conditions named: infantilism, masculinism, and feminism.

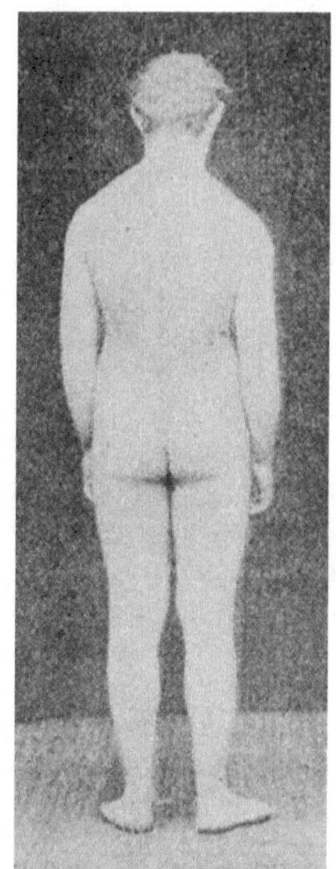

FIG. 103.

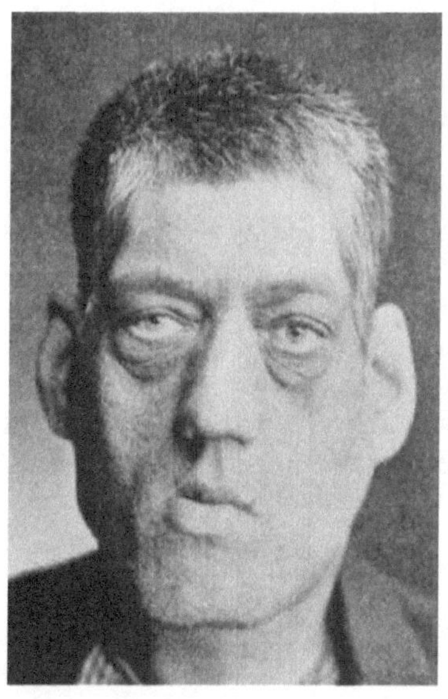

Among the most striking manifestations arising from arrest of development in certain directions with possible hypertrophy in others, are the conditions known as giantism and dwarfism (*see* Frontispiece). Both these conditions may be expressions of atavism to no very remote ancestors and present little if any evidences of degeneracy. In other cases degeneracy may be well marked, and the condition be due to imperfect gland action, such as disorder of the pituitary body, which causes very frequently an enlargement of many of the bones of the body, and very often a uniform enlargement of all the bones. Indeed, as Marie has said, giantism is acromegaly occurring during the period of adolescence. In many instances the opposite condition, dwarfism, occurs during infancy from causes which check the further growth of the body, although the general functions remain unchanged. Dwarfism is very apt to be attended by preservation of the intellectual faculties without evidence of degeneracy, other than the egotism shown in extreme vanity. Moral defects are, however, more apt to occur in dwarfism than in giantism, in which last condition mental defect is apt to occur, varying from a simple good-humoured stupidity to feeble-mindedness. In proportion as the central nervous system has been affected will the stigmata of degeneracy appear in both conditions. As the line between disease and disordered function is not thinly drawn in these cases, disorders like rickets or local bony tendencies to extensive growth may coexist with both conditions. Infantilism is peculiarly apt to occur with giantism, and while less frequent in dwarfism it also occurs, but is then especially apt to be associated with rickets.

Closely akin to these conditions are leontiasis ossium and acromegaly, both of which are characterised by similar trophoneurotic defects. The first of these conditions may occur precedent to puberty and cease in its completion. Kiernan has observed this in the case of an imbecile on Ward's Island, who lived until the age of 75, after spending more than sixty years in the charitable institutions of New York. His ancestry was of the criminal and defective classes. Acromegaly is characterised by abnormal growth, chiefly in the bones of the head, face, and extremities. As a rule, the disorder begins at the completion of puberty, although it occasionally occurs at the onset of the climacteric. The illustration given (Fig. 104) presents the characteristic features of the disease. In this case there are local evidences of congenital defect. The prevailing trend of opinion is that this condition is due to irregular action of the pituitary body which controls osseous development.

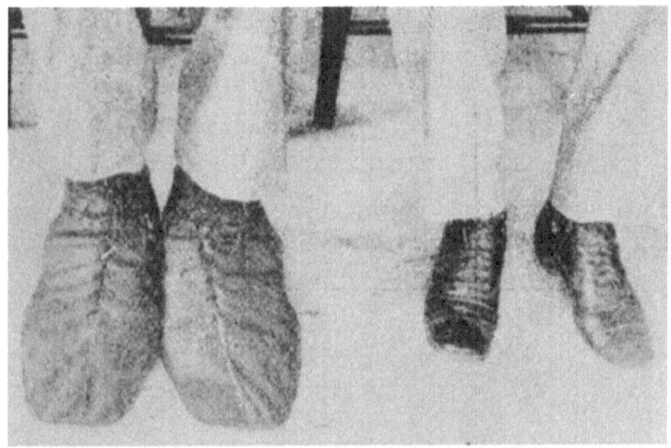

FIG. 105.

As already pointed out in the chapter on Heredity and Atavism, the arrests of development may affect one side of the body, while the other pursues the direct course of development. This may show itself in over-growth, as well as in under-growth, on the affected side. The person may appear, even from the centre of the forehead down, as if the halves of the bodies of two different persons had been joined in one. Conditions may vary from this extreme type to a state in which a lack of proper nerve and blood supply on the undeveloped side predisposes to attacks of disease, as already pointed out.

Not rarely does it happen that acromegaly attacks the side most deficient in nerve supply. The same is true of allied disorders affecting the growth of the muscles.

The conditions of development may be such that both sides are equally defective in nerve supply, so that when acromegaly occurs it may attack both sides equally. This is particularly apt to be the case with the lower extremities, and enlarged feet (Fig. 105) are not an uncommon result.

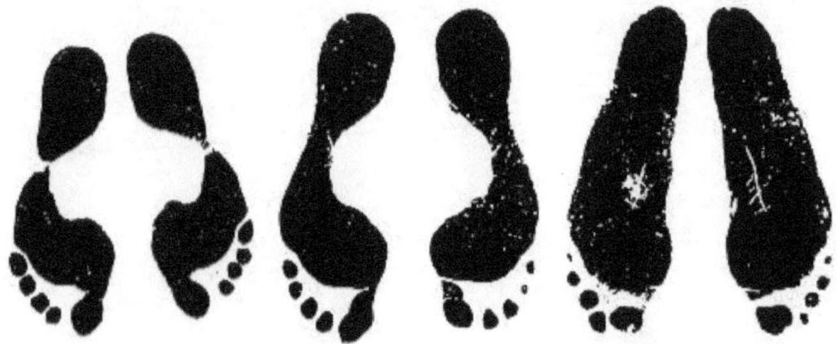

FIG. 106.

The feet, in addition to the condition already described as being common in both extremities, exhibit special stigmata of their own in consonance with the evolutionary advance which the foot has shown as compared with the hand in man's evolution. In the lower races the hollow of the foot does not exist, and the condition known as flat-foot occurs (Fig. 106). This is usually associated with low instep. It occurs among the stigmata of degeneracy, and is not rarely associated with grave moral defects and intellectual distortions. It and other feet degeneracies have been found frequently among paranoiacs, moral imbeciles, and prostitutes. This is particularly true of the prehensile power of the foot.[235]

CHAPTER XV

DEGENERACY IN REVERSIONAL TENDENCIES

THE hair of the head and body may never develop from the condition of down (lanugo) present in the new-born. The hair over the sexual organs may alone remain in this condition, not showing itself at puberty. In women the hair may be unusually developed on the face and chest. It may also cover the whole body, a condition which is normal in the Ainus of Japan. It may develop, as already shown, very markedly in the lumbar regions.

Speech may be markedly disturbed, reverting to the condition of Haeckel's Homo-alalus in the shape of deaf-mutism, which is one of the extreme expressions of degeneracy. Not less than 93 per cent. of the cases of congenital deaf-mutism possess deformities of the head, face, jaws, and teeth. The mere fact of the exceedingly primitive structure of the internal auditory mechanism has abnormal or defective hearing power as a consequence. Many cases of congenital deaf-mutism owe their origin to this, inasmuch as the auditory mechanism is not in a condition to appreciate sound, even though the individual may not have been born deaf, and the whole auditory apparatus subsequently degenerates. A mental defect is sometimes superadded, thus aggravating the case. Upon general principles, since deformities of the head, face, jaws, nose, antra, vaults, &c., are common in neurotics and degenerates, stigmata of the ear-bones must occasionally take place. From the complicated structure of the ear, lesions must often result from such deformities. The deaf- mutism here considered is the result of congenital conditions not produced by disease. Dumbness may result from congenital defects of the tongue or deformities of the larynx of an atavistic or a degenerate type, but degeneracy rarely extends so deeply into the organism as in the case of deaf-mutism. No greater error is committed than the confusion of deaf mutism secondary to ear disease with the congenital type.

The most prominent reversional tendencies occur in the genitals. One very common condition is retention of the testicles within the abdomen (*cryptorchidism*), which has been already pointed out, and may represent the last expiring trace of degeneracy. The testicles may, however, be perfectly normal in structure and function. In the female the uterus may present every type of mammalian uterus from the marsupial up. The female may also revert (as more rarely the male) to the condition of the reptiles and oviparous mammals in which the urinary organs and bowels empty into a single opening, the cloaca. This condition has been found in the female offspring of degenerate families, who are otherwise normal and who have produced children, despite the cloaca.

Another reversion is the occurrence of breasts without nipples, resembling those found in the oviparous mammals. The breasts in degenerates, as already shown, are frequently multiple, sometimes because the law of individuation is reversed, but more often as a reversion to the many-breasted condition (*polymastia*) of the precursor of man.[236] The human kidney and liver may revert not merely in function alone to the sauropsida, but also in structure.

The human heart may present in degenerates all types from the pulsating vessel found in the lancelet up to that of the mammal. The imperfect types of these sometimes perform their functions properly, except under strain. In other cases mixture of arterial and venous blood results, producing the so- called "blue babies."

Under the teachings of the extreme disciples of Morel, it has been assumed that the family of the degenerate tends to irrevocable extinction. On the principle of individuation already outlined from Spencer, degeneracy, through its tendency to generalise rather than specialise function, causes too rapid development of cells which tend to extinguish each other, thus preventing proper ovulation; and, in the next place, the same condition prevents proper development of the ovum if formed and fecundated; and, finally, causes too numerous simultaneous developments of ova, which would tend to destroy each other. The same cause produces also premature extrusion of ova. At the same time, however, under given conditions, this principle also tends to produce reversions in type in the shape of too frequently repeated and abnormally multiple births. It has been noted that even the ancestors of those predisposed to phthisis have numerous families and many children at a birth albeit most of these die ere reaching the sixth year. Marandon de Monteyel[237] finds that multiple and frequently repeated pregnancies often occur among the families of hereditary lunatics. This has been corroborated by Kiernan[238] and Harriet C. B. Alexander,[239] of Chicago, in connection with the hereditary lunatics in Cook County. They found that 90 families of the hereditary insane averaged 11 children each. Six families had 5 children, 4 had 7 children, 8 had 8, 10 had 9, 14 had 10, 8 had 11, 4 had 12, 4 had 13, 4
had 14, 3 had 16, 3 had 17, 4 had 18, 3 had 19, 5 had 20, and 1 had 21 children, each. Twins, triplets, and quadruplets were six times as frequent as among normal families. Manning has found similar conditions among the hereditary insane in Australia. Valenta, of Vienna,[240] has noted this also among epileptics. He reports the case of an epileptic mother who had 36 children, including six twins, four times quadruplets, twice triplets. Her

daughter, also an epileptic, bore 32 children before she was 40, including quadruplets twice, triplets four times, and twins once. Similar, though less striking, statistics occur with other classes of degenerates with proportionate frequency when the sterilising effect of certain diseases to which they are specially liable is taken into account. The general acceptance of the opinion as to large families being a test of advance in evolution seems strange when the extent and force of the action of the principle of individuation is taken into account, and when it is remembered how prolific are the lower vertebrates as compared with the higher.

The origin of tumours on the principle now adopted depends essentially on that reverse of the principle of individuation, illustrated in plural births.

One most striking expression of nutritive degeneracy is hæmophilia or the diathesis of the "bleeders." This, as Potain has pointed out, is not met with except in families which are subject to nutritive or graver degeneracies. Dent has shown that definite mental peculiarities, especially an inability (stronger than unwillingness) to tell the truth, are especially common in bleeders.[241] Hæmophilia was frequently encountered in the Valois[242] family, and has been met with in the descendants of Ernest the Pious of Hanover. The condition, as Osler,[243] of Baltimore, points out, is characterised by a tendency to uncontrollable bleeding, either spontaneous or from slight wounds. The hereditary transmission in this disorder is decided. In the Appleton-Swain family, of Reading, Mass., there have been cases for nearly two centuries. Instances have already occurred in the seventh generation. The usual mode of transmission is through the mother, who is not herself a bleeder, but the daughter of one. Atavism through the female is the rule. The daughters of a bleeder, though healthy and free from any tendency, are almost certain to transmit the disposition to the male offspring. The affection is much more common in males than in females, the proportion being estimated at 11 to 1, or even 13 to 1. The tendency usually appears within the first two years of life. It is rare for manifestations to be delayed until the tenth or twelfth year. Families in all conditions of life are affected. Bleeders, like other degenerates, may have large families; the members usually have fine soft skin. In all probability, as the researches of Cohn show, this condition is due to incomplete inhibition, resultant in excessive activity of the blood-making organs. Such inhibition is, of course, cerebral, and hence, as a later acquirement, readily affected by degeneracy which may find its chief expression in this defect.

Among the conditions that have been recognised as an expression of degeneracy is gout, which, as Fothergill long ago pointed out, is a reversion to the condition found in the sauropsidian liver and kidneys. Cullen had previously expressed the opinion that gout is a neurosis. Later researches tend to show that this neurosis is one controlling nutritive tissue change. The condition may occur early in childhood as well as at the periods of stress. The same is true of conditions like arthritis deformans, all of which may be the sole expression of degeneracy in an individual who exhibits many marked stigmata. Another expression of nutritive degeneracy is the senile atrophy of the skin described by Souques.[244] In a case of this kind under my care the patient, a twenty-six-year-old man, was born with club-foot. He has some musical talent. He is a marked degenerate. The skin is thick, coarse, and dry, giving him a very old appearance on account of its shrivelled condition. The ears are undeveloped, eyes small and sunken; excessive development of the cheek-bones; hair coarse and stiff; face arrested in development, possessing a partial V-shaped arch. The width outside first molar is 2; outside second bicuspid, 1·75; width of vault, 1·50; height of vault, ·58. One of the prominent features of degeneracy noticed in this case was the lack of hair upon the face.

Disorder of the thyroid produces both dwarfing cretinism, and a myxœdematous condition of the subcutaneous tissues, increasing the quantity of the jelly-like material in these, and therefore approximating some conditions found in the invertebrates. Ichthyosis (the skin disorder producing the "fish men" of shows) is frequently an expression of degeneracy, often associated with deficient limbs and monsters in the same family.

FIG. 107.

A condition due to heredity (involving an arterial change called arterio-capillary fibrosis) underlies many disorders like cirrhosis of the liver, kidneys, and other organs. It is usually an expression of premature senescence. Certain families for this reason exhibit a tendency to an early appearance of old age (Fig. 107), a tendency which, as Osler remarks, cannot be explained in any other way than that in the make-up of the machine bad material was used for tubing.

Obesity or lipomatosis is a nutritive expression of degeneracy especially noticeable in the second dentition, at puberty, and sometimes at the climacteric. As Féré has shown, lipomatosis (first noticed by Cruveilhier) is an expression of stress at the period of evolution. Youthful obesity occurs in descendants of degenerates. In my experience it is attended by great liability to disease and systemic weakness when under morbid influence. These lipomatosic children are liable to rheumatism (more properly gout) and great hemorrhage from slight causes. Youthful obesity is sometimes, as Féré remarks, associated with precocious maturity and resultant early senescence, but more often with extended infantilism, as in the case of Dickens's "fat boy."

In connection with this question of obesity I examined 267 corpulent school children and adults. Nearly all had marked stigmata of degeneracy; 92 per cent. had deformed ears to a marked degree; 66 per cent. had arrested development as compared with their age, while 12 per cent. presented excessive development; 34 were too young to show the final form and size of the jaw. Of the 34, in about 33⅓ per cent., the molars, incisors, cuspids and bicuspids were present; 96 per cent. of these had small teeth. Of the remaining 233, 87 per cent. had arrested development of the upper jaw, 22 per cent. of the lower jaw, 64 per cent. had V or saddle-shaped arches or their modifications and protruding teeth; 17 per cent. had hypertrophy of the alveolar process; 83 per cent. had small teeth; 27 per cent. had extra tubercles upon the molars; 82 per cent. had stenosis of the nasal cavity more or less marked; 36 per cent. had deflection of the nasal septum to the left, and 29 per cent. to the right; 21 per cent. wore glasses for eye defects. In 58 per cent. there was enlargement of the thyroid gland, and in 7 per cent. arrest of development of the same.

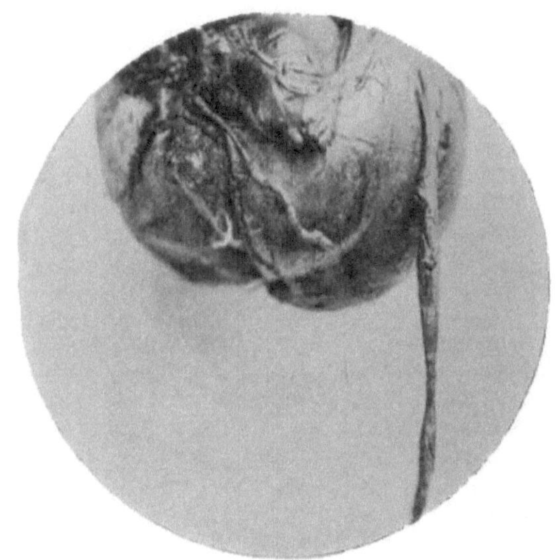

FIG. 108.

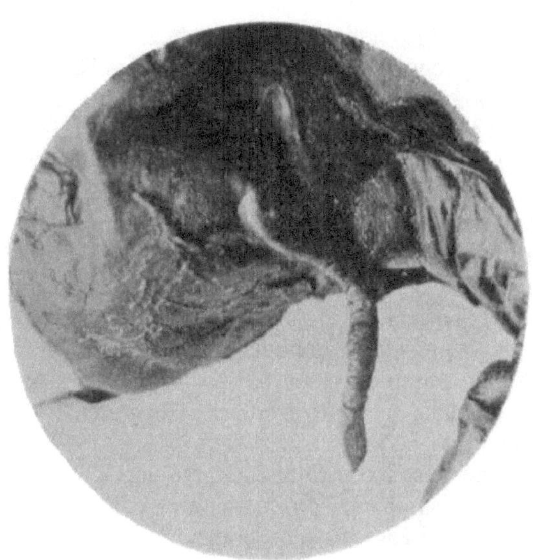

FIG. 109.

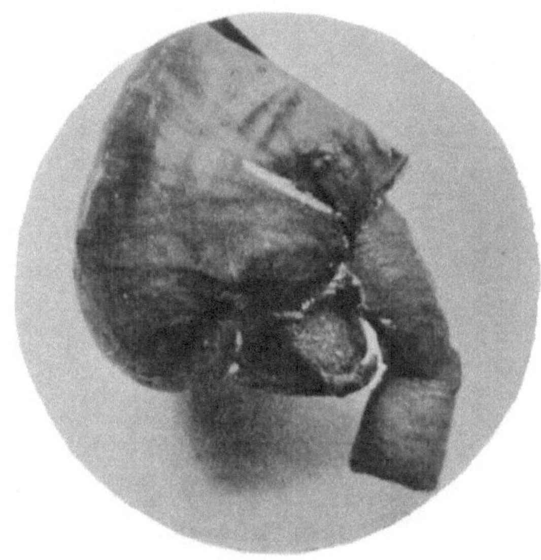

FIG. 110.

Among the structures of reversionary type that have attracted most attention of late years is the appendix vermiformis. This, as elsewhere shown, is a rudimentary offshoot which is extremely variable. Man retains this structure as a relic of having been at one time a vegetable feeder. In the koala (Australian native bear), a vegetable-feeding marsupial, it is more than thrice the size of the body. In the carnivora it has entirely vanished. In man, where it is sometimes absent and sometimes is as largely developed as in the orang, it is commonly from four to five inches in length and about a third of an inch in diameter. The appendix is poorly supplied with blood, which predisposes it to attacks by microbes because of the absence of leucocytes to fight these, and also because being, so to speak, a blind ally of the intestine, microbes find in it a suitable culture medium for them. The secretions of the appendix are very apt to decompose: hence a culture medium. The extreme variability of this disappearing organ may be judged from the Figs. 108, 109, 110. As it is best developed in degenerates, it constitutes in them one source of predisposition to death from blood poisoning or from sudden shock. The location of this organ also tends to facilitate disease. In degenerates it may be situated at any point upon the end of the big bowel, varying from two to three inches. This little bowel is worse than useless in man, being a source of serious danger. It is an instance of checked development of the same kind which causes the human liver to take on sauropsidian peculiarities. Man in this particular as well as the orang is lower than the carnivora, who have lost this worse than useless organ. Its tendency to disappearance in man indicates once more the truth that degeneracy of an organ is often, through the law of economy of growth, for the benefit of the organism as a whole.

I may conclude this outline of human reversionary tendencies by mentioning that merycism, or rumination, has been very frequently found among imbeciles, paranoiacs, hysterics, and epileptics.

CHAPTER XVI

DEGENERACY OF THE BRAIN

ONE illustration, and a very striking one, of the influence of degeneracy on the brain is the durencephalous child which so often appears in degenerate families. Here the cerebral hemispheres and everything but the medulla and pons may be absent, while the rest of the body is in a comparatively normal state of development. Starting with such an extreme expression of degeneracy in the brain, a wide but closely linked range of deficiencies may be found in the brain of degenerates, involving even in some almost normal individuals more than simple deficiency. What was pointed out by Spitzka,[245] of New York, twenty years ago concerning the brain of hereditary lunatics, is equally true of the brains of the other degenerate branches of the same tree. The conventional notion associating idiocy and imbecility with quantitative deficiency of the forebrain only is, as Spitzka remarked, a very imperfect one. The researches of numerous observers have shown that qualitative defects (using the term qualitative in its wider sense to cover both morphologic and histologic aberrations) are as common, and are more characteristic features of the degenerate brain. These defects may be enumerated under the following heads: 1. Atypical asymmetry of the cerebral hemispheres as regards bulk. 2. Atypical asymmetry in the gyral development. 3. Persistence of embryonic features in the gyral arrangement. 4. Defective development of the great interhemispherical commisure. 5. Irregular and defective development of the great ganglia and of the conducting tracts. 6. Anomalies in the development of the minute elements or neurons (as the cells and associating of fibres are now generally called) of the brain. 7. Abnormal arrangements of the cerebral vascular channels. All of these conditions, separately or in the combination of several of the features above mentioned, are occasionally found in the brain of paranoiacs, moral imbeciles, criminals, deaf-mutes and other degenerates. Of the first type the brain (Fig. 111), from the practice of Kiernan, is an excellent illustration. This brain came from a paranoiac criminal who died in the Chicago (Cook County) Insane Hospital. A very similar brain was observed by Kiernan in one of the paranoiacs dying in the New York City Insane Hospital. Similar brains have been observed in deaf-mutes[246] whose mental status passed muster because of the allowance made for mental deficiency due to deaf-muteness. A brain showing as great asymmetry was found in the case of a French physician of standing who was a member of a mutual autopsy society. He proved, however, to have had degenerates in his ancestry and had exhibited peculiarities which showed that much of the degeneracy due to this ancestry had been corrected by proper training. The defects enumerated under Spitzka's second head are also observable in the illustration given. The gyres are not only asymmetrical as to their number in the two hemispheres, but also as to their size. The contrast between this brain and the ideally normal one of the mathematician Gauss[247] (Fig. 112) could not well be greater. Both of these as regards complexity of gyres contrast very decidedly with both the fœtal brain given by Bastian (Fig. 113) and the idiot brain (Fig. 114) of a patient of Kiernan. The persistency of embryonic features in the gyral arrangement is excellently illustrated in Fig. 115, which represents the brain of an imbecile examined by Spitzka. Here the convolutions in general were few, large, and well marked.[248] The occipital and parietal lobes preponderated in mass as compared with the temporal and frontal. The latter were greatly hollowed out on the orbital face, and the gyri here found were few, simple, and atypical. On the whole the convolutions of the right hemisphere were better marked and the secondary folds more numerous than those of the left hemisphere, and the type of the convolutions presented differences on the two sides. The most pronounced differences were exhibited in the island of Reil and in the occipital lobe. The island of Reil on the left side had fewer and flatter gyri than that of the right side, and resembled in its general aspect the first impression of the brain of an orang-outang. The right island had six folds better marked than those of the left side, but their type was more decidedly radiatory, which was in relation with the unusual shortening of the insular field. The external perpendicular occipital sulcus which Bischoff never found in the adult human brain (but which has been found persistent in a case of imbecility with moral perversion by Sander and in a sane neurotic individual by Meynert) was finely marked upon the right side of the brain under consideration. The fissure was very deep, its posterior wall was slightly bevelled, and covered several secondary gyri of its anterior walls. It differed in position from the similar fissures described by Meynert and Sander in that it did not, as in these cases, unite with the internal perpendicular occipital sulcus and thus simulate the arrangement found in the anthropoid apes. It was merely the unobliterated external occipital fissure of the embryo, and, as in the latter, its medial end if prolonged would have fallen behind the internal perpendicular occipital sulcus. The anomaly consisted therefore in the preservation of an embryonic feature. The arrest of development involved the generally better developed hemisphere. On the left side gyri and sulci were few and simple but typical, the external perpendicular occipital sulcus being interrupted by a broad crossing gyrus. On transverse vertical sections through the hemispheres the average vertical thickness is found to be the same on both sides and normal. The great ganglia were of relatively large dimension, and the white mass of the hemisphere, aside from the internal capsule and the other detachments mediating the connection of the cortex with lower centres, relatively reduced. The caudate nucleus appeared to be of bolder contour on the right side. The right lenticular nucleus presented a larger section area by about 25 per cent. than its fellow of the opposite side. It was much shorter, however, like the insular territory of the same side, and in corresponding sections the posterior end of the left lenticular nucleus was struck while the right was absent. The right nucleus was rounder, the left more triangular in contour in corresponding altitudes. The olivary bodies were asymmetrical, the right one being flatter and smoother than the left. On transverse sections no difference between the olivary nuclei beyond that which occurs in healthy persons could be found; the asymmetry was ascertainably one of prominence only. There was one morphologic appearance noticeable in the fourth layer of the paracentral cortex. This consisted of the presence of round bodies comparable to the nuclei of nerve cells within a thin or no mantle of protoplasm, and presenting every gradation from the free nuclei of the neurolgia, so called, to nerve cells with imperfect processes. These bodies in the human cortex represent imperfectly developed nerve cells and are normally found in the cortex of lower animals. The barren layer or ependyma of the cortex was in places twice as thick in this brain as in the brain of normal beings. This ependyma is the histologic factor of the enormous weight of macrocephalic brains. In a macrocephalic case coming under the observation of Kiernan, of Chicago, in which the brain weighed 68 ounces, the ependyma was five times the normal thickness. The conditions to which Spitzka refers are more or less constantly found in degeneracy. The readiness with which any form of the degenerate series may undergo a metamorphosis into another in the course of hereditary transmission is not, Spitzka remarks, interpretable in any other light than that of the transmission of structure defects either intensified or mitigated in the course of such transmission.

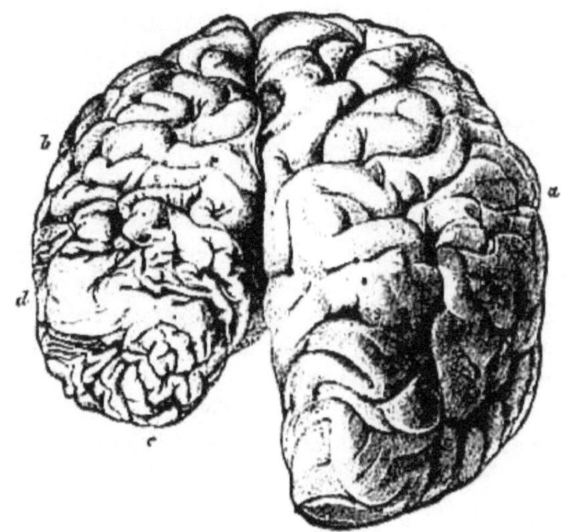

FIG. 111.

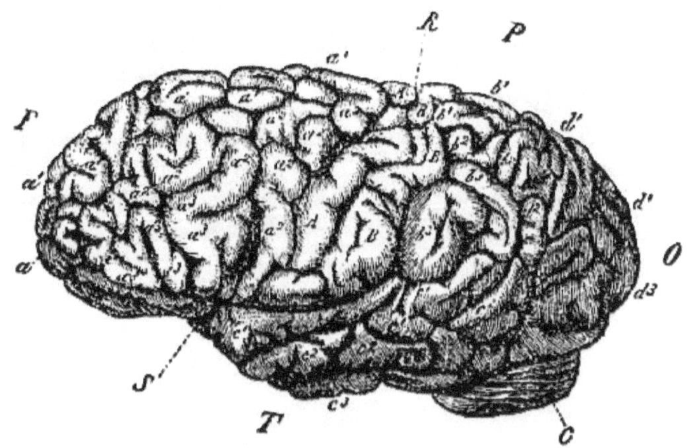

FIG. 112.

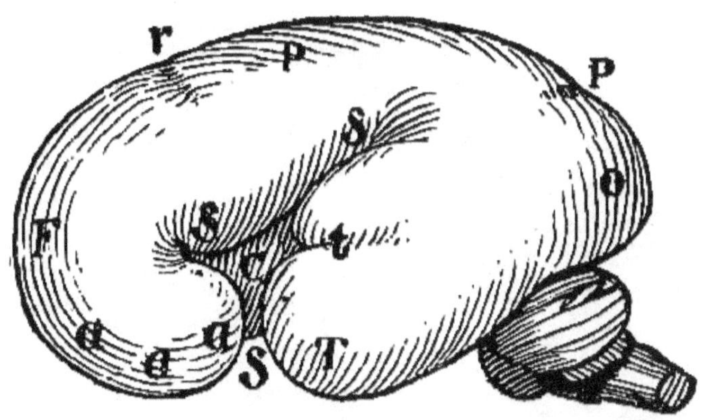

FIG. 113.

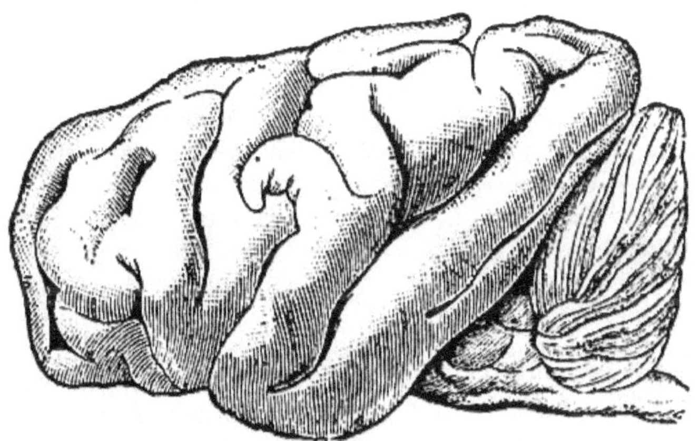

FIG. 114.

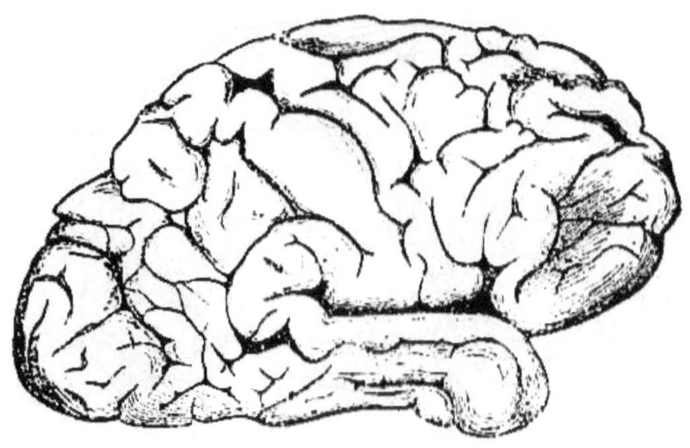

FIG. 115.

Transmission of many of these cerebral defects occurs at the moment of conception. The embryonic mechanism of these defects, and the influence which fœtal and maternal impressions and injuries exert on the development of the nerve centres, furnish valuable argument by analogy in support of conclusions regarding the degeneracy group. Embryologists imitate known natural teratological states of the nerve centres by artificial methods. By wounding the embryonic and vascular areas of the chick's germ with a cataract needle malformations are induced, varying in intensity and character with the earliness of the injury and its precise extent. More delicate injuries produce less monstrous development. It is particularly the partial varnishing or irregular heating of the egg-shell that results in the production of anomalies comparable to microcephaly and cerebral asymmetry. The constancy of the injurious effect of so apparently slight an impression as the partial varnishing of a structure not directly connected with the embryo at all, suggests a most plausible explanation of maternal and other impressions acting on the germ. The delicate problems in this connection may be inferred from the observations of Dareste that eggs transported in railroad cars, and thus subject to the vibration and repeated shocks of a railroad journey, are checked in development for several days. A less coarse molecular transmission taking place during the maturation of the ovum or its fertilisation, or, finally, during the embryonic stages of the more complex and hence more readily disturbed and distorted human germ, would account for the disastrous effects of insanity, emotional explosions, and mental or physical shocks of either parent on the offspring.

For the majority of cerebral deformities the causes of the deformity must exist in the germ prior to the appearance of the separate organs of the body. Artificial deformities produce analogous results because they imitate original germ defects either by mechanical removal or by some other interference with a special part of the germ. Early involvement of the germ is shown in the fact that the somatic malformation in degeneracy often involves other parts of the body than the nervous axis: defective development of the uro-genital system, deformities in the face, skull, irregularities of the teeth, misshapen ears and limbs.

Those who seek for the source of the arrested or perverted brain development in the reaction of an abnormally growing and ossifying skull on the skull contents are in error. The premature ossification theory does not hold good even for the microcephali; it is to be doubted if it ever had any justification in view of the often open character of the sutures. Taking the well-studied cases of asymmetry, the variability of a single factor shows that caution is needed in referring cerebral anomalies to any single influence. In Muhr's case (cited by Spitzka) the atrophic cerebellar hemisphere was on the same side with the atrophic cerebral hemisphere. The internal carotid artery of that side was of lesser calibre and the entire skull half shortened. Here the lagging behind in growth of one half of the skull appears on first sight to explain the retarded development of the corresponding halves of the cerebrum and cerebellum. In view of the atypy of the gyri, however, an atypy not to be explained purely on mechanical grounds, it is more reasonable to believe that the imperfect development of certain vascular channels was either concomitant or secondary to a primitive anomaly of the cerebral hemisphere. The retarded skull growth would have to be looked upon as a tertiary occurrence and the cerebellar defect as a final ensuing result. Ordinarily with defective development of one cerebral hemisphere the cerebellar defect is on the opposite side, herein following the course of the anatomical connections of that development and of the secondary degenerations. The deviation from this rule in Muhr's case was due to the entering of the abnormal skull-shape, itself secondary to other defects, as an element influencing brain growth at a special period of development. An abnormal shape of the skull, generally associated with a cerebral defect, and hence valuable as a physical sign presumably indicating mental anomalies, may exert an important modifying influence at a late period on the contained brain, but the grosser defects in the cerebral architecture must antedate the period of skull growth and be deeply planted as an original intrinsic fault in the brain blastema itself. The researches of His have shown how important for the definitive shape of the body and its organs are the position of individual cells, the portion of the germ area, the convexity and length of germ curves and the relative rate of growth of different germ areas. And as the experiments of other embryologists have established the possibility of producing monstrosities analogous to cerebral defects by altering the conditions ever so slightly, the general conclusion follows that the fundamental error of development at the foundation of malformations associated with degeneracy is to be located at a very early period of embryonic, or possibly of ovuline life. Certain of these anomalies are due to a disturbance of the balance between the growth of the epiblast and mesoblast derivatives of the brain, others to a disharmony in the development of related associated brain segments; in the severer cases both elements are combined.

It is not difficult to perceive the relation existing between a defective brain weight, paucity of the gyri, deficiency of properly developed cortical cells and such an elementary form of mental aberration as simple imbecility. The subject of the relation between structure and function gains in interest when we leave this domain of simple mental weakness to analyse the relation between structural defects and the positive symptoms of insanity and degeneracy—that is, moral perversion, mental obliquity, delusions, and morbid impulses. Such symptoms are not limited to the higher forms of the degenerate series; they occur, though less constantly and less markedly, in the lower forms.

C. K. Mills,[249] of Philadelphia, on examination of imbecile, paranoiac, and criminal brains, found atypical asymmetry as to gyral and fissure development present. The features of this atypical asymmetry were the existence of a Sylvian fissure shorter on one side than the other, both absolutely and comparatively, and also a more vertical direction of the fissure on one side than on the other, greater exposure of the insula on one side with marked differences in the development of its fissures and gyri, confluence of the central fissure with the Sylvian on one side only, and great tortuosity or bridging of the former fissure in one hemisphere, unusual narrowness, straightness of complication of the precentral or postcentral gyrus on one side; marked difference in the simplicity of complexity of the frontal lobes, great simplicity of the orbital surface on one side, differences in the parietal fissure as to length and interruption, a smaller parietal or marginal or angular gyrus on one side, very great difference in the degrees of confluence and interruption of the fissures in general, exceeding great length vertically of the supertemporal or parallel fissure on one side, unusual differences in the size of the precuneus and cuneus.

A. W. Wilmarth,[250] of Philadelphia, Pa., after a careful study of idiots and imbeciles ranging in intellectual power from the idiot, properly so-called, to the juvenile criminal, paranoiac, and "ne'er-do-well," finds that the brains of these vary greatly along the line pointed out by Spitzka and Mills. One type of brain in this class of children is very simple in its outward configuration. The convolutions are usually coarse, but little convoluted and comparatively free from secondary folds. The fissures tend to assume a confluent type. Another variety, found chiefly among the lowest grades, might well be termed "atypic." A brain without a corpus callosum is a marked example. In the frontal lobe of the right hemisphere the first frontal convolution is quite regular. Below this from the centre of the lobe seven fissures passed in different directions, cutting the tube into a number of radiating convolutions, entirely different from its usual appearance. The short fissure of Sylvius (about three inches in length) passed upward, turned sharply, and passed almost directly behind. Two parallel gyri curved around its posterior extremity. The arrangement of the convolutions of the temporal and parietal lobes were so exceedingly irregular and complex that it was impossible to classify them. In the occipital lobe, on the contrary, the gyri were complete in number and of regular arrangements. In the left hemisphere the arrangement of the frontal convolutions was more regular, but the temporal and parietal lobes presented the same complicated area of surface folding, bearing but little resemblance to the normal brain. The tendency of the convolutions to arrange themselves in parallel curves around the posterior extremity of the fissure of Sylvius was well shown in the brain of a boy of exceedingly low intellect. The frontal lobes in this brain are proportionately large; the convolutions straight, especially the third frontal, the fissures shallow. In the left temporal lobe they are nearly obliterated from pressure of fluid in the ventricles. The ascending frontal convolution on each side appears to be wanting. On the left side a large bridging convolution crosses the middle of the fissure of Rolando. Confluence of fissure is a decided feature of idiot brains. Even where confluence is not complete, the tendency of the principal fissure to cut through separating convolutions is very evident. Were the cases where confluence is nearly complete included, the number would be considerably augmented. The fissure of Sylvius passed into the fissure of Rolando in one case on both sides, in another on one side only. In two other cases they were connected by deep secondary fissures. The interparietalis has its origin in the fissure of Sylvius in four cases on both sides, in five cases on one side only. The calcarine fissure passed completely across the gyrus frontitatus on both sides in two cases, on one side in four cases. In one case the first occipital convolution sank nearly beneath the surface, the next occipital gyrus projecting over it, forming a parietal operculum. There also seems to be a strong tendency to form annectant gyri in the upper part of the parieto-occipital fissure. In no less than six hemispheres of 15 brains were these supplementary gyri found more or less complete. In one case on both sides, in five cases on one side, the parieto-occipital fissure cut through the first occipital convolution into the interparietal fissure. A tendency of the transverse occipital fissure to approach the parieto-occipital fissure is very apparent, though in no case do they coincide. The folds of the cerebral cortex, from a lack of the stimulus of healthy growth, sometimes revert to forms resembling those found in other groups of the animal kingdom.

The fundamental factors of thought and action, as Spitzka terms them, are two: perceptions and motor innervation. These are, in other words, the units of thought and action. They can be properly referred to nerve cell groups as their anatomical seat, and, as far as intellect is in question, to the cell group represented in the more or less diffused and dovetailing areas of specialised function in the cortex cerebri (Fig. 116). But the largest hemisphere known, with the most crowded and most highly developed nerve cells, and the most extensive connections with the periphery, and the most perfect projection of that periphery in its intricately convoluted mass would, functionally speaking, represent nothing but a mass of pigeon-holed impressions stored away without method and without purpose, useless to the organism were it not for those arched fibres uniting the different cortical centres with each other.

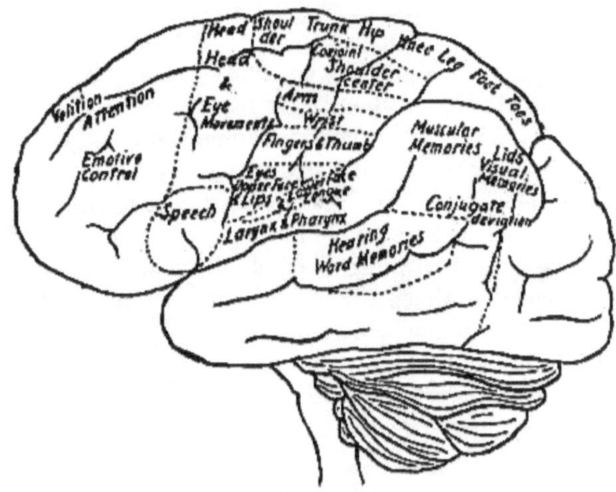

FIG. 116.

These fibre constitute by far the greater part of the white centrum oval of the hemisphere. The total transverse section of the crus and the fibre masses from the thalamus and basilar ganglia, does not comprise more than one-third of the entire mass. In the lower animal this relation is different. The projecting fibres, such as those of crus and capsule and the great ganglia, are not as massive as in man, but they are nearly equal to, and in still lower forms exceed, those connecting the gyri with each other. Hence the chief point of contrast noted on examining a transverse frontal section through the cerebral hemisphere of a man and an ape consists in the mass of the centrum ovale of Vieussens. The whole substance in man actually appears hypertrophied when compared with that of lower animals. It is the associating fibres which mainly mediate that complex co-ordination of the separate units of thought and action which constitute the anatomical basis of the highest mental functions (Fig. 117). The study of the human mind does not resolve itself merely into an analysis of individual faculties such as simple perceptions and motor innervations, but above all requires the establishment of their synthesis into the complex abstractions on which the ego depends.

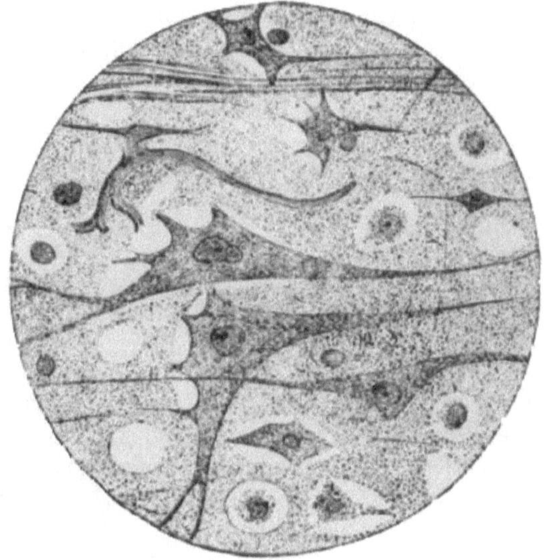

FIG. 117.

Neither anatomic nor physiologic researches are calculated to demonstrate just what associating fasciculi or what groups of such fasciculi are subservient to any particular co-ordination. Where, for example, the cortical area for vision overlaps that of the centre for forearm and hand, the associating fasciculus underlying the debatable land is subservient to the co-ordinations employed in writing and drawing. In like manner a similar associating bond extending from the centre of auditory word symbols to that of the tongue and lip centres may be considered a chief factor mediating the speech co-ordinations. A child originally has no adequate notion of distance or perspective, but will, in the first week of life, grasp at objects fifty feet away. Its first ideas of space are gathered from its own skin sensations; it learns to distinguish between single impressions when touching foreign bodies, and associated double ones as when it touches a part of its own body. In great part this may even be accomplished by an active infant during the last months of utero-gestation; it has learned thus to separate the conception of its own body from the confused chaos which all impressions originally constitute to the infant; the next lesson is to learn that to reach certain objects it moves a certain distance, while others are immediately in reach. It then discovers, therefore, that the discrimination by the eye is possible, since intervening objects which it has learned to measure by its own body or bodily movements as a gauge permit an approximate judgment of distance, in aid of which comes experiment in the shape of time requirements, since to go so far requires such time, while to go further requires a much greater. The crude ideas of space at this time must involve areas in the cortex devoted to motion and to general sensation situated in the Rolandic region. Those devoted to visual impressions are largely situated in the occipital region, and those devoted to time may be located in the frontal lobes. Further analysis of the more elaborate sense of space possessed by adults, involving the play of equilibrium and the appreciation of movement and direction in foreign objects, shows that cortical areas situated in nearly every part of the hemispheres are subsidiary to it and connected by fibre tracts of different lengths and courses. It is evident, therefore, that the mal-connection of cortical centres is at the root of various tropho-neurotic, nervous, mental, moral and other perversions exhibited in degenerates. Deformity and deficiency of the corpus callosum in some degenerates is but an expression of general defect of associating tracts. Convolutional aberration in others is but an expression of imperfect development of end stations and fibre systems. All mental and moral disturbances are associated with perversions of the functions of the cerebral hemisphere, but the converse, that cerebral hemisphere lesions only are the essential accompaniments of mental symptoms evinced during life, is not true. Lesions of the pons, the crura, and thalami are accompanied by more or less complete obliteration of consciousness, blurring of the perception, confusion in the intellectual sphere, even where the lesion is not of such a character as to disturb the neighbouring ganglia by pressure. Two explanations are possible of this phenomenon. Either the vaso-motor centre for the cortical vessels is under the control of isthmus ganglia partially, and hence isthmus lesions by irritation or destruction of the centre excite or paralyse the vascular tubes of certain cortical districts, or pathologic interruption of the great nerve tracts involves functional disturbance of cortical end stations. The first explanation is applicable in cases where general and widespread disturbance, somnolence, excitement, or depression are found. The latter where the disturbance is partial in character. If all avenues of sensory perception be closed unconsciousness in the way of sleep speedily follows. Interruption of the perception tracts is followed by corresponding phenomena, though less extensive when occurring in the isthmus territory. That an irritative lesion in the line of the centripetal tracts can influence cortical life is shown by thalamus lesions in which hallucinations are sometimes present. Here the cause of the hallucinations is in the lower centre, but the entry of these into the intellectual sphere can take place only in the cortical termination of that tract, since at this point only through the connecting associating tracts can it become a part of the ego.

Meynert traced an enormous division of the crus directly to the frontal lobe and the lenticular nucleus, and showed that this portion through the transverse fibres of the pons was of necessity connected with the cerebellum, and that far other functions are to be located in the cortex than merely muscular innervation, visual and auditory perceptions. The restiform columns derived from spinal fibres enter the cerebellum and terminate chiefly in its hemispheres. The cortex of these hemispheres is connected by radiatory fibres, with the dentated nucleus, which is a recipient of fibres of the auditory nerve. The cortex of the cerebellar hemisphere receives fibres both from the sensorial periphery of the body and the semicircular canals. From this reception area the transverse fibres of the pons originate and enter the crus. It is these which enter the frontal lobe and lenticular nucleus. In no respect does man so much differ from the ape as in the quantitative development of these fasciculi. Their development is intimately associated with the mass of the frontal lobe, and there is every reason for considering them the channel of information of the equilibrium and possibly of the senses of space and time, on which the scope of the mind is so closely dependent. Lesions in these tracts may disturb these sensations, and the entire mental architecture may totter with the withdrawal or weakening of so important pillars. The congenital asymmetry of the peduncular tracts observed in certain cases of mental and moral perversion are not without bearing on the symptoms of those cases. And this explanation would be adjunct to the principle of mal- development of the associating tracts here advanced in explanation of other symptoms of these same states. It is a logical truism that complex cerebral functions have a complex substratum. Nothing could be more unphilosophical, for example, than to speak of "intellectual cells" (Denkzellen) in the cerebral <u>cortex</u>. Simple elements can have but simple functions; complex functions require a union of numerous simpler elements in a complex structural combination.

Such symptoms as epileptic explosions are admittedly connected with no demonstrable anatomical aberration, and yet when epileptic explosions of a certain type are found associated with a cortical lesion they are to be regarded as symptoms of that lesion. Morbid projects, delusions, and moral perversion are simply functional perversions of a properly built cerebral mechanism or the outcome of a visible structural defect. And when the latter is palpably attributable to an error in development and occurs with a certain constancy in similar cases, a fundamental relation must be assumed between the defect and the general tenor of the symptoms.

There is a great difference clinically between the effect of congenital and acquired lesions. When porencephaly (a deformity originally studied by Heschl) dates from infantile or fœtal life, imbecility is always present during life; but where it is developed in the matured brain imbecility does not necessarily result.

Deficiencies in the cerebral vascular system underlie the pathological phenomena on the basis of infantile cerebral paralysis, and allied hereditary and congenital states. The degenerate conditions in the spinal cord are essentially those described by Spitzka as occurring in the brain. Vascular states, either as to irregularities in the number of vessels or in the vessels themselves, underlie, as in the case of the cerebral palsies, hereditary ataxias and other congenital and hereditary spinal cord disorders.[251]

CHAPTER XVII

DEGENERACY OF MENTALITY AND MORALITY

IN the mental and moral degeneracies there is a complete transition from the durencephalic monster through the microcephalus, the idiot, the imbecile, and the feeble-minded to the mentally normal individual. Between the feeble-minded and the normal individual occurs a group whose general characteristics is, as was pointed out by Magnan, a disharmony and lack of equilibrium, not only between the intellectual operations, properly so-called on the one hand, and the emotions and propensities on the other, but even between the intellectual faculties themselves. A degenerate may be a scientist, an able lawyer, a great artist, a poet, a mathematician, a politician, a skilled administrator, and present from a moral standpoint profound defects, strange peculiarities and surprising lapses of conduct. As the moral element—the emotions and propensities—is the base of determination, it follows that these brilliant faculties are at the service of a bad cause, of the instincts and appetites which, thanks to the defects of the will, lead to very extravagant or very dangerous acts. In other cases the opposite occurs. Degenerates of irreproachable character show strange defects in their intellect. They often have a feeble memory in certain directions. Sometimes they cannot understand figures, or music, or drawing. In a word, an otherwise normal individual's intelligence is lacking as regards certain faculties. The centres of perception are unequally impressionable, unequally apt to gather together impressions, only certain impressions are registered and leave durable images; certain relations, certain associations between different centres, are perverted or even entirely destroyed.

The mental stigmata of degeneracy, therefore, may be divided into those involving the moral elements (in which case there is no very striking intellectual disorder) and those involving the intellectual elements, in which the conditions may be divided into states where intellectual disorder alternates with periods of complete lucidity or with neuroses (periodical insanity, neuroticism, hysteria, and epilepsy), and states in which the intellectual disorder is a permanent quantity (paranoia, one-sided genius, imbecility, and idiocy). Great as is the apparent gap between idiocy and one-sided genius, on the one hand, and between idiocy and crime, on the other, this gap is, as already stated, filled by numerous closely interlinked forms, dependent on the proportionate removal of checks (which the race has acquired during evolution) on the explosive expressions of egotism and mentality. The removal of these checks is dependent on the removal or weakening of the power of associating tracts, to which reference has been made in connection with the degenerate brain. The idiot, capable only of purely vegetative functions, who would perish were food not placed far back in his mouth, is one step lower than the normal infant, who is essentially, as has been remarked, an egotistic parasite. On slightly increased development this idiot, with the powers of a rather low animal, gains food and satisfies its instincts. These instincts at this stage may manifest themselves in the explosive manner characteristic of the undomesticated and non-social animals. With these instincts may appear others which man has long lost; thus an idiot girl (who was delivered of an infant when alone) gnawed through the umbilical cord in the manner of animals, thus effecting separation and preventing hæmorrhage. At still a higher stage the imbecile may manifest destructive instincts, may steal without the signs of remorse displayed by a housebred dog, or may kill without recognising the results of killing. The intellect may be comparatively developed in certain imbeciles in comparison with the ethical defects. For lack of proper associating fibres, the imbecile may be unable to acquire those higher associations constituting the secondary ego, in the most elevated sense. To this class ultimately belong the instinctive homicides, torturers, sexual criminals and thieves, so frequently found among the juvenile offspring of degenerate stock. In them the primary ego is strong, and the restraints of the secondary ego, which perceives the rights of others, weakened or completely absent. This class forms the germ of the congenital criminal whom no discipline can tame, and who is incapable of being taught the dangers of his procedures under the law of the land. Between this class and the paranoiac there is at once a curious likeness and distinction. The lack of proper associating powers prevents the moral imbecile from recognising any rights of others. The same lack in the paranoiac prevents him from recognising the force and rights of other people in opinion. The moral imbecile has lost the greatest acquirement of the race in evolution, that acquirement which fully recognises the secondary ego in accordance with the sublime precept, "Do unto others as ye would that they should do unto you."

For practical purposes the division of criminals given by Tyndall is sufficient. Crime is essentially an anti-social factor, and violations of law can be regarded as crimes only in proportion as they are anti-social. The essential character of crime is its parasitic nature. Parasites, in a general way, may be divided into those which live on their host, without any tendency to injure his well-being (like the dermodex in the skin follicles); those which live more or less at his expense, but do not tend to destroy him; and, finally, those which are destructive of the well-being of man and lack proper recognition of individual rights which constitutes the essential foundation of society. The first type is impurely represented by the idiots, imbeciles, lunatics, paupers by deprivation, blind, crippled, senile, insane, and deaf mutes. Society, either indirectly or directly, has been the source of the parasitic state of many of these, and hence, as also in the case of law-made criminals, such parasitism really takes nothing from society. The second class is represented by prostitutes, sexual degenerates, paupers, and inebriates. Some of these, however, could be put into the third class, among those moral lunatics and criminals who fail to recognise that individual rights constitute social order. Prostitutes, paupers, and inebriates have this in common, that crime in them has taken the line of least resistance. The great ethical defect in the prostitute is not lack of checks on explosive sexual propensities so much as the use of these last as a method of living by her wits. In essence prostitution is the expression of the criminal tendency manifested by the confidence operator. The researches of sociologists like Chaplain Merrick,[252] of the Millbank Prison, London, show that at least one-half of the prostitutes leave their homes voluntarily to take up a "life of pleasure." Pauline Tarnowsky[253] finds that in Russia prostitution is crime in women taking the line of least resistance. The prostitutes, like the other criminals, are divisible into criminals on occasion (vice, monetary reasons, &c.), accidental criminals, law-made criminals, weak-willed criminals, and insane criminals. The proportion of the law-made and accidental criminals among the prostitutes is much less than among other criminals, as Merrick has shown. Seduction stands very low in the list of causes. The proportion of the occasional criminal type is very large. Pauline Tarnowsky concludes from her researches, which my own tend to verify, that the prostitute, as a rule, is a degenerate being, the subject of an arrest of development, tainted with a morbid heredity, and presenting stigmata of physical and mental degeneracy fully in consonance with her imperfect evolution. C. Andronico, of Messina, Italy, arrived some time previously[254] at the same conclusions as those of Tarnowsky. Tarnowsky found that 44⅓ per cent. of the prostitutes had skull deformities, 42^2 face deformities, 42 ear deformities, and 54 teeth deformities. Andronico found among 230 prostitutes the following anomalies: Flat nose, 20; handle-shaped ear, 35; vicious implantation of teeth, 10; convergent strabismus, 2; facial asymmetry, 4; prognathism, 7; receding forehead, 35. Grimaldi, in a study of 26 prostitutes, had similar results to those of Tarnowsky. Lombroso, in an examination of 50 prostitutes, found exaggerated jaws, 27 times; plagiocephaly, 23 times; nasal asymmetry, 8 times; exaggerated zygomæ, 40 times. Tarnowsky found that in

150 prostitutes, taken at random from those answering to the necessary conditions (uniformity of race, ability to give their family history and years of residence in licensed houses), there were present signs of physical degeneracy in 87. Among the abnormalities were oxycephaly, platycephaly, stenocephaly, plagiocephaly, and heads with marked depression either at the bregma or the

lambda. The majority had a marked development of the external occipital protuberance; in an equal number of virtuous women it was present but four times. These and other anomalies were thus distributed among the 150 prostitutes: Malformation of the head (oxycephaly, plagiocephaly, &c.), noticed in 62; development of the occipital protruberance, 62; very receding foreheads, 18; hydrocephalic, 15; various anomalies of the face (prognathism, asymmetry), 64; ogival palatine vault, 38; congenital division of palate, 14; vicious implantation of teeth, 62; Hutchinson's and Parrot's teeth, 19; absence of lateral incisors, 10; Morel ears, 16; defective ears (detached from head, deformed, &c.), 47; anomalies of the extremities, 8.

In my researches in the same class, with the assistance of Harriet C. B. Alexander and J. G. Kiernan, the subjects chosen were those committed to the Chicago House of Correction. They are the least intelligent of Chicago's professional prostitutes. The number examined was 30. As regards the race they included 13 Celtic-Irish, 5 Irish-American, 3 Scandinavian, 1 German, 1 German-American, 2 American, 1 English-American, 1 Latin-Swiss, 2 Negro.

It should here be remembered that the "fine" system of Chicago places only the "obtuse" class in the Bridewell. One was seventeen years old, two eighteen years, one nineteen years, five between twenty and twenty-five years, three between twenty-five and thirty, six between thirty and thirty-five, five between thirty-five and forty-five, one was forty-six years old, two were fifty-five, three sixty-one, and one sixty-five. There were eighteen blondes, ten brunettes, and two negroes. Four were demonstrably insane and one was an epileptic.

In sixteen cases the zygomatic processes were unequal and very prominent. There were fourteen other asymmetries of the face. Three heads were Mongoloid (one Irish-Celt, one Swiss, and one Scandinavian). There are Mongoloid race types in the regions where all three come from. Sixteen were epignathic and eleven prognathic. In one there was arrested development of the lower jaw, and in four arrested development of the face bones. The nose was abnormal in six. There were sixteen brachycephalic and thirteen mesaticephalic skulls. There were no dolichocephalic skulls. There were three with oxycephalic skulls, of whom one was a Celt, one a German, and one a Scandinavian. There were eighteen dome-type skulls, of whom seven were Irish-Celts, five Celtic-American, one English Anglo-Saxon, one American Anglo-Saxon, and one German-American. There were four tectocephalic skulls, of whom one was an Irish-Celt, one an Anglo-Saxon American, and one a Scandinavian. There were three platycephalic skulls, of whom two were Celts and one a Scandinavian. There was a plagiocephalic German and a stenocephalic Celt. One skull had a protuberance at the bregma. Twelve occiputs were flattened, and in four of these there was no tubercle; eighteen had an enormously developed occipital protuberance. The percentage of deformities of the jaws was large. Twenty-nine had defective ears. Normal ears were present only in a member of a family which had furnished one mother and two sisters to the institution.

The direct hereditary history of prostitutes is excellently illustrated in Marie Duplessis, idealised by Alexandre Dumas in *La Dame aux Camélias*. Her paternal grandmother, who was half prostitute, half beggar, gave birth to a son by a country priest. This son was a country Don Juan, a peddler by trade. The maternal great-grandmother was a nymphomaniac, whose son married a woman of loose morals, by whom a daughter was born. This daughter married a peddler, and their child was Marie. She had the confidence-operator tendencies of many of her class. She died childless, early in life, from consumption.[255] With their ancestry, habits, perverse instincts, prostitutes cannot be cured or reformed by the enforcement of municipal ordinances. Though those of criminal and congenital type be taken from their surroundings and placed where they can earn an honest livelihood, they soon go back, voluntarily, to their old mode of life.

An allied class, belonging to a still blacker phase of biology, are the sexual perverts. The congenital form associated with the stigmata of degeneracy, as already shown, is an expression of the defective line whence the victim has sprung. The congenital types are, like the similar types of the prostitute, victims of inherited defects. The sexual pervert may be divided into precisely the same classes as other criminals. The congenital type often links degenerate lunatics, epileptics, &c., with a born criminal class.

Between the criminal and the insane is a debatable line occupied by moral imbeciles, reasoning maniacs, &c. There are many insane persons in whom the principal deviation from the normal consists in disorder of the moral faculties. In most closer inspection generally reveals signs of degeneracy. The seeming immorality is the striking factor of the case and superficially the mind otherwise appears clear and rational by contrast. As Krafft-Ebing has shown in these cases, the most striking features are moral insensibility, lack of moral judgment and ethical ideas, the place of which is usurped by a narrow sense of loss or profit, logically apprehended only. Such persons may mechanically know the laws of morality, but if such laws enter their conscience these persons do not experience by any real appreciation, still less regard, for them. These laws to them are cold, lifeless statements. The morally defective know not how to draw from them motive for omission or commission. To this "moral colour-blindness" the whole moral and governmental order appears as a mere hindrance to egotistic ambition and feeling, which necessarily leads to negation of the rights of others and to violation of the same.

These defective individuals are without interest for aught good or beautiful, albeit capable of a sentimentality which is shallow cant. Such persons are repellent by their lack of love for children or relatives, and of all social inclinations, and by cold-hearted indifference to the weal or woe of those nearest to them. They are without other than egotistic care for questions of social life or sensibility to either the respect or the scorn of others, without control of conscience and without sense or remorse for evil. Morality they do not understand. Law is nothing more than police regulation. The greatest crimes are regarded as mere transgressions of some arbitrary order. If such persons come in conflict with individuals, then, hatred, envy, and revenge take the place of coldness and negation, and their brutality and indifference to others know no bounds.

These ethically defective persons, when incapable of holding a place in society, are often converted into candidates for the workhouse or the insane hospital, one or the other of which places they reach after they have been, as children, the terror of parents and teachers, through their untruthfulness, laziness, and general meanness, and in youth the shame of the family and the torment of the community and the officers of the law, by thefts, vagabondage, profligacy, and excesses. Finally, they are the despair of the insane hospital, the "incorrigibles" of the prisons, and (Krafft-Ebing might have added) the veritable burdens of the poor-house. If intellectual insanity or crime do not claim them, pauperism or criminality is likely to be their destiny. The moral imbecile may, however, keep within the law, and as in the instance of the "Napoleon of Finance," cited elsewhere from Kiernan, may achieve business success. His descendants often, however, evince degeneracy in an aggravated form. Many of the supposed reformers of various alleged social evils are often of this class. Their morbid egotism takes the direction of cant and sentimentality, so common at certain states in evolution, as points of least resistance. Like Guiteau, the assassin of President Garfield, they aim at doing a "big thing for humanity and myself," the humanity being concentrated in "my" ideas. The moral lunatic needs but a slight twist intellectually to become the paranoiac in whom there is, as Spitzka has pointed out,[256] a permanent undercurrent of perverted mental action peculiar to the individual, running like an unbroken thread through his whole mental life, obscured, it may be, for these patients are often able to correct and conceal their insane symptoms, but it nevertheless exists, and only requires friction to bring it to the surface. The general intellectual status of these patients, though rarely of a very high order, is moderately fair, and often the mental powers are sufficient to keep the delusion under check for practical purposes of life. While many are what is termed crochety, irritable, and depressed, yet the sole symptoms of the typical cases of this disorder consist of the fixed delusions. Since the subject matter of the delusion is of such a character that these patients consider themselves either the victim of a plot or as unjustly deprived of certain rights and position, or as narrowly observed by others, delusions of persecution are added to the fixed ideas, and the patient becomes sad, thoughtful, or depressed in consequence. The patient is depressed logically, as far as his train of idea is concerned and his sadness and thoughtfulness have causes, which he can explain, and which are intimately allied with that peculiar, faulty grouping of ideas which constitutes the rendezvous, as it were, of all the mental conceptions of the patient. Nay, the process may be reversed, and the patient, beginning with a hypochondriac or hysteric state, imagines himself watched with no favourable eye. Because he is watched and made the subject of audible comments (hallucinatory or delusional), he concludes that he must be a person of some importance. Some great political movement takes place; he throws himself into it, either in a fixed character that he has already constructed for himself, or with the vague idea that he is an influential personage. He seeks interviews, holds actual conversation with the big men of the day, accepts the common courtesy shown him by those in office as a tribute to his value, is rejected, however, and then judges himself to be the victim of jealousy or of rival cabals, makes intemperate and querulous complaints to higher officials, perhaps makes violent attacks upon them, and being incarcerated in jail or asylum, looks upon this as the end of a long series of persecutions which have broken the power of a skilled diplomatist, a capable military commander, a prince of the blood, an agent of a camarilla, a paramour of some exalted personage, or finally the Messiah Himself. All through this train of ideas there runs a chain of logic and inference in which there is no gap. If the inferences of the patient were based on correctly observed facts and properly correlated with his actual surroundings, his conclusions would be perfectly correct. For years and years many such patients exhibit a single delusive idea as the only prominent symptom. There is hereditary taint in most of these subjects, who are strange in disposition from infancy. As children they frequently shun society and indulge in day- dreams. Their bodily growth is normal, but even trifling disease takes on a cerebral tinge. They may show talent in special directions, but their intelligence rarely passes out of the puerile stage. They often brood over a feminine ideal, a girl who has never encouraged them, and whom they persecute with absurd plans of marriage.

Connecting the paranoiac with the moral imbecile are the so-called "reasoning maniacs." Here the intellectual power is less than either that of the moral imbecile or of the paranoiac, twisted though the intellect of the latter be. Loquacious or unusually taciturn, heedless or morbidly cautious, dreamers, wearisome to all brought in contact with them, capricious and unmitigated liars, their qualities are often, in a certain manner, brilliant, but are entirely without solidity or depth. Sharpness and cunning are not often wanting, especially for little things and insignificant intrigues. Ever armed with a lively imagination and quick comprehension, they readily appropriate the ideas of others, developing or transforming them and giving them the stamp of their own individuality. But the creative force is not there, and they rarely possess enough mental vigour to get their own living. Passing without the slightest transition from one extreme to the other, they felicitate themselves to-day on an event which they sneered at the night before. In the course of a single second they change their opinions of persons and things, novelty captivates and wearies them almost in the same instant. They sell for insignificant sums things they have just bought, in order to buy others which, in their turn, will be subjected to like treatment; and, strange to say, before possessing these objects, they covet them with a degree of ardour only equalled by the eagerness they exhibit to get rid of them as soon as they become their own. To see, to desire, and to become indifferent are three stages which follow each other with astonishing rapidity.

The intense egotism of these persons makes them, as W. A. Hammond remarks, utterly regardless of the feelings and rights of others. Everybody and everything must give way to them. Their comfort and convenience are to be secured though every one else is made uncomfortable or unhappy; and sometimes they display positive cruelty in their treatment of persons who come in contact with them. This tendency is especially seen in their relations with the lower animals.

Another manifestation of their intense egotism is their entire lack of appreciation of kindness done them or benefits of which they have been the recipients. They look upon these as so many rights to which they are justly entitled, and which in the bestowal are more serviceable to the giver than to the receiver. They are hence ungrateful and abusive to those who have served them, insolent, arrogant, and shamelessly hardened in their conduct toward them. At the same time, if advantages are yet to be gained, they are sycophantic to nauseousness in their deportment towards those from whom the favours are to come.

The egotism of these people is unmarked by the least trace of modesty in obtruding themselves and their assumed good qualities upon the public at every opportunity. They boast of their genius, their righteousness, their goodness of heart, their high sense of honour, their learning and other qualities and acquirements, and this, when they are perfectly aware that they are commonplace, irreligious, cruel, and vindictive, utterly devoid of every chivalrous feeling, and saturated with ignorance. They know that in their ratings they are attempting to impose upon those whom they address and will even subsequently brag of their success.

It is no uncommon thing for the reasoning maniac, still influenced by his supreme egotism and desire for notoriety, to attempt the part of reformer. Generally he selects a practice or custom in which there really is no abuse. His energy and the logical manner in which he presents his views, based as they often are on cases and statistics, impose on many people, who eagerly adopt him as a genuine overthrower of a vicious or degrading measure. Even when his hypocrisy and falsehood are exposed he continues his attempts at imposition, and when the strong arm of the law is laid upon him, he prates of the ingratitude of those he has been endeavouring to assist, and of the distinctiveness and purity of his own motives.

Closely akin to that instability of inter-association resulting in loss of proper checks on action in the types just described, is the sentimentalism which often covers real hardness, but which charms and allures the mass.

This has essentially the same psychological basis as the suspicional tendencies and pessimism with which it is so often associated. Suspicional tendencies arise from states of anxiety resultant on instability of association, dependent on lack of associating fibres. Pessimism (so frequently present in the otherwise healthy degenerate) is often, as Magalhaes has shown, nervous instability with alternations of irritability and prostration. The subject is supersensitive; impressions call forth intense and prolonged reactions followed by exhaustion. The state is characterised by a general hyperæsthesia, which naturally results in an excess of suffering. From instability and hyperæsthesia results discord between the feelings themselves, between the feelings and the intelligence, between the feelings, the ideas and volitions. Discord between the feelings shows itself in a great variety of paradoxes, contradictions, and inconsistencies. To the pessimist possession of a desired object does not atone for former privation. Pain or unsatisfied desire is replaced by the pain of *ennui*. With inability to enjoy what he has are coupled extravagant expectations regarding that which he does not have. He is extremely susceptible both to kindness and to contempt. He passes suddenly from violent irritability to languor, from self-confidence and vanity to extreme self abasement. His intense sensitiveness results in intellectual disorders. For this involves a great vivacity of the intuitive imagination, which favours the setting up of extravagant ideals, lacking in solid representative elements. Hence a gap opens between his ideal and the actual. He can never realise the ideal he pursues and so his feelings are of a sombre hue. From this excessive realism results a state of doubt, a certain distrust of all this rational objective knowledge. It assumes another form in extreme subjectivism. The pessimist is haunted by images of the tiniest religious scruples, suspicions, fears, and anxieties, resulting in alienation from friends, seclusion, misanthropy. The pessimist is further characterised by an incapacity for prolonged attention, a refractory attention and a feeble will. These result in inaction, quietism, reverie, self-abnegation, abolition of the personality, annihilation of the will, amounting sometimes even to poetic or religious ecstasy. Pessimism is frequently associated with a morbid fear of death. The tramp is one phase of the degenerate in whom the restless wandering tendencies of the neurasthenic and paranoiac are added to the parasitic tendencies of the pauper, and the suspicional egotism of the "reasoning maniac."

The one-sided genius is a link between the neurotic, the epileptic, the paranoiac, the hysteric, and the imbecile. Cases crop up in which all these elements are so mingled as to create a puzzle where they shall be placed. In some cases, in accordance with the general law that physiologic atrophy is accompanied by hypertrophy in other directions, the intellectual powers other than along certain lines may be remarkably deficient. Moreover, the intellectual power due to healthy atavism is increased by the degeneracy in certain directions. Without going into the question, raised by Lombroso,[257] as to genius being an epileptoid neurosis, sufficient evidence exists to show that ill-balanced genius often coexists with defects in a large number of directions. The coexistence of genius with imbecility and even idiocy has been well illustrated by Langdon Down, who cites numerous instances thereof.[258] Defect in genius, whether of the imbecile stamp or otherwise, accompanied by deficiency, is not expressed in the genius, but in its deficient accompaniment. Even the mental instability of the highest type of defective genius is closely akin to that of the neurotic.

The hysterics, as has been shown by Des Champs,[259] are neurotic women in whom an aggravated sensibility exists. Neurotic women are divisible into three categories according to the predominance of one of three centres— cerebral, genital, and neuropathic. These types may be pure or intermixed. The general characteristics are an absolute want of equilibrium in sensibility and will power. There exists mobility of humour in direct relation with facile impressionability to external influences or to internal states. The nerves vibrate to all sentiments coming from within or without, and all are registered without proper relation. One fact chased by another is forgotten. Another produces a momentary hyperexcitation, which takes place of the truth, whence it is that falsehood is instinctive, but the patient protests her good faith if accused of the same. This lack of equilibrium leads to a decided modification of the mental faculties. Intellectual activity is over excited, but in diverse degrees and variable ways, according to the particular tendencies adopted. Absorbed by a preoccupation or controlled by an idea, they become indifferent to all else. Their ideas are abundant, and they rapidly pass from the idea to the act. Their vivid imagination, coupled with a bright intelligence, gives them a seducing aspect, but their judgment is singularly limited, attenuated, or false. They judge from a non-personal standpoint excellently. They are quick at discovering the faults of even their own relatives, but faults rightly attributed to themselves are repudiated. Their memory is capricious. They forget their faults and their acts under impulse, albeit these may be consciously done. The cerebral type is led by the intelligence. She has little or no coquetry; what coquetry there may be is the result of intention and temporary. There is an ethical sense, frankness and nobility in her ideas, disinterestedness and tact in her acts, and she is capable of friendship. Her tastes carry her to male pursuit, in which she succeeds. She becomes often what is called a "superior woman," and too often what is called an "incomprehensible woman." She has but little guile. To the sensual type voluptuousness is the aim of life and the centre of her acts and thoughts. She is well endowed with guile and extremely diplomatic. She is full of finesse, but not very delicate. Her lack of scruple often spoils her tact. She is ruseful, dissimulating, and unconsciously mendacious. She despises friendship and needs watching. If circumstances permit she loses all delicacy, reserve and modesty. She is destitute of scruples. Her crimes are coolly remorseless. The neuropathic type is one to which the grasshopper is a burden. Her nerves are always on edge. She is a heroic invalid who displays the air of a martyr about trivialities.

The character of the neurotic, as Kiernan remarks, recalls the observation of Milne-Edwards concerning the monkey character. Levity is one of its salient features, and its mobility is extreme. One can get it to shift in an instant from one mood or train of ideas to another. It is now plunged into black melancholy and in a moment may be vastly amused at some object presented to its attention.

Neuroticism in man differs in no respect from that in woman except that anæsthesia, paralysis of emotional origin, and conscious convulsions are less common. The male neurotic could be subdivided precisely as Des Champs has the hysteric. Neurotics are often long-lived, peculiarly resistant to certain acute and fatal disease, and are frequently retentive of their youthful appearance, which is to a certain extent an evidence of their resistance to the wear and tear of life and advancing old age, and due to emotional anæsthesia. Recognition of the neurotic tendency often induces the individual to take better care of himself. The youthful appearance may be due largely to arrest of facial development at an early age, the face thus retaining the child character throughout life. Considering, therefore, this class of neurotics, which does not include those afflicted with the more serious nervous disorders such as epilepsy, they may be looked upon as the victims of evolutionary processes that are constantly going on in the race and under civilised conditions.

Neurotics are not met with to any extent among barbarous races, but are numerous in civilised communities, where the weak are preserved from early death and then subjected to the struggle for existence. Neurotics are individuals naturally imperfect in some directions, but by the law of economy of growth they are often superior in others. Their disordered nervous functions and hyperæsthesia are not, necessarily, indicative of inferiority of general organisation compared to their ancestry. They may simply imply a more rapid advance in some one direction in the development of the nervous system than can be kept up with by the remainder. These defects may in some cases be the advance guards in the progress of the development of the race.

As the nervous system controls nutrition in all departments of the organism, anomalies occur with erratic nervous functions in such individuals. In these neurotics are often found defective development involving the bony and other structures. They have fine and delicate features, small jaws and defective teeth. These are the results of general systemic modifications connected with the neurotic state. The arthritic diathesis occurs also; it is one of the underlying conditions of many neurotic manifestations, often responsible for acquired bony deformities, not infrequently involving the jaws to some extent.

Neurotic degenerate symptoms from a mental standpoint are noticeable long before deformities of the osseous system are developed. They show themselves in mental weakness, extreme stupidity, and precocity. Under the first class the child is obstinate, quarrelsome, malignant, even immorally inclined, and is often spoken of as being wicked or vicious. Harriet C. B. Alexander[260] says the ruling instinct in the child of three or four is self- gratification. It destroys what it dislikes. Among the earliest manifestations of morbid mental activity in childhood are hallucinations, which depend on already registered perceptions.

In many instances even moral agencies produce sudden explosions of mental disorders. The inherited tendencies of childhood predispose to these attacks. As Clouston has shown, neuroses and psychoses not requiring hospital treatment are by no means uncommon in the too sensitive child with hereditary taint. Children of this class have crying fits and miserable periods on slight or no provocation. As Clouston has also shown, precocity, over-sensitiveness, unhealthy strictness in morals and religion for a child, or too vivid imagination, want of courage, thinness and craving for animal food, are common characters. These children are over-sensitive, over-imaginative, are too fearful to be physiologic, and tend, as a general thing, to be unhealthily religious, precociously intellectual, and at first hyperæsthetically conscientious.

The other class of children, as a rule, are very handsome babies and children. The brightness is noted by parents at a very early age, and they extol their many clever qualities and sayings. The tendency is for the parents to cultivate these precocious qualities and believe it to be the proper thing to encourage them; while in early life this class may possess the peculiarities of the other class and also show those of degeneracy. These children are the best scholars in the schoolroom and learn their lessons with apparently little or no study. They are usually thin, frail children, and very nervous. Very little food is taken and much of that is not assimilated. Especially is this true of the lime salts, which form bone and tooth structure. These lime salts are excreted through the kidneys and salivary glands. This is easily demonstrated by an examination of urine, mouth, and teeth. Large collections of tartar are always found in these cases. Children of both classes are sure to show stigmata of degeneracy. This period of degeneracy commences at the sixth year, or at about the time the first period of brain development ceases. The bulk of the brain has obtained its growth. In some the child commences to improve mentally very fast. In others mental development is slow. In still others it ceases altogether. From the time the second set of teeth begins to develop until the twelfth year, neuroses of development and stigmata of degeneracy are stamped upon the head, face, nose, jaws and teeth, and later any of the conditions mentioned under the heads of nutritive degeneracy and local perversion tendencies may appear.

Closely akin to these states are expressions of degeneracy manifesting themselves with some approach to regularity in periods, as in epilepsy and the periodical insanities. The periodical insanities may be simply emotional states of exaltation (as in mania), of extreme depression (as in melancholia), of stupor, or of mental confusion. They may show themselves in periodical acts, as in dipsomania. This condition differs from the condition called inebriety in the fact that it is a periodical expression of degeneracy whose form has been accidently determined, but which would exist even were its form changed. The differences are excellently outlined by Dana,[261] who divides intemperate drinkers into four classes: Periodical inebriates or dipsomaniacs, pseudo-inebriates, common drunkards and victims of delirium inebriosum. The disease in the first class is a periodical insanity. In the pseudo-inebriates the desire for drink is only one of many manifestations of a weakened constitution or inherently unstable nervous system. The third type are those which approximate the occasional criminals. Another periodical insanity is kleptomania, in which insane stealing occurs at intervals of greater or lesser regularity. Nymphomania or satyrasis is a periodical insanity in which there is an insane impulse for sexual intercourse. Pyromania is a periodical tendency to commit arson. All of these periodical conditions may occur alone or in combination with other degeneracies.

Closely related to the periodical insanities are the epileptic states which play so large a part in many of the phenomena presented by the degenerates. In the epileptic the mental rather than the gross nervous expression merits attention. From what has already been said about epilepsy, it and the periodical insanities are in no small degree the effect of mal-development of the fore brain as compared with the centres of organic life. The great convulsive centre is, according to Spitzka,[262] the reticular grey matter of the brain isthmus, particularly of the pons and medulla. All characteristic features of the full epileptic onset can be produced in animals deprived of the related cerebral cortex. It needs but a slight puncture with a thin needle to produce typical convulsions in the rabbit, and some of the convulsive movements reported by Nothnagel have not only shown the true epileptic character but also that peculiar automatism noted in aberrant attacks. It is in this segment of the nervous system that all the great nerve strands conveying motor impulses, both of a voluntary and automatic and some of a reflex character, are found united in a relatively small area, and just here a relatively slight irritation might produce functional disturbances involving the entire bodily periphery.

The experiments of physiologists have shown that if a sensory irritation of a given spinal nucleus be kept up, after having produced a reflex movement in the same segment, any reaction beyond the plain of that segment is not in the next or succeeding planes but in the medulla oblongata. The motor reaction then manifests itself in laughing, crying, or deglutitory spasms, and, if the irritation be of the severest kind, epileptic or tetanic spasms in addition. Now the occurrence of laughing, crying, or deglutitory spasms could be easily understood if the molecular oscillation induced by the irritation were to travel along the associating tracts from the given spinal segment to the nuclei of the medulla oblongata. For in the medulla are found the nerve nuclei which preside over the facial, laryngeal and pharyngeal muscles. It is not easy at first to understand how tetanus and epilepsy, that is, spasms consisting in movements whose direct projection is not in the medulla oblongata but in the cord, can be produced by irritation of the former.

There are scattered groups of nerve cells in the medulla oblongata which have either no demonstrable connection with the nerve nuclei, or are positively known to be connected with the longitudinal associating strands. These cells hence can safely be regarded as representing a presiding centre over the entire spinal system. No spinal centre exerts any influence even remotely as pronounced as that of the entire cord. This applies to man and other mammals. That the elaboration of the medullary centre was as gradual a process as that of other higher differentiations is illustrated by the case of the frog, whose medulla has acquired the faculty of reproducing general spasms while the spinal cord itself retains this property also; hence here the predominance of the medulla is not so marked as in mammals.

The reticular ganglion of the oblongata is not in the adult a part of the central tubular grey matter, but has, through originally developing from it in the embryo, become ultimately isolated from its mother bed. It constitutes a second ganglionic category, and the association fibres bringing it in functional union with the spinal grey (first category) in lower animals and shown to have assumed the position of projection fibres in the higher, constitute a second projection tract; both together are a second projection system. The scattered grey matter of the medulla has great importance. Anatomically it is (though its cells be scattered diffusely as a rule) a large ganglion with numerous multipolar cells of all sizes, many of them gigantic, sometimes exceeding the so-called motor cells (which they simulate in shape) of the lumbar enlargement in size. Scattered in the "reticular substance" of the medulla from the upper end of the fourth ventricle to the pyramidal decussation, they merit the collective designation of reticular ganglia.

The cells of the reticular formation are known to be connected with the nerve nuclei, on the one hand, and with longitudinal fasciculi, which, since they run into the cord, terminate either in the grey matter or the nerve roots directly, for nerve fibres do not terminate with, as it were, blind ends. Now in the mammalian brain the reticular ganglion lies scattered among fibres which come from the higher centres, and the interpellation might be made whether, after all, the reticular ganglion be not a mere intercalar station for fibres derived from a higher source. Originally the ganglion was an independent station. In reptiles this body of cells is too considerable to account for a termination in them of the few cerebral fibres possessed by these animals. And, on the other hand, the vertical strands are notably increased in their passage through the field of the medulla oblongata.

The medulla oblongata with its reticular ganglion seems to be the great rhythmic centre. In fish the movements of the operculum and mouth, in sharks those of the spiraculum, in perenni-branchiate amphibians the branchial tree, in the infant the suctorial muscles, in all vertebrates the movements of deglutition, of the heart and respiratory muscles, all movements presenting a more or less regular rhythm, are under the control of the medulla oblongata. The early differentiation of this part of the cerebrospinal axis is related to the manifestations of rhythmic movements in the embryo and their predominant importance in lower animals. The possibility should not be excluded that a rhythmic movement may be spinal, nay even controlled by peripheral ganglia (heart of embryo). A higher development, however, implies the concentration of rhythmic innervations at some point where that anatomical association may be effected which is the expression of the mutual influence these movements exercise among themselves.

Two sets of phenomena must be borne in mind in studying the physiological pathology of the epileptic attack. First, the condition of the epileptic in the interval. Second, the explosion itself. Too much attention is paid to the last, too little attention to the first. The constitutional epileptic is characterised by a general deficiency of tone associated with exaggerated reaction and irritability. Thus the pupils are at once widely dilated and unusually mobile. The muscular system, though generally relaxed, manifests exaggerated reflex excitability. The mental state is characterised at once by great indifference and undue irascibility. In the same way the vascular system is depressed in tone in the interval with rapid marked changes under excitation. The state of the nervous system as a whole Spitzka forcibly compares to that of an elastic band which, being on the stretch continually, is apt to rebound violently when one end is let go. Under normal circumstances the band is less stretched and hence not as liable to fly so far when the check is removed.

An irritation which, in health, produces restlessness of the muscular system, accelerated respiration and pulsation and various mental phenomena within the normal limits, in the epileptic results in more intense phenomena in the same direction. The nervous irritability of the epileptic manifests itself in one direction especially. An important vaso-motor centre for the brain vessels exists, possibly diffused through an area somewhere between the thalamus and subthalamic region above the pyramidal decussation below. The irritability of this centre results in sudden arterial spasm in the carotid distribution (so characteristic a feature of the fit onset); simultaneously with the contraction of the vessel the pupil undergoes an initial contraction, and relaxation instantly results in both cases. The sudden interference with the brain circulation produces unconsciousness, and destroys the checking influence of the higher centres on the reflexes in a manner analogous to any shock affecting the nerve centres. In the meantime, while there has been a sudden deprivation of arterial blood and a sinking of intracranial pressure so far as the great cerebral masses are concerned, there has been as sudden an influx of blood to the unaffected district of the vertebral arteries whose irrigation territory is now the seat of an arterial hyperæmia. The result of this is that the great convulsion centre, the medulla, being over-nourished, functional excess, that is, convulsion, occurs unchecked by the cerebral hemispheres, which are disabled by their nutritive shock. The unconsciousness and coma of epilepsy more resemble shock than they do cerebral anæmia or syncope. The impeded return circulation of venous blood now comes into play. The contraction of the neck muscles explains this obstruction and especially the accumulation of venous blood in the cerebral capillaries of the medulla.

True epilepsy presents an enormous number of sub-groups, exhibiting every variety of deviation from the ideal convulsive form, and the existence of these forms tends to demonstrate the views just expressed. In ordinary petit mal the initial arterial spasm has but to be confined to the surface of the hemispheres, leaving the thalamus ganglia undisturbed, and it can readily be understood how the momentary unconsciousness or abolition of cortical function can occur without the patient falling, his automatic ganglia still carrying on their functions. At the same time with the lesser spasm there would be a less extensive sinking of intracranial pressure with less consecutive collateral hyperæmia of the lower centres and therefore no convulsion.

In certain cases the arterial spasm fails to affect the entire cortical surface simultaneously; some one trunk may be more pervious, and as afflux of blood may occur in its special field where certain impressions and motor innervations are stored, the result will then be that the function of the relatively well-nourished territory will be exalted. If it be a visual perception territory, sights, colours or luminous spectra will be seen; if it be an olfactory territory, odours will be smelt; if a tactile centre, crawling, tingling and cold sensation are felt; if a speech centre, cries, phrases, and songs may be observed. This explains the manifold epileptic aura, which is simply an isolated, exaggerated, and limited cortical function. The recurrence of the aura is readily explicable on the ground of the well-known physiological law that any nervous process, morbid or normal, having run through certain paths, those paths will be the paths of least resistance for that process to follow in the future.

These conditions will be greatly exaggerated in proportion to the deficiencies in the associating tracts and will often, in turn, pervert these. The sexo-religious and other mental states of epilepsy often closely mimic normal mentation and serve to disguise the intense depth of degeneracy which epilepsy implies.

In their explosive, unchecked character the morbid restlessness of the neurotic, hysteric, and criminal depend upon like brain disorder to that of the epileptic, except that consciousness is not involved, and with conscious acts are intermingled those preceding from the lower automatic processes described. Consciousness, however, is sometimes lost in part, whence frequently the defects so often noticed in the thoughts of the degenerates.

The two following cases which have come to my notice illustrate the obliteration of the function of limited areas of the brain. A young lady, aged 22, of refinement and highly accomplished, was engaged to be married. One evening her *fiancé* called; she failed to recognise him and he remained ever after a stranger to her. In every other respect her mind was seemingly normal. She died of tuberculosis. In another case a young lady, an expert stenographer, while riding her wheel, fell striking her head against a stone. She remained unconscious for some days, and was quite ill for three or four months. After her recovery she was much surprised to find that she knew nothing about her former employment, although her brain was perfectly normal in other respects.

CHAPTER XVIII

CONCLUSIONS

SINCE, as Weismann[263] admits, interference with the nutrition of the germ plasm will result in the production of variations, the fact is evident that even according to the Weismannian principle the nutrition of the parents will determine the power of the embryo to pass through the various embryonic stages up to the developed child. Impairment of nutrition may check this development at any standpoint, and may thus produce any or all of the defects due to degeneracy. Weismann has no doubt about the inheritance of a "tuberculous habit whose peculiarities are certainly transmissible." Practically, therefore, even according to Weismann, that most emphatic critic of the transmission of hereditary defect, a condition of nervous exhaustion is produced in the parents which may be transmitted as a whole to the offspring, or may simply so affect the ovum as to produce various arrests in development with hypertrophies elsewhere. The influence of nervous prostration in the father may be overcome by conditions in the mother tending to help development. As her share in the germ plasm is most emphatic, not only at the time of the formation, but also during the entire development of the embryo, production of degeneracy will largely depend on her nutrition. The influence of healthy atavism is much more emphatically exerted through the female, albeit even in the male it may overcome the nervous exhaustion of the ancestor so far as reproduction of it is concerned.

While many are called, few, owing to healthy atavism, are therefore chosen for complete degeneracy. Although heredity plays a large part in the degeneracy of the individual, still environment in many cases exerts a greater influence in determining, according as it strengthens or weakens healthy atavism, the depth of degeneracy. Treatment, therefore, both of the individual and of the family is largely a question of prophylaxis or prevention.

In prophylaxis of the family the first indication is to stop the production of degenerates. Two measures have attracted considerable attention, and from their seeming simplicity have met with much favour. The first is regulation of marriage. This, as a means of preventing degeneracy, has been much over-estimated. Laws claiming to regulate marriage have ignored two factors. In the first place the graver degeneracies only are taken into account. From what has been shown as regards the tendency of the degenerate to intermarry, and from the fact that restraints on marriage inevitably result in illicit relationships of permanent character (equally productive of degenerates whose defects have been increased by the condition in which they are born), the only procedure likely to be of value in this relation is to regard marriage simply as a contract designed for certain ends and permit its annulment for fraud, for concealment of defects (intentionally or otherwise) incompatible with the procreation of healthy children. In its essence this is the English common law theory. Its principle is recognised by the divorce codes of various continental European countries. Furthermore, it is on this principle that the Pope not infrequently annuls marriages, divorce not being recognised by the Church of which he is the head. It is certainly best for the stability of the family that unhealthy unions should have the least permanency possible.

Another element in prophylaxis, castration, ignores completely the rights of individuals under the English common law (and, so far as the United States is concerned, a provision of its constitution). Although sacrificing these important guards against that degeneracy in the body politic which inevitably reflects itself in degeneracy in the individual, this procedure fails to accomplish its end, since it ignores completely the principle of transformation in heredity. The distance between the criminals (whom it is proposed to castrate) and the hysteric offspring of good family is not so great that the progeny of one will not be as degenerate as the progeny of the other. Whatever may be said of the value of this procedure as a deterrent, its use as a prophylactic is comparatively small.

Much better results are obtainable by guarding women from the factors of degeneracy during puberty and during matronhood. Many nations whose laws ostentatiously regulate marriage in a manner most oppressive to individual liberty entail by their customs over-work in a spasmodic manner during puberty and during matronhood. Nations whose customs permit women and dogs to be harnessed together as beasts of burden, to carry the hod and to dig trenches for sewers, gas, and waterpipes, cry out very loudly against the dangerous license of the English-speaking nations in permitting women to intrude on male occupations. There is no doubt but that women (and it may be said a large majority of men) are now through evolution unsuited to occupations involving spasmodic expenditure of force, and well suited to those implying continuity. As Bachhofen, Reclus, and Otis T. Mason have shown, two-thirds of the occupations of this last type have been created by women. Man, as Havelock Ellis demonstrates, in accordance with the law of evolutionary advance, is adjusting himself to these occupations. Attempts to regulate employment of women in unhealthy trades are a step in the right direction so far as prevention of a factor of degeneracy is concerned, since it can be carried out without that disregard of personal liberty which is more dangerous in such attempts at regulation than the defect to be regulated.

The periods of menstruation and pregnancy in degenerate women require (from what has been said on maternal impressions) special attention suited to the individual, and not prescribed indiscriminately for all classes. An excellent illustration of the dangers of Procrustean prescription is the instance where the vegetarianism of the mother during pregnancy was followed by the production of ill-nourished offspring. Diet during pregnancy undoubtedly can exercise a great influence for good, but this diet must ignore the "longings" of pregnant women, which are simply the bulimia, or abnormal appetite for food, produced by irritation of the medulla.

In dealing with the toxic factors the question of legal regulation of the opium and alcohol habits requires attention. There is very little doubt but that the routine prescription of alcohol and opium (in the shape of paregoric and soothing syrup) by the laity for painful menses, teething, toothache, &c., underlies many cases of degeneracy in the offspring. This prescription is the more dangerous because it is recommended in the hidden guise of nostrums by hysterics with blatant alcoholophobia. One of the most energetic female advocates of the legal prohibition of alcohol beverages endorsed very emphatically the nostrum of one of her hysteric supporters which contained 50 per cent. alcohol and 1 per cent. each of cocaine and morphine. As the persons largely under the influence of such endorsement were hysterics whose zeal for reform was largely an expression for desire for notoriety, the dangers of its use during menstruation cannot well be over-estimated. To reach this serious source of degeneracy from alcohol and the narcotics, statement on each bottle of the exact composition of nostrums should be exacted by law.

Government could exercise a potent influence for good on alcohol abuse by improvement of sanitary conditions in the tenement or apartment house districts. Experience in New York and elsewhere has shown that improvement in tenement houses produces decided decrease in the number of dram shops in tenement-house neighbourhoods. The earlier tenement-houses in New York, as elsewhere, were originally dwellings intended for one family. As these were replaced by houses specially built for tenements, with proper sanitary arrangements and improved ventilation, not only did a tremendous decrease occur in the infantile death-rate, but a decrease also in the patronage of dram shops. In many instances it was apparent that alcoholic abuse had grown out of poverty. Foul air and crowded quarters had begotten not only a desire for stimulants but a desire for social intercourse. The dram shop met social needs as a club. It is along this line that Government can make best use of its police powers.

The Government, in exercise of its police powers directed to sanitary ends, could enable the trade unions to secure improved sanitation in shops in which occupations unhealthy by themselves or because of environment, are carried on. In this way improved sanitation of unhealthy occupations could be best secured.

The prophylaxis of degeneracy in the mother and father may be summed up as simply the prevention of a state of neurasthenia, or nervous exhaustion, whether this condition (involving the functions of growth, motion and sensation, which, as Marinesco has shown, exist in every neuron and its processes) exhibit itself in the general nervous system or in the organs connected with alimentation, elaboration, and excretion. Every factor of acquired degeneracy produces what is practically this condition of neurasthenia ere exerting any influence in the production of degeneracy. In other words, the neurasthenia of the ancestor becomes the neurosis of the descendant. Therefore the neurasthenia requires in its treatment in the ancestor the removal of the exciting cause and the treatment of the effect by physiologic rest in the truest sense of the word. In a general way, therefore, the ordinary principles of hygiene applied to each individual case will suffice to prevent development of this neurasthenia. The part of Government in this is very small. It is true here that, as remarked by Johnson—

> "How small of all that human hearts endure,
> That part which kings or laws can cure!"

Training of the individual rather than governmental regulation must be the factor to prevent degeneracy in the ancestor. Indeed governmental regulation by injuring self-reliance (that factor so easily destroyed and so hardly regained) may itself be a potent factor in degeneracy.

Prophylaxis of degeneracy in the individual should commence with the birth of the child. Whatever may be said of hypothetical ante-natal training, there is no doubt that considerable benefit can be accomplished during the first months of life. As the great aim of training is to secure self-control, it must be obvious that to accustom an infant to expect attention at every moment it cries, whether the cry be the expression of need or not, is to weaken, not to strengthen, its self-control. Furthermore, regularity in bodily functions is a great source of strength. The child can be trained during the first months of life by careful attention to its wants on the one hand, and as careful inattention to its caprice on the other, so that all its functions become equably regular and automatic. With this regularity many of the factors underlying caprice, peevishness, and anger can be prevented in the earliest months of life. Unless there be enormous deficiency in the associating fibres a good start can then be made toward the creation of a secondary ego. It is at this period and during that of the first dentition that training is too often neglected or perverted in such a way as to strengthen the primary ego at the expense of the secondary. At this period the extent of training needed may be judged by the amount of stigmata, few though they be, present in the child. With the period of the first dentition certain mental and nervous stigmata manifest themselves. If the child be liable to convulsions on the slightest causes, if it manifest screaming fits without apparent reason, if it be frequently assailed by night terrors, serious attention is needed, and this attention should be directed not only to its mental and nervous condition, but also to its functions of assimilation, elaboration, and excretion. Here dangerous degeneracy may show itself which is not apparent elsewhere. The training of the child should be conducted along the lines recommended during the first months of life. The essential principles governing this have been excellently outlined by Jules Morel.[264] The treatment of all degenerates, and consequently their preservation from the evils that threaten them, ought to begin in their earliest infancy. First avoid exaggerating hereditary predisposition when serious neurosis has occurred in the parental line. Too often such a conclusion is adopted, and hope of recovery in the descendants is abandoned because one of the parents or the grandparents was affected with insanity by reason of organic disease of the brain. Preliminary examination of the neurotic needs to be made before one is enabled to judge as to the effects of heredity. Only after a careful examination can the extent of heredity be determined. The proof will be beyond doubt when in parents and in their children stigmata of anatomic and physical degeneration are abundantly found.

In dealing with the question of the education of the child, the signs of fatigue expressed in the ears and face should receive attention. Attempts are being made in the schools of Chicago and elsewhere to determine these. The following schedule prepared by Colin A. Scott for the Chicago Public Schools is an excellent means towards this end:—

> *Eye*:—Each eye should be examined separately and in a good light. Hold a card over one eye while the other is being examined. In using the optometer, find the place where vision of the dots is the easiest and most distinct. In using Snellen's test card, place the pupil at the distance marked upon the card. Have him begin at the top and read down as far as he can, first with one eye and then with the other. He should be able to read a majority of the test type. Test with optometer, and in reporting use the number on the stem preceded by F for far-sightedness, and N for near- sightedness.
>
> Place the card for astigmatism at the distance marked upon it. Cover one eye and ask pupil to indicate, without moving nearer,

the circles which appear blacker or lighter than the others. Bring the card nearer and find at how many feet distant he still sees any of the circles darker or lighter than the others. At a sufficient distance every one betrays some degree of astigmatism, which is of consequence as a defect only when capable of detection within the distance indicated upon the card. Outside of this point astigmatism may be reckoned as absent and marked 0 in the report. Note if the pupil suffers habitually from inflamed eyelids, and inquire if he complains of tired and painful eyes or headaches after reading, studying, or using his eyes in other similar ways. Note any other defect of formation or position of either eye. Test the movement of the eyes by moving a coin to about eighteen inches of the eyes.

Test each ear with the same watch in the same place and position. Establish the normal degree of hearing for your room under these conditions. Describe each ear in the report as—(1) normal; (2) slightly hard of hearing; (3) hard of hearing; (4) considerably deaf; or (5) deaf. As a further test, place the pupil at a distance and ask him to repeat a number of words or letters. In all of these tests care must be taken to avoid the possibility of suggestion in asking questions or by other means. Note if the child is a mouth-breather, or gives other signs of adenoids or enlarged tonsils. Notice circulation in each ear.

Signs of Fatigue, &c.:—In no case should it be said in the presence of a young child that he is nervous or defective in development or nutrition.

Note the position and balance of the body in standing and sitting, and whether the movements are—(1) habitually restless and fidgety; (2) note especially the balance of the head; and (3) position and occupation of the hands, showing nervousness or not;
(4) note any twitching or marked lack of motor control in any part of the body; (5) note whether the pupil flushes periodically or frequently; is the pupil (6) easily excited or (7) fatigued by task in school or at home? Inquire if the pupil has frequent "morning tire" (number of days per month) or headaches not connected with serious defects of the eyes. (8) Is he unduly irritable or irascible? Are there any other signs of lack of emotional control—for example, (9) being too easily impressed; or (10) with an undue tendency to tears, or uncontrollable laughter?

Note the general condition of bodily nutrition (this by no means depends directly upon food), and the number of signs of failure in physical development (height, weight, &c.)

Researches along this line in Germany and England have shown that the fatigue produced by studies varies, and that it is possible by arranging sequence of studies to remove fatigue produced by one study through the rest furnished by another. It has been found that biology exhausts least and mathematics and grammar most. While there is undoubtedly a spirit of emulation stirred by these last two studies which is injurious, the limited associations affected by them are further a source of fatigue as well. The numerous associations of biology afford points of rest on the one hand while not tending to emulation on the other. It is this spirit of emulation, with its attendant alternation of worry and hope, that causes so many of the acquired nervous disorders of the adult, and which hence is obviously much more potent for evil in the child.

Physical and mental training in the special asylums for imbeciles and idiots gives such splendid results that it is surprising that parents, and especially those charged with bad heredity, are not encouraged and advised by their physicians and friends to try from the first year of the child's life special measures for their preservation. If a persevering physical and psychic management of the weak-minded gives such admirable results in asylums, it would be still better if the child could be trained from the earliest period of its life. This subject is ignored by the public, and in every case not sufficiently appreciated. First of all try to preserve patients of a nervous or of a weak constitution. They should know in what state of health they are living, they must be informed of the great danger of matrimonial union with a person of the same tendencies, and especially when consanguinity exists between them. The greatest care is to be given to children of this class. Experience has already led to the conclusion that mental and physical overwork increases this defect: hence young brains must not be over-excited with worry or emotionalism. The will of children ought to be cultivated and strengthened. Their minds should be methodically educated. The bodily functions should never be artificially stimulated in any way, to increase unduly the assimilation of the food. Development of the intelligence, the sensibility and the physical training, should be looked after in the same way. Once a plan of living is laid down it should be followed. Success depends on this. The great influence of hygienic conditions (air, light, food, dress, habitation, sleep, muscular exercise, &c.) should not be forgotten, for without them efforts made for mental training are useless. By putting these methods into execution an increase of the congenital taint is prevented, and such methods perceptibly amend the psychopathic depreciation which in the usual way of living would certainly become worse. The object very often thus secured is double;

aggravation has been prevented, amelioration has been obtained.

In dealing with nervous exhaustion produced by the infectious diseases, the dangers of the convalescent period are not sufficiently taken into account. Parents are but too apt from mistaken motives of economy to dismiss the physician at the onset of convalescence. It is precisely at this period that the system hovers between permanent systemic defect and recovery. Proper diet and proper training at this time will often prevent the checking of puberty development, and hence a breakdown under the stress of that period. The same is true of the convalescent period from such diseases in adults. Many a mother has thus injured her constitution and given birth to degenerate children in marked contrast with the normality of the children born before.

Frequently efforts are unsuccessful either because the family physician and the educator have no time to superintend treatment, or because they are unable, for many reasons, to individualise treatment properly. Hence the high value of well-organised special boarding schools for the degenerate.

The special aim, says Koch, is to teach the patient to govern himself, to repose confidence in himself. To reach this end a great deal is required of him who undertakes the treatment. He has to exercise himself with patience. He must know how to divide the time for work and the time for rest. For many of these ill-balanced subjects variety is wanted as well in physical work as mental training.

Those charged with these remedies, exercising good judgment, are soon able to distinguish the more favourable cases from the more difficult. They can soon say that a favourable remedy for the one may be noxious for another, and *vice versâ*. Tonics, spirits, cold baths, &c., and even hypnotism may be tried, but great caution is to be exercised, and these remedies should never be employed except by prescription of physicians.

Even subjects of congenital mental instability suffering from obsession (imperative ideas) without delusions are not inaccessible to treatment. In these cases naturally the most important part belongs to the medical treatment as in most mental cases. The more serious cases, dating from the first youth and aggravated in proportion to the age, are not to be completely cured. The progressive evolution can be stopped and patients ameliorated in such a way that improvement makes their life bearable.

The same results can be obtained with less degenerate subjects. Success occurs often when patients are enabled to understand the nature of their sufferings, to discern that their disease does not belong to insanity, that it is unlikely to lead to mental disease. This understanding is one of the best of all anodynes. Donders, of Utrecht, said to one of his patients suffering from optic hyperæsthesia of neurasthenic origin: "What medicine cannot do, time and oftentime hygiene realise." The intelligent patient having thus received assurance of his sight, good hygiene and mental rest soon after produced a cure. Acquired mental depreciation may exist from the first years of the child's life. These depreciations in proportion to their intensity are characterised by fatigue and even nervous exhaustion accompanied with physical weakness and functional trouble in one or more organs of sense, by pathological debility of the intelligence and impaired memory especially for recent facts, difficulty of comprehension and of associating ideas and judgment, as well as worries, fears, despairs, especially in cases of intoxications by morphine, cocaine, bromides, coffee, &c. These are increased by irritability and excitability when the troubles arise from onanism, puberty, or other periods of transformation in the sexual life.

Fight from the first the symptoms of predisposing and occasional causes, because if aggravation be prevented recovery is possible. Especially in these depreciations must the physician utilise all his knowledge and prove that only mental science is sufficient to cure such patients. Not only has he to guide the intellectual life, and life of sensibility and will, but he has also to remedy the morbid physical conditions, to superintend the general régime, times of work and rest, air, light, dressing, preservation from alcoholic and other excesses.

One great element of possible danger of the first importance is training in the sexual sphere. To avoid and at the same time to enlighten is the problem presented. In dealing with this problem the great requirement, balance, not repression, must be kept in mind. Masturbation is very frequently an expression not of mental or moral deficiency, but of purely local (first in at least most cases) physical conditions. Irritation (from the presence of worms in the rectum or vagina, an intensely acid state of the urine, or constipation) to male foreskin and female clitoris has produced a local itching, the attempt to relieve which has led to masturbation. Granting all that has been said about the deteriorating effects, especially in degenerates, the source should first be sought here. Attention to these physical states will often prevent the development of this practice and its resultant moral deterioration.

In dealing with the sexual appetite the fact should be remembered that encouragement of healthy modesty is a duty in both sexes, and pre-eminently so in the male. Too much of what is called "sexual purity" is very often an expression of sexual perversity. While great stress has been laid on the evil effects of association between boys, too little stress has been laid on the danger of the training of boys by women. The sexual history of boys often demonstrates that their initiation into the sexual life was first at the instance of women older than themselves, often servants, but not rarely sexual "purists" or persons whose ostentatious religiosity covered a sexual perversity. In the healthy association of the sexes there is very little danger, but in such morbid association there is great danger, the more that the morbid conceals itself under religiosity and the allied phases of sexual perversion. Great stress has been laid on the dangers of co-education, but the growing opinion is that education limited to one sex is the source of even greater dangers to both boy and girl. It is a matter of common observation among genito-urinary specialists, alienists and gynecologists, that much of the alleged "purity" so ostentatiously displayed by graduates of colleges limited to one sex, is often the offspring of a sexual perversion which, whether congenital or not, has been fostered by the environment of one sex without the modifying, healthy influence of the other.

In dealing with these cases the stigmata first likely to attract the physician's attention are in the milder cases those of the jaws, teeth, nose, throat, ear, and eye. Rapid decay of the teeth often leads to the discovery not merely of constitutional degeneracy, but also of the effects of certain strains which aggravated this. Dentists, mouth, throat, ear, and to a lesser degree eye specialists, are hence in a position to detect degeneracy at its outset. If they do not put the cart before the horse, and refer the constitutional symptoms to the local disturbances, they are in a position to be of eminent service to the race.

What Jules Morel has said of the more evident degenerates is equally true of the others. Education should be conducted along the lines which Froebel indicated when he pointed out that play is the child's work, and that a development of this work is the natural problem for education. Extension of the general training of the whole body, from the properly conducted kindergarten to the school, is the principle on which all education should be conducted. This is recognised by advanced educators, as previously it had been recognised by the physician confronted with the effects of school strain resulting from the opposite theory. Manual training is a principle long adopted by idiot schools, where training of certain muscles through both mental and physical methods precedes intellectual training alone. Manual training may, however, be the source of equal dangers with the excessive abuse of intellectual training which preceded it. In the education of the degenerate, as in the education of the other members of the race, the true source of success is to avoid "the falsehood of extremes."

INDEX OF AUTHORS

Agassiz, 43

Aitken, Sir W., 86

Alexander, Harriet C. B., 57, 151, 285, 320, 335

Amabile, 61, 109

Amadei, 20

Annandale, 263

Andronico, 319

Anstie, 83

Aquinas, St. Thomas, 6

Aristotle, 5, 6, 10, 11, 66

Attmyer, 12

Aubry, 77

Augustine, St., 6

Awl, 144

Ayres, Howard, 201

Bacon, Francis, 3

Bacon, Roger, 6

Bachhofen, 349

Baer, Von, 13, 70, 172

Bannister, H. M., 87

Bastian, 297

Bauer, S., 47

Beach, Fletcher, 25

Bemiss, S. M., 81, 86

Benedikt, 22

Berwig, Elise, 60

Billod, 143

Bischoff, 298

Bjornstrom, 20

Bock, 204

Boëthius, 4

Bourgeois, 86

Bremer, L., 117

Brigham, 8, 18, 21, 144

Broca, 18

Brown-Sequard, 48

Bruce, 204

Buchanan, 214

Buffon, 5, 67

Bullard, 115, 116

Bulwer, 122

Bureau, 109

Burnett, 45

Burton, 3

Byron, Lord, 78

Calkins, 109

Campagne, 18, 176

Camper, 12, 181, 183, 185, 187

Carpenter, G. T., 245

Carson, 61

Catlin, 173

Charrin, 65, 71, 72, 122

Chiarrurgi, 8

Christopher, W. S., 145, 150, 156

Clapham, Crochley, 176

Clark, C. K., 142

Clouston, 25, 336

Cohen, M. A., 47, 48

Cohn, 287

Conger, 88, 89

Coolidge, F. S., 71, 122, 268

Cope, E. D., 52, 179

Lucas, Prosper, 12, 200

Luys, 78

Macaulay, 5

Macdonald, Jas., 21

Magalhaes, 330

Magnan, 20

Manning, 87

Marestang, 137

Marie, 278

Marro, 89

Marsh, 200

Marshall, 17

Mason, O. P., 349

Maudsley, 17, 24, 25, 66

Maupas, 41, 44, 80

Maupertius, 263

Mattison, 61, 109

McFarland, A., 21

McBride, J. H., 21

Meige, 274

INDEX OF SUBJECTS

Hare-lip,

UNWIN BROTHERS, THE GRESHAM PRESS, WOKING AND LONDON.

"The most attractive Birthday Book ever published."

Crown Quarto, in specially designed Cover, Cloth, Price 6s.
"Wedding Present" Edition, in Silver Cloth, 7s. 6d., in Box. Also in Limp Morocco, in Box.

An Entirely New Edition. Revised Throughout.

With Twelve Full-Page Portraits of Celebrated Musicians.

DEDICATED TO PADEREWSKI.

The Music of the Poets:

A MUSICIANS' BIRTHDAY BOOK.

Compiled by ELEONORE D'ESTERRE-KEELING.

This is an entirely new edition of this popular work. The size has been altered, the page having been made a little longer and narrower (9 × 6½ inches), thus allowing space for a larger number of autographs. The setting-up of the pages has also been improved, and a large number of names of composers, instrumentalists and singers, has been added to those which appeared in the previous edition. A special feature of the book consists in the reproduction in fac-simile of autographs, and autographic music, of living composers; among the many new autographs which have been added to the present edition being those of MM. Paderewski (to whom the book is dedicated), Mascagni, Eugen d'Albert, Sarasate, Hamish McCunn, and C. Hubert Parry. Merely as a volume of poetry about music, this book makes a charming anthology, the selections of verse extending from a period anterior to Chaucer to the present day.

Among the additional writers represented in the new edition are Alfred Austin, Arthur Christopher Benson, John Davidson, Norman Gale, Richard Le Gallienne, Nora Hopper, Jean Ingelow, George Meredith, Alice Meynell, Coventry Patmore, Mary Robinson, Francis Thompson, Dr. Todhunter, Katharine Tynan, William Watson, and W. B. Yeats. The new edition is illustrated with portraits of Handel, Beethoven, Bach, Gluck, Chopin, Wagner, Liszt, Rubinstein, and others. The compiler has taken the greatest pains to make the new edition of the work as complete as possible; and a new binding has been specially designed by an eminent artist.

Crown 8vo, about 350 pp. each, Cloth Cover, 2/6 per Vol.;
Half-Polished Morocco, Gilt Top, 5s.

Count Tolstoy's Works.

The following Volumes are already issued—

A RUSSIAN PROPRIETOR.	WHAT TO DO?
THE COSSACKS.	WAR AND PEACE. (4 vols.)
IVAN ILYITCH, AND OTHER STORIES.	THE LONG EXILE, ETC.
MY RELIGION.	SEVASTOPOL.
LIFE.	THE KREUTZER SONATA, AND FAMILY

MY CONFESSION.
CHILDHOOD,
BOYHOOD, YOUTH.
THE PHYSIOLOGY OF
WAR.
ANNA KARÉNINA. 3/6.

HAPPINESS.
THE KINGDOM OF GOD
IS WITHIN YOU.
WORK WHILE YE HAVE
THE LIGHT.
THE GOSPEL IN BRIEF.

Uniform with the above—
IMPRESSIONS OF RUSSIA. By Dr. Georg
Brandes.

Post 4to, Cloth, Price 1s.
PATRIOTISM AND CHRISTIANITY.
To which is appended a Reply to Criticisms of
the Work.
By Count Tolstoy.

1/- Booklets by Count Tolstoy.

Bound in White Grained Boards, with Gilt
Lettering.

WHERE LOVE IS,
THERE GOD
IS ALSO.
THE TWO PILGRIMS.
WHAT MEN LIVE BY.

THE GODSON.
IF YOU NEGLECT THE
FIRE, YOU
DON'T PUT IT OUT.
WHAT SHALL IT PROFIT
A MAN?

2/- Booklets by Count Tolstoy.

NEW EDITIONS, REVISED.

Small 12mo, Cloth, with Embossed Design on
Cover, each containing
Two Stories by Count Tolstoy, and Two
Drawings by
H. R. Millar. In Box, Price 2s. each.

Volume III.

Volume I.

contains—
WHERE LOVE IS,
THERE GOD IS ALSO.
THE GODSON.

Volume II.

contains—
WHAT MEN LIVE BY.
WHAT SHALL IT

PROFIT A MAN?

contains—
THE TWO
PILGRIMS. IF
YOU NEGLECT
THE FIRE,
YOU DON'T
    PUT IT OUT.
  Volu
me IV.
contain
s—
MASTER AND MAN.
  Volume V.

COUNT TOLSTOY'S LONGEST AND MOST MAGNIFICENT WORK.

Issue in TWO Double Volumes, Price 7s. per Set.

War and Peace.

By COUNT TOLSTOY.

(Contains 1600 pages. Printed in very clear type.)

This is not only one of the finest, but probably one of the longest novels ever written, occupying, as it does in this edition, 1600 large and closely printed pages. Notwithstanding its vast length, its multitude of figures, the number of events it deals with, the interest of *War and Peace* is not only intense, but unbroken throughout the immense march of the story, so that no reader, great though the undertaking is, will fail to read to the end once he has started on the book. The eminent French critic, Vicomte E. M. de Vogüé, writing on *War and Peace*, says:

"As you advance in the book, curiosity changes into astonishment, and astonishment into admiration, before this impassive judge, who calls before his tribunal all human actions, and makes the soul render to itself an account of all its secrets. You feel yourself swept away on the current of a tranquil river, the depth of which you cannot fathom; it is life itself which is passing, agitating the hearts of men, which are suddenly made bare in the truth and complexity of their movements."

At the end of the second volume, a complete Synopsis of the story is given, also a list of the principal characters (of which there are about one hundred).

COMMEMORATION VOLUME.

Crown 8vo, Cloth Elegant (the Cover specially designed), price 2s. 6d.
With 35 Full-page Illustrations.

"DIAMOND" JUBILEE EDITION.

Our Queen:

The Life and Times of Victoria, Queen of Great Britain and Ireland, Empress of India, etc.

By the Authors of "General Gordon," "Grace Darling," etc.

This important work provides an exhaustive history of the life of the Queen, from her infancy to the present year in which she commemorates the sixtieth year of her reign. Any account of the life of the Queen would be imperfect that did not take into account the immense march of progress—political, industrial, and scientific—and the many memorable events which her reign has witnessed. In the course of its narrative this volume deals with these events in an impartial and enlightened spirit; it provides, in fact, a complete and authentic history of our own times in their religious, social, literary, artistic, and scientific aspects, together with biographical records of the many men and women of eminence of the Victorian era. Perhaps in no respect have such great strides been made as in the extent of the territory over which our Queen rules. When she ascended the throne, her sway extended over 1,387,000 square miles (including colonies and dependencies); now the empire has an area of 11,130,000 square miles, it being thus eight times as large as at the beginning of the reign. The vast interest of the subject of the work need not be commented on, an interest which will be both intensified and universally felt during the present year, and which it is the object of this attractively and earnestly written book to worthily and adequately satisfy. The many portraits which it will contain will add effectively to the value of the work.

An Edition of this Work on large paper (Demy 8vo) with Coloured Illustrations, price 5s., is also published.

BOOKS OF FAIRY TALES.

Crown 8vo, Cloth Elegant, Price 3/6 per Vol.

ENGLISH FAIRY AND OTHER FOLK TALES.

Selected and Edited, with an Introduction,

By EDWIN SIDNEY HARTLAND.

With Twelve Full-Page Illustrations by CHARLES E. BROCK.

SCOTTISH FAIRY AND FOLK TALES.

Selected and Edited, with an Introduction,

By SIR GEORGE DOUGLAS, BART.

With Twelve Full-Page Illustrations by JAMES TORRANCE.

IRISH FAIRY AND FOLK TALES.

Selected and Edited, with an Introduction,

By W. B. YEATS.

With Twelve Full-Page Illustrations by JAMES TORRANCE.

THE CONTEMPORARY SCIENCE SERIES.

NEW VOLUME

Crown 8vo, Cloth, Price 6s.

Hallucinations and Illusions:

ASTUDY OF THE FALLACIES OF PERCEPTION.

By EDMUND PARISH.

This work deals not only with the pathology of the subject, but with the occurrence of the phenomena among normal persons, bringing together the international statistics of the matter. It discusses fully the causation of hallucinations and the various theories that have been put forward; and further, it examines and adversely criticises the evidence which has been brought forward in favour of telepathy.

NEW EDITIONS.

Crown 8vo, Cloth, Price 6s. With Numerous Illustrations.

Man and Woman:

A STUDY OF HUMAN SECONDARY
SEXUAL CHARACTERS.

By HAVELOCK ELLIS. Second Edition.

"... His book is a sane and impartial consideration, from a psychological and anthropological point of view of a subject which is certainly of primary interest."—*Athenæum*.

Crown 8vo, Cloth, Price 3s. 6d.

FOURTH EDITION, COMPLETELY
REVISED.

Hypnotism.

By Dr. ALBERT MOLL.

"Marks a step of some importance in the study of some difficult physiological and psychological problems which have not yet received much attention in the scientific world of England."—*Nature*.

Great Writers

A NEW SERIES OF CRITICAL
BIOGRAPHIES.

Edited by ERIC ROBERTSON and FRANK
T. MARZIALS.

A Complete Bibliography to each Volume, by
J. P. Anderson, British Museum, London.

Cloth, Uncut Edges, Gilt Top. Price 1s. 6d.

VOLUMES ALREADY ISSUED.

LIFE OF LONGFELLOW. By Professor Eric
S. Robertson.
LIFE OF COLERIDGE. By Hall Caine.
LIFE OF DICKENS. By Frank T. Marzials.

LIFE OF DANTE GABRIEL ROSSETTI. By J. KNIGHT.
LIFE OF SAMUEL JOHNSON. By Colonel F. GRANT.
LIFE OF DARWIN. By G. T. BETTANY.
LIFE OF CHARLOTTE BRONTË. By A. BIRRELL.
LIFE OF THOMAS CARLYLE. By R. GARNETT, LL.D.
LIFE OF ADAM SMITH. By R. B. HALDANE, M.P.
LIFE OF KEATS. By W. M. ROSSETTI.
LIFE OF SHELLEY. By WILLIAM SHARP.
LIFE OF SMOLLETT. By DAVID HANNAY.
LIFE OF GOLDSMITH. By AUSTIN DOBSON.
LIFE OF SCOTT. By Professor YONGE.
LIFE OF BURNS. By Professor BLACKIE.
LIFE OF VICTOR HUGO. By FRANK T. MARZIALS.
LIFE OF EMERSON. By RICHARD GARNETT, LL.D.
LIFE OF GOETHE. By JAMES SIME.
LIFE OF CONGREVE. By EDMUND GOSSE.
LIFE OF BUNYAN. By Canon VENABLES.
LIFE OF CRABBE. By T. E. KEBBEL.
LIFE OF HEINE. By WILLIAM SHARP.
LIFE OF MILL. By W. L. COURTNEY.
LIFE OF SCHILLER. By HENRY W. NEVINSON.
LIFE OF CAPTAIN MARRYAT. By DAVID HANNAY.
LIFE OF LESSING. By T. W. ROLLESTON.
LIFE OF MILTON. By R. GARNETT, LL.D.
LIFE OF BALZAC. By FREDERICK WEDMORE.
LIFE OF GEORGE ELIOT. By OSCAR BROWNING.
LIFE OF JANE AUSTEN. By GOLDWIN SMITH.
LIFE OF BROWNING. By WILLIAM SHARP.
LIFE OF BYRON. By Hon. RODEN NOEL.
LIFE OF HAWTHORNE. By MONCURE D. CONWAY.

LIFE OF SCHOPENHAUER. By Professor
WALLACE.
LIFE OF SHERIDAN. By LLOYD SANDERS.
LIFE OF THACKERAY. By HERMAN
MERIVALE and FRANK T. MARZIALS.
LIFE OF CERVANTES. By H. E. WATTS.
LIFE OF VOLTAIRE. By FRANCIS ESPINASSE.
LIFE OF LEIGH HUNT. By COSMO
MONKHOUSE.
LIFE OF WHITTIER. By W. J. LINTON.
LIFE OF RENAN. By FRANCIS ESPINASSE.
LIFE OF THOREAU. By H. S. SALT.

LIBRARY EDITION OF 'GREAT
WRITERS,' Demy 8vo, 2s. 6d.

Ibsen's Prose Dramas

EDITED BY WILLIAM ARCHER

*Complete in Five Vols. Crown 8vo, Cloth,
Price 3s. 6d. each.
Set of Five Vols., in Case, 17s. 6d.; in Half
Morocco,
in Case, 32s. 6d.*

*'We seem at last to be shown men and women
as they are; and at first it is more than we can
endure.... All Ibsen's characters speak and act
as if they were hypnotised, and under their
creator's imperious demand to reveal
themselves. There never was such a mirror held
up to nature before; it is too terrible.... Yet we
must return to Ibsen, with his remorseless
surgery, his remorseless electric- light, until
we, too, have grown strong and learned to face
the naked—if necessary, the flayed and
bleeding—reality.'—*SPEAKER (London).

VOL. I. 'A DOLL'S HOUSE,' 'THE LEAGUE

OF YOUTH', and 'THE PILLARS OF SOCIETY.' With Portrait of the Author, and Biographical Introduction by WILLIAM ARCHER.

VOL. II. 'GHOSTS,' 'AN ENEMY OF THE PEOPLE,' and 'THE WILD DUCK.' With an Introductory Note.

VOL. III. 'LADY INGER OF ÖSTRAT,' 'THE VIKINGS AT HELGELAND,' 'THE PRETENDERS.' With an Introductory Note and Portrait of Ibsen.

VOL. IV. 'EMPEROR AND GALILEAN.' With an Introductory Note by WILLIAM ARCHER.

VOL. V. 'ROSMERSHOLM,' 'THE LADY FROM THE SEA,' 'HEDDA GABLER.' Translated by WILLIAM ARCHER. With an Introductory Note.

The sequence of the plays *in each volume* is chronological; the complete set of volumes comprising the dramas presents them in chronological order.

Library of Humour

Cloth Elegant, Large Crown 8vo, Price 3s. 6d.
per Vol.

'The books are delightful in every way, and are notable for the high standard of taste and the excellent judgment that characterise their editing, as well as for the brilliancy of the literature that they contain.'—BOSTON (U.S.A.) GAZETTE.

VOLUMES ALREADY ISSUED.

THE HUMOUR OF FRANCE. Translated, with an Introduction and Notes, by

ELIZABETH LEE. With numerous Illustrations by PAUL FRÉNZENY.

THE HUMOUR OF GERMANY. Translated, with an Introduction and Notes, by HANS MÜLLER-CASENOV. With numerous Illustrations by C. E. BROCK.

THE HUMOUR OF ITALY. Translated, with an Introduction and Notes, by A. WERNER. With 50 Illustrations and a Frontispiece by ARTURO FALDI.

THE HUMOUR OF AMERICA. Selected with a copious Biographical Index of American Humorists, by JAMES BARR.

THE HUMOUR OF HOLLAND. Translated, with an Introduction and Notes, by A. WERNER. With numerous Illustrations by DUDLEY HARDY.

THE HUMOUR OF IRELAND. Selected by D. J. O'DONOGHUE. With numerous Illustrations by OLIVER PAQUE.

THE HUMOUR OF SPAIN. Translated, with an Introduction and Notes, by SUSETTE M. TAYLOR. With numerous Illustrations by H. R. MILLAR.

THE HUMOUR OF RUSSIA. Translated, with Notes, by E. L. BOOLE, and an Introduction by STEPNIAK. With 50 Illustrations by PAUL FRÉNZENY.

THE HUMOUR OF JAPAN. Translated, with an Introduction by A. M. With Illustrations by GEORGE BIGOT (from drawings made in Japan). [*In preparation.*

COMPACT AND PRACTICAL.

In Limp Cloth; for the Pocket. Price One

Contributors—J. Langdon Down, M.D., F.R.C.P.; Henry Power, M.B., F.R.C.S.; J. Mortimer-Granville, M.D.; J. Crichton Browne, M.D., LL.D.; Robert Farquharson, M.D. Edin.; W. S. Greenfield, M.D., F.R.C.P.; and others.

The Secret of a Clear Head.
Common Mind Troubles.
The Secret of a Good Memory.
The Heart and its Function.
Personal Appearances in Health and Disease.
The House and its Surroundings.
Alcohol: Its Use and Abuse.
Exercise and Training.
Baths and Bathing.
Health in Schools.
The Skin and its Troubles.
How to make the Best of Life.
Nerves and Nerve-Troubles.
The Sight, and How to Preserve it.
Premature Death: Its Promotion and Prevention.
Change, as a Mental Restorative.
Youth: Its Care and Culture.
The Gentle Art of Nursing the Sick.
The Care of Infants and Young Children.
Invalid Feeding, with Hints on Diet.
Every-day Ailments, and How to Treat Them.
Thrifty Housekeeping.
Home Cooking.
How to do Business. A Guide to Success in Life.
How to Behave. Manual of Etiquette and Personal Habits.
How to Write. A Manual of Composition and Letter Writing.
How to Debate. With Hints on Public Speaking.
Don't: Directions for avoiding Common

Errors of Speech.
The Parental Don't: Warnings to Parents.
Why Smoke and Drink. By James Parton.
Elocution. By T. R. W. Pearson, M.A., of St. Catharine's College,
    Cambridge, and F. W. Waithman, Lecturers on Elocution.

THE SCOTT LIBRARY.

Cloth, Uncut Edges, Gilt Top. Price 1s. 6d. per Volume.

VOLUMES ALREADY ISSUED—

 1 ROMANCE OF KING ARTHUR.
 2 THOREAU'S WALDEN.
 3 THOREAU'S "WEEK."
 4 THOREAU'S ESSAYS.
 5 ENGLISH OPIUM-EATER.
 6 LANDOR'S CONVERSATIONS.
 7 PLUTARCH'S LIVES.
 8 RELIGIO MEDICI, &c.
 9 SHELLEY'S LETTERS.
10 PROSE WRITINGS OF SWIFT.
11 MY STUDY WINDOWS.
12 THE ENGLISH POETS.
13 THE BIGLOW PAPERS.
14 GREAT ENGLISH PAINTERS.
15 LORD BYRON'S LETTERS.
16 ESSAYS BY LEIGH HUNT.
17 LONGFELLOW'S PROSE.
18 GREAT MUSICAL COMPOSERS.
19 MARCUS AURELIUS.
20 TEACHING OF EPICTETUS.
21 SENECA'S MORALS.
22 SPECIMEN DAYS IN AMERICA.
23 DEMOCRATIC VISTAS.
24 WHITE'S SELBORNE.
25 DEFOE'S SINGLETON.

26 MAZZINI'S ESSAYS.
27 PROSE WRITINGS OF HEINE.
28 REYNOLDS' DISCOURSES.
29 PAPERS OF STEELE AND ADDISON.
30 BURNS'S LETTERS.
31 VOLSUNGA SAGA.
32 SARTOR RESARTUS.
33 WRITINGS OF EMERSON.
34 LIFE OF LORD HERBERT.
35 ENGLISH PROSE.
36 IBSEN'S PILLARS OF SOCIETY.
37 IRISH FAIRY AND FOLK TALES.
38 ESSAYS OF DR. JOHNSON.
39 ESSAYS OF WILLIAM HAZLITT.
40 LANDOR'S PENTAMERON, &c.
41 POE'S TALES AND ESSAYS.
42 VICAR OF WAKEFIELD.
43 POLITICAL ORATIONS.
44 AUTOCRAT OF THE BREAKFAST-
TABLE.
45 POET AT THE BREAKFAST-TABLE.
46 PROFESSOR AT THE BREAKFAST-
TABLE.
47 CHESTERFIELD'S LETTERS.
48 STORIES FROM CARLETON.
49 JANE EYRE.
50 ELIZABETHAN ENGLAND.
51 WRITINGS OF THOMAS DAVIS.
52 SPENCE'S ANECDOTES.
53 MORE'S UTOPIA.
54 SADI'S GULISTAN.
55 ENGLISH FAIRY TALES.
56 NORTHERN STUDIES.
57 FAMOUS REVIEWS.
58 ARISTOTLE'S ETHICS.
59 PERICLES AND ASPASIA.
60 ANNALS OF TACITUS.
61 ESSAYS OF ELIA.
62 BALZAC.
63 DE MUSSET'S COMEDIES.
64 CORAL REEFS.
65 SHERIDAN'S PLAYS.

The Canterbury Poets.

IMPORTANT ADDITIONS.

WORKS BY ROBERT BROWNING.

VOL. I.

Pippa Passes, and other Poetic Dramas, by Robert Browning. With an Introductory Note by Frank Rinder.

VOL. II.

A Blot in the 'Scutcheon, and other Poetic Dramas, by Robert Browning. With an Introductory Note by Frank Rinder.

VOL. III.

Dramatic Romances and Lyrics; and Sordello, by Robert Browning. To which is prefixed an Appreciation of Browning by Miss E. Dixon.

BINDINGS.

The above volumes are supplied in the following Bindings:—

IN GREEN ROAN, Boxed, with Frontispiece in Photogravure, 2s. 6d. net.

IN ART LINEN, with Frontispiece in

Photogravure, 2s.

IN WHITE LINEN, with Frontispiece in Photogravure, 2s.

IN BROCADE, 2 Vols., in Shell Case to match (each vol. with Frontispiece), price 4s. per Set, or 3 vols. 6s. per Set.

And in the ordinary SHILLING BINDINGS, Green Cloth, Cut Edges, and Blue Cloth, Uncut Edges (without Photogravure).

The Three Volumes form an admirable and representative "Set," including a great part of Browning's best-known and most admired work, and (being each of about 400 pages) are among the largest yet issued in the CANTERBURY POETS. The Frontispiece of Vol. I. consists of a reproduction of one of Browning's last portraits; Mr. RUDOLF LEHMANN has kindly given permission for his portrait of Browning to be reproduced as a Frontispiece of Vol. II.; while a reproduction of a drawing of a View of Asolo forms the Frontispiece of the third Volume.

The World's Great Novels.

Large Crown 8vo, Illustrated, 3s. 6d. each.

Uniform with the New Edition of"Anna Karénina."

A series of acknowledged masterpieces by the most eminent writers of fiction.

THE COUNT OF MONTE-CRISTO. By ALEXANDRE DUMAS. With Sixteen Full-page Illustrations drawn by FRANK T. MERRILL, and over 1100 pages of letterpress, set in large clear type.

THE THREE MUSKETEERS. By ALEXANDRE

DUMAS. With Twelve Full-page Illustrations by T. EYRE MACKLIN, a Photogravure Frontispiece Portrait of the Author, and over 600 pages of letterpress, printed from large clear type.

TWENTY YEARS AFTER. By ALEXANDRE DUMAS. With Sixteen Full-page Illustrations by FRANK T. MERRILL, and 800 pages of letterpress, set from new type.

LES MISÉRABLES. By VICTOR HUGO. With Eleven Full-page Illustrations, and 1384 pages of letterpress.

NOTRE DAME. By VICTOR HUGO. With numerous Illustrations.

JANE EYRE. By CHARLOTTE BRONTË. With Sixteen Full-page Illustrations, and Thirty-two Illustrations in the Text, by EDMUND H. GARRETT, and Photogravure Portrait of Charlotte Brontë. Printed in large clear type; 660 pages of letterpress.

Tolstoy's Great Masterpiece. New Edition of Anna Karénina.

ANNA KARÉNINA: A NOVEL. By COUNT TOLSTOY. With Ten Illustrations drawn by PAUL FRÉNZENY, and a Frontispiece Portrait of Count Tolstoy in Photogravure.

"Other novels one can afford to leave unread, but *Anna Karénina* never; it stands eternally one of the peaks of all fiction."—*Review of Reviews*.

LONDON: WALTER SCOTT, LTD., PATERNOSTER SQUARE.

Footnotes:

[1] *Alienist and Neurologist*, 1895.

[2] Folklore of Shakespeare.

[3] *Anatomy of Melancholy*, sixth edition, 1652, part i., sec. ii., mem. i., sub. sec. vi.

[4] *From the Greeks to Darwin*, p. 25.

[5] *Works*, Sydenham Society Edition.

[6] *Histoire Naturelle*, edition 1761.

[7] *Zoonomia*, "Generation," vol. i.

[8] *Diseases of the Mind*, p. 46.

[9] *Traité des Dégénérescences Physiques, Intellectuelles et Morales de l'Espèce Humaine*, 1857, p. 3.

[10] Traité de Pathologie Comparée.

[11] La Psychologie Morbide dans ses Rapports avec la Philosophie de l'Histoire.

[12] *Alienist and Neurologist*, January 1892.

[13] *Traité Physiologique et Philosophique de l'Hérédité Naturelle*, 1847.

[14] Les Forçats.

[15] The Mysteries of Paris.

[16] Les Vrais Mystères de Paris.

[17] *Annales Judiciares*, 1840.

[18] *American Journal of Insanity*, April, 1846.

[19] *Criminal Jurisprudence and Cerebral Development*, 1841.

[20] *De la Formation de Type dans les Variétés Dégénérés*, 1864.

[21] *Chapters on Evolution*, p. 349.

[22] Wiley, *Origin of the Vertebrates.*

[23] Degeneration.

[24] *Die Ursprung der Wirbelthier*, 1875.

[25] *Psychiatrie*, 1859.

[26] *Psychologie Morbide*, 1889.

[27] *Archiv f. Psychiatrie*, 1868.

[28] Cited by Griesinger, edition 1845, p. 252.

[29] *Recherches sur les Idiots*, 1860.

[30] Cited by Havelock Ellis, *The Criminal*, p. 29.

[31] *Gulstonian Lectures*, 1870.

[32] See, for instance, Art. "Microcephaly," *Dict. of Psych. Medicine*, and, especially, Mingazzini's study of the morphology of cerebral hemispheres, *Il Cervello*, 1895.

[33] Psychologie Naturelle.

[34] *Journal of Mental Science*, 1870.

[35] *American Prison Association Report*, 1866.

[36] *Deterioration and Race Education*, 1876.

[37] *Report of the New York Board of Charities*, 1876.

[38] *W. S. Tuke Prize Essay on the Somatic Ætiology of Insanity*, 1877.

[39] *Allgemeine Zeitschrift f. Psychiatrie*, 1869-78.

[40] *Journal of Mental Science*, 1873.

[41] *L'Uomo Delinquente*, 1876.

[42] *Journal of Nervous and Mental Disease*, January, 1878.

[43] Studien au Verbrecker-Gehirnen.

[44] *Chicago Medical Review*, July 1, 1881, p. 310.

[45] *Two Hard Cases*, 1882.

[46] *Trial of Charles J. Guiteau*, vol. ii.

[47] Every Asylum Report of the Gray School gave statistics of hereditary transmission.

[48] Medical Jurisprudence.

[49] Mental Disease.

[50] *American Journal of Neurology and Psychiatry*, vol. ii.

[51] *Alienist and Neurologist*, 1882.

[52] *Canada Medical and Surgical Journal*, Feb., 1882.

[53] *Medical Times*, May 20, 1882.

[54] *Transactions of Pennsylvania Medical Society*, 1882.

[55] Selection dans les Aristocracies.

[56] *Journal of Mental Science*, 1879.

[57] *Canada Medical and Surgical Journal*, Feb., 1882.

[58] *Journal of Mental Science*, April, 1878.

[59] Evolution and Disease.

[60] *Medicine*, 1897.

[61] *Brain*, 1894.

[62] Ray Lankester, *Degeneration*.

[63] *Man and Woman*, pp. 23, 390.

[64] *Human Embryology*, p. 567.

[65] E. S. Talbot, *Etiology of the Osseous Deformities of the Head, Face, Jaws, and Teeth*.

[66] *Evolution of Sex*, p. 129.

[67] *St. Louis Clinical Record*, 1878-81.

[68] *Germ Plasm*, pp. 431, 565.

[69] *American Medico-Surgical Bulletin*, August 15, 1893.

[70] *Circumcision*, p. 204.

[71] *Medicine*, July, 1898.

[72] *Medical Record*, vol. xlii.

[73] *Organic Evolution*, p. 178.

[74] *Comptes rendus*, 1882, xciv., p. 697.

[75] *Transactions of the American Neurological Association*, 1877.

[76] *Journal of Nervous and Mental Disease*, 1877, p. 544.

[77] Factors of Organic Evolution.

[78] Hereditary Traits.

[79] *Journal of Nervous and Mental Disease*, 1877, page 548.

[80] *Sensation et Mouvement*, chap. xiv.

[81] Harriet C. B. Alexander, *Transactions Chicago Academy of Medicine*,

January, 1895.

[82] *Medical Classics*, July and August, 1888.

[83] *Chicago Medical Journal and Examiner*, 1883-4, p. 426.

[84] *Somatic Ætiology of Insanity*, p. 41.

[85] *Medicine*, September, 1898.

[86] *Review of Insanity and Nervous Disease*, March, 1891.

[87] *American Journal of Obstetrics*, October, 1882.

[88] *American Medico-Surgical Bulletin*, July 15, 1896.

[89] *American Journal of the Medical Sciences*, October, 1856.

[90] *La Famille Névropathique*, 2nd ed., 1898.

[91] *Transactions American Neurological Association*, 1877.

[92] *Transactions de l'Institut Pasteur*, 1896.

[93] *La Psychologie Morbide.*

[94] *On the Mind*, 1805.

[95] *Pathology of the Mind.*

[96] *Lehrbuch der Psychiatrie.*

[97] *La Famille Névropathique.*

[98] *Dégénérescence de l'Espèce Humaine.*

[99] *St. Louis Clinical Record*, 1878-81.

[100] *Neurological Review*, vol. i., 1886.

[101] *La Famille Névropathique.*

[102] *Medicine*, June, 1898.

[103] *Bulletin Medical*, 1887.

[104] *Medicine*, September, 1897.

[105] *Annales Medico-Psychologique*, March and April, 1869.

[106] *Marriage and Disease*, pp. 186-7.

[107] *Annalles Medico-Psychologiques*, S. 7, t. xvi.

[108] *Maladies Mentales*, p. 215.

[109]

"The darkness of her Oriental eye
    Accorded with her Moorish origin
(Her blood was not all Spanish, by the by;
    In Spain, you know, this is a sort of sin).
When proud Grenada fell, and, forced to fly,
    Boabdil wept; of Donna Julia's kin
Some went to Africa, some stayed in Spain,
Her great-great-grandmamma chose to remain.

"She married (I forget the pedigree)
    With an Hidalgo who transmitted down
His blood less noble than such blood should be;
    At such alliances his sires would frown,
In that point so precise in each degree
    That they bred in and in, as might be shown,
Marrying their cousins—nay, their aunts and nieces,
Which always spoils the breed, if it increases.

"This heathenish cross restored the breed again,
    Ruined its blood, but much improved its flesh;
For, from a root, the ugliest in Old Spain,
    Sprung up a branch as beautiful as fresh,
The sons no more were short, the daughters plain."

[110] The origins of the prohibition of incest have lately been fully discussed by Durkheim, *L'Année Sociologique*, 1898.

[111] *Psychological Dictionary*, "Consanguinity."

[112] *Bulletin de L'Académie de Médecine*, t. xxi. p. 746.

[113] *American Medical Bi-Weekly*, vol. xii., No. 13.

[114] *Mental Hygiene*, p. 25.

[115] *Intermarriage of Relations*, p. 40.

[116] *Edinburgh Medical Journal*, October, 1865.

[117] *Marriage of Near Kin*, p. 218.

[118] *American Journal of Insanity*, 1869-70.

[119] *Marriage and Disease*, p. 266.

[120] Cited by Ribot, *Heredity*, p. 292.

[121] Cited by Huth.

[122] *Allgemeine Zeitschrifft für Psychiatrie*, B. xxvii.

[123] *L'Encephale*, October, 1882.

[124] *Detroit Lancet*, September, 1882.

[125] *Journal of Nervous and Mental Disease*, 1883.

[126] *Australian Medical Gazette*, 1886.

[127] *Il Manicomio*, May, 1886.

[128] *Alienist and Neurologist*, January, 1887.

[129] *La Pubertà*, 1898, pp. 242-60.

[130] *Archives d'Ophthalmologie*, 1887.

[131] *Transactions International Medical Congress*, 1887, p. 264, vol. v.

[132] *Lancet*, January to March, 1883.

[133]

> "For Englishmen to boast of generation
> Cancels their knowledge, and lampoons the nation.
> A true-born Englishman's a contradiction,
> In speech an irony, in fact a fiction.
>
> And here begins the ancient pedigree
> That so exalts our poor nobility.
> 'Tis that from some French trooper they derive,
> Who with the Norman bastard did arrive.
> The trophies of the families appear.
> Some show the sword, the bow, and some the spear,
> Which their great ancestor, forsooth, did wear.
> These in the herald's register remain
> Their noble mean extraction to explain;
> Yet who the hero was no man can tell,
> Whether a drummer or a colonel;
> The silent record blushes to reveal
> Their undescended, dark original.
>
> These are the heroes that despise the Dutch
> And rail at new-come foreigners so much,
> Forgetting that themselves are all derived
> From the most scoundrel race that ever lived;
> A horrid crowd of rambling thieves and drones,
> Who ransacked kingdoms and dispeopled towns;

The Pict and painted Briton, treacherous Scot,
By hunger, theft, and rapine hither brought,
Norwegian pirates, buccaneering Danes,
Whose red-haired offspring everywhere remains,
Who, joined with Norman-French, compound the breed
From whence your true-born Englishmen proceed.

And, lest by length of time, it be pretended
The climate may this modern breed have mended,
Wise Providence, to keep us where we are,
Mixes us daily with exceeding care.
We have been Europe's sink, the jakes where she
Voids all her offal outcast progeny.
For ages, fugitives from neighbouring lands
Have here a certain sanctuary found;
The eternal refuge of the vagabond,
Wherein but half a common age of time,
Borrowing new blood and manners from the clime,
Proudly they learn all mankind to contemn,
And all their race are true-born Englishmen."

[134] *Ethnology*, p. 201.

[135] *Alienist and Neurologist*, 1892, 1895, 1896.

[136] *Origin of the Aryans.*

[137] *Ethnology in Folklore.*

[138] *Journal of Nervous and Mental Disease*, 1886.

[139] *Origin of the Aryans.*

[140] *Alienist and Neurologist*, January, 1892.

[141] Cited by S. Laing, *Human Origins*, pp. 38-41.

[142] *Anthropology.*

[143] *Alienist and Neurologist*, October, 1896.

[144] *Origin of the Aryans.*

[145] Talbot, *Osseous Deformities.*

[146] *Osseous Deformities of the Jaw*, p. 30.

[147] *Hybridity and Heredity*, p. 307.

[148] Cited by Keane, *Ethnology*, p. 265. See also Johnston, *British Central*

Africa, 1897.

[149] *Journal Am. Medical Ass.*, vol. xx., 1893.

[150] *La Razza Negra*, p. 20, 1864.

[151] *Man and Woman*, pp. 25, 390.

[152] Johnson, *Chemistry of Common Life*, vol. i. p. 239.

[153] *Detroit Lancet*, September, 1882.

[154] *Observations on the Brain and Mind*, p. 10, 1798.

[155] The Opium Habit.

[156] *Review of Insanity and Nervous Disease*, 1890.

[157] *Annual Universal Medical Sciences*, 1895.

[158] *Annual of the Universal Medical Sciences*, 1892; and (for Summary of Etienne's Report on the offspring of the young married women in the Nancy factories), *British Medical Journal*, April 23, 1898.

[159] *Annual of the Universal Medical Sciences*, 1889.

[160] *Annual of the Universal Medical Sciences*, 1895.

[161] *Lancet*, November 30, 1891.

[162] *Neurologisches Centralblatt*, 1887.

[163] *Chemistry of Common Life*, vol. ii.

[164] *Lead Diseases*, American edition, 1848.

[165] *Journal of Nervous and Mental Diseases*, 1881.

[166] *American Journal of Obstetrics*, October, 1882.

[167] *Birmingham Medical Review*, January, 1887.

[168] C. E. Paddock, of Chicago, cites very analogous cases.

[169] *Variation of Plants and Animals under Domestication*, vol. i. p. 37.

[170] Keane, *Ethnology*, p. 203.

[171] *Lectures on Man*, 1868.

[172] *Man and Woman*, chap. iv.

[173] *Annual of the Universal Medical Sciences*, 1892, K. 18, vol. v.

[174] *Annual of the Universal Medical Sciences*, 1892.

[175] Boies, *Pauper and Prisoner.*

[176] *New York Medical Journal*, vol. lxii.

[177] *American Journal of Insanity*, 1887.

[178] La Pellagra.

[179] *Journal of the American Medical Association*, vol. xxii.

[180] Psychology of Childhood.

[181] *Journal American Medical Association*, vol. xxii.

[182] *Alienist and Neurologist*, 1897.

[183] *Illustrations of Insanity*, 1817.

[184] *Pepper's System of Medicine*, vol. i.

[185] *Journal of Mental Science*, 1886-87.

[186] Nervous Diseases of Children.

[187] Diseases of the Stomach.

[188] *Embryology*, p. 465.

[189] Virchow, *Gesam. Abhandlg., Wis. Med.*, 1856.

[190] *Report New York City Asylum for the Insane*, 1875.

[191] Kiernan, *Alienist and Neurologist*, January, 1891.

[192] *Annales Medico-Psychologiques*, 1849.

[193] Anthropology.

[194] *American Journal of Insanity*, July, 1895.

[195] *Revista Sperimentale*, xxii.

[196] *Human Embryology*, p. 468.

[197] *American Naturalist*, 1883.

[198] *Oral Deformities*, p. 480.

[199] *Medicine*, September, 1897.

[200] For cases see, *e.g.*, Gould's *Anomalies*.

[201] Bland Sutton, *Evolution and Disease*, p. 193.

[202] *Osseous Deformities*, p. 398.

[203] *Journal of Morphology*, vol. v.

[204] *Arb. Zoolog. Institut*, Wurzburg, iii.

[205] The Amphioxus.

[206] *Sajous' Annual*, 1889.

[207] *Sajous' Annual*, vol. iv., 1892.

[208] *Journal of Nervous and Mental Diseases*, 1878.

[209] *La Famille Névropathique*, p. 156.

[210] *Medicine*, May, 1898.

[211] For further particulars, see "The Degenerate Ear," by Eugene S. Talbot, *Journal of The American Medical Association*, January 11, 1896.

[212] Minot, *Embryology*.

[213] Minot's *Embryology*.

[214] *The Descent of Man*, p. 15.

[215] Frigerio's measurements of the auriculo-temporal angle were taken with a specially devised instrument from the pinna to the mastoid. Buchanan's were apparently taken from the anterior edge of the mastoid to the helix, giving the angle of the external face of the whole ear.

[216] See "Degenerate Jaws and Death," by Talbot, *Journal Am. Medical Association*, vol. xxvii. p. 134.

[217] Osborn.

[218] Talbot, "Mouth breathing not the cause of contracted jaws and high vaults" (*Dental Cosmos*, 1891).

[219] Per cent.

[220] Féré, *La Famille Névropathique*, p. 158.

[221] Ibid., *Nouv. Icon. de la Salpêtrière*, 1890.

[222] *Jour. de l'Anat. et de la Phys.*, 1893, p. 564.

[223] Cited by Gould in *Anomalies*.

[224] Gould, *op. cit.*

[225] Gould, *Anomalies*, p. 272.

[226] *Revue Internat. des Sciences Med.*, November 1886.

[227] Achondroplasia, or imperfect development of cartilage with resulting imperfections in the extremities, has come under my observation. The first case, a man of 38, had a face arrested in development and the appearance of a ten-year-old boy. His jaws were small with a protrusion of the lower. His arms were absent. The hands were full sized and attached to the shoulder. Another case was that of a member of the Spanish nobility in whom degeneracy was

stamped on the entire body. He was short in body and had an enormous head. The jaws were undeveloped with a V-shaped arch. His left hand was located near the shoulder.

[228] *Alienist and Neurologist*, January, 1898.

[229] *Medicine*, January, 1898.

[230] Wharton, *Proc. Royal Society of Ireland*, 1863.

[231] *British Medical Journal*, January 25, 1897.

[232] Meige, *L'Anthropologie*, T. 6, Nos. 3, 4, 5.

[233] Havelock Ellis, *Psychology of Sex*, vol. i. "Sexual Inversion."

[234] Otis T. Mason, *Smithsonian Contribution to Knowledge*, 1888.

[235] Julien, *Monatschrift für Prakt. Dermatologie*, March, 1898.

[236] *Annual of the Universal Medical Sciences*, 1892.

[237] *L'Encephale*, 1883.

[238] *Neurological Review*, 1886.

[239] Malthusianism and Crime.

[240] *Wiener Med. Wochenschrift*, February 13, 1897.

[241] *British Medical Journal*, April 23, 1898.

[242] "Stigmata of Degeneracy in Royal Families," *Jour. Am. Med. Assoc.*, vol. xxvii. 1894.

[243] Practice of Medicine.

[244] *Progrès Medical*, July 15, 1888.

[245] *Somatic Etiology of Insanity*, 1877.

[246] Ziegler, *Pathologic Anatomy*.

[247] Vogt, *Lectures on Man*. The lettering refer to the text of that work.

[248] *St. Louis Clinical Record*, vol. viii. p. 66.

[249] *Journal of Nervous and Mental Disease*, 1886, p. 54.

[250] *Journal of Nervous and Mental Disease*, 1886.

[251] In the foregoing, and to some extent in the following, chapters it has been necessary to touch on many complicated questions of brain function, more or less outside the main topic of this book. The aspect of such questions is, however, constantly changing in the light of new investigations, and our

knowledge is still far from certain in many most important respects. For excellent statements of the prevailing views of brain localisation, brought up to date, the reader may be referred to the special sections of the latest editions of Foster's *Physiology*, or of Waller's *Physiology*; Donaldson's *Growth of the Brain* may also be consulted.

[252] *Work among the Fallen*, summarised in *Journal of Mental Science*, 1892.

[253] Études Anthropométriques sur les Prostituées.

[254] *Archivio di Psichiatria*, 1882.

[255] And see the biography of Marie Duplessis by Georges Soreau in *Revue de France*, 1898.

[256] *St. Louis Clinical Record*, 1879-80.

[257] The Man of Genius.

[258] *Journal of Mental Science*, 1886.

[259] *Review of Insanity and Nervous Diseases*, 1891.

[260] *Alienist and Neurologist*, July, 1893.

[261] *American Journal of Insanity*, 1893-4.

[262] *New England Medical Monthly*, 1881.

[263] Germ Plasm.

[264] *American Journal of Insanity*, 1893-4.

Transcriber's Notes:

Images have been moved from the middle of a paragraph to a nearby paragraph break.

The text in the list of illustrations is presented as in the original text, but the links navigate to the page number closest to the illustration's loaction in this document.

Punctuation has been corrected without note.

Other than the corrections noted by hover information, inconsistencies in spelling and hyphenation have been retained from the original.

9 783732 625666